Husband to Feminize

by Brad Pri

Book 2: Cuckold Husband. No Holes Barred

"How did I end up helping my wife cuckold me?" John asked himself. John thought he'd grabbed the brass ring by marrying Tonya, a knockout seemingly out of his league, until she revealed that he'd never satisfied her sexually. He was faced with a desperate choice: let her be unhappy, lose her, or ... become a knowing cuckold. His fateful choice led him down the rabbit hole to increasing domination by his awakened bride, participation in his own cuckolding, feminization—and what else?

In Book 1, Johnny let his wife Tonya take a lover with his blessing. Johnny discovered that this sparked a dominant side of his wife, who began to relish her control over him. Johnny was shocked to discover that her kinky side excited him. He was startled to find that the more she taunted him and the more outlandish things she demanded, the more turned on he became. Now that it seems no holds (or holes) are barred, where will this journey end?

Already Tonya has replaced Johnny with a dildo, fucked Johnny with a dildo, and made Johnny drink her urine and wear panties and negligees. She found a well-endowed lover, Brian, a courier who delivers to her company. She's had Johnny eat cream pie after Brian's visit. She's given her anal cherry to Brian, and then engaged in an orgy with Brian's well-hung friends Calvin, a black man, and David, a blond surfer dude.

We rejoin Johnny the day after the orgy, a mere three weeks after he first learned of how he was failing to meet his wife's sexual needs. How far they've come in that short time! But that's only the beginning of where they will go!

Content warning: This work contains sexually explicit language and scenes. It is intended for mature adults who are not offended by themes of marital infidelity, female domination, humiliation, cross-dressing, cross-gender behavior, group sex, bisexual behavior, urolagnia, and anal sexuality.

-Day 20 Thursday-

Although I was exhausted, I found myself wondering how long it would be until Tonya fucked Brian and his buddies again. It turned out that I didn't have long to wait for that answer.

About 3 pm my cell phone rang. I saw that it was Tonya's phone. I answered it, but no one replied. It took me a few seconds to realize that I was overhearing a conversation between two people on the other end. I heard Tonya's voice.

"Calvin, I'm so glad you were free to come over! I was getting lonely, home alone all day."

"Sure thing, baby! We can't have a pretty lady like you getting lonely, can we?" Then there was some rustling and smacking. I could just picture Calvin with his tongue down Tonya's throat.

"I'd never had a black man until last night! I had to try it again! But this time I want to take my time and really appreciate it. Get those clothes off! I want to taste that licorice stick of yours!"

"What do you like best: the licorice or the creamy filling?" Calvin replied.

"Mmm!" Tonya moaned. "The licorice is so good! Mmmm!" <Slurping sounds.>. "I can't decide: the creamy filling now, or save it as a sauce for my clam sandwich? Hmmm."

"Oh, baby!" Calvin huffed.

"Mmmm!" Tonya enthused. "I forgot how good a real cock feels in my mouth! Not like sucking on that little straw of my husband's. This is a big, hard, warm, throbbing hunk of man!"

It was all too easy to picture what was happening in my bedroom. I squirmed as my dick tented my pants uncomfortably. I sat frozen at my desk, the cell phone pressed to my ear.

"Lie back, Calvin. I've got to feel that black cock in my white pussy! I mean it's been over twelve hours that it's been empty!" Sounds of moving, bed creaking.

"God, it feels so thick, like it will never fit! I'll just need to get it regularly until my cunt adjusts to man-sized cocks again. Unh! Let me get some pussy juice on the head."

"Oh, God, that feels so good!" Calvin hissed.

"Unh! Unh! Aurrgghh! Oh! So ... nice ... and ... full! Whoa there, boy! Give me a chance to get used to it."

"Your cunt is so hot and tight, girl!"

"Let me ride you, Calvin! I'm gonna fuck you this time!" The bed started to creak rhythmically. "So good! So good!" Tonya panted.

My hand was rubbing the front of my pants, but I had to get out of there. Muting my microphone, I walked quickly to the bathroom and secreted myself in a stall. I ripped my pants and panties down and grabbed my prick, giving out an ecstatic groan.

The bed was creaking in a faster rhythm now and animalistic grunts and moans came from both lovers.

"God, Calvin. I love your big, black cock!" Tonya thrilled.

"Fuck me, white bitch! Take my black seed into your cheating cunt!" Calvin urged. His insults seemed only to inflame Tonya's lust: I clutched my rampant cock harder and groaned quietly. I could imagine his ebony body and her white skin and I could picture his long rod deep within her pink womb.

"Come, damn you!" Tonya beseeched him. "Come with me now!" I wondered if she were talking to me too, that she might guess that I was jacking off to the sounds of their fucking.

"Oh! Oh! Oh, God! Oh, God!" Tonya strangled out as her orgasm crashed in on her.

"Take it, bitch! Here it fuckin' comes! Fuck! Oh, fuck! Oh, shit! Shit!"

I pictured his cream jetting out of his black phallus, shooting deep into my wife's belly, his black swimmers ravenously searching for a white egg to impregnate. I pumped my dick furiously to that image and with a gasp I shot my load across the stall to hit the door and fall onto the heap of my pants and panties at my feet!

For a moment I was paralyzed, lost in the ecstasy of my own orgasm. Coming out of my daze I looked in embarrassment at my scum dripping down the stall door and soaking into my clothes.

"Fuck! Fuck shit!" I swore and grabbed a ball of toilet paper and began desperately trying to wipe up the mess. A glob was right on the front of my pants. The sticky consistency of semen made me sure it would leave a stain. I mopped up as much as I could, then I fastened my pants. I turned down my phone as went to the sink and tried to get more off with a wet paper towel. Of course that only left a larger wet spot on my pants, making it look as if I'd peed myself!

I walked back to my desk, hoping no one would notice my wet pants or how long I'd been gone. If anyone asked, I'd tell them I'd spilled some pop.

I turned the volume back up and was surprised to find that the call was still connected.

"Oh, Calvin," I heard Tonya coo, "do you think you got any more fat black cock for my other hole? I'd hate for it to tighten all the way back up, after all the good work you fellows did to stretch it out for me. I figure I'm going to need some ass-fucking a couple times a week to keep it ready for action."

"God, what a slut! You can't get enough!" Calvin exclaimed, but I was pretty sure Tonya'd take that as a compliment. "Why don't you lick your white pussy juice off my black cock and then give Calvin a few minutes to catch his breath! Then see if you can't get it to stand to attention?"

"Mmmm," Tonya replied, and I heard slurping sounds. "Mmmm!"

"You like how that pole tastes, all covered in your pussy juice? You ever eaten a pussy?"

"Unh-unh," Tonya grunted, her mouth obviously full.

"Maybe I should bring one of my girlfriends over and watch you eat her out, eh? Then she can watch you take my cock up your ass. Might make her jealous. And maybe give her some ideas, I hope! Oh, yeah," he enthused. "That's good. You give Calvin some lovin' and then you can suck Calvin nice and hard."

"Oh, Calvin, I'm so happy that I've got all these big beautiful cocks back in my life. I'm like a kid in a candy store. Mmm!" I could tell from the sounds that she was switching back and forth now between sucking and kissing her black lover. It was strange, but knowing they were kissing made me more jealous than Tonya blowing him! Cocksucking was just sex: kissing seemed more ... intimate? Fucking was his job: loving Tonya up was my job! Get off my patch, dude!

I heard Calvin grunt and I could guess that he had rolled over on top of Tonya. I could picture his huge black body enfolding Tonya's voluptuous white curves! The hums and smacks told me they were kissing and hugging and a wave of jealousy rippled through my body!

"I love those milky white tits, girl!" Calvin enthused and Tonya's moans told me he was suckling her perfect breasts again as he had done last night. But this time he could take his time, instead of having Brian eager to fuck Tonya's ass! The image of his ebony face sucking her alabaster mounds sent sparks through my brain!

"Oh, Calvin! You're driving me wild! I can't believe I settled for my husband's boy-dick for two years when there are real men like you out there. Last night convinced me. I'm never going back. I'm going to have all the dick I can get—black, white, yellow, brown—as long as they are big!"

"Oh, you got it bad, girl! You got cock-hunger. Let Calvin fill you up again!"

"Lube me up, Calvin! My ass is needing it! Oh!" she grunted, probably from his fingers invading her ass. "Oh, yeah, baby. Grease me up. God, I can't wait! Last night I was afraid I couldn't take it, but now I know I can and how fucking good it feels! My ass is tingling for it!"

I could picture his fingers plunging into her, stretching her, working the lube into her gorgeous ass. My cock started to stir again. I got self-conscious at how long I'd been just sitting there holding the phone up to my ear without talking, I started to fake conversation as I walked back to the bathroom.

"Yeah, right. OK, tomorrow. 3 o'clock? Sure," I pretended, with the mute still on my phone.

The bathroom was empty, so I grabbed a paper towel and went back inside my favorite stall. I dropped my pants and panties and grabbed my still-sore dick, which amazingly sprang to life again. Not the big, manly, full-throated life that Calvin's cock was full of, but the pathetic, little boy, wanker life that my shortcomings consigned me to.

"Here comes Calvin, baby! Ready or not!"

"Oh, God! Ouch! Ouch! Easy!" Tonya cried. "Ow! God, you're so big! Maybe I can't do it again, so soon."

"You're gonna take it, baby! You got Calvin all hot again and he's gonna fuck your white ass!"

My cock strained at those words and my hand flew up and down. It was my own wife, but somehow the idea that he might be somewhat forcing her excited rather than horrified me. I was gripped by pure lust. My cock wanted someone to get fucked.

"Take it, baby! Take Calvin all the way up your butt!"

"Unh!" Tonya yelped. "Oh, God. Oh, fuck, too big.... Unh! Unh!"

"I can feel it, baby! Your ass is like a damn glove! And I'm fucking it!" The bed creaked and Calvin grunted and panted. I could picture it, his black prick sawing in and out of her lily-white ass, Tonya's face a grimace of concentration, on the edge between pain and pleasure.

"Oh! Oh! Shit..," Tonya moaned and now I couldn't tell if it was out of discomfort or lust. "Oh, God, Calvin! Oh, fuck me! Fuck my white ass! Shit! Oh, I love it!" So lust it was.

"Your ass is so tight! So hot!" Calvin said, his voice rough with tension. "Now that I've come once, I'll fuck your white ass all day!"

"Oh, fuck!" Tonya screamed. "Oh, fuck! Fuck! Fuck! Fuck! Ohhhh! Arrgghhh!" I knew she was coming with that black baseball bat up her bum.

But it didn't stop. I could hear Calvin pounding away and Tonya cries just going on and on.

"Oh, God! Oh! Oh! Fuck me! Fuck me! Fuck me!"

My penis was sore but I continued to whack it. The lustful fire in my brain was fighting against the recency of my last orgasm and the pain of my self-abuse. I couldn't even get fully hard, but I still felt I was on the edge of coming,

"God! Oh!" I heard Calvin's baritone. "Oh shit! Oh shit! Ohhh!" and I knew he was spilling his seed deep in my wife's rectum. My own dick throbbed and a convulsion shook me. Instead of a jet, I could only manage a dribble of sperm, which spilled down my hand. Dutifully I quickly raised my hand to lick the mess off my fist. The thought flashed through my mind: I wonder what would his black sperm would taste like?

I momentarily felt a flush of vicarious triumph at Calvin's re-conquest of my wife's backside. How I wished I deserved that Promised Land! I felt admiration for Calvin, rather than jealousy, and a strange gladness that at least <u>he</u> could enjoy Tonya's anal charms. But I knew that I did not deserve entry there and that I never could. I wasn't man enough. I was a Little Leaguer who could only admire the real pros from the stands.

As my arousal drained away, my post-orgasmic letdown crashed in on me. I felt the shame of being in the bathroom stall, beating off at work for the second time in a day. And I was listening to my wife giving herself eagerly to another man instead of doing my job. God! How pathetic I was!

But even as my self-esteem ebbed away, it made me all the more beholden to Tonya. I should be all the more grateful that she tolerated me at all. I was nothing! She could do so much better than me! I couldn't see why, but she said she still loved me, even though she apparently planned to let a parade of other men enjoy fucking her fore and aft.

But far from cursing her, I blessed her. She was a saint to accept me and still love me. A saint despite cum running down her leg. I whimpered in awe of my luck. I was a useless wimp, but this goddess loved me! I could only keep loving her! That a woman like that even <u>allowed</u> me to lick the spunk out of her pussy made me lucky!

The sound of someone else entering the bathroom roused me from my reverie. I could hear cooing and cuddling going on at the other end of the phone, but I figured the main show was over and closed my phone. With awkward embarrassment I quickly cleaned my hand with toilet paper and dabbed off my reddened dick. I walked straight to the sink and rapidly washed my hands and exited.

I looked at my watch and was shocked that it was already 4:15. I'd spent over an hour on the phone and jerking off. I felt wasted but a fever took me over. I had to see Tonya. I had to show her my devotion. I wanted to prostrate myself before my goddess and suckle at her divine pussy and ass. Without a word to anyone I just grabbed my things and almost ran out of the building. I drove home in a trance, telling myself over and over how much I loved Tonya, like a mantra.

Turning down our street I was shocked to see a strange car in our driveway behind Tonya's. Calvin's car, of course. He was still here! I kept driving and went around the block. I was desperate with impatience to see her, to throw myself at her feet and declare my love. The car was still there. What should I do? I drove around the block and pulled over. I'd wait ten minutes and then checked again.

After five minutes I couldn't stand the waiting and I started up the car and circled the block. I gnashed my teeth at the sight of the red car in the drive. I went around the block and parked again, this time determined to wait the full ten minutes. I looked at my watch fifty times. After ten more minutes I pulled around the block and exulted to see an empty space in our drive.

I ran into the house. I couldn't wait to see Tonya, as if I were afraid she might not be there. She wasn't in the kitchen or the living room, so I guessed she was still in bed. I burst into the bedroom.

"Johnny! What a nice surprise! You're so early! You didn't run into ... my guest, did you?"

"No, I waited until he left. I was around the block. Oh, Tonya, I couldn't wait to see you! I love you so much!"

"Wow, that's not usually the greeting a gal gets when he husband finds her in bed with her holes full of someone else's cum! I love you too, baby! What's come over you?"

I took her in my arms. "I don't deserve you, but I'm so happy to be your husband anyway. I want to show you how much I love you!"

"I can think of a way," Tonya teased and threw off the covers. She pulled her knees back to her chest, exposing her puffy, gooey pussy.

I threw myself at her gash, taking a second to enjoy the intoxicating smell of her arousal, mixed with the potent smell of Calvin's semen. I fervently kissed her cunt lips and began to lick up the heady mixture of her juices and Calvin's spend. My tongue probed her slit, sucking out the remains of Calvin's cock cream.

As the taste of another man's cum filled my mouth and nose, I was almost delirious at the now-familiar flavor. I was eating cum, sucking down cum! Was I disgusted? No! It thrilled me! A shiver went down my back and my hair stood on end. A warm, satisfied, exultant feeling filled me!

"Oh, that's so nice, Johnny. So nice to have you love up on my pussy after a big cock has hammered it. Your lips and tongue are so soothing, so gentle, so loving. It's so relaxing. The fucking is so frantic, so wild. But this is so nice. You make me feel safe and loved."

This was music to my ears. I was doing something special for her, even if I couldn't fuck her satisfactorily.

She pulled her knees back further, exposing her anus. Taking my cue, I kissed her oozing anus, licking up the lube and semen. I drove my tongue into the ring of her sphincter, probing as far as I could into her ass and sucking up all the juices I could. After a long time of my feasting on this, Tonya pulled me up to cuddle with her.

"It's OK that I had Calvin over, then, I guess? You don't resent it? I mean, it wasn't something we'd discussed, not part of our deal."

"Tonya, you deserve a man ... men ... who can satisfy you. You deserve that pleasure. I don't want to deprive you. I love you so much, I want you to have everything. I guess that you need men like Calvin or Brian or Dave. And men like that deserve women as beautiful and desirable as you! I'm lucky just to be your husband. I want to show you that I love you no matter what!"

"Oh, Johnny! I'm the lucky one, to have a husband who will suck my pussy and ass, even when they are full of other men's cum! Or maybe even prefer it that way, eh? Did you like that black cock cream? Did you enjoy your phone call? Did you pull your little dickie out and jack off because it excited you that a big black stud was fucking your wife? And that you'd get to eat that cum? How many times did your little dickie squirt?"

Her description embarrassed me—and the fact that she was so sure she knew what I would do. I muttered, "Twice," and swallowed.

"Good! Where did you do it? Did you rub your dickie right at your desk or what?"

"I went to the bathroom."

"So you could really wrap your fingers around your little willie properly and really milk it while the black man's big cock was giving your wife orgasm after orgasm. Oh, that's priceless! I can just see you huddling in the bathroom stall like a boy who's found his father's Playboy! Hah!" she laughed derisively. "I bet that felt good, didn't it?"

"Yes, it felt good!"

"Get it out! Let me see your little peepee! I'll bet it's sore. From all that wanking. Let me see it."

I was embarrassed, but I unbuckled my pants and skimmed down my panties. Tonya took my again-firm penis in her hands.

"Look at it! Hard again after all that jerking off! Licking my cum-filled pussy and ass really excites you. Too bad it can't be your cum in there, eh? Look how red it is, though! Let Tonya soothe it."

She dipped her hand into the still-open lube jar and dabbed it onto my chafed shaft. Taking it into her hand, she began to masturbate me. It felt so much better than my dry jerking off earlier.

"Too bad you can't fuck me like those guys can. A good fuck is so nice: it brings two people closer together." Her hand felt so good on my penis! She was stroking me slowly, gently, almost hypnotically. "I felt so close to Calvin this afternoon! His cock was inside me, so deep inside me. And not just in my pussy. In my ass: there's something even more personal about that. He was giving me such pleasure and I was giving him pleasure. It's such a giving of oneself. A good fuck connects people so deeply, so completely." She continued to slide her hand up and down my greasy shaft, maddeningly slowly and gently.

"Oh, Tonya, I want that with you! I want us to be that close!" I choked out.

"But what can we do. Your little weenie just isn't big enough. How can we fuck?"

"You can fuck me!" I cried. "You can use the dildo. We can fuck, like you did with Calvin. We can feel that close."

"I don't know, baby. Maybe. If you really wanted it, as bad as I wanted Calvin's cock."

"How can I show you?"

"You go get it. You put it on me. Then show me how much you want it."

I clambered over to the nightstand and got out the dildo and harness. I was so eager that I clumsily slipped the harness up her legs and under her hips. I slipped the dildo into the ring and cinched the harness firmly. Tonya reached out and grasped the dildo by the base, planting it against her pubic bone. She closed her eyes and gave a murmur of satisfaction. She started to stroke the cock, pressing the base against her mound.

It was a mind-blowing sight: my wife transformed from an ultimately desirable female into a startling hermaphrodite. She became instantly doubly sexy: all the eroticism of her curvaceous female body joined to the primal masculine power of the impressive phallus protruding from her groin.

"I'm the man now. You're the boy—or girl, I guess. Take your clothes off. Let's compare bodies. No, better: I'll take your clothes off. You'll be the passive, submissive one and I'll seduce you, dominate you, make you beg, and then take you!"

We got out of bed and I felt almost shy as Tonya reached out to stroke my nipples through my shirt. Then she began to unbutton my shirt and remove it. The reversal of roles made me uncertain, tentative. I just stood there, passive, letting her work on me. I felt so weak and helpless! She dropped my shirt to the floor and bent to suck at my nipples. Her massive cock bumped into me and slid against my hip as she suckled one nipple and then the other, sending electricity zapping through my body. I groaned. When she sucked my nipples it made me feel even weaker, more feminine.

Tonya poked her dildo against my cock and then dipped to thrust it between my legs suggestively, rubbing my balls from below. Sparks were going off in my brain as I saw her huge penis touching my modest one. A moan escaped my lips and I started rolling my hips with her thrusts.

Tonya pulled back and lightly stroked my dick again.

"How cute!" she squealed derisively. "It's almost like a real penis, just smaller! Not much compared to a real cock though." She turned to bring the dildo next to Little Johnny for comparison. Her cock was longer, thicker, easily twice the mass of mine.

"Which one looks like it could really do some fucking, Johnny? Which could really satisfy? Which would you rather get fucked by?" She aggressively thrust her cock against mine, pushing it out of the way. I swallowed and licked my lips, but no words came out.

"Go ahead, feel them both. Wrap your fingers around my cock. Feel the size of it, the weight of it, the firmness of it."

I reached out and took it in my hand. I'd stroked my own plenty enough to know there was no comparison. It felt like a baseball bat against my palm. I began to worry again how I my ass could accommodate it.

"It's so big," I murmured.

"So satisfying," Tonya continued, a dreamy, far-off look in her eyes. "Now touch your little peepee," she ordered.

I let go of her and took my shaft in hand. It seemed thin and small by comparison, although the warmth of it was nice.

"Which one is for fucking?"

"Yours...," I admitted meekly.

"And so what would you say yours is made for?"

"For wanking. It's made for beating off," I conceded.

"Yes, more like a clit than a penis! So what do you think? Who should fuck who?"

"You ... you should ... fuck me," I croaked out.

"Should you ever fuck me? Would that little prick be any good for fucking?"

"Noooo!" I moaned. "I'm not man enough."

"That's right! Every time you 'fucked' me, you were really just masturbating against my pussy, you little wanker!" She reached out and started to caress my dick, which felt wonderful. "But I don't know if you want it bad enough. I'm awfully tired. I've already had my fucking for today. I don't know if I want to go to the trouble."

"Oh please!" I yelped. "I do want it! I need it! I want to feel you, to connect with you. Please ... fuck me!" I begged.

"Then show me how much you love this cock, my cock. Worship it. Make me want to take you!"

'Take you.' That phrase fired my lust. Yes, that's what I wanted. I wanted her to take me, to conquer me. I wanted to be her possession, to show her I was hers through and through.

How else could I worship her cock? I fell to my knees and brought it to my lips, kissing the head, then down the shaft. Then I took the head in my mouth. The thickness of it shocked me again. It easily filled my mouth. I sucked on it and pressed it against the roof of my mouth with my tongue. It started out cool, but the Cyberskin began to warm gradually. I drooled saliva on it, making it slick and silky.

"What if it were real, eh, Johnny? What if it were a man's cock: warm, pulsing with his blood, oozing pre-cum on your tongue? Brian's cock, or Calvin's, or David's? Wouldn't you like that?"

Her suggestion scared and thrilled me at the same time. So forbidden, so perverse, but my cock swelled with arousal. I couldn't keep the images out of my head: the men's cocks I'd seen on the computer screen, fleshy, rampant, drooling. I'd seen Tonya take them in her mouth. Could I do that? Would I? Did I actually want to? The very question spurred me on. I took Tonya's cock in as far as I could, sucking on it, banging it against my tonsils.

"I guess that answers my question!" Tonya taunted me as I moaned around the rod in my mouth. She entwined her fingers in my hair and began to thrust gently in and out. I felt her take control, making me let her fuck my mouth. I fought to suppress my gag reflex as she hit the back of my throat.

"That's it: imagine you're sucking off one of my boyfriends. He's just fucked me and I need you to get him hard again so he can fuck my ass. That's how you'll show us that you really accept it, that you want him to fuck me. And you love sucking his cock: it is so gorgeous, so manly, so everything you wish you could be. You admire him, look up to him. So you want to worship his cock, the symbol of his sexual power. Sucking on it lets you enjoy that power, bask in it. It's like being the bat boy at the baseball game. These are the weapons of your heroes and you get to touch them, take care of them, even excite them.

"You can feel him hardening in your mouth. You can taste his pre-cum oozing. Your mouth is exciting him. It feels so good! He likes what you are doing: you are serving your hero. And pleasing your wife."

Tonya's voice was like a hypnotist's. I was adrift in a dream world where all this was happening. I was seeing and feeling and wanting everything she said. My pulse was racing. I felt hot, feverish. The cock in my mouth was real, warm, throbbing.

"And best of all, you find yourself aroused! This man's cock is making you hot! Your own little penis is hard, pulsing. You are turned on by sucking a man's penis!" I groaned. "Yes! I think I'd like to see that, Johnny! I definitely want to see you suck a man's cock. Maybe many men's cocks! And you're getting there, Johnny!

"Would you do that, Johnny? If I asked you to suck a man's cock, would you do it, for me?"

"I ... I'll do whatever you ask," I stammered.

"Excellent! Because if you ty it, I think you'll like it! I can hardly wait! Now let's get your cunt ready for him, too. Show me how much you want a cock fucking you! Then maybe we'll have man make love to you too!"

Tonya pulled me up by my hair and laid me on the bed. She reached out for my penis and found the knob glistening with pre-cum. She rubbed the goo all over the head of my cock, drawing a gasp from me.

"You like this! You like sucking cock and dreaming of sucking off my boyfriends! Good! That's very good! You make an excellent cuckold,

Johnny." While she talked, she milked more of my seepage out and used it to lubricate my dickhead. The wet slickness felt wonderful. If I hadn't already shot my wad twice earlier, I'd have come in 30 seconds.

"You just lie there, little Johnny. I'll be back in a jiffy." I gasped as she let go of my penis: I wanted it to go on and on. I lay there in a sexual haze. I was dimly aware of water running in the bathroom. Tonya returned holding the enema bag and hung it off the headboard. She scooped up a dab of lube and grasped my dick again, taking my breath away. In a few strokes she had my cock throbbing with need.

"Oh, your little clit is so hard, Johnny! But it's your cunt that is really in need, isn't it? Show me your boy-cunt, Johnny. Show me where you need me to fuck you!"

As Tonya continued to masturbate me, I pulled my legs up to expose my asshole. Her right hand scooped up a dollop of lube. While she continued the maddening massage of my erection, she smeared lube around my anus, toying with my ring.

"Ohhh!" I moaned and squirmed in anticipation. She dipped one finger into my rectum, while simultaneously pulling luxuriously on my greasy member with her other hand. She coordinated her assault, combining her stroking with the tickling and teasing of my anus. I started to grind my hips and purr.

Without stopping her hand job she grabbed the enema nozzle and I felt it slip into my bottom. In a trice she twisted the valve and warm water flowed into me. I tensed for a second but the warmth of the water soon relaxed me.

"Doesn't that feel good? Tonya's getting your ass all nice and warm and relaxed, so that you'll be ready for fucking." She closed the valve and slipped the nozzle out, holding a finger across my pucker. Now she was only holding my cock, barely massaging it.

"OK, now up and to the bathroom. Hurry back!"

With a groan I reluctantly stirred myself and quickly went into the bathroom and released the enema. A string of pre-cum stretched off the end of my cock like spider silk.

I hurried back to lie down on the bed. Tonya immediately grabbed my dick again and ordered me to pull my legs up. Wasting no time she plopped a fingerful of lube on my asshole and pushed a finger into my rectum, spreading the lube in all directions. She sawed the finger in and out: it felt like nothing. She grabbed more goo and I felt two fingers push at my anus. I strained to open myself and felt them push in, stretching the opening tightly. I grunted and willed my sphincter to relax, to let Tonya in. She started to gently fuck my bottom with her fingers.

"Open up, Johnny. Show me you really want me to fuck you. Show me you have a cunt that really wants cock." She grabbed up more lube and plunged two fingers back in more easily now. She worked her fingers in a circle, stretching in every direction, opening me up. I felt her knuckles against me, her fingers buried all the way.

Tonya kneaded my cock with her other hand, stoking my arousal, confusing my brain whether the sparks were coming from my cock or my ass.

"Beg me to fuck you, Johnny. Tell me how much you need cock."

I groaned at the effort to speak, to form thoughts.

"Please ... fuck ... me. I need it. I want your cock in me, just like you had Calvin's cock in you today. Fuck me like he fucked you!"

"You want to be my bitch? You want me to use you?"

"Yes!" I admitted. "I want to be yours! Take me! Fuck me into your sissy bitch!"

Tonya's fingers stretched into me, finding my prostate. I groaned as she sent voluptuous sexual jolts up my cock. She began to stroke my prostate insistently and it was so intense it was almost painful. I was writhing in ecstasy, throwing my head from side to side. She just held my cock, concentrating her assault on my backside.

"Oh, Tonya!" I moaned, too overcome to say more. "Oh! Oh! Tonya! Tonya!"

"What do you need?"

"I need cock! Cock in my ass! Please fuck me!" Wordlessly she pulled out her fingers and I panted in need. I opened up my eyes to see her lubing up the dildo, turning it into an obscene gleaming ramrod. But I was so horny that I did not quail at the idea of it stretching me. I'd do anything to get that wonderful stimulation again.

Tonya knelt behind me and I pulled my knees tighter to my chest, offering her a clear shot at my rectum. I already felt warm and loose from her fingers and I willed myself to be a cunt for her cock.

I felt the head of the dildo against my sphincter and again I was amazed at how huge it felt. I pushed down with my muscles, trying to open up for it, but my ass protested the stretching. Tonya massaged my sphincters with tiny thrusts, coaxing rather than raping me. But she pushed forward insistently and I winced at the taut stretching of my anal ring. She nudged back and forth and then thrust into me, breaking past the inner ring.

Oh God, it felt so big! Tonya continued to thrust gently in and out, but my ass still felt tight. She took my neglected cock in her hand and I groaned with the welcome distraction. She masturbated me for a few moments, leaving her cock still buried in my ass. Then she started to fuck me again, a little harder, a little deeper.

"You want it! You want to be fucked! You're a girlie man without a real cock. You want a big cock in you, to fuck you, to own you. Only you wish it were a real cock, that you were being fucked by a man! You're a faggot, aren't you?"

Her words shredded my ego but inflamed my lust. I groaned at the implications. With every stroke her cock was sliding in more easily and more deeply. I thrilled as it touched my prostate and I pushed down to rub my gland against her shaft. She buried herself to the hilt and now every thrust slid against my prostate, sending delicious sparks through my whole nervous system.

My ass was feeling warmer and warmer, looser and. looser. Yes! I wanted it. I needed it.

"Oh God, Tonya! Fuck me! Please! I'm your cunt!"

With that Tonya began to fuck me in earnest, with long, deep strokes. My ass was opening and loosening and I thrilled at the feeling of that massive cock going in and out of me easily. It was a feeling of surrender: my body was surrendering to Tonya. It felt wonderful, like a runner's high: full of energy but at the same time relaxed. Every thrust twinged against my prostate achingly, excitingly. Every withdrawal let me catch my breath and every thrust was a welcoming, ending with another wonderful poke at my prostate. I was in heaven.

"Is this what you really want, Johnny? Not to fuck your wife, but for her to fuck you? Do you like my cock? Does it feel good?"

"Auurrgh, it feels ... so good!"

"You love it, don't you? What if it were a real cock, a man's cock? Flesh and blood, throbbing with his excitement! Imagine! He'd be lusting for you! He'd be feeling your hot ass squeezing him. You'd feel his excitement as he fucked you harder and faster! You'd know you were pleasing him, that he was loving how your ass felt around his cock. Does that thought make your weenie even harder?"

I didn't want to, but I couldn't help picturing what she suggested. No! Was that a thrill of arousal going through me? Was the idea of making love to a man really exciting me? I didn't want that, did I? What would it feel like, a real flesh-and-blood cock, to let a man dominate and use me?

"And think of the best part: feeling him come inside you! When he has the orgasm you gave him! Imagine the feeling of his cock pulsing inside you, feeling every contraction, his cum shooting inside you like a volcano! There's nothing like it, Johnny! And knowing that you caused that. That you inspired lust in a man, that he wanted you!

"Beat off to that idea, Johnny! Take your cock and jerk yourself off, imagining my cock is a man fucking you! One of my boyfriends proving what a complete cuckold wimp you are! Do it!"

And what rippled through me was another unexpected thrill of excitement. A man's cock! Flesh and blood. His flesh inside me. Oh, my God, that was darkly exciting! Some deep secret place in my heart or soul or brain responded and sent a wave of sexual warmth through me!

In a sexual frenzy I took my greasy penis and began to stroke it as Tonya pounded into my ass. I closed my eyes and imagined it was

Brian's cock, hot and throbbing, on the edge of orgasm. I imagined him thrilling to his triumph, fucking his girlfriend's husband, unmanning him, proving he was the alpha male. I thrilled at the idea that my ass was pleasing him and that his orgasm would be my triumph. I'd be draining his seed and his strength from him. His orgasm would be my pinnacle: when I felt him spurting I'd know that I had served him and my wife well! My mistress and.... My master....

"You're a faggot, Johnny! That's why you can't fuck me! Say it! 'I'm a faggot!' "

I'd say anything by this time. I was insane with lust.

"Say it!"

"I'm ... a ... FAGGOT!!!"

"Yes!" Tonya crowed, ramming her cock into me furiously.

"Argghh!" I screamed and cum bubbled up out of my dick. My ass spasmed around the dildo, but my cum weakly oozed out, more clear than milky, since I'd already come twice that afternoon.

Tonya held the cock deep within me, watching my prick twitch and leak. She smiled and looked flushed with victory, knowing that I'd been imagining a man fucking me as I had come, just as she'd told me to. She knew that would be one more humiliation, one more layer of my manhood stripped away. Not only had I let her fuck me, but I'd let a man fuck me in my imagination and it had aroused me to orgasm! But did she guess how deeply it had touched me?

She started to gently nudge my ass with the dildo and I groaned. With my orgasm passed, the height of my arousal no longer made the cock a welcome intruder. It felt huge, foreign, and my ass was sensitive. But slowly she resumed a fucking rhythm.

"If I'm going to fuck you, it can't always only be when you want me to. I get to fuck you when I want to. I get to exercise my 'husbandly' rights. Look, your cock's still hard! It still wants more. Maybe I'll want all my boyfriends to have a go at you. They won't stop without having their turn just because you've had your orgasm!"

I pulled my legs up obediently, opening my ass wider so she could resume plowing into me.

"Wives have had to put up with husbands demanding their conjugal rights whether they were in the mood or not. God knows I've put up with your squirming on top of me, poking me with that little worm of yours when it was doing nothing for me. At least I have the courtesy to fuck you with a proper cock!"

As she continued to ream my gaping ass, I drifted down into a head space of even more abject surrender. Tonya knew her cuckold psychology. This ass-fucking was going beyond role reversal and gender bending. She was showing that she was in charge and that I was hers to use and abuse. And I was accepting it.

As she continued to abuse my ass I found myself feeling more and more weak and helpless—but filled with warmth and love for her! She was taking me where I'd never known I could go and I had no choice but to trust her, to open myself to her, to follow her, and to love her with all my heart and all my body. This dildo was plunging into my ass, but it was claiming my heart and soul for Tonya.

She was smart to keep fucking me like this. I had no choice but to surrender completely. I was completely defenseless, so all I could do was let go and let myself be used. And I found myself floating on a blissful cloud! No ego, no will, just ... acceptance!

"I love you, Tonya!" I cried as she raped my ass over and over. "I love you!" I started to cry, my legs pulled tightly to my chest to allow her to fuck me, with my cum still pooled on my stomach. "I love you!"

"I know!" she said as she continued to fuck me like a machine. "Tell me again!"

"I love you! I worship you! I don't care if you fuck me, or fuck other men, or suck their cocks, or they fuck me, or I suck their cocks! I still love you more and more!"

"I know, baby!" she choked out and she was crying too. "I know you really love me!" she said, her voice straining with the effort of fucking me. "I love you too!"

She buried the cock in me and leaned down and we were kissing. I could feel the dildo pushed up against the top of my rectum and we kissed long and deeply.

"I love you," I whispered. "More than ever."

"And I love you more each day, Johnny," she replied.

With great care Tonya started to withdraw the dildo from me. My ass ached with the feeling of emptiness. It felt as if you could stick a football in there.

Tonya wiped at the cum and smeared it on the greasy end of the dildo and down the shaft. She brought it to my lips and I immediately took the head in my mouth and sucked the cum and lube off. I grabbed the cock and licked up and down it.

"That's what my lovers' cock with be like when they pull out of my ass or pussy. All covered in their own cum. A tasty treat for you to lick off, eh?"

She grabbed a handful of tissues and wiped the lube from my abused anus and rear end. She grabbed more tissues and wiped off my sensitive cock. To my surprise she lay down next to me with the dildo still on and began to kiss me. We cuddled and kissed like that, the dildo awkwardly pressed between us.

"Don't you want to take the harness off?" I asked.

"No, I think I'll keep it on. I like it. It's a real feeling of power! I like having the big cock in our family! It makes me feel like the boss."

"OK," I conceded and marveled at Tonya's transformation.

I hated to spoil the mood, but I couldn't help myself.

"Um...."

"What?"

"What you said. What you told me to say. Did ... did you really mean it?"

"What?" Tonya asked, just to be contrary, knowing what I meant.

"That ... that I'm a ... faggot? Do you really think I'm a faggot?"

"It would explain a lot, wouldn't it? How you like to be fucked, how much eating cum turns you on."

"But I love you! You turn me on! Women are very sexy to me!"

" 'I think she doth protest too much!' But don't you think Brian's cock is very sexy? Doesn't his cock turn you on too?"

That was the scariest thing she could ask. Because ... it did.

"Does that mean I'm a faggot?"

"Who knows? Maybe you are really a faggot deep down. Maybe you aren't. I guess we'll find out. We'll keep trying things until we find out. But the important thing is that no matter what, I'll still love you. So just keep an open mind. And an open ass! And mouth!"

She laughed and kissed me and that broke the tension. I still didn't have an answer. It still worried me, but I could put it away for now.

We spent the rest of the evening in our bathrobes. The front of Tonya's robe was penetrated by the dildo, jutting out lewdly through the front slit. Every time I looked at it I felt a twinge of perverse arousal at the strange hermaphroditic figure she cut. Her voluptuous body and feminine robe jarred against the rampant phallus protruding from her groin. When she walked she seemed to swagger, as if the dildo were the prow of a ship cutting a swath before her. But it also reminded me of Brian's cock and a little shiver went through me as I pictured it.

Before bed she asked me to fellate her for a few minutes. She told me it would be "good practice" and also remind me of "my place" in our new relationship. She felt my reluctance to fellate a piece of rubber.

"Imagine it's Brian's cock then," she told me ad then complimented me on my improved enthusiasm. I tried to protest that I wasn't doing it any differently, but beneath my protests was the knowledge that she was right. It was more exciting to imagine I was submitting to her lover.

To my surprise Tonya crawled into bed still wearing the dildo. We kissed with it poking into my groin. Tonya reached down and pulled my half-hard cock up against hers, pressing the underside of my dick against the underside of the dildo.

"Look how little yours is compared to mine! Yours really is just a big clit, isn't it? But it's cute, like it's my cock's little brother. Well, <u>baby</u> brother." She held them like that, squeezing my cock against hers and jiggling the dildo up and down, almost fucking my cock with hers. It felt sort of nice.

Then she had me roll over and she spooned me, placing the dildo between my legs and rubbing it up against my ass crack.

"I like fucking you, Johnny. I hope you liked it, because we're going to do it some more. Did you like it?"

"Yes, Tonya dear. I loved feeling you inside me. I felt so ... helpless, but it was OK, because it was you and you love me. I ... sort of liked ... feeling helpless."

"That makes sense to me. That's a feminine feeling, being passive, helpless. More and more you're letting go of that struggle to be strong, to be manly. It must be a relief to surrender to. your feminine instincts.

"But it might not always be me That's fucking you, Johnny. And it might not be for love, either. It may be just for sex."

"I don't know if I'd like that," I said, but something quivered inside me. I'd be a sex object. Oh! Why did that idea excite me?

"Hush, Johnny. We'll see what happens. I'll never force you to do something. But I may ask you to do things you don't think you want to do, just because I want you to do them. And you might find you like them once you try them. But I will never force you. It will always be up to you in the end."

"OK."

"I want so much for you, Johnny! I want you to experience everything that excites you, deep inside, no matter whether you think you 'should' want it or whether other people think it's wrong. I want you to feel all the joy and excitement you can! Just let Little Johnny lead you. If it makes him hard, it's good, no matter what anybody thinks. Listen to Little Johnny. Follow him. Now hush and go to sleep."

"Good night."

Tonya's dark hints worked on my imagination. Images of Brian's cock and the videos from the cuckolding sites flitted through my head. Cuckold husbands sucking the wife's lover clean. Sucking him to make him hard for her. Opening their mouths to take his ejaculation straight onto their tongues. And ... prostrating themselves while he ... fucks them. Makes the cuckold his bitch.... Cocks, cocks, cocks. Big, hard, beautiful cocks....

-Day 21 Friday-

I woke the next morning. I'd forgotten about the dildo until I rolled over and it was between us. Tonya sensed my movement and cuddled up to me, poking me again. I reached down and pulled it between my legs, up against my testicles. It tickled my taint and felt huge between my legs. I couldn't believe I'd taken it up my ass.

Tonya lay on her back and told me to straddle her in a 69 position and to practice sucking her. I took the dildo in my mouth and washed it with my tongue.

"Get used to having it in your mouth. Take it deep as you can."

Tonya couldn't resist my backside squirming above her face. She popped the lid of the lube and slipped a finger in my ass. She twiddled my abused prostate, then stuck two fingers in, twisting this way and that. My cock sprung to attention.

"We don't want this hole to get all closed up again!" A minute later she said, "Get up and kneel by the bed." I thought she was going to face-fuck me again, but she slipped off the harness.

"Chin back, mouth open. We'll call this the 'toilet position.' " She straddled my face and soon I felt the hot spray of her urine filling my mouth. I swallowed without thinking anything of it, feeling only a gladness to be used by her and a warmth spreading from my stomach from her gift. My cock filled with warmth as well.

"We're a good fit for each other, Johnny," Tonya said, looking down at my hardening penis. "Our psyches fit together, just like Brian's cock fits my cunt!"

After the last 36 hours, going back to work again was like waking up from a dream. But every time I went to the john and saw my women's panties encasing my crotch, I was reminded it was all real. In fact, in some ways it was work that seemed more like dream world. At work I felt as if I were a spy going undercover. Here I had to pretend to be "normal," to hide the fact that I was a pantied cum-lapping urine-drinking sissy cuckold. That was my new real life, but no one outside must know.

At dinner it seemed as if we were continuing the "normal" masquerade. Tonya told me with amusement how she'd "admitted" to everyone at work that she'd really been hungover, not sick.

"But I didn't tell them what I was hungover from!" she laughed.

But the normal interlude was short-lived. Tonya had me help her undress and then she asked me to lick her pussy and ass. Her pussy smelled so good that I knew that she'd been aroused that day.

"Calvin told Brian about our 'afternoon delight.' I was a little worried that Brian would be jealous. After all, big-dicked guys aren't usually as generous with their women as you little fellas have to be! But he thought it was hot! Of course it was originally his idea to invite Calvin and David to join us, but some guys want to call all the shots and don't want anything going on to the side.

"But Brian was totally OK with it! He was just surprised that I'd be up for anything after the fuck-a-thon we had Wednesday night, much less for more anal sex. Brian's really perfect for me: a great cock and a generous spirit too. Of course no one's as generous as my Johnny! Brian at least gets his turn, and he's not my husband either.

"Oh that's so relaxing when you lick my pussy and ass so gently and lovingly. You must have been a girl in your last life!"

To my surprise Tonya asked me to get out the dildo and harness and again she fastened it on. But this time she got out a frilly negligee instead of her robe. The cock sticking out from under the lace and frills of her lingerie shorted out circuits in my brain. She bade me lie down next to her and she rolled to hug me, the dildo pressing against my hip.

"Baby, I've been thinking a lot today. I bet you could smell what I've been thinking about when you ate my pussy! I don't see how we can keep up this charade of my supposedly sneaking around behind your back to fuck my boyfriends."

That 'boyfriends—plural' jangled every time she said it. It wasn't going back to just being Brian. And it didn't sound as if it were just about sex either, as much as it once did. It sounded more and more like a relationship. Or relationships, maybe.

"I'm not going to want to settle for a night here and there, just when we can invent a plausible story for you to be out of the way. Even if it were every Wednesday, I'm not going to be able to wait a whole week to get some of the big-cock fucking. You can see that, can't you?"

"Um, I guess ... um ... sure," I stammered.

"Not only that, but I'd like to be able to relax, to fall asleep with one of those hunks next to me in bed and to wake them up with a morning blow job on one of those glorious meat poles.

"And it's not fair to you. As much as you like to jerk off watching a real man fuck me, I miss having you there, being part of the action. There's things I'd like to see happen that aren't going to happen with you in another room."

"Like what?"

"Oh, I think you know, but let's leave that for another time! What I'm saying is, I think we need to stop pretending we're going behind your back."

"You're going to tell them everything? That I've been spying on them and videotaping them without their knowledge?! They could be pissed! They could probably sue us—and that would be the least of it. They could tear me limb from limb!"

"No! Relax, silly! I'm not going to tell them you've known all along! I'll tell them that you caught us. Brian is already worried that you're bound to catch on sooner or later. I'll just tell him it was sooner. Calvin's afternoon delight gives us the perfect opportunity. I'll say you came home early because you were worried about me being home sick and you found Calvin here. Heck, that's actually the truth. They say that's the secret of convincing lying: use as much of the truth as you can."

"But if I've caught you, isn't that going to end it?"

"Sure, it would—if you were a normal manly husband! But you're my little-dicked wimp husband. I'll tell them that I threatened to leave you rather than stop seeing them. I'll tell them that I blamed your, er, shortcomings for my infidelity, and I ridiculed you for being unable to satisfy me like they can. I'll say you broke down and begged me to stay with you and that you said that I could have as many lovers as I want as long as I wouldn't leave you."

'Talk about sticking as close to the truth as you can,' I thought to myself.

"Yes! I'll tell them you completely fell apart, blubbering and begging, that you'd say anything and agree to anything to keep me from leaving. So I decided to push my advantage. I told you I refused to sneak around at all, that I would have these men right in our home and fuck them in our bed, right under your nose and that you would have to accept it.

"In fact, we'll say I told you that if this were going to work, you'd have to accept this as my perfect right. You'd treat them as our guests, since they'd actually be doing you a favor, satisfying your wife's needs that you could not. And I'll tell them that you agreed to it all, in tears, on your knees, trembling in fear that I'd walk out on you if you didn't."

Something about this "story" unsettled me. My stomach was full of butterflies. I remembered all too vividly my actual anguish and fear when Tonya had revealed what a complete failure I was as a lover. I had been in terror that our marriage was over and I had begged her to stay no matter what it took. But a part of my mind was also realizing that this 'story' was sketching out new rules for our future far beyond what we'd discussed before. I was expected to accept any number of men in our bed, coming and going as they pleased, and that I'd have to humiliate myself by condoning it happening under my own nose and treating these men as guests in my bed!

But what could I do? In actual fact I <u>was</u> exactly in the position that Tonya was supposedly "concocting" for her "story." She called all the shots. I had to do whatever she said or I'd risk losing her altogether.

"What if they don't want to do it? What if they can't handle knowing that I know? What if they don't want me there?"

"Hell, they've all three fucked me in front of each other already. I didn't notice any stage fright! I think you forget the psychology of the alpha male. They'll probably get off on lording it over you. Besides, I've got the pussy—and ass, for that matter—that they want to fuck, so I'm in the driver's seat. Are they going to give up a chance at that? Remember, most men will do anything their cock tells them to do.

"But how do you like this angle? I'll tell them we have to do it with you right there because we need to humiliate you and crush your ego. That doing that will make you helpless to change your mind. We won't tell them it turns you on. That would make it sound a little gay. But I can sell them that we need to weaken your spirit and defeat you. That will appeal to their male ego, to be the conqueror rather than a gigolo."

"But what if it turns out that I don't like being there? What if it is too humiliating to be there, the defeated husband?"

"But that's why I want you to be there: to acknowledge that defeat, to face it head on. Your little-dick ego won't be able to hide, won't be able to pretend you're the man you wish you were. Humiliation is what we want: it is the death throes of that part of you that wants to pretend to be the big man, the stud. Humiliation is good—the stronger, the deeper, the better. It's our signpost that we are going the right way!

"Humiliation is actually the point. Well, fucking is the point, but humiliation is the way to get there. As humiliating as it is to hide and jerk off while you watch your wife fuck other guys—and then eat their cum out of her pussy—it'll be ten times as humiliating to look those guys in the eye and hand your wife over to them! You could never go back to thinking you're 'the man of the house' after that!

"You think you know how big Brian's cock is now, but wait until you're in the same room face-to-face with it! That'll make it so much more real to you. It'll be the difference between watching a basketball game on TV, knowing some guy is 7 feet tall, versus standing next to him and feeling him tower over you. You'll be able to compare your little willie to his man-cock with your own eyes.

"Imagine it! You'll be able to smell how excited I am, hear the squishing of him pumping in and out of my pussy, feel the heat coming off our bodies. You'll be standing by meekly while another man possesses your bride's womb just a few feet away! It will be glorious humiliation! It'll be like drinking Jack Daniels instead of Ripple wine. It'll blow your mind! You'll be so turned on you won't be able to help but beat your meat in time with Brian's thrusts!"

She took my very stiff cock in her hand.

"Look how hard you are even as I describe it! As terrifying as that scene is to your false pride, it excites you terribly! Or is it 'wonderfully'? You need it and we need it. It is a natural step in killing the delusion that you are my man, of pretending to yourself that you could ever were my man. You're my husband, Johnny, and I love you to pieces, but you need to know that you can't be my Man."

As if to remind me why I couldn't be her man, she pushed the dildo up against my dick. She grabbed the dildo and my cock in her hand, squeezing their undersides together. She began to gently thrust the dildo against my penis, bizarrely "fucking" my cock with her much larger one. Once again I was rendered passive and helpless, as the stimulation was so delicious and strange that I was overcome.

"Tell me you'll do it, Johnny. Tell me I can call Brian and tell him that tomorrow night he's going to fuck me in front of you!"

The stimulation was so intense that I could barely speak, but we both knew what I was going to say.

"Uh.... Uh.... Yessss! Unh! OK. Whatever you want. Ohhh!"

"Good boy!" Tonya said softly and immediately let go of my penis. She got up and said brightly, "I've got to call Brian and tell him the good news! And make plans for tomorrow night!" leaving me in frustration. "Go ahead and finish yourself off if you like, but be thinking of that. Be thinking of what it will be like to be right there in the same room, allowing a better man to fuck your wife. Thrill to that. Come thinking of that, wanting that, burning for that!"

She left the room and I clutched at my oozing penis. I felt shame: here I was, about to masturbate while my wife called her lover! Was I that desperate? Was I a mechanical toy—"Stick the coin in the slot and watch him beat his meat"? Did I have that little pride or self-control? God knows I'd come enough times in the last 36 hours, I hardly "needed" it. Maybe I'd just show her that I wasn't a puppet on a string.

But my eyes lit on the jar of lube. It would feel so good to feel my slippery hand stroke my throbbing cock! I was so close, it would only take a minute. Tonya's already given me permission. Heck it sounded as if she wanted me to.

My hand reached out to the jar almost as if it had a mind of its own. My cock certainly had a mind of its own! It didn't seem to care who Tonya was fucking. Or, worse, it seemed as if it preferred Tonya fucking other men. Maybe Tonya was right—maybe masturbation really was my preferred sexual activity. Maybe I was more in love with my own hand than with her!

'If so, so be it!' I thought to myself as I opened the lube. I hesitated on the precipice for a second, then my fingers dipped down into the jar.

"Fuck it!" I said to myself. "No, beat it, I guess!" I spread the lube over the glans and down the shaft and sighed with deep pleasure. My hand enveloped my cock and I began to slide it up and down hypnotically.

Tonya didn't have to tell me what to think about while I masturbated. Her order was only meant to deepen my humiliation, because she knew exactly what I'd be fantasizing. I had to think about it because the picture excited me tremendously, just as she had predicted.

I imagined seeing Brian's cock with my own eyes, mere feet from me, seeing its size, seeing it stiffen and throb with masculine power! I'd be fascinated, in awe, almost reverent. I imagined him cupping Tonya's breasts possessively and looking over at me, his unspoken words saying, "You're not stopping me! I'm pawing your wife and you're just sitting there letting me. What a pathetic wimp!"

I imagined Tonya spreading her legs and I could see her cunt lips swollen, opening for him, so eager. I could smell the scent of her excitement so strong that it reached me across the room. And I pictured his cock poised at her opening, almost as if to say, "Last chance to stop me!"

I gasped as I imagined his cock plunging into her. I felt on fire as I thought, 'It's done! He's taken her!' My hand flashed over my slick penis. In my mind's eye I saw myself masturbating there too, right in front of them, beating off across the room while Brian fucked my wife better than I ever had. That was the ultimate humiliation: not only did I allow it, but I thrilled to it!

And then I was back in reality, cum jetting over my belly. For a few moments I was in ecstasy, and then I started to come down. There I was, my hand a greasy mess, cum squirted over me. I'd given in, let my lust rule me again. But it felt so damn good! If I were a pathetic wanker, I might as well enjoy it. I knew that I'd do this again, and again, and again.

I scraped up the pearly cum onto my fingers as best I could. It looked disgusting there and for a moment I considered sopping it up with tissues. But I'd feel guilty for disobeying Tonya, so I licked it up as quickly as I could, as she'd ordered me always to do.

I looked down at my shriveled penis. What a little worm it was now, all deflated! Not much better when it was hard, I guess. How could any woman lust after that?

Once again Tonya became my lifeboat in a sea of self-pity and self-disgust. Tonya loved me; Tonya married me despite It all! What a miracle! Tonya's love saved me. If a parade of men and miles of strange cock was what it took to keep Tonya happy, that was a small price to pay to be in her life.

I took some tissues and cleaned up the lube and pulled a robe on. I could hear Tonya speaking low and intensely into her phone. She still wore the dildo, but I could see that she'd slipped a hand under the base of the dildo and was fingering herself as she talked to Brian! Whatever they were talking about was turning her on, for sure. I wasn't in the mood to eavesdrop on their conversation, so I went into the other room and turned on the TV.

Tonya stayed on the phone with Brian for a long time. I wondered if he were dismayed at the news that they'd been found out. But that would be nothing compared to the news that their affair would continue with her husband as an audience! That might take some fancy talking by Tonya to get Brian to go along. But I knew first-hand how persuasive she could be!

Finally she came in, the dildo bobbing before her as she walked. She sat next to me and reached into my robe, inspecting my little dick and discovering its shriveled condition.

"I see you took care of yourself. Good boy." Then she put her arms around me and hugged me with excitement.

"He bought it! He's willing to come over tomorrow night and he's willing to let you be there while we fuck! Oh, it's going to be so exciting! I can't wait for you to be right there when he sticks his cock up my pussy! God, it's making me wet just thinking about it! Shit! Lie down! I want to fuck your face!"

She unbuckled the harness and pulled the dildo aside, then straddled my face, suffocating me with her wet and fragrant pussy. I started to lick and suck her musky slit, but true to her word she started bucking and scrubbing her gash across my face, practically using it like a washboard. She was very turned on and aggressively wanting to wring her orgasm out of me, not passively waiting for me to bring her off. I tried my best to lick and suck her while she hunched her pelvis into me. She was frantic for her come and soon her cries and shudders told me she had reached it.

"Oh, God, that felt good!" she exulted. "Now relax me with a little gentle ass-licking." She turned around and settled her ass on my face, her starred anus winking at me. "I expect Brian will want to fuck my bottom too tomorrow. In fact, I think I will insist on it, to show you he's welcome to places you've never been! So make sure I'm nice and loose and ready for him!"

I never needed much prompting to eat out Tonya's luscious ass. The feeling of her rounded globes encasing my face was heavenly and the earthy scents of her backside would have put the starch back into Little Johnny if he hadn't been beyond exhausted. I loved the feeling of her puckered ring squeezing my tongue and then giving way and letting me spear into her bowel. Although she was still tight I could feel that she was opening up wider and more easily every time we did this.

"Oh, Johnny, you're so good at ass eating! I could rent you out to the girls in the neighborhood! That feels so nice!

"And now for a little practice with my other sex organ!" She rebuckled the dildo harness and crawled over me, her head toward my feet. She held the dildo above my nose. Knowing what she wanted I craned my neck to reach it.

"That's right," Tonya encouraged. She gently moved the cock until it filled my mouth. "Don't try to take too much. We don't want you to choke." There was something touching about her tone, gentle and encouraging. She was a concerned teacher guiding her student. It was almost heartwarming as long as you didn't think too hard about the fact that she was trying to teach her husband to suck cock.

"This is something you can really be proud of, something you can really be good at, not the false pride of thinking you could be a manly man," Tonya explained. "You can be a great cocksucker—no special equipment needed, just desire and dedication."

I felt the dildo hit the back of my throat. I felt myself start to gag. My eyes teared up. I had to pull my head back and cough.

"Poor baby!" Tonya sympathized. "Make love to that cock! Kiss it. It is the cock of your lover. Kiss it and make a wish: that it were a real live cock, warm, pulsing with blood, trembling to shoot creamy sperm down your pretty throat. Close your eyes and wish!"

The cock loomed above me, shiny, wet with my saliva. I closed my eyes and kissed it. I imagined a man's cock slipping into my mouth. To feel his cock twitch with excitement ... and then ... to feel it jerk with orgasm and shoot his seed into my mouth....

I was lost in the fantasy. In the heat of my arousal the idea did not seem disgusting or frightening. It seemed ... hot! I kissed the dildo lovingly as Tonya directed, then pulled it against my cheek with my hands.

"Yes, Johnny! Yes! Imagine that!" She reached down and grasped my little willie, trying to torment it into yet another erection. She swung herself around and lay on top of me, the dildo sandwiched between our bellies.

"God, I love you, Johnny!" she kissed me hard and assaulted my mouth with her tongue. She continued to kiss me hard and to writhe on top of me, rubbing the dildo into my belly.

"You may not be much of a man, but other than that you're a perfect husband for me! You make me happy in so many ways I'd never even imagined a month ago. Even your little no-good-for-fucking weenie makes me happy! It makes you so excited when you masturbate and that makes me happy. It makes you excited when you see me fuck another guy, and that makes me so glad. It even makes you want to suck a cock and take a cock up your ass. It pops up like a signal flag to show me how much you really want that, even if you don't want to admit it. So I love this little baby cock!" She kissed me again, tenderly this time. "And I love you."

She kept the dildo on for the rest of the night and fell asleep with it in between us.

## -Day 22 - Saturday

I was as nervous as the first time Tonya's slept with Brian, maybe more so. Even though that had involved another person in our fantasies, this was the first time for me to "go public" as a cuckold, even if Brian would be the only witness. It was another level. Tonya said it would be another "breakthrough" in our exploring the new dimensions of our marriage.

"God, Johnny, we're setting ourselves free! We're throwing off the chains of convention! We're doing what makes us happy, instead of what the 'rules' tell us we should want. It's intoxicating! If you want to beat off in front of us, go ahead! If you want to suck Brian's cock, do it! I won't tell you that you can't, that it's 'too gay.' If it makes Little Johnny hard, just do it!"

She really was stuck on this 'gay' thing. I felt a shudder of shame every time she said something like that. But every time my little dick got as hard as a rock! If I were naked, Tonya would pointedly look at my stiffy and if I were dressed she'd feel me through my clothes and raise an eyebrow at finding me hard, to let me know she knew. But why? Why should the idea of seeing or touching or sucking Brian's cock make me hard?!? I'm not gay....

"This is making me nervous! What am I going to do, sit here waiting for him to ring the doorbell?"

"No, I've already thought of that and I agree with you. That would be just too awkward. I decided that my meeting him somewhere else and coming back here would be better. So I told Brian I'd meet him at the club like we did Wednesday. We'll have a drink or two to get loosened up and get over the butterflies, and when we're horny to jump each other's bones, then we'll come back here."

I wasn't sure if that would be any easier, but Tonya had it all arranged, so I went along. I was insane with conflicting emotions. Half of me dreaded that evening and half of me couldn't stand for the hours to pass. For the first time Tonya forbade me to masturbate that day.

"The hornier you are, the better," she said. "That'll put Little Johnny in charge and he'll tell you just what to do!" I kept myself frantically busy with chores, just to try to keep my mind from thinking.

Tonya went out and bought yet another foxy outfit for the occasion. I was tempted to beat off while she was gone, but I sensed that somehow she'd know, so I held back. The dress she got was thin, clingy, and barely covered her tits and cunt. She bought a silver sequin-spangled thong, so that no one could miss seeing her panties when she dipped or twirled dancing. She put on dramatic make-up and blaze red lipstick. Everyone at the club would know that Brian was getting lucky that night.

"Do I look hot enough, Johnny?" she asked.

"Tonya, four guys are going to come in their pants when you walk in the door!"

"Good, then. That's the look I was going for!"

"Not the happily married woman look, then?" I replied.

"Well, I'm married, and I'm happy, so I guess this is how some happily married women dress!" she said, kissing me on the cheek and immediately wiping her lipstick off my skin. "I'm a married woman who's happy that her husband's taking her to meet her stud boyfriend! What married woman wouldn't be happy about that?"

Put that way it almost sounded noble rather than sordid. I was a devoted husband doing what made his wife happy. What could be wrong with that?

When we got to the club it was already crowded with the Saturday night revelers. As we surveyed the throng I had to remind myself I was supposed to be the cowed husband, reluctantly delivering his wife into debauchery to avoid a divorce, who'd just found out his wife had already been cheating on him. I adjusted my mindset to play my part: angry, hurt, and scared.

To my surprise it was not just Brian waiting for us: there were Calvin, David, Audrey, and one of her girlfriends. So I wasn't to be humiliated just in front of Brian alone!

Already I started to feel embarrassed. Three people here knew I was a cuckold and now they presumably knew that I knew. I started to blush and stammered out a greeting. I saw each man look at me with what? Curiosity? Wariness? Pity? Scorn?

Brian brashly reached his hand out to greet me and I automatically took it. He looked me in the eye and grinned a shit-eating smile! Then Calvin and David shook my hand in turn, greeting me as if I were a long-lost buddy.

"Johnny! Great to see you again! (Great fuck your wife is! Thanks for bringing her! Thanks for being such a good sport!)" It made me think of the jocks greeting the guy who had snuck a case of beer out of his parents' basement fridge.

"Tonya!" Audrey said with real surprise in her voice. "Look at you! All foxed out! What's gotten into you lately, girl?" That had Brian and his buddies falling out laughing. 'Our cocks is what's gotten into her!' was what they were thinking. Tonya sat right next to Brian and planted a big French kiss right on his mouth! I could see Audrey's eyes go wide and I knew she wasn't in on this. What must she be thinking? I felt a wave of humiliation go through me: Audrey was seeing me stand by while my wife carried on with another man. But my cock was swelling to a half-boner!

"Johnny, you should get this round," Tonya ordered me. "I want a margarita. See what everybody else wants." She wasn't wasting any time putting me firmly in my place.

I came back with a pitcher of beer and a pitcher of margaritas. Tonya kissed me on the cheek when I sat next to her, but she was leaning against Brian, plastered to his side. I felt my jealous instincts rise and I had to talk to myself.

'You can't compete with him,' I said to myself. 'He's' your natural superior. Be glad she even lets you suck her pussy after. She's doing you a favor to let you watch so you can jerk off while he fucks her. You're the intruder here, not him. You're lucky you can even come along for the ride.'

As these words sunk in I lulled myself into a dreamy detached state. I looked at Brian and Tonya. They made a nice couple. A more even match than Tonya and me. I wasn't bad looking, but Tonya was a "9" and I was maybe a "6." Brian was a really handsome, muscular man. I looked over at David and Calvin. David was a Nordic blond who could be a ski model. Calvin was an athletic black man with a chiseled profile. These men were in Tonya's league. I was lucky to be the bat boy.

Hell, if you took a certain perspective I was lucky. I was the kid who'd won the raffle to be the home team's honorary bat boy. I got to sit in the dugout with the pros. I was the envy of all the boys who were in the stands, wishing they could be the bat boy! It was my place to serve the pros as best I could. I could feel the lure of "sub-space" I had read about on S-M websites.

Tonya had been right to force this next step. I needed a lot of practice to accept my place. And it could only be done by facing it and feeling this jealousy, by enduring the embarrassment in public. By eating the humiliation.

With a start I remembered that I wasn't supposed to be a willing cuckold. I was supposed to be a reluctant, coerced, wronged husband. I shook myself out of my cocoon and got back to playing my part. I stared a frown at Tonya snuggling up to Brian and I squirmed in my seat. Tonya took the cue.

"You don't mind if I dance with Brian, do you, honey?" she said a little too loud and with a subtly sarcastic edge.

"What?! Oh, uh ... no ... I guess not. Whatever you want."

"I should think you'd be relieved. I mean, you're not that much of a dancer. Brian's a much better dancer than you. That won't make you jealous, will it?"

I looked down at the table.

"No, I guess not. Go ahead." I saw David and Calvin look at each other and stifle a guffaw. They either already knew about the "arrangement," or else they were getting off thinking I was clueless to the innuendo.

Tonya and Brian walked to the dance floor, Tonya's ass-hugging dress showing off her body with every step. It was a fast dance and Tonya was wriggling like a pole dancer, her wares barely held in by her skimpy dress.

I stared them down with a look of mortification and anger. Calvin and David decided to rub it in.

"Wow, look at Tonya go! What a hot momma!" Calvin gushed.

"She can dance with me any time!" David leered.

"Whoa! I've never seen her go to town like that!" Audrey declared. "I don't know what's gotten into her!"

"Brian!" David and Calvin said and fell over each other laughing. "I mean, he's such a good dancer it inspires her to match his, er, energy, I guess," Calvin rushed to explain away their remark. They both looked at me and my face was burning with embarrassment. I had only expected to deal with Brian tonight. I hadn't anticipated being made a laughingstock in front of Brian's buddies.

"You better do something, John," Audrey prodded. "If you don't slow Tonya down this might turn into something more than dancing!"

"Yeah, John, are you gonna let her carry on like that?" Calvin jibed.

"They're just dancing. It's a free country. I'm not that into dancing, so I don't mind if she enjoys herself."

"Yeah, Tonya was telling us about how you don't dance very well!" Calvin continued to stick it to me. "It's really nice of you to let her dance with other men so that she can really enjoy some good dancing!"

"I'll drink to that!" David enthused and raised his glass. "To John, a really good sport!" He and Calvin clinked their glasses and shared a laugh, while Audrey and her friend drank to the toast with a quizzical look.

"Well, I guess not every man would be OK with it, but Tonya and I trust one another." I said to try to put a brave face on it.

"But I hear that the way you dance, Tonya doesn't really have to worry about you dancing with another woman!" Calvin joked.

"No, I suppose not. But I, er, enjoy seeing her happy."

"I guess we'll see," Calvin said mysteriously, and I was almost certain now that Calvin and David knew what was going to happen later! I wanted to shrink out of sight! Having Brian know was going to be hard enough, but having to endure the grins and smirks of these two was awful. Were they planning to come over too? Did they expect me to submit to another orgy tonight? As always, I felt a shiver of fear go through me at the thought, but my cock got hard even as my cheeks burned!

The music had turned to a slow dance and I knew what I would see when I found Tonya and Brian in the crowd. They were molded together like Siamese twins, crotch to crotch. The crush of dancers blocked them from view for a while and then when they came back around they were kissing! There could be no doubt they were giving each other tongue. It was so hot that I got turned on watching them!

"My God, look at her!" I heard Audrey whisper to her friend. "Doesn't she know she's married? Shit, even if she were single I'd tell her to get a room! Maybe she's mad at John and this is some payback thing. Or maybe she's trying to make him jealous. But I don't see that working. John's just not the type to fight back."

'Yeah, he's the dickless wimp type,' I thought to myself. Is that how everybody saw me? "John's such a nice guy. Tonya's lucky to have such a devoted husband. I mean, he's no tiger, but he'll be home every night and she'll never have to worry about him going out on her. Mr. Dependable, that's John." Ugh! No wonder she was turning to other men. Were her girlfriends taking bets on how long it would take before she went out on me?

"Still enjoying seeing Tonya enjoy herself, John?" Calvin jabbed. What was up with him? Didn't he see which side his bread was buttered on? Why was he egging me on? Did he want to see a fight? Or was it like Tonya said, they saw it as a conquest and were getting off on knowing that I <u>wouldn't</u> fight, that they could lord it over me and revel in defeating me?

"Like I said, it's a free country," I replied and took a drink of my beer. I decided to start playing it as the defeated husband, resigned to his helplessness, drowning his sorrows. It would be easier than playing the tense, resentful, prickly husband. And it let me get in touch with my real feelings. I was trying to eat my humiliation like a good boy and take solace or even feel noble, that I really was sacrificing for Tonya's happiness.

Tonya and Brian came back flushed and exuberant from their dance. Tonya shooed me to move into the booth to make room for them, Brian on one side and me on the other again. But Tonya was pretty much ignoring me and focused on Brian and making no attempt to hide that.

"Pour me a margarita and Brian a beer, honey," Tonya ordered.

"Yeah, I bet you're pretty thirsty after that workout," Audrey said, arching her eyebrows at Tonya.

"Oh, Audrey! Brian and I are just friends! We just like to dance."

"Yeah, we saw you getting friendly!" Audrey replied.

"Oh, it's just innocent flirtation!" Tonya maintained. "Johnny doesn't pay it any mind, do you, honey?"

"No, it's nothing," I said in a flat voice, staring at my glass in resignation.

"See?" Tonya said. And with that she turned and gave Brian another passionate kiss.

"Shit! I need to get myself a friend like that—tonight!" Audrey said in a stage whisper.

"C'mon, then, let's you and me dance!" Calvin said, grabbing Audrey by the hand. David invited Audrey's friend to join them, leaving Brian and Tonya and me at the table.

"I must say, you're being really civilized about this, John," Brian said as soon as the others were out of hearing. "I was a little weirded out about this, but you're being pretty cool."

"Well, that's the way Tonya said it had to be. It wasn't really my idea, was it?"

"No, it was my idea," Tonya interjected, "and John's going to do as he's told, because it really was his little problem that made this necessary, wasn't it, Johnny?"

"Yes, dear," I conceded with a sigh.

"Now that doesn't mean you can't enjoy it, though. Wasn't your little peepee getting hard as you watch me dry hump Brian out there? Isn't it a turn-on to see your wife as a hot seductress?" Tonya reached over and rubbed the front of my pants, stroking my hard-on through the fabric.

"And, Brian, isn't it a turn-on to be able to carry on with another man's wife right in front of him and he can't do a thing about it?" She reached over and stroked the front of Brian's crotch, eliciting a shudder and quiet moan from him.

"Oh, yeah!" Brian sighed in acknowledgment.

"My, look at me!" Tonya cried. "Two men hard for me." She continued to stroke each of us in unison, her actions partially hidden by the table. "Whatever will I do with them? Which cock will I suck and fuck? This little one?" she said, looking toward me, "But it's so little. Or this big one?" she said, turning toward Brian.

"It feels nice and long and thick. I bet it would feel so good up my pussy! But it feels so big! John, do you think I could get this big cock up my ass? You know we've never had anal intercourse, so I've never even taken even your little dickie up my ass. Could I fit this big manly cock up there?"

"I'm sure I don't know," I said, but my excitement from Tonya's stroking was making my voice a little unsteady.

"What about you, Brian? Do you think my ass could take this man-meat?"

"Oh, yes!" Brian gasped.

"But if it did, it would be so tight and so full! Would you like to see that, Johnny? See if your little wifey could take a big thick cock up her little pink butt-hole?"

I closed my eyes and swallowed. Having Tonya play with us both, in public, with no one the wiser, and her talking so filthy, it was a massive turn-on for both Brian and me.

"I don't know!" I whispered.

"Brian, Johnny's never seen his wife take a big cock up her ass. Would it be OK if he watched? I think it would be so educational!"

"Yes," he choked out. "If you want."

"Oh, I do want! I want it very badly, because once he's gone along with that, I don't see how he can object to our sucking and fucking whenever and however we want! Especially if he gets off on it, if it excites him so much he wanks his little wiener while you're fucking me, which I'm pretty sure he's going to do. I think he's going to be so turned on watching his bride get fucked by a real man that he won't be able to help himself!"

"Oh, God!" I whimpered. "Can we go home right now? I can't take much more of this!"

"You're so turned on by the idea you can't wait to see Brian fuck me? You want to rush home and watch it? See I told you," Tonya said, tuning to Brian. "What do you think, Brian?"

"God, yes! Let's go!" he said, squirming beneath Tonya's stroking hand.

"Well, then, it's unanimous, because I can't wait to get a big cock in my pussy! Home, James!" Tonya said imperiously to me.

Tonya decided we'd take Brian home in our car and leave his car at the club. Tonya got in the back seat with Brian, relegating me to chauffeur duty. Brian and Tonya almost immediately started making out in the back seat as I drove them to our home. Then I heard a zipper and Brian moaning. In the rear view mirror I could see Tonya's head bobbing up and down. She was blowing him in the back seat before we'd even gotten home!

"Mmm!" Tonya purred, "It's so nice to have a kielbasa in your mouth after so long with only cocktail wieners!"

Fortunately the drive was soon over. I pulled into our drive, but Tonya didn't stop right away. I watched intently in the rearview mirror in silence.

"I don't know which I like better, baby: your mouth, your pussy, or your ass. They're all so good," Brian told Tonya.

"Well, that was just an appetizer. You'll get to decide before the night is over!"

Brian awkwardly stuffed his wet and stiff prick into his pants and limped into the house. I was thankful that Tonya immediately took charge when we got in the house.

"I want you both naked right now and come sit next to me on the couch." She kept her seductive outfit on, emphasizing her control. We each stripped quickly. I couldn't help but stare at Brian's cock. As Tonya had predicted, it was even more impressive at close range than in the pictures or on the videos. Against my will my own dick started to harden. I saw Brian smirk at my modest endowment.

Tonya took my penis in her hard and lightly toyed with it.

"See what I had to work, Brian? And Johnny," she said, reaching out with her other hand to cradle Brian's meat, "can you blame me for being excited by this? I can see that even as a man, you appreciate a beautiful penis when you see one. You were getting hard just looking at it!"

"It's ... it's just the situation...," I protested.

"Look at it! Isn't it magnificent?" She squeezed it and gave it a couple strokes. "Look at yours. Which do you think would give me more pleasure? Which would feel the best in my pussy? His or yours?"

"His...," I admitted in a defeated voice.

"And as my husband, don't you want me to be pleased? Isn't it your duty to make me happy? Can you make me happy with this little dick? Can you fill my cunt and make me scream with joy?"

"No!" I croaked out.

"Why not?"

"Because ... I'm too small. I'm not ... man enough...."

"So you admit you've failed me as a husband?"

"Yes!" I whispered. But a strange ripple of arousal went through me! To admit I was less of a man ... a failure—in front of my wife's lover ... it excited me!

"But this cock! This is a real man's cock. Stand up, both of you. I want to compare them."

With a fuzzy head I stood up and Tonya had us stand face to face, our erections jutting out like lances ahead of us. Tonya took each cock in her hand and pulled us forward until our cocks were side by side, almost touching!

The proximity of that big prick made me nervous—but excited! It was as if sexual energy radiated off his penis. Brian's dwarfed mine, like a full-grown man standing next to a six-year old! Mine was like a baby penis next to his. I was almost afraid to look at it, as if that would make me gay, but it fascinated me at the same time.

"This cock feels so good going in my pussy, Johnny! It fills me up, it touches me in places your dickie has never been." She closed her eyes. "It makes me feel complete. I want to melt. I feel possessed, helpless. Happy.

"And when it's in my ass.... Oh, that's fuller than full. That's turned inside out. It makes me crazy! It turns me into an animal. A cavewoman. That cock is the club the cartoon caveman carries. It knocks me out!

"Do you want that for me, Johnny? Do you want me to feel that good, to be that happy? Do you want to make that happen for me, even if it can't be you that does it?"

I looked at her and I couldn't speak. I felt small, not my cock, but my whole self, as if I were shrinking under their gaze. She had never spoken so directly about what she felt with Brian. It dazed me.

"Johnny, I want you to feel it." She took my hand in hers and placed it on Brian's cock! I had never touched another man's cock before!

"Feel it! Squeeze it! Feel how thick it is! Feel how hard it is! Feel how hot it is!"

I felt as if I were in a dream, but I did as she said. My hand was trembling as I wrapped my fingers around his shaft. I was touching another man's penis! I looked at his cock and my hand as if I were watching someone else. My eyes were riveted on this penis.

Brian's cock was almost silky, with the skin stretched so tight by his hardness. The softness of the skin was exciting and it moved easily over the hardness of the erection beneath it. It felt so thick in my grip and so big that it felt heavy in my hand. The head was stretched tight as I pulled the skin down the shaft and a pearl of pre-cum formed at the slit.

I felt—what? I felt small and weak. It was as if all strength were draining out of me and Brian were growing stronger. And I felt ... awe. This was the cock every man wished he had.

And I felt excited! Not just the excitement of the situation: I was sexually turned on! I looked at my hand wrapped around a man's penis and I couldn't believe how much it aroused me! It was as if electricity were flowing into my fingers!

"Do you want me to fuck that cock tonight? Do you want to give me the best gift a husband could give his wife? Do you want to give me the gift of ecstasy? Do you want to show me that kind of love and share with me the joy this cock can give me?"

I looked at the cock in my hand, and then at Tonya's imploring face and then for a moment at the man whose cock I held in my hand.

"Yes!" I whispered and my voice shook. I wanted that so much! I couldn't wait!

"Say it. Say it out loud," Tonya commanded.

"Yes, I want you to fuck him. I want him to give you all the pleasure I can't!"

"Why?"

"Because I'm not man enough! Because I'm a failure!"

"No, honey. Because you love me! Because you want the best for me even if it hurts you! Because you take pleasure in my joy, even if that joy is in the arms of another man. You want me to take joy in the arms of another man!"

I don't know why I spoke but the words were torn out of me.

"I'm not good enough for you," I croaked. "You should fuck him. He's a real man. He's the man you need, not me!" It almost felt like a relief, like a weight off my shoulders to say it out loud. Maybe Tonya was right.

It was a relief to quit trying, to stop pretending to be a man. To dwindle down into ... whatever I was.

She wrapped her hand around Brian's shaft, overlapping my hand and leaned forward and kissed me. Then she turned and kissed Brian while we still held his penis together. The warmth of her hand on mine and the warmth of Brian's penis were mind-blowing. I couldn't believe it but I was jacking another man's cock! I kept slowly pumping it even as my wife was kissing him!

"Johnny, feel my cunt. Feel how wet it is. Feel how much joy you are giving me tonight!" I released Brian's penis and slipped my hand under her dress, pulling her thong to one side. I touched her nether lips and my fingers came away sopping with her juices.

"Now taste the juices my cunt has wept for another man! Taste how eager your wife is to make you a cuckold before your own eyes!"

In a trance I put the fingers to my mouth and tasted the strong taste of her arousal. She pulled off her dress and pulled her thong off and lay back on the couch.

"Johnny, I want you to lick my pussy and make it wide open for Brian's gorgeous thick cock. Brian, come here and kiss me and suck my breasts while Johnny gets my cunt ready for you!"

Brian, to his credit, didn't let this bizarre situation faze him a bit. He fell to mauling my wife's beautiful breasts and kissing her. Her pussy already leered at me, swollen with arousal. I smelled the overpowering aroma of her excitement and I was eager to taste more of her cunt. I fell to my knees and it felt right that I crawled to her. It was fitting that I was kneeling on the floor like a slave and Brian was next to her. Her pussy lips pressed hot against mine and they were heavy and stiff with her lust. I feasted on them, all the more excited at the thought that Brian's cock would soon be parting these folds!

"That's it, hubby. Get your wife all wet and open," Tonya told me. "Brian's pretty big. He needs a lot of room."

Out of the corner of my eye I could see Tonya clutching Brian's penis, caressing it to a fever pitch. My own hand still tingled where I had been holding Brian. His cock was mere inches from my face!

"Oh, Brian, I need your cock in me! I have to feel it in my cunt!"

Brian was more than happy to oblige, but Tonya held her arms out to stop him.

"Wait! Johnny, do you really want me to fuck him?"

"God, yes!" I cried, my face glistening with Tonya's juices.

"Then I think you should put him in me. Take his cock and put it at my cunt!"

I was in a fever. I would have done almost anything! I reached out and took Brian's thick erection in my hand and, trembling, I held it to Tonya's obscenely eager pussy. I couldn't believe I was touching another guy's penis! His shaft was warm and I could feel the hardness of it. Oh, my God, this was turning me on so much! My hand tingled, as if his penis were electrically charged. And my own meager penis jumped at the contact. Tonya reached out and stayed my hand, leaving me gripping Brian's cock on the verge of her vagina.

"Johnny, I think you should ask Brian to fuck me. After all, he's doing your job for you. Ask him nicely to fuck your wife properly, since you can't do it."

"Oh, God! Please babe!" Brian begged, desperate to bury himself in her welcoming flesh.

I turned my eyes from the rampant cock poised at my wife's entrance and looked up at Brian's face. I was holding another man's penis and looking him in the eye! I swallowed in a dry throat and croaked out, "P-please, would you please fuck my wife ... since I ... can't satisfy her?" I dropped my eyes back to the rod quivering in my hand. His penis felt hot in my palm. I was holding another man's erection!

"God, this is hot!" screamed Brian and, with my hand still gripping his shaft, he thrust at Tonya. My eyes went wide when I saw how, even in her heat, Tonya's cunt could barely stretch to accommodate his tool! Her vagina was stretched tight around his shaft. He did not relent but continued to press in and Tonya grunted in pain / pleasure.

Suddenly I realized that I still had my hand around his shaft and pulled my hand away as if I'd been burned. He pulled out an inch to spread her juice around her opening and then he thrust into her again. Again her cunt resisted and only two-thirds of his shaft was in her. Her pulled back again and then nailed her, driving all of his organ into her.

I couldn't take my eyes away! It was so close, so real. The scene in front of me was pure lust. Tonya cried out in satisfaction. I could smell her and feel her heat from two feet away! I saw Brian's shaft draw out of her, glistening with her secretions. He was fucking my wife right in front of me, inches away from me! I was an official cuckold now: a willing, participating cuckold. I could hear his grunts of exertion from driving his cock into her. It was totally different from the video. It was as if their sexual electricity was radiating into the air. I couldn't take my eyes off that magnificent penis, like the cobra hypnotizing its prey. God, I loved it!

My dick was throbbing with excitement, pre-cum oozing out of my slit. Tonya had thoughtfully put a jar of lube on the side table and I fumbled with the lid in my eagerness to coat my prick with it. I gasped at the sensation as my hand greased my tiny organ and I began to stroke myself. I closed my eyes and shuddered. It felt so good!

"Look at Johnny, Brian!" Tonya whispered. "He's beating his meat while his wife fucks another man! He's not angry, not violent. He's turned on! He likes it! It's exciting him so much he has to masturbate! That's what his little winkie is best for!

"Are you enjoying yourself, baby? Do you like watching another man fuck your wife? Is it turning you on, to see your wife make you a cuckold?"

I closed my eyes in shame, but my hand didn't stop pumping my penis.

"Tell us, Johnny. I want to hear you say it. Does it make your little peepee hard to see a real man fuck your wife's cunt? Tell us!"

I looked down at the ground.

"Yes!" I hissed out.

"No, look at me! Look at Brian. Tell us!"

"Yes!" I said, looking up with a mortified expression. "God, it's so sexy! Yes, I like it! Yes, it is exciting me! His cock, it's so ... sexy! God help me, I don't know why! I must be some kind of pervert! I've never been more turned on!"

"Yes, some kind of pervert. No real man would do that. But I love you, Johnny, so go ahead and jerk off! I want you to enjoy yourself too. God knows, you should get something out of this, since you can't fuck me and you have to watch your wife be unfaithful."

Tonya pulled Brian's face down to hers and kissed him deeply.

"Oh, God, Brian, your cock feels so good in me! Show him how a real man fucks! Show him how a real man satisfies a woman! Make me your woman and make him your bitch!"

"Oh, God!" Brian cried and I knew that Tonya had pushed all the right buttons to make him wild. She was giving him her cunt and making him the victor over another man, all at the same time. It was his birthday and Christmas together. He could steal another man's wife and defeat a rival just by using his penis: the fantasy of every stud.

I was amazed that Brian hadn't already shot his load after all the build-up, but I suppose having me there and Tonya's little speeches were a distraction. But now he was concentrating and pounding her cunt with long, hard strokes. Tonya was no longer dividing her attention: she was consumed with absorbing the punishment he was giving her pussy, pulling her knees back to open herself as wide as possible. She was arching her back to meet his thrusts, giving a tiny gasp as he buried himself in her, ramming her pubic bone with his own.

I was mesmerized by the sight. My world became the joining of their sex and the silky feeling of my hand on my dick. I slowed my strokes to luxuriate in the delightful sensations coming from my engorged penis. Long strings of pre-cum were drooling off the end to the floor. I started to feel the tension building in my groin and I knew my spend was moments away.

I looked at my wife's face and I knew she was being transported to a land where I had never taken her. His cock was her world. He was wringing supreme pleasure from her cunt. Her hips were writhing under him in an uncontrollable animalistic rhythm. This was what Nature designed sex to be, a savage meeting of cock and cunt! This was real fucking and it took my breath away. What I had called fucking had as much to do with this as tiddlywinks did with football. Brian was a man and Tonya was his rightful prize.

Tonya started to orgasm. Her head was whipping side to side and she was growling and moaning.

"Oh, fuck, Brian! Oh, God! Oh, it's so good, so good! Unh! Unh! Oh! Oh! Fuck me! Fuck my bitch cunt!" Her legs were twitching and she hunched her pelvis into him.

It was magnificent. I felt pulled along into the maelstrom of their fuck. It was like hearing a beautiful symphony or seeing a work of art. I felt grateful to be allowed to be a small part of it. I felt in awe of them, of their power, of their beauty. I was a witness to their passion. I didn't just feel it in my cock. I felt it in my heart. Tonya was right: as strange and twisted as this might seem to others, Tonya and my sharing this was an act of love!

As that thought crossed my mind I gasped and cum shot out of my penis. I only had a split-second to reach out my free hand and I only caught a part of the jet, which flew out with startling power, landing on the coffee table and rug.

I thought Tonya was oblivious to me, but she heard my shout and opened her eyes briefly, smiled a Mona Lisa smile and blew me the tiniest kiss, just between her and me. Then she closed her eyes and let Brian's cock transport her again.

"The wanker's shot his load, baby! Show him where a real man plants his seed!"

That was all it took to fire Brian's lust. He started thrusting frantically in short hard strokes. Then he froze and bellowed.

"Ugh! God! Arrggghhh!" he shouted, more like pain than joy, as if his seed were being ripped from him. "Oh fucking God! Shit! Shit! Ohhh!" He writhed and then collapsed on top of her.

Tonya wrapped her arms around him, hugging him to her bosom.

"Oh, Brian, that was wonderful!" Tonya panted. She was talking to him, but she was looking right at me. "Look at the wanker! He's made a mess!" Brian cocked his head and saw my palmful of cum and the strings on the table and dripping off the end of my dick, and shook his head in distaste.

"I think he should clean it up. I think he should lick up his own mess."

"Ew, no, that's gross, Tonya!" Brian reacted.

"If you think that's gross, that's just a warm-up for what's next. Go ahead, lick it all up, hubby, or I won't let you put Brian's cock up my ass!"

God! As unhorny as I was from just having shot my wad, that threat still scared me! I did want to put his cock up her ass! I dearly wanted to!

I'd have walked over hot coals to do it! God, I wanted just to feel his hard cock in my hand again. Licking up my cum in front of another man was nothing if it meant I could plant that magnificent cock in Tonya's beautiful ass!

Brian watched with wide eyes as I dipped my face to my hand and swallowed the strip of ejaculate there.

"Shit, man! No!" he hissed. He shook his head as I licked the jism off the coffee table and even the rug. It embarrassed me, but it felt somehow like an achievement, to prove I would do it, to lower myself even more in Brian's eyes.

Tonya whispered to him, but I knew she purposely did it loud enough so that I could hear too, but low enough that Brian would think it was a secret.

"It's part of our plan," she whispered. "You have to go along with it. We have to degrade him so that he'll be so humiliated that he can't object to anything we want to do! Follow my lead, even if it shocks you. I know him: I know what he needs and I know he'll do it."

Tonya rolled Brian off her and he collapsed next to her on the couch. She closed her legs with a hand pressed to her pudendum.

"Come look at a well-fucked cunt, Johnny! You've never seen one before, at least not that you knew!" She hunched her hips up and spread her legs. I crawled over between her knees. The scent of sex was overpowering, not just pussy smell, but the foreign smell of Brian's semen as well.

"Look at it, Johnny! Isn't it sexy? Look how red and puffy it is! That's what a pussy looks like when it's been stretched and used by a nice thick cock, really open and pounded. Look how it gapes open, how wet and gooey it is! Isn't it beautiful? Isn't that the way you always want to see your wife's cunt, so satisfied? Don't you always want to see it that way, forced open by the big cock of a real man? Don't you want to see it dripping with cum, blessed by the seed of an alpha male?

"Doesn't it smell so nice? Not just the pussy juice, but the smell of a real man's potent sperm. Doesn't it smell good enough to eat? Don't you just want to taste it, to taste what a satisfied, well-fucked pussy tastes like?

"This pussy's been unfaithful to you, Johnny. It's broken our wedding vows. I swore in a church, before a minister, in front of our parents to be faithful only to you, to never let another man's cock in there. But I've done it. Not just tonight. Not just Brian either. It's fucked Calvin and David too. This pussy just can't get enough big cock.

"But this pussy needs to know that you still love it, even filled with another man's spunk. It needs to know you still love it even while it still tingles with the orgasm from another man, even with another man's cum dripping out of it."

She took my face between her hands and pulled my face up to look her in the eyes.

"Kiss it, Johnny! Kiss my unfaithful cunt! Let this cunt know, let me know, and show Brian that you forgive this cunt for making you a cuckold. Show me that you're so hopeless that you still love me even though I've fucked another man and I'm going to go on fucking other men, lots of other men!"

I looked at her cunt. White semen was oozing out, starting to drip down her lips toward her crack. It glistened with her spend and Brian's. The lips stood out, still engorged, but a little more floppy, red and sore-looking. But to me in that moment it was beautiful! It was like a flower blossoming, opening up to give its nectar. I gazed at it and I loved it! That was the core, the center of my Tonya. Defiled by another man? No, anointed, consecrated with the virile seed of a better man. In that moment I was taking Communion, being baptized into the Church of the Unfaithful Cunt.

I wanted nothing more In that moment than to taste the cum of a real man. With reverence I bent and placed my lips at the opening, where a glob of Brian's cum gathered ready to plop out. I kissed Tonya hot nether lips and sucked that cum into my mouth.

"Yes!" Tonya exulted in triumph. "Taste it, baby! That's the fruit of the fuck you just witnessed. That's Brian and me mixed together, the taste of our love! Savor it! Love it!" I heard Brian grunt a sound of amazed disgust.

I buried my face in her folds. I lapped up the juice that oozed out of her pussy and then I buried my tongue in her, probing to taste more! Brian groaned. I tasted it, the bittersweet—wonderful!—taste of another man's cum. I knew that taste, unforgettable, undeniable. I was eating another man's semen! And I loved it! I shuddered with humiliation and lust mixed together.

"Brian, look how much he likes it! Get it all, baby! Get every drop of Brian's manly juices! Maybe there's some of his testosterone in there, to make more of a man out of you, instead of cunt-lapping cum-sucking wimp!" Tonya's switch back and forth between loving, exhorting, and degrading whipsawed my brain, but I knew that was deliberate, to get me so confused I'd do or feel whatever she wanted.

"Do you like my cream pie, baby? Did Brian and Tonya make a tasty cream pie for you?" I just kept licking as my answer.

"Look at his winkie, Brian! He does like your cream pie! He's getting hard again from eating his cheating wife's sloppy cunt!" And indeed my traitorous dick was filling up again mere minutes after my orgasm.

"I bet he'd like another treat!" Tonya archly hinted. She pulled me up by my chin and pushed my face toward Brian's crotch. She reached out and grabbed his now-limp but still impressive unit.

"I don't want you just to love my cummy cunt. I want you to love this gorgeous cock too, Johnny, I know you're not gay—or at least I don't think so—well, maybe bi…. But anyway, even if you are straight, you've got to love this cock! It's beautiful and it's made your wife so happy.

"And we need to get it cleaned off, but even more, we need to get it all hard again so it can fuck my ass! And you really, really want to see this cock in my ass now, don't you? But this cock's so tired from the hard fucking it gave me. It's going to take some work to get it nice and hard and you're the only one who isn't tired from fucking."

Tonya took my face in her hands again and did her, 'I really mean it, you have no choice,' looking me in the eyes thing.

"I want you to kiss this cock and show Brian you love what his cock did for my pussy. And then I want you to lick off his cum and my cum. And then I want you to suck him hard so he can fuck my ass! Show me what a good cocksucker you can be and make your wife happy!"

I'd only 15 minutes ago touched another man's cock for the first time and now she was asking me to give him a blow job! She'd teased me and made me jack off fantasizing about it, but now was the moment of truth! I'm not supposed to do that. Everything I'd ever been told that it was wrong for a man to want that.

I wondered what Brian was thinking and I looked up and he was smiling with anticipation! So I guess it wasn't too gay for him! Tonya had nailed it: he was enjoying my humiliation. He was proving he was the alpha male. Getting blown didn't make you gay: giving the blow-job is what made you gay.

Tonya reached down and took my half-hard cock in her hand. She was gently stroking me, like a horse whisperer with a skittish colt. She bent down to whisper in my ear.

"Look at it! Isn't it a fine cock? You know you want it! You want to feel it in your mouth. You want to love it with your tongue. You want to feel it swell between your lips! It's covered with my pussy juice! It's been so far up my cunt, it's squirted straight into my womb. You want it. That's what you girlie boys want, to feel the power of a real man, in your hand, in your mouth, in your ass!"

She bent his shaft toward my mouth. I noticed with amazement that it didn't look as limp as it did a minute ago. Brian was getting excited by this! I felt a little thrill of pride that the prospect of my mouth on him might be arousing his manhood.

"Manhood." His manhood. The sound of that excited me! I wanted his manhood! My mouth tingled. It was watering. I was hungry ... for cock! I wanted to taste it, I wanted to feel it swell. I wanted to feel the heat and the hardness of it!

"If you love me, you'll do this, because this makes me so happy," Tonya urged. "You want me to be happy and so you want this hard and hot and in my ass!"

I lowered my head to the glistening knob and, trembling, I planted a tentative kiss on it. My lips tingled where they touched him. I was kissing another man's penis! I felt a hot thrill in my chest. It was soft and spongy.

"Yes!" Tonya thrilled and squeezed my cock in encouragement. She began to stroke it lightly.

The glans was sticky and not as smooth as it had felt earlier when it was completely hard. My brain in overload, I tentatively licked at it, scraping my tongue around the head and then up the shaft, like licking a lollipop. I thrilled as it twitched in response and savored the now-familiar taste of Tonya's juices and Brian's cum. I was actually <u>doing</u> it: I was licking a man's cock!

Now for the moment of truth. I'd dipped my toe in the water, but it was time to jump in the pool. I could hardly believe it, but with a deep breath I opened my mouth and took his cockhead in my mouth.

It was big! It filled my mouth with soft warmth. I thrilled to feel the blood pumping and the head getting bigger and harder! Tonya kept massaging my dick, but I was more excited by feeling Brian's penis stiffening. I felt my mouth fill with saliva and I began to spread it around his head with my tongue.

Oh my God! I was officially a cocksucker. I had another man's penis in my mouth. I was sucking him. My head was rushing, as if I were drunk. But I had another feeling of ... pride? Accomplishment? I'd done it, what Tonya'd wanted, what I'd been afraid to do, what I'd been tempted to do. I was sucking a cock! I'd climbed the diving board and jumped off the high dive!

I sucked as much of the shaft as I could into my mouth, feeling it bump against the back of my throat. I bobbed my head on his cock, slurping my lips around the shaft as I withdrew it and plunging it against the back of my throat.

'I've got a cock in my mouth. I'm sucking a cock,' I screeched silently in my head. I felt a shudder go through me. My whole body was vibrating.

I grasped his shaft in my hands to give myself better control and began sucking and licking. I reached my tongue out for the sensitive ridge on the underside of his penis, just below the knob and I was rewarded by hearing Brian gasp.

"Oh, Johnny, you're doing it!" Tonya exulted. "Good boy!"

This was so much better than sucking the dildo! This cock was warm, the skin was soft, and it was throbbing and pulsing with Brian's arousal! I felt the hair on the back of my head stand up and a thrill went down my back. I was loving how his penis felt in my mouth! I was loving being a cocksucker! I was so turned on by it!

"Oh, shit! Mmm!" he moaned. "You sure he's never done this before?"

"Oh, Johnny, he likes it! You're doing a great job! Oh, I'm so proud of you! You are making me so happy right now!" She squeezed and stroked my dick deliciously and I redoubled my efforts.

"Oh, Johnny, doesn't it feel so good in your mouth? It's so big and hard and warm and slick."

I could only grunt "Uh huh" with my mouth full. I began to pick up some of my slobber and stroke his shaft with my hand while my mouth worried his cockhead. I tickled the underside of his shaft with my tongue and then ran the tip of my tongue around the sensitive rim of his knob. I was exploring his whole penis with my mouth. I wanted to savor every ridge, every vein! It did feel good! It was sexy! God, it even tasted good! It was arousing me to have this potent organ in my mouth! It didn't matter to me right then that he was a man and I was a man. I loved it!

"Shit, babe, I think he's gonna put you out of business for blow-jobs! I'll be sneaking around to see him behind your back if this is a preview of what he can do! I guess only a guy can really know what feels best to a dick, since he's got one himself."

"Well, a scale model of one!" Tonya laughed.

"Sure, but it's a working scale model. Oh, shit, that feels wonderful! Watch out, Johnny, or you might get a surprise!"

At that Tonya gasped and reached her free hand down to her pussy and started toying with her clit. The idea of Brian erupting in my mouth obviously excited her! She was clearly delighted at the enthusiasm Brian was showing for my blow-jobs. She'd been worried it would be too gay or too kinky for him. Perhaps she'd had to get him over the hump with her excellent use of psychology, but now he was evidently a convert!

"As hot as that idea is, I have plans for that hard-on, so don't go too far, Johnny."

I realized to my chagrin that I was really getting into sucking Brian's cock! Knowing how good a mouth could feel, I was getting into giving him all the pleasure I could. But I was also feeling pleasure! There was no doubt that it was a gorgeous specimen of a cock. It was thick and heavy and oh-so-slick with my saliva. I delighted in running my tongue up and down the smooth skin and feeling him quiver. It was big but that made it all the more pleasant to wrap my lips and tongue around it!

My recently spent cock was hardening. It was so wrong: by having sexual contact with another man I had gone over the edge into forbidden territory. I couldn't believe how much I was enjoying this! It was almost as if by sucking this superior man's penis I were absorbing his sexual power.

I looked at his again-stiff cock and felt admiration for Brian. He was hard again so soon after a tremendous orgasm. I knew how big, because I'd just sucked his huge cum out of my wife's cunt. I felt like a boy looking up to his favorite sports hero. It felt right that I was kneeling before him, as if I were worshipping him. It felt good to submit to him!

"Does my little hubby like sucking a big cock? Is it nice to have a big cock to play with after all these years of only getting to play with a little baby cock? Tell me!"

I took his cock out of my mouth, but I kept licking it.

"God, it is a really nice cock. I wish mine were as big as this!" I answered. "It feels nice in my mouth. It's … so … sexy." I was telling the truth, but it sounded so gay coming out of my mouth that I blushed.

"I think I may know another reason he doesn't fuck you like you want, Tonya," Brian chuckled.

"You're enjoying this way too much, Johnny!" Tonya agreed. "Back off! That's my cock! I think it's time to adjourn to the bedroom. Looks like Brian's ready for the next course."

I relinquished Brian's cock reluctantly. Looking at it, hard and wet, I felt a pang of hunger to have it back in my mouth!

Tonya led us into the bedroom, one on each side of her, one of her hands on each of our cocks. With the spell broken temporarily, I was feeling sheepish about how eagerly I'd sucked Brian. What was the matter with me? But part of me couldn't wait until I could do it again!

Tonya interrupted my internal struggle.

"Look at my ass, Johnny? Isn't it nice? Wouldn't you like to get it all relaxed and loose so I can get Brian's big cock up there and you can see me get fucked up the ass?" She lay on the bed, but kept Brian standing next to her so she could keep a hand on his penis and stroke him lazily. She drew her knees up, exposing her rosebud, which still showed signs of her reaming of two days ago. A thin film of pussy juice and jism had trickled down from her pussy to dampen it.

"Eat my ass, Johnny. Get it ready for Brian to ass-fuck me!"

She grabbed my weenie and maneuvered me around into a 69 position, so she could continue to milk my shaft just as she was milking Brian's. I lowered my head between her cheeks and kissed her rear entrance gently and lovingly. Then I tongued it and began to suck on it and probe inside. The pussy-jism smell began to be spiced with an earthier smell from her rectum. For some reason that excited me and I drove my tongue into her, trying to see how far I could get it in.

"Oh, that's marvelous, Johnny! You so love to eat my dirty asshole too! Your tongue is so gentle, not like Brian's nasty cock! You are a gentle soul, Johnny. I'm so lucky to have both of you: a gentle partner to take care of me and a strong virile man to fuck the bejeezus out of me! "

Tonya turned to mouth Brian's cock, keeping him nice and hard for the second act. She turned away from him, but kept one hand on that phallus. She bade me to come around to the side of the bed where she turned her head to kiss Brian's cock.

"Now you," she said, pushing his prick toward me. I kissed it as she had. I was happy to get my mouth on it again! My cock twitched at the perversity of it. Then she licked up one side and nodded at me to lick up the other.

"Now both sides at once!" she suggested. She held Brian's cock between us and we each licked up one side. When we got to the top, she closed her lips around one half of the head and I did the same, so out lips half-met, with Brian's cock held between our two mouths.

"Oh, shit, you guys are blowing my mind!" Brian cried, but the smile on his face told me he was meaning that as a good thing.

"Half-men like Johnny are fascinated with real men and their cocks, Brian. I sensed he might take to this pretty well." I blushed and drew back. Tonya might be reminding me not to act too happy about it, for fear of scaring Brian off, although I guessed he was too fascinated and turned on to stop now. But I suppose we had to wonder what he would tell Calvin and David. Their comments might freak him out when he was removed from the situation and not so horny. I decided I'd better go back to acting a little more reluctant again. I stepped back.

"Maybe we should move on, Tonya," I suggested.

"Can't wait for the next act, eh?" Tonya teased. She excused herself to go to the bathroom and give herself an enema. "Keep him hard for me while I'm gone, Johnny!"

"Why don't you get the lube out, Johnny?" Brian said, taking Tonya's part. "Get my cock all lubed up so I can fuck your wife's ass!"

Wordlessly I let go of his cock and retrieved the lube jar. I realized that my own cock was already shiny with the grease I had put on it earlier. That embarrassed me again. I took the lid off and with trembling fingers I pulled up a generous glob of lube and awkwardly dabbed it on his rampant erection.

That seemed worse, even wimpier to be dabbing it on like a fairy, so I grabbed it in my hand and began smearing the lube all over his cock. I realized to my chagrin that I hadn't taken enough lube: I'd taken enough for my cock, but I'd need at least twice that much for Brian's weapon. I scooped up another fingerful and coated his whole shaft and head thickly. I told myself I was just making sure it was spread just right, but in fact I was enjoying the feel of his cock filling my hand and the slippery feel of his greased shaft. The thrill of having control of this gorgeous penis was turning me on. My palm was tingling where his cock was sliding over my skin!

I realized that Brian hadn't said anything and I looked up and his eyes were closed and he was obviously enjoying my ministrations. My own cock jumped as I pictured the scene, us alone in the bedroom, with me masturbating my wife's boyfriend! But I didn't want to stop! I was loving it!

"Why don't you lube yourself up, as long as your hand's greased up?" Brian said quietly and I looked at him in surprise. He was suggesting I stroke myself, which was actually pretty perceptive, as I was dying to touch myself, in fact. The thought flitted through my head, 'I can see why Tonya likes him he's a pretty nice guy, for a wife stealer.'

Dropping my head in embarrassment I said, "Yeah, thanks." I shuddered as waves of pleasure rolled over me at the feel of taking my jutting erection in hand and feeling my greasy fingers slide up and down the shaft, just as they had been stroking this god-cock moments before.

"OK, that's enough. Back to work," Brian commanded me. He thrust his cock in the direction of my hand. Greased up, it looked even bigger and somehow, meaner, ready for action. I took it and began to slowly slide my hand up and down the shaft. I was fascinated by it, seeing the veins stand out and seeing the spongy outer sheath compress and move against the hard inner core. I felt a rush of warmth percolate up my back, standing my hairs on end. I was slipping into "sub-space," enjoying the sensation of serving a man who was so much stronger, more dominant than me. My ... master?

"Oh, my God! That's darling!" Tonya shouted, fascinated at the tableau. "No, don't stop! My two boys, enjoying each other! It's precious! Don't move! I have to get a picture! And a video!" She grabbed up her phone and began to snap pictures furiously, telling us to smile, for me to hold Brian's cock out at the camera, getting close ups and full-body shots.

"Look how hard you both are! And your cocks are both shiny! It's like they're different sizes of the same model: one's a small and one's an extra-large! Johnny, you're so clever to get Brian all lubed up for fucking my ass! You're a go-getter when it comes to cuckolding yourself!"

"It was Brian's idea," I protested. "And you said to keep him hard."

"But Little Johnny's telling me you are enjoying it! Lubing my lover up to rape your wife's ass turns you on, you dirty boy! And I thought you were doing this so I wouldn't divorce you!"

"Tonya, don't even talk about that!"

"Well, I'm sure we won't have to. As hard as your cock's been this whole night, you'll be asking me to fuck other men when I'm not even in the mood! I can see it: 'Not tonight, dear! I just can't fuck another man for you tonight! My cunt's just worn out! You'll just have to jerk off on your own. Or ask one of them to let you suck them off or fuck you up the ass!'"

"Tonya!" I cried.

"Oh, I'm just joking, Johnny! My rectum's all eager, so Johnny, as long as your hand's all greasy already, why don't you lube up my ass? That way you'll get to stick something up there, even if it's only your fingers!"

Tonya lay on her back and pulled her legs up, exposing her backside. I complied with her orders, picking up the jar and dipping up a glob of lube and smearing it on her puckered hole. One finger went in with almost no resistance. Tonya murmured in satisfaction as I spread the lube all around inside her, stretching her sphincters sideways to loosen them. I dipped up more lube and stuck two fingers in her. The earlier fucking must have relaxed her, as two fingers went in almost as easily as one.

"Shit, this is fantastic!" Brian enthused. "Your own husband is prepping you so I can fuck you up the dirt road! I've died and gone to heaven! Maybe I'll move in here!"

That thought made my heart skip a beat. That was the one thing that could still scare me. Tonya might not leave me, but would I be displaced in her affections? Would Brian or these other lovers intrude into our lives to the point where I'd be superfluous, moved to the sidelines?

"Don't get ahead of yourself, buddy boy!" Tonya chided. "You're pretty and all, but your still just a nice fuck up till now. And speaking of fucking, why don't you two fix me up?"

I figured Tonya was asking me to put Brian in her again. She moved onto her hands and knees, presenting Brian with a wonderful view of her gorgeous ass cheeks. She took each cheek in her hands and spread her ass lewdly, quivering with anticipation of Brian spearing her. Brian crawled up in the bed on his knees and I reached out and took his slippery penis in my hand!

The sight of Tonya offering her glistening distended asshole like a target and seeing my own hand aiming Brian's cock at that opening short-circuited my brain! I trembled with excitement. How prescient Tonya was to involve me in her cuckoldry! I was delirious with excitement! My cock felt like a hot dog on the grill, ready to split open it was so hard! I wouldn't trade places with anyone this second, not even Brian!

"Oh, God!" I sighed to myself. I thought my head might explode.

I held Brian's magnificent cock to Tonya's anus and he pushed against the muscle. I still held his throbbing cock in my hand and he slid through my fingers, pushing forward. Tonya's ass resisted and I saw the whole backside area sink as he pushed slowly.

"Oh, God, he's so big!" Tonya cried. "I feel so tight!"

Brian backed up a hair and I felt his cock slide against my palm. It felt like we were partners: Batman and Robin (well, maybe I was Alfred), Green Hornet and Kato. I was rooting for him to slam home, to bury himself in her ass, as eager as if it were my own cock poised at her entrance. We were fucking her together. Well, except that I wasn't fucking anybody....

He nudged against her sphincter, prodding it. I could feel his cock was hard as steel and I could feel her ass giving way slightly. He drew back a half-inch and then thrust forward. Tonya yelped as the head stretched open her ass. He wiggled back and forth, giving her an instant of relief and then pressing the attack again.

I felt every twitch, every movement, as if he were fucking my hand at the same time. I found myself taking his shaft in my grip and pressing him forward. I felt as if I were stabbing Tonya's ass with Brian's cock.

"Oh! Oh! Ow! Ow!" Tonya hissed as the head slipped past her first ring and her ass gripped just behind the rim of his head. Brian continued to expertly jiggle back and forth, massaging her asshole, sending her the message to relax, open up, and prepare for the next assault. He pushed forward and his cock burst through the second ring and he was halfway in her. I reluctantly released my grip on his cock, breaking our connection, clearing the way for him to start sawing in and out of her ass.

"Oh shit! Oh shit! Stop for a second!" Tonya pleaded. "I know it's gonna feel great, but I've got to get used to it first!" Brian obediently waited, in fact, pulling back a little. Again I was impressed with his patience and consideration as a lover. No wonder Tonya trusted him! It must take steely control not to rape that ass with abandon now. But he wanted to be able to do this again ... and again ... and again ...  and again.... And maybe he ... cared for her? 'Don't go there!' I told myself.

"Let me do it," Tonya ordered and she began to rock back and forth, massaging her ass with his cock. I saw her concentrate and bear down on his cock, pushing herself back, trying to impale herself on his fleshy sword. She paused to let her muscles accustom themselves to this unnatural invasion and then heaved back again, swallowing another inch of his shaft.

I stared with rapt attention at the tight ring where her ass gripped his member. Her anus was red and squeezed tightly into his flesh, drawn like a rubber band around his shaft. I quivered to imagine the exquisite feelings the clutching of those muscles at Brian's cock must be producing. What would...? What would it be like for ... me ... to...? Be fucked ... like that? Oh, God! I wasn't imagining I was Brian: I was imagining I was Tonya! 'But he's so big!' I thought. The slow progress of Tonya's ass down his cock began to remind me of an anaconda swallowing its prey whole.

"Oh, God! Oh, my ass! It is so full of cock! Oh, I feel so tight, so stretched!" Tonya cried. "I want to take it all! I want you to take my ass, to own me! I'm your bitch, Brian! Oh, God! It's so hot, so thick, so deep inside me!" Tonya was practically babbling in lust. She started to rock back and forth, fucking herself in his cock in short strokes, every time trying to force him a little deeper inside herself.

"I need it all! I need to take your cock all the way in my ass! I want to feel you all the way up inside me!"

Brian took that as his cue to thrust forward and bury himself in her. She yelped and pulled away and he grabbed her hips and pulled her back, driving himself in until his thighs slammed into her butt cheeks. She tried to pull away, but he held her, buried in her ass to the root.

"Oh, God! It's too deep, too big!" Tonya cried.

"You're gonna take it, bitch!" Brian growled. He started to fuck her in earnest now, no longer the gentle lover, but now the dominant alpha male.

"Oh, God! Oh, God!" Tonya cried. She held still and let Brian fuck her ass, reaming her over and over.

My heart cried out as I saw this man violating my wife, my bride. He was using her, taking her, heedless of the wrongness of using her back passage like a cunt, but only caring that it felt good to his raging hard-on, that the warmth and grip of her tortured rectum pleased his cock.

But my own dick was going wild at the same time! The lust that motivated Tonya to let Brian violate her anus for his pleasure fired my own twisted arousal. The pure sexuality of the act drove me wild! I took my already greasy hand and began to pump my own cuckold dick. I shuddered with pleasure and closed my eyes at the overwhelming excitement.

When I opened my eyes, Tonya was no longer passively enduring his thrusts but was meeting them with her own.

"Oh! Fuck me! Fuck my dirty ass! That ... feels ... so ... fucking ... good! Use my ass! Make me your whore! Oh, God, I want it! I want your cock up my fucking ass!"

Tonya's urgings drove Brian into a frenzy. He slammed into her as if he were trying to make her regret her words, but she only writhed in ecstasy at his assault. Her ass no longer resisted his thrusts but welcomed them. Truly he had conquered her body and was using it savagely.

My brain bounced back and forth between observer and participant like a schizophrenic kaleidoscope. Part of me was an eye with a penis, the ultimate voyeur watching the best pornographic movie. Part of me was aware that here I was, inches away, watching another man force his penis up my wife's ass, using a passage never designed for sex, overpowering her protesting muscles for his perverse pleasure.

'What am I doing?' part of my brain cried. Did I want to let this continue? Did I really want to be a bystander in my own bedroom? Or did I want to trade places with Brian, forcing my own dick up my wife's rectum? Or ... did I want to ... trade places with Tonya?

I took my cock in hand and stroked it and my cock answered all these questions. Yes, I wanted to watch Brian violate my wife. He was the better man, the deserving conqueror of this forbidden country. I admired him, wanted to watch his magnificent fucking. I wanted his superior penis to plumb places my poor dick could never reach, to give her the ultimate pleasure. And yes, I wanted to beat my meat to the rhythm of two perfect sexual animals in anal coitus! And part of me knew the pleasures of being fucked and was racked with envy to be fucked by a man's cock!

My lubed hand was flying over my cock, wringing delicious pleasure from the depraved scene before my eyes. I could only take so much stimulation. With a start I felt my orgasm arrive at the base of my cock and a second later cum was squirting out into the palm of my free hand.

Tonya reached beneath her and twiddled her clit. Brian could feel her anus twitch as her fingers ignited her orgasm.

"Oh, shit!" Brian yelled as he felt her orgasmic spasms pulse through her rectum, as if designed to wring the cum out of his cock. A second later he slammed into Tonya's bowels and coated her colon with his sperm. "Fuck! Fuck! Shit! Fuck!" he swore as his cock convulsed in the tight confines of his lover's ass.

"Stay in me!" Tonya cried as she collapsed to the bed. Brian fell on top of her, his cock still buried in her. "I love to feel it wedged in there, it fills me up, so I can feel every inch of it, feel how thick and hot and slippery it is! I can feel your cum way up in me."

"God, babe," Brian hoarsely exclaimed, "your ass is like a vise around my cock! It squeezes me all around, like compression shorts for my schlong! That is dynamite!"

"Oh, Brian, I want to be your anal whore! I want you to fuck my ass whenever you want. I've got an 'Open' sign permanently lit for you. Call me at 3 am, on Christmas morning, during Thanksgiving dinner and I'll bend over and spread my cheeks. This ass is all yours!"

Tonya spoke as if Brian were the only one in the room. She was so caught up in the throes of anal passion that she'd forgotten she'd just put on a show for her lawful husband. I stood there, my palm full of my own semen and my other hand on my wilting dick. With my lust temporarily sated, I was acutely aware that I was a fifth wheel. I quickly licked up the gooey pool on my hand so that Brian wouldn't notice what I was doing.

"I bet you enjoyed that too, didn't you, Johnny? Did you beat your meat while a real man fucked your wife's ass? Did seeing a man properly butt-fuck your wife make you shoot your dick-spittle into your hand?"

"Yes," I muttered in a meek voice.

"And did you lick up your mess like a good boy?"

"Jesus, Tonya! You're something else! That's gross!" Brian exclaimed.

I sighed in resignation and admitted, "Yes, Tonya."

"Good! I really do want you to enjoy this too. It must be so exciting for you to see a real man who knows how to fuck, how to take pleasure and give pleasure! Oh, Johnny, to feel that cock up my ass.... It feels like an invasion at first. But then, when he's all the way in and he's pounding away and I know he's not going to stop fucking until he comes no matter what—oh then, Johnny! Then it's like a demon possesses me! I surrender and my ass opens up and then it's as if his cock is fucking every cell in my body at once!" Tonya sighed with delight.

Brian grunted and Tonya sensed that he was wanting to get off of her and relax.

"OK, babe, you can pull out now. But lie next to me for a bit. Johnny's got his clean-up duty!"

Brian gently pulled out and I saw Tonya's ass gape open like a mouth! Her anal ring was almost as red as her lipstick and I could see right into her rectum for a second, shiny with lube and....

"Would you like another suck on Brian's nice fat cock, Johnny? I think you should thank him for ass-fucking your wife and letting you watch. I think you should beg him to taste his delectable penis again. After all, he's done something you can't do for me. He's been very generous with his gifts."

I looked over at Brian, lying exhausted on the bed. His cock was limp, but still bigger than mine was fully erect. It shone with lube and a drop of cum hung from the tip. I looked intently at it and struggled to define the feeling that filled my chest. It was fascination. And ... desire.

"Um ... er...," I hesitated.

"Go ahead! Ask him nicely. You want to taste it again, don't you? You want to feel it in your mouth again. And you certainly want him to let you watch next time, don't you?"

Oh, God, she was right! I did! The idea of sucking his cock again was not repulsive at all. It had been ... um ... pretty ... wonderful...!

"Um ... well ... please, um, Brian ... may I suck your cock? I'd like to clean it and, er, thank you for..."

"...ass-fucking...," Tonya prompted.

"...ass-fucking ... my wife so well."

"Very good!" Tonya said.

"That would be very nice, Johnny," Brian replied. "Tonya assures me that you've never sucked cock before, but from the sample you gave me earlier, I'd say it comes naturally to you! You're quite a good cocksucker already! They say there's no substitute for enthusiasm. You can't beat a man who loves his work! Good cocksucking is 90% enthusiasm. You can tell when the girl is really enjoying sucking your prick. And I could tell by your hard-on and your energy that you really loved it! So it'd be my pleasure."

I knew he was probably only trying to rub it in, to go along with Tonya's instruction to humiliate me. But it was a little too close to the mark. To my consternation, I had enjoyed sucking Brian's cock to a startling extent. And a part of me couldn't somehow help but be a little bit proud if I were good at it too!

Brian scooted forward in much the same position as in the living room, with his ass just on the edge of the bed. I knelt between his legs. The intimacy of being squeezed between his thighs was mind-blowing! As I took his limp but heavy member in my hands I was acutely aware that I was on my knees in an attitude of supplication. But I didn't mind it. It felt ... right. He was my superior. It was right for me to be bowing down to him.

I squeezed his cock up from the base, milking a glob of cum from the tip, which I gently licked off. Brian moaned softly: his cock was still hyper-sensitive. I took the head into my mouth and cradled it there, thrilling to the way it filled my cavity! Oh, God, this felt good! I savored its soft-meaty consistency. I took as much as I could into my mouth and wrapped my lips around the shaft, sucking it like a straw as I pulled my head away.

"Oh!" Tonya gasped. "So gentle! So loving! So ... feminine, the way you do that!"

"He knows what feels good to a man," Brian agreed. "My cock's pretty tender right now. Gentle feels good."

"Yes!" Tonya concurred. "That's just what it was like when he sucked your cum out of my pussy. Gentle, soothing. He's so tender and loving. That's just what my pussy and ass need after your battering ram!" She stroked Brian's stomach lovingly and they were two lovers sharing an intimacy and I was their trusted servant.

I sucked gently on Brian's cock a few more times, tasting each drop of semen I managed to coax out of his slit. The taste of his cum was strong. Then I started to lick up and down his thick shaft with broad strokes, lapping up the lube and remnants of the cum he'd dumped in Tonya's bowels. There was no pussy juice this time, only spunk and the oily taste of the lube.

It was too soon to expect Brian would harden again, but he seemed to still be enjoying my efforts, shown by his slight smile and closed eyes. His cock seemed at least not to have lost all of its starch. I guessed that if I'd kept it up I could have coaxed another erection out of him. That idea was surprisingly arousing!

"My turn!" Tonya announced, addressing Brian. "You can't hog him!" she said with a mock slap at Brian. "He's my husband after all! And my ass is the star of this show!"

She made me lie on the floor. To my surprise she did not immediately sit on my face, but hovered her ass a few inches over it.

"Open wide, cucky!" she urged. I gazed at the starburst of her anus, amazed that although clearly stretched and reddened, it had sealed itself up again. I saw it twitch and I knew what was coming. She was going to squeeze Brian's cum into my mouth!

Brian had swung around to witness this spectacle.

"Oh, shit!" he exclaimed.

"Exactly!" Tonya laughed.

"What an evil she-devil!" Brian said, shaking his head. "And what a wimp!"

I saw Tonya's sphincter spread and a gooey mass bubbled out and dropped in a glob on my tongue. As I swallowed, the strong taste of Brian's cum and lube was mixed with the earthy musk of Tonya's ass. I saw her anus contract and then convulse again, spurting another load. A warm feeling spread over me as I thought of the fact that I was swallowing yet another dose of a man's semen! It didn't bother me. I hungered for it!

"Isn't that good, baby? That's our gift to you! The gift of Brian's and my passion for each other. You're the only person in the world we would share that with, but I want to, because you're my husband and I love you too! I'll let David and Calvin fuck my butt, but you're the only one I'll let suck cum out of my ass! That's my special treat just for you!"

I watched as Tonya's sphincters rippled as she worked to squeeze as much of Brian's cum out of her rectum as she could. When no more emerged, she was content to settle onto my face and let me lick the mixture of lube and cum from her anus. I probed her bunghole with my tongue. It slipped in almost as easily as into her cunt, so stretched were her poor muscles by the thickness of Brian's penis.

"God, is there anything he'll shrink from, Tonya? He'll stick his tongue up your butt?" Brian marveled.

"Oh, I think his only limit is our imagination, Brian! He loves me and he's terrified of losing me. That's a formidable combination. But the real mind-fuck is that humiliation seems to turn him on! So the lower he sinks, the higher his little flagpole rises. So he's actually happy to do things his big brain abhors. But the little brain in his pants runs the show! Look! Even listening to us talk about him this way is turning him on! His tiny peepee is twitching!"

And she was right. Her discussing me with her lover as if I were a lab experiment was demeaning, but it was sending thrills through my groin! And the embarrassment of their seeing that made my little willie grow!

"What else would you like to see him do? Do you want to experiment" Tonya continued. "Do you want to see if he'll drink my piss? Wouldn't that be a nice chaser for his cum / ass dessert? Do you think he'd let me use his mouth like a toilet?"

"Oh God, Tonya! He wouldn't, would he? That would be too much! Won't it make him sick?"

"I wouldn't put it past him. I think we'll run out of ideas—or stamina—before we'll reach his limit!"

Tonya rose off my face. She winked at me so that Brian couldn't see. She knelt next to me, placing one hand on my cheek, sticky with Brian's cum, and one hand on my hardening cocklet. She looked me straight in the eyes, like a hypnotist.

"Johnny, you've been wonderful tonight. You've been the best cuckold husband a slut-wife could ask for. My gosh, you've done everything I've asked you, things you never dreamed you'd do.

"Now I want you to prove your love another way. I want to piss in your mouth. I want to use your mouth like a toilet. And I want you to drink my pee down. I won't force you to do it, but I want you to do it and I want you to tell me that's it's OK. You'll make me so happy if you will be my toilet! Brian doesn't think you'll do it, but I think you will, because you love me that much. Show Brian how much you love me."

All this time she was stroking my penis. Even though I'd already drunk her urine many times, I admired the power of her mesmerism. It thrilled me to know that I would have said yes to whatever she asked me in that way, so alluring were her words.

"Brian thinks that drinking my piss is too low, even for you, that no man would debase himself so far. But I've told him that nothing is too low for you, that there is nothing you would deny me. Am I right? Would you make yourself my toilet? May I piss in your mouth right now?"

I did not answer aloud. I merely lay back down and opened my mouth and waited for her to straddle me. Tonya squatted over my mouth and beamed at me.

"I want to see my piss as it goes in your mouth! Oh, Johnny, you make me so happy!"

I saw her concentrate and then a golden stream gushed out onto my tongue. It was hot and salty.

"Oh, God! You're doing it!" Tonya exulted, as if we'd never done it before. When my mouth was full, she halted her stream to let me swallow.

"Now drink it!" she said excitedly, and I did as she asked. "You're drinking my piss! You're my toilet! You're my cum-eating, cocksucking, ass-licking, piss-drinking cuckold! Can you go any lower, Johnny?" With that she resumed pissing into my mouth with renewed delight.

"Oh, man!" Brian exclaimed. "I'd never believe this night if I hadn't seen it with my own eyes! I'm still not sure I believe it! How can he do that?"

Tonya continued until she'd emptied her bladder. Then she lowered herself to let me lick the last drops of urine from her pussy. As I breathed in and out, the smell of urine filled my nose.

"Look at his dick!" Brian cried. "It's getting hard again! Drinking piss turns him on!"

"Yes and no," Tonya begged to differ. "It's debasing himself for me that turns him on. It's proving he's not really a man that turns him on!"

Tonya stood up. Somehow my being on the floor looking up at her towering over me seemed fitting. She stuck out one foot and toyed with my half-erect penis.

"Time for you to go to your room, Johnny. Brian's going to stay the night. We'll see you in the morning." She lay back down with Brian on our king-size bed and they began to cuddle as I got up and went to the guest room.

"Ha ha!" I heard Brian guffaw as the door closed. "Kicked out of his own bed! Haw!"

"It's my bed now, baby!" Tonya corrected him.

I retreated to the guest room—maybe "my room" would be more accurate now. Ever the glutton for punishment I opened the laptop to check on the spy camera. I saw Tonya and Brian kissing. Very cozy. But Tonya must have been reading my mind, for a minute later she got up and moved a tissue box in front of the camera lens, blocking my view! I could still hear, but they were speaking low enough I couldn't make out what they were saying. No doubt Tonya wanted to rub in my exclusion from their "love nest."

I rewound the video file and found that the whole scene since we went into the bedroom had been well captured, although it was of necessity a stationary wide shot. The views of Brian and Tonya fucking were by now old hat. But seeing myself hold Brian's cock up to Tonya's ass sent shock waves through me.

Yet even that was nothing compared to watching myself kiss, lick, and suck on Brian's penis! You see other people on the internet all the time, but you never see yourself. My cock throbbed as I watched myself and I remembered the feel of his penis in my mouth: the warmth, the size, the slickness, the electricity of his sexual organ connecting with me. I played those few minutes over and over.

My dick cried for release yet again! I'd already come twice, but reliving the boundaries we'd crossed fired my libido! In a frenzy I operated the video editing software, quickly making myself a "highlight reel": myself greasing Brian's cock to ass-fuck my wife, my holding his cock to her ass while he penetrated her, sucking his cock clean after, Tonya squeezing his cum out of her ass into my mouth, and then finally pissing into my mouth.

I set the highlights to play in a loop and lubed up my cock. I sighed with delight as my hand slid over my slippery dick and my eyes drank in the perversions I had been a party to that night. My earlier comes kept my orgasm at bay and I slowed my stroke to drag it out so I could enjoy the video. But I finally released another meager puddle into my palm.

I licked up my spurt faithfully and turned off the computer in self-defense, unsure whether I could resist the temptation to watch it all night. Naked, I crawled between the sheets.

I was a cocksucker. I'd sucked another man's penis. Cocksucker. Faggot. True, my wife had pushed me, prodded me. But no one had held a gun to my head. I'd sucked another man voluntarily.

And what was really scary was that I'd loved it! I shivered and got goosebumps as I recalled all the sensations and feelings. It had been impossibly thrilling! My whole body had vibrated with excitement just from touching another cock and then having it in my mouth.... Licking it. Tonguing it. Sucking on it. It'd been amazing! The power of it was almost frightening.

I knew now that I would be doing it again. It was too exciting to resist. I had to have more of that.

With that thought I fell asleep exhausted.

-Day 23 Sunday-

Toward morning I had a dream. Tonya and I were in bed naked, playing with each other, kissing and fondling. I latched onto one breast with my mouth and began to suckle. I drew it deep onto my mouth and felt the nipple press against the roof of my mouth.

But then somehow it was pressing to the back of my throat. Her breast was filling my mouth. It started hammering against the back of my throat. It felt too long and too pointed. I felt a ridge. Then I realized it had become a penis! I continued to suck on it and it continued to fuck my mouth, until I felt a shudder and the taste of hot cum filling my mouth. I swallowed and swallowed greedily.

And then suddenly the penis was a breast again and the cum was oozing out of Tonya's nipples. In the dream I looked up and Tonya was feeding me from her full breasts, but the milk was cum. I sucked and sucked at her teat and her breasts just continued to give forth cum instead of milk. And in the dream I loved it! The cum was sweet, creamy. Gallons of it!

"Baby," came Tonya's voice. "Wake up, baby. You must have been exhausted! Brian and I have been up for a while. In fact, we've been rather busy, so I have something for you."

I was still in a fog, halfway between the dream and reality. I tried to close my eyes and go back to sleep, but Tonya straddled my head and brought her fragrant pussy to my face. The accumulated juices of many orgasms and Brian's fermenting deposits filled my nose with an overpowering scent.

Tonya pressed her cunt lips to my lips. It was a short leap from the cum-filled breasts of my dream to the cum-filled vagina in my mouth. In a dream daze I suckled at her pussy as I had at the fantasy breasts and drank down the same cum-flavored nourishment. In my half-asleep stupor I purred a satisfied 'mmmm' as I feasted on her gooey snatch. My cock, already aroused from the dream, became fully erect. I was beginning to love the taste of cum!

Tonya seemed amused at my sleepy enjoyment of her present and was content to let me dreamily lap her cunt for some time before she eventually dismounted.

"Wake up, sleepy cuck-boy! Fucking makes my boyfriend hungry. Time for you to make us breakfast!"

That brought me out of my dream. The reality of where I was and who was there came flooding in. I dragged myself out of bed and to the kitchen.

Tonya had pulled on a filmy robe, left open so that her breasts and pudendum were on display for Brian's admiration. Brian was attired in a thin happi coat, also left open, displaying his proud equipment unashamedly. He leaned against our kitchen breakfast bar on one of our tall stools.

"Good morning, Johnny. Slept well, I hope," he greeted me heartily.

"Good morning," I mumbled, my eyes avoiding his.

Tonya, always alert to the currents in the situation, quickly stepped in to orchestrate.

"Johnny, I think it would be a good idea to make some little gestures to help you get comfortable with our new relationships. I think you should acknowledge that Brian is the master of the house when he's here, and to acknowledge that you are in no way pretending to be the man of the house, or even male, except in a technical sense.

"I think you should greet him every day by kneeling at his feet. And I think it would be appropriate for you to honor the symbol of his superiority by kissing his penis."

I looked at Tonya to see if she were serious. I could see that she was. I uncertainly moved toward Brian. He grinned and turned himself to face me, separating his knees to make room for me to kneel. I snuck a glance at his face but then kept my eyes downcast as I tentatively knelt in front of his chair. My traitorous dick stood out in front of me, already hardened to half-mast. I stared at Brian's meat, hanging limp in his lap, and I bent to place a dry kiss squarely on its head. As much as my background and upbringing rebelled, the prospect did not dismay me!

"That's right!" Tonya praised me. A flash went off and I blinked. She'd taken a picture of me kissing his cock!

But I wanted more! I couldn't believe the lure this penis had for me. I felt a hunger in my stomach and in my mouth. I lifted the head and slipped it into my mouth! I sucked on it lazily and a joy filled my chest!

"Oh, my God!" Tonya said, surprised despite her herself. She watched amazed as I continued to nurse on Brian's cockhead. Brian just watched and shook his head in disbelief. I heard him sigh though.

I wanted more! It felt so good to have this man-meat in my mouth. I didn't want to let it go. I wanted to nurse on it, like the cock-breast in my dream. Tonya thought she was pushing me to acknowledge Brian as my master and superior, but she never guessed that I was already most of the way to accepting that myself! It felt right to be kneeling before this man who was everything I would never be: strong, manly, a sexual god. It was almost an honor to serve him.

"OK, that enough!" Tonya declared. "That's very good, but we're hungry for other kinds of sustenance!"

I awkwardly rose to my feet and Tonya informed me that they wanted a farmer's breakfast: eggs, bacon, and pancakes.

"I've already had enough sausage this morning!" Tonya laughed. She brought out a frilly apron and fastened it on me. Brian chuckled at my expense.

"With your horny little dick sticking out all hard, I'm afraid it'll get burned on the stove!" Tonya explained.

While I made breakfast I marveled at my own actions. Where had that come from? I had really wanted to do that! I'd do it again in a second if they'd let me! What was happening to me? I felt an empty place, a yearning ... for Brian's cock! It was like the box of chocolates that called your name, that you couldn't stop thinking about.

They retired to the dining room while I prepared breakfast. Tonya had me serve them coffee while the food was cooking. They read the paper like a couple on their honeymoon. I brought them their breakfasts, setting the plates in front of them like a waiter. It didn't feel wrong. I was their servant—and lucky to be here at all!

"You can sit at the breakfast bar and have your breakfast, Johnny. But wait! I'll get you some juice!"

Tonya held a large juice glass in her hand. She squatted next to the table, smoothly bringing the glass to her crotch. A second later her golden urine was whooshing into the glass. When it was two-thirds full she pulled it away and handed it to me. I could feel the warmth of her pee through the glass.

"You enjoyed it so much last night, I thought you'd like to start your day with a drink!"

Remembering that I was supposed to be new to this I pretended to be nonplussed, but then I held it to my lips and drank it all down in several swallows. Brian shook his head in disgusted amazement.

"Good boy!" Tonya exclaimed. She reached under my apron and gave my erect penis a squeeze to reward me. "Now go have your breakfast. It smells wonderful!"

I ate my breakfast while Tonya and Brian talked and laughed with each other. With their lust temporarily slaked, I noted with a small twinge of jealousy that they seemed to enjoy each other's company, not just each other's bodies. After all the sucking and fucking, I'd forgotten how much Tonya had liked Brian right off the bat, even when they were just having lunch.

"Johnny, be a dear and refill our coffees? We're going to go out on the back porch and finish the paper." I was glad to see that they both tied their robes, although I wondered what our neighbors would make of the handsome stranger here on a Sunday morning in a bathrobe.

I was pointedly not invited to join them, so I busied myself with cleaning the kitchen while they chatted and mowed their way through the fat Sunday paper. After all, one doesn't invite the help to sit down with the family.

Even though (or because?) it humiliated me to be treated like their servant, I decided I'd better bring them more coffee. I hesitated at the door, realizing that I still only wore the frilly apron, which only covered my front and made me look like a ridiculous sissy. But I wasn't sure I had permission to get dressed yet. So I swallowed hard and stepped out onto the porch.

"Oh, Johnny, you're a dear! What a good host—well, not really a host, I guess—more like a hostess!"

As I poured more coffee for each of them, Tonya reached up under my apron and grasped my penis, half-hard again from the humiliation of the situation. Her hand felt marvelous and the feel of the breeze and sun on my naked backside was titillating.

"I love your outfit, Johnny," Tonya said as she continued to milk my dick. "It provides just the right touch of feminine frills that makes it clear that you're no he-man ... more like a she-man.... And it gives me such full access to everything." She extended her other hand and stroked my ass suggestively.

"Doesn't John have a cute little ass, Brian? It's so nice and smooth." She continued to caress the globes of my ass while she lazily pulled on my little willie maddeningly.

"Yeah, but his mouth is his best feature!" Brian laughed.

"But you haven't even felt his ass yet!" Tonya jibed.

"Well, I've felt his mouth, and it's a great mouth!" Brian replied.

"Maybe one of these days you'll have to compare the two," Tonya murmured. She slipped her hand between the cheeks of my ass and stroked across my anus. I rolled my hips in response. She put one finger on my asshole and started to massage it in small circles. I rocked my hips and moaned. "Most effeminate men have a strong streak of anal eroticism," she intoned suggestively.

"Brian's going to have to be leaving soon, Johnny," Tonya told me, never stopping the hypnotic rhythm of both hands under my apron. I was starting to sink into a lust daze from what she was doing. "We've had a marvelous time and you've been absolutely wonderful. Brian and I have been talking about what would be a fitting ending."

Tonya looked me in the eyes.

"I want you to suck Brian off before he goes! Give him an orgasm with your mouth. He loved how you sucked him, and you've already eaten his cum out of me. But I want you to feel the thrill when he spurts and feel that hot cum hit the back of your throat, to taste it full-strength. And I want you to feel the excitement of knowing that he's coming for you, that you're the one who gave him that orgasm. It's one of the best feelings in the world and I want to share that with you, baby!"

I groaned as the image of that went through my head and Tonya's hand on my penis and her finger on my asshole made me wild. 'No, no no!' a voice in my head said. 'You're not gay! You're not supposed to do that! It'll make you gay!'

"I bet you really are dying to do that. I'm betting the idea really excites you! Well, I give you my permission. I give you permission to suck off my boyfriend! I want you to. I want to see your mouth on his cock and know that you're not just playing with it, but that you're not going to stop until he blows his cookies for you!"

Tonya's words and hands were driving me into a frenzy. I could feel a hunger building up in me, a lust to do it. The idea of sucking off this sex god excited me! I could imagine the electricity of feeling his penis throbbing, quivering, getting ready to blast his seed. I could almost feel the spasms as his cock convulsed. I could feel the hot lava of his eruption.

Brian untied his robe and let it fall open, revealing the gorgeous package at his crotch. He took his half-hard cock in hand and lazily pumped it, tempting me with it. 'Look at it. You know you want it,' he seemed to be saying. I suspected he was getting off on the idea of being a sexual god, with a phallus so wonderful that both men and women wanted it. He was the King.

"Will you? Do you want to?" Tonya asked.

"Yes!" I croaked out, my throat dry with lust and anxiety. But I wasn't just saying what Tonya wanted me to say.

"Say it!" Tonya barked.

"I ... want to suck him off! I want to taste his cum!" I hissed between gritted teeth, the admission torn out of me. I cringed at my own words, squeezing my eyes shut in shame.

"Outstanding!" Tonya crowed. "I knew it! I don't know if you are bisexual, Johnny, but I suspect you're going to a hell of a cocksucker one way or the other! And who knows what else? Maybe you can just love cocks without loving the men they're attached to."

Tonya let go of my cock and led me back into the living room. Brian sat on the couch and lay back, throwing his robe open and spreading his knees wide. Tonya removed my apron.

"I want to see your little stiffy throb and drool while you suck Brian's cock!"

I saw our video camera set up on a tripod. I looked at Tonya.

"It's your first man, Johnny! The first time you bring a man to orgasm. That's a moment you will want to relive over and over!" She picked up her phone from the table. "I want to get some close-ups too."

That almost pulled me back from the brink, but I was too much under Tonya's spell to resist. I had tunnel vision for Brian's cock now.

Tonya guided me to kneel between Brian's knees. She set the video camera running and then knelt down to take some pictures of Brian's half-hard tool.

"Look at it. It's already bigger than yours and it isn't even hard! Isn't it beautiful? That's what a cock should be! Anyone, man or woman, would have to admire it. And for the next little while, it's going to be all yours!

"Make love to it, Johnny! Kiss it, caress it, lick it, stroke it. Feel it grow, feel it throb. Excite it until it explodes! Make it give you its man-juice. Make that beautiful cock yours!" She didn't have to seduce me though. That penis fascinated me. It was like a magnet attracting me.

I leaned down and kissed the tip. I shuddered with the feel of its soft sponginess and the heat of the blood starting to fill it. Everything I'd ever been taught said this was wrong. This was a man's sex and I was a man. But a thrill went through me, that I was breaking that taboo! A man's lips on a man's penis! It was like touching two electric wires together. The thrill went straight to my little cock.

"Oh God!" I groaned under my breath.

"Isn't it delicious?" Tonya cried. "You want it so bad it hurts!"

I felt in a frenzy but also the feeling was so intense that I had to hold my breath. It was so powerful that I could only stand it by going slow, taking in a little bit at a time. I kissed the side of the head so gently, so I could feel every nerve, every pore of the skin. I kissed the other side gently. I kissed the sensitive spot right below his slit. I kissed the top of the head. I kissed the tip again.

"Jesus!" Brian swore and he threw his head back. His cock began to swell.

I kissed all around the rim of his cock and then I licked lightly all around the rim. Then I began to tickle the ridge on the underside of his shaft, licking up lightly.

'A man's cock! A man's cock! I'm sucking another man's cock!' was going through my head over and over! I wasn't preparing him for Tonya or cleaning up after her. A man and I were having sex. I was having sex with him. Oh God, it was terrible, but so terribly exciting! I couldn't believe it how aroused I was!

I teased his frenulum with my tongue tip and Brian sucked in his breath and moaned. I trembled too. I wasn't just obeying Tonya. I was enjoying this, savoring every moment. My first cock!

I began to lick his shaft and cockhead more thickly, coating it with my saliva. I couldn't hold back any longer: I had to taste him again. I took his cock deep in my mouth and Brian let out a sigh of satisfaction.

His cock was fully erect now. God, this felt good! The rubbery hardness of it felt marvelous in my mouth. I pressed his meat against the roof of my mouth, feeling it give. I licked hard up the underside, squeezing it against the roof, like squeezing the paste out of a toothpaste tube. I flashed on the memory of my cum-breast dream and started to suck on his cock as if it were a teat. Brian hissed and his hips bucked.

"Oh, God!" Brian moaned.

It felt so good in my mouth! It tasted so good.

"Oh, shit, this is hot!" swore Tonya as she snapped picture after picture. "I knew I wanted to see you suck cock!" I peeked sideways and saw she'd opened her robe and had a hand stroking her pussy lips.

I began swirling my tongue around the head of Brian's cock, twisting my head this way and that to caress the head wetly. I grabbed the base of his shaft in one hand and began to pump him slowly while I alternately sucked and licked his cockhead. I knew he'd already come this morning, so there was no urgency. I could savor this penis as long as I liked.

I wanted more! I wanted more of his cock. I crammed it against the back of my throat, trying to get as much as I could into my mouth! I felt myself gag and tears sprang to my eyes. I backed off but sucked it down again as far as I could. He was so long and thick that I could only take about half of it.

I saw that Brian had his head thrown back and he gripped the couch cushions tightly in his balled fists. His face was a grimace of either pain or ecstasy. I thrilled to see the effect I was having on him! I was proud to see that I was pleasing him! He was in my power. My mouth and hands were his world.

I could feel the heat of his cock in my mouth. His skin was stretched tight with his coursing blood. His cock throbbed with every beat of his heart and it twitched with mounting arousal as my tongue and lips found his sensitive spots.

I was vibrating with my own sexual arousal. His cock was like a dynamo of sexual energy and my mouth was absorbing it. Every stroke of his penis in and out of my mouth was like stroking my own penis. My brain was bursting with lust, even though my own cock remained untouched. I almost felt as if I could come just from sucking him! It was so satisfying to know how much pleasure I was giving him!

Brian began to quiver and his pelvis began to jerk. He started to thrust upward, driving his cock into my mouth. He was groaning and his breathing was ragged.

"Get ready, baby! He's gonna come!" Tonya shouted.

"Oh! Oh!" Brian cried.

I felt his cock suddenly swell even thicker and harder. The moment was electric. It was as if his penis were on fire! His hips stopped jerking and he held his breath. I knew I was on the verge of a new day.

"Unh! Unh! Unh!" he grunted. I felt the spasm as hot cum flooded my mouth. His cock was alive, spewing the very stuff of life. In my mouth! I vibrated with excitement. He was coming in my mouth! I was overwhelmed with a feeling of triumph! I'd done it!

"Fuck! Fuck! Fuck! Oh, shit!" Brian shouted. Pulse after pulse shot his man-seed into my throat. I clamped my lips around his shaft and tried to swallow. I could feel his hot cum oozing down my gullet to my stomach! I held his hard, quivering rod between my lips without moving, knowing that his cock was supersensitive right now.

"Oh, Johnny!" Tonya sighed. I looked out of the corner of my eye and she had one hand squeezing a nipple and the other rubbing her clit like mad.

"Oh shit!" Brian gasped. "Oh shit! Christ! Oh God! What a fucking blow job!" He was out of breath, gasping for air. Tonya shuddered and grunted and I knew she had brought herself to orgasm only a little after Brian.

I was reluctant to let his cock go, but I knew he was too sensitive for anything but the gentlest caress. I gently sucked to try to milk the last drops of cum. I lightly drew his penis out of my mouth, raking it clean with my lips as it withdrew.

The taste of Brian's cum in my mouth now was much stronger than I had ever tasted before. It was hot and unmixed with Tonya's juices or anal lube. It was not a pleasant taste, but neither was it repulsive. I wondered if it were a taste that would grow on me.... It wasn't bad. But it was the taste of excitement! That taste told me I'd made another man come!

God! I'd blown another guy. How did I feel? What was it like? I felt ... what? Like I'd accomplished something. Like I'd ... done something I wasn't sure I could do. Like I'd hiked Pike's Peak. I'd been scared to do it. But I'd done it. I'd made it. And I was ... OK. I guess. I felt ... proud?

Tonya bent down to me and kissed me full on the mouth. She probed my mouth with her tongue and sucked at my lips and I knew she was seeking the share Brian's cum with me.

"Oh God, baby, I can taste him in your mouth! You sucked down his hot, manly cum! You sucked him dry! I'm proud of you! That was the hottest blow job I've ever seen!"

"Fuck!" Brian interrupted. "I don't think I can walk! That fucking whacked me!" His praise was so spontaneous. "Babe, you're gonna need to get me a fucking wheelchair!"

I had just had oral sex with another a man, but Tonya and Brian were acting as if I'd won a medal.

"Poor baby! Brian's come and I've come, but look at Little Johnny! He's stiff as a board still. Look like there's still one person who hasn't come."

I looked at Tonya and wondered if she were offering me some kind of relief. Was she offering to give me a blow job or hand job?

"Here's the lube, baby. Why don't you jerk yourself off? We'll wait. I know that you've got to have been awfully excited by getting to play with a big cock. It shouldn't take but a minute to get a little spurt out of your peepee. Go ahead."

That was my sex life now, to relieve myself. 'That's what little willies are for,' I could hear Tonya saying, 'for jerking off.'

My face hot with shame, I accepted the lube from Tonya and began to grease my little worm. As aroused as I was, I wasn't going to turn down an orgasm.

"Sit down, baby. Relax and enjoy it," Tonya directed. She cuddled next to Brian and they kissed, but then they both turned toward me, like the audience at a show.

I sat on the chair opposite the couch and began to masturbate. I'd whacked off last might right next to them, but they'd been so preoccupied that it seemed almost private. Now I felt their gaze burning into me. My cock didn't seem to mind at all though. It was painfully erect and my slippery hand felt wonderful.

"Look how much he enjoys it!" Tonya remarked to Brian. "It certainly could be that Johnny enjoys his masturbation just as much as we enjoy our fucking. Maybe his nerve endings are packed together tighter because he's so small. They say a clit has just as many nerve endings as a penis. That's why they're so sensitive. Maybe a mini-penis is like a big clit."

Hearing Tonya talk about me like that, as I weren't there, was surreal. I've heard about masochists going into their "sub space." I felt something similar, that I was in my "lust space," where none of the normal rules applied, where anything goes as long as it feels good to my peter.

"Taste Brian's cum in your mouth, babe. Breathe it in and savor that aroma. His cock came in your mouth. You sucked off a man!"

"And you sucked him off good!" Brian chimed in. "God, that was some blow job! A-plus!"

"Your mouth was so good, his cock thought it was a cunt. It couldn't help itself! Think of it!"

Of course, Tonya hardly needed to say that. I couldn't think of anything else! But her saying it aloud ripped down the curtain. It said, 'I know what you're thinking. You can't hide. I know that sucking Brian's cock is making your cock hard.'

"Oh, Johnny, don't come just yet! Brian, I have a genius idea! Oh, my God, this is great! Get over there and press your cock against his! Let him come with your cocks together!"

"Haw!" Brian laughed and I knew Tonya's found her perfect partner in crime. He got off on humiliating me as much as Tonya did. The gayness of it did not faze him. It was as if, in his mind, he was so quintessentially the stud that nothing he did with me could touch him. He had Teflon heterosexuality. But the gayness stuck to me, dragged me down below a snake's belly. I was the guy with cum in his mouth, wearing a frilly apron, whoring out his own wife, not him.

Brian had a better grasp of engineering than Tonya.

"Wait, babe, he needs to come over here. He has to sit between my legs, to get our crotches that close together."

I hesitantly got up and sat between his legs, wrapping my legs around his torso. Our cocks came together in the middle, underside to underside. Tonya's genius had struck again. This terrifyingly intimate, practically like fucking more than masturbation. But also it brought our penises side-by-side for that invidious size comparison. Even though my cock was fully erect, Brian spent organ still dwarfed it.

I looked at Tonya, unsure what she wanted to happen next.

"Well, Johnny, grab them both. What did you think, that Brian was going to beat you off? That's your job!"

I grasped the two shafts. Brian's was thick enough that I couldn't wrap my hand completely around these Siamese twins. But the sight and sensation of the sensitive underside of my cock pressing against his ridge sent a shudder through me. I began to pump up and down and I was blown away by the awesome feeling. I gasped.

"Oh! He likes it!"

Brian stared at the two penises, like a deer in the headlights. The bizarre sight fascinated him and struck him dumb.

I groaned at the magical electricity that seemed to flow from his cock, but I suppose it really came from my perverted mind. I'm sure it was my imagination, but it felt as if his penis was an electrode pouring sexual current into my poor dick (and my poor brain). I squeezed our penises harder, as if I wanted to meld them into one super-penis. I couldn't believe how good it felt! I loved seeing them together, our two cocks. I loved rubbing myself against his penis!

I stared in awe at his cock. It was so powerful. So ... beautiful. And his body. I sat on his thighs and they were thick and hard. He was so strong, so manly. It was so mind-blowing to press my pitiful weenie against his gorgeous phallus!

"Oh shit!" I softly gasped as the eroticism overwhelmed me. It was so good, I was trembling!

"It's like his penis is fucking your penis, Johnny!" Tonya squealed.

I knew I couldn't last much longer. Even though I was stroking slowly, my orgasm was building. I felt it arrive at the base of my cock and then cum was jetting out of my penis. I convulsed and the gooey mess splashed down onto our joined dicks. Another glob bubbled out of my slit and cascaded down, like topping on a sundae.

"Oh God!" I strangled out and I held our two cocks frozen, looking in horror at the mess I'd made.

"Oh, Jesus!" Tonya cursed and her hand parted her pussy lips and collected the moisture there.

I shuddered with disgust at what I'd done. As always the post-orgasmic letdown cleared the sex-induced frenzy from my brain. But it could not obscure the scariest thing: holding Brian's cock next to mine was the single most sexually exciting thing I'd ever felt!

"Lick it up, Johnny," Tonya demanded. Her voice had a snarky edge, as if this were yet another victory over me. 'Look what I made you do!' it seemed to say. 'Look how low I've gotten you to sink! Now you have to pay the piper!'

Some of my cum coated my hand and I let go of our cocks and licked it off dazedly. My own cum tasted bitter to me in my humiliation. I scraped up more off my cock and sucked it off my hand. I went to scrape off Brian's cock, but Tonya grabbed my hand.

"No! You lick that up!" she insisted.

I had to climb off the couch and crouch at Brian's feet. I took his cockhead in my mouth and sucked and licked my spunk off it. Despite my letdown, it still felt ... what? ... comforting? ... to have Brian's penis between my lips! Then I licked his cock up and down the shaft. Some of my jism had seeped down into his pubic hair and I had to bury my lips in his curls and suck at the base of his penis to get it off. Brian's cock was deflated, but it held a not-quite-limp firmness that told me he enjoyed this clean-up job.

"Now kiss it, babe. Kiss it thanks and kiss it goodbye for today."

I didn't know if Tonya meant two kisses or one. To be sure I kissed Brian's penis twice. Tonya meant to humiliate me, but my kisses were heartfelt. I felt as if I were worshipping that magnificent cock!

"You're welcome!" Brian laughed. "My pleasure! Mine entirely!" I felt a strange warmth go through me as I sensed that he'd be back for more soon.

Tonya swept open her robe and his and pressed her naked bosom to his chest and her bush to his groin. They kissed deeply.

"Get his clothes, Johnny!" Tonya commanded. I scrambled to gather his things and then he quickly dressed. I realized then that I'd have to chauffeur him back to his car! Tonya and I dressed. They cuddled and kissed in the back seat while I drove. Tonya kissed him long and hard in the club parking lot while I sat there waiting. Then Brian jumped into his car and sped off.

Tonya stayed in the back seat, content to keep me in the chauffeur role a while longer.

"Oh, Johnny, I'm so happy! I was so nervous about how that all would go, but it couldn't have gone better! Having you there made it even better. Knowing you were actually handing me over to another man, approving another man to do the dickwork instead of you—that made it so deliciously wicked! Actually seeing your frustrated little wiener stiff and seeping an arm's reach away while another man's cock plunged into my cunt—that made my pleasure so much keener!

"Tell me, Johnny: when he was fucking me, did you feel jealous or were you glad that it was him instead of you? Did you want to push him aside? Or were you grateful that he was doing your job for you?"

I stared straight ahead down the road. I knew what the answer was, but I hesitated to admit it. What would Tonya think of me?

"I was glad," I strangled out. "I was relieved a little, I guess. I didn't have to worry about failing you. I knew he'd please you." There, I'd said it. I felt a pressure off my chest. Whether she hated me or scorned me or accepted me, I couldn't take it back.

"Of course. Sure, I can see that," she said. "You feel like a fake, a fraud. You know you're not a real man, but everyone expects you to be. With a real man to pinch-hit for you the pressure is off. You're free to masturbate and really enjoy it! You're not cheating your wife's gain: she's taken care of.

"It's like pre-failing! You can't succeed as a man, so why try? Let the men be the men and the wimps be cuckolds. 'Be all that you can't be ... in the Cuckold A-a-army!' "

I felt a sinking feeling. She seemed accepting of my answer and yet I'd still lost. One thing she'd said certainly rang true: being able to masturbate openly, with Tonya's approval or even encouragement, without guilt or deceit, was exhilarating. I could totally give myself to it without reservation. I wondered if she were right, that some men's sexual pinnacle is fucking, but maybe for a man like me masturbation was the ultimate pleasure. Masturbating while another man fucked her had been satisfying in a way I'd never felt before. But the feeling I had when Brian's and my cock had touched....

Tonya was quiet the rest of the way home. I was deep in thought too. What did it mean that when I jerked off next to Tonya and Brian's humping bodies, that I felt closer to Tonya than in all the times we'd fucked? It was as if sharing that experience generated some kind of bond that we couldn't produce just the two of us.

What did that mean? It meant that Brian's cock was the magic ingredient. His cock drove Tonya to ecstasy and watching that cock fuck Tonya drove me to ecstasy. A big manly cock was the key.

Looking at it that way made me feel a little less alarmed at how aroused I'd been touching Brian's cock. No wonder I'd practically worshipped it. The cock was the sexual powerhouse of our threesome, right? It didn't make me gay that it excited me, did it? It was exciting. It was the magic wand of our cuckold marriage.

I parked the car and we went back into the house. Just inside the door, Tonya turned and took me in her arms, crushing me with a hug.

"Oh, Johnny, I feel so close to you right now! We're a team! We're on a big adventure into the unknown and now we're doing it together! We're out there beyond anything we've ever done or that anyone we know has ever done. Hell, it's beyond anything we even imagined! There's no rules, no guidelines, we're playing everything by ear. It's terrifying but exciting! All we have to go by is each other: our love for each other, our commitment to each other! And we are sticking together, supporting each other. I've never loved you more than I love you right now!"

She kissed me hard and hugged me again.

"How could a husband show any more love for his wife than you have? You swallow your false pride, you sacrifice your manhood, offer it up on a silver platter for me! You actually put another man's cock in my cunt with your own hands! You lubed another man's cock so it could fuck my ass! My God, Johnny, that takes devotion! That takes strength. That takes courage." She kissed my brow and held my head to her bosom.

"Even though you were watching before, even though you were in the same house, it still felts if I were doing it on my own and you were just letting me. Now this time you were <u>there</u>, you were <u>participating</u>. That made it so much better, so much more meaningful."

She took my face between her hands and looked me straight in the eyes.

"Johnny, I can hardly explain to you what it meant to me, meant to our relationship, to see you take another man's cock in your mouth! For me! To cross that line, to ignore all your homophobic fears, to break all those taboos to please me! To make him hard again so he could cuckold you again! What wife could not love a husband who would do that for her?

"But then to actually make love to his cock, to bring him to orgasm, to let him cum in your mouth and to suck down his hot cum...." She crushed my head to her chest again. "To actually engage in homosexuality for my pleasure, to excite and impress me—well, that, Johnny, makes me love you so much! To go there, to risk being gay for me, that touches my heart. I couldn't have a better husband than you!

"Another thing that has brought us closer is how we've opened up to each and shared our deepest, darkest secrets! I shared my secret that your little dickie wasn't satisfying me and how I longed for a real man's cock. Just today you opened up more and shared your secret shame of failing me and how it's actually a relief to you to farm out the job of fucking your wife to other men.

"Tell me, Johnny: what was it like for you to suck another man's cock? What was it like to feel him spurt right into your mouth?" Then she hesitated. "Did you like it?"

This question made me nervous. That was the scary question. Not, "Would I do it?" We'd already answered that. But.... If I <u>liked</u> it, that was a whole other matter. Except what really made me nervous is that I already knew the answer. I looked at Tonya with terror in my eyes.

"I did," I said in a strangled, tortured voice. "Oh, Tonya! I did! I ... I ... really ... really liked it!"

"Oh, Johnny!" Tonya said in seriousness. She took me in her arms. "That's wonderful!"

"Wonderful? No! Isn't that something to be ashamed of?"

"No. Well, yes, I suppose. I guess it is shameful. But that is the magic of what we have together. Not only can you admit that you can't satisfy me, but you've even admitted to me you secretly lust for other men's cocks! I feel honored to be entrusted with such shameful secrets!"

I felt myself getting emotional, a little choked up. My eyes felt dewy. She made it sound so noble, so loving. I did feel closer to her. We were outlaws, and that meant we only had each other. Who could we talk to about this, but each other? No one else would understand. We shared a secret and that was a strong bond.

I loved her so much that a fear grew within me. What if we were to lose this? What if she left me for one of these studs? I hugged her back in desperation.

"Don't leave me, Tonya! I couldn't live without you! Are you going to fall in love with Brian? If he makes you so happy and he's so much better a man than me, I'm afraid you'll decide to be with him for good and you'll leave me! If I'm really gay somehow, why would you stay with me?" I was near to tears.

"Oh, Johnny! I'm never going to leave you! Aren't you listening to me? I love you! Brian is sex. It's great sex and I'm never going to give that up, but it isn't love. And if you get off on sucking a man's cock or even getting fucked by a man, I don't think that means you don't love me. I'm telling you that what we're doing is making me love you more, not less! I need big cocks and good fucking, but you do things for me those studs will never do. I'll show you!

"Baby, it might seem strange, but I really want to piss in your mouth right now!" Tonya admitted. "No stud is going to do that. I feel so much love for you and I feel so close to you and pissing in your mouth just makes me feel even closer. It's like I'm giving you a part of myself, a secret, intimate, dirty, shameful part of myself, Something no one else would accept. And you're accepting me, right into your insides, almost into your soul, making my dirty urine a part of you.

"I want to feel your mouth on my pussy. I want to see you offering yourself as my toilet, eager to serve even my basest needs, no matter how much it lowers you."

She lowered her panties as I dutifully lay myself down on the floor. I saw her smile brightly as I opened my mouth like a baby bird.

"Ah!" she sighed. "My human toilet! My personal port-a-potty!" She raised her dress and squatted down to me, spreading her pussy lips with her fingers to expose her tiny pee hole. Her cunt was redolent with the smells of her repeated arousals of the past 24 hours and the remains of Brian's several deposits, the most recent only that morning. I breathed it in deeply, wishing I could bottle this fragrance, the essence of sex and satisfied lust.

Tonya hovered there, not settling on my mouth, but suspending herself just above me, as if my mouth really were only a toilet. I saw her muscles strain and then I saw her pee hole widen and a golden stream jet out. The hot urine hit my tongue and frothed into my mouth, soon filling it. I struggled to swallow while not closing my mouth as Tonya continued to gush pee without pause. The stream started to abate after the second mouthful and then became a dribble with an occasional squirt.

Tonya lowered herself so I could lick the last drops off her. I kissed and licked her pink flesh. I snaked my tongue into her cunny and was rewarded with the lingering taste of Brian's spunk, now pungent after fermenting inside Tonya.

"Kiss me!" Tonya commanded urgently. "I want to smell my piss on your breath!" I exhaled into her nose and then she kissed me fervently.

"Oh God!" she exclaimed. "I don't know why that excites me so much! I'm pissing in your mouth and you're just lying there drinking it! My piss is filing your tummy now! It's deliciously dirty! Don't brush your teeth! I want to smell that all day! I'm not going to shower: I want my cunt to stink with the remains of Brian's and my fucking!"

Just then the phone rang. It was my parents inviting us over for Sunday dinner at their place. I wanted to make up an excuse not to go, but Tonya said we should go: "Man—or woman—does not live by fucking alone, Johnny! We can't stop living the rest of our lives just because you want to masturbate all day watching videos of other men fucking your wife! Or is it that you want to watch yourself sucking off Brian all day?"

I begged Tonya to shower before we went to my parents, but she refused.

"Are you afraid they'll smell my stanky pussy? I don't think they'll be getting their noses down there!"

I was determined to take a shower myself before we went. Tonya came in the bathroom and insisted that she "inspect" my ass before I got in the bath. She had me bend over and grab my ankles while lubed up a finger and probed my backside. It was a humiliating position to be in and I felt like I was being treated like a child. But my cock didn't mind: as always, it inflated as Tonya tickled my rectum.

"If you're really going to be clean, we'll have to give you an enema, babe. I want to start you on a program of anal hygiene, so that you'll be 'fuck-able' at a moment's notice." I had to delay my shower while she prepared an enema bag. She announced that she was going to have a buffered saline solution in a jug under the bathroom sink, so that we'd always have a soothing, nonirritating enema solution at hand.

She had me lie on the bathroom rug and she injected the enema into my bowels and supervised that I held it for what she deemed was long enough before I evacuated. Then she had me "assume the position" again while she checked that my rectum was empty. She took the opportunity to massage my prostate: "I've read it's good for men to have their prostate massaged: it may prevent an enlarged prostate or even prostate cancer." I'm not sure what her rationale was for fondling my again-rigid cock while she did so, except probably to create an association between anal invasion and sexual arousal in my mind!

The rationale for ending up with two fingers up my ass wouldn't have been to check me for "cleanliness." I suspect it was more to establish the idea that she would invade my body when and where and how she liked and I had no right to object. Of course I'd be unlikely to object, as her finger-fucking of my ass, coupled with her stroking, had my head in orbit and my cock drooling pre-cum.

"Look at your cock, babe! You so love having your ass played with! What a shame it would be if we had never discovered that you like to be fucked up the ass! We have to take advantage of that 'ass-et' regularly!

"Do you think all men would enjoy being fucked if they didn't have a hang-up about it making them gay? Or is that only a turn on for guys who have some sissy leanings? Do you think Nature might have designed it as a compensation for small-dicked guys? You know, since they can't get as much pleasure out of fucking girls, they should get more pleasure somewhere else?

"Oh, I know! Maybe since their dick doesn't stick out very far, some of their nerve endings are buried that otherwise would have been on the outside if they had a man-sized cock? And they, like, stick farther back toward their asshole instead? And that's why they like having big long things stuck up their ass?"

I suspect Tonya detected that if she kept this up much longer, I would have shot my wad, as she suddenly declared she was done, leaving me with a swollen dick and a greasy ass. She charged me with showering quickly, as it was nearly time for us to leave to get to my parents. As I lathered up my erect cock and greasy ass, I considered finishing the job myself, but I decided that if Tonya had wanted me to do that, she'd have done it herself. I surmised that it was her intent that I be horny, although to what end at a family dinner, I couldn't guess.

As we drove to my parents' house, Tonya continued the focus of the conversation on my cuckold status.

"Do you think they'll notice any difference? You know, nature has designed us with the prime directive to reproduce, to pass on our genes. If parents ignored the possibility that their daughter-in-law might be screwing other men, they'd be at a disadvantage. After all, then how could they know if her children were really their grandchildren? They could be showering resources and attention and inheritance on a bastard, who had none of their genes!

"So maybe nature has equipped parents with cuckold detectors! You know, we don't know much about human pheromones. We know other animals respond powerfully to them and can detect them at concentrations of one part in a billion. Could it be that parents unconsciously can smell semen and tell if it has the 'family smell'? Or could they smell that my pussy has been so aroused that it never could be sex with my own husband that could make me that hot? Or could a cuckold husband give off pheromones that indicate fear and submission? What do you think?"

"Tonya, it's just Sunday dinner! We've done it dozens of times! They're not going to be thinking or asking about our sex life!" I sputtered out. But Tonya had got me thinking and I couldn't get her ideas out of my mind. I could just hear my parents: "We hear Tonya's cut you off and she's screwing any guy with a decent size peter. Are you taking precautions to be sure none of these studs knocks her up? Does this mean you're not going to giving us any grandchildren? I hope none of these guys gives her the clap!"

As I imagined my cuckoldry becoming public knowledge I felt waves of humiliation wash over me. But I felt my cock hardening in my pants.

Tonya's speculation made me feel paranoid when we got to my parents' house. I felt awkward, like I had a scarlet C for Cuckold on my forehead. Putting it in a family context made me feel even smaller. My mini-dick didn't only mean I was letting Tonya down, but in turn I was letting my parents down too.

But if anything, Tonya seemed lit up. She was friendly, bubbly, happy. She'd always gotten along fine with my folks, but today she was a real charmer. Some people say you can tell when a woman is "well-fucked." I was starting to believe it, if Tonya's performance was any indication. She seemed so alive that I started to wonder if she'd been living with a lot more frustration and anger because of my deficiencies in the bedroom than I'd realized. If getting some man-sized cock could make her this happy—not just in bed but in general, I felt guilty that I'd been depriving her of that.

Another change in her behavior was that, although she was quite affectionate with me—holding hands, pecks on the cheek—she was also somewhat domineering that afternoon. She ordered me about, telling me to sit here, to get her a drink, to take her dishes away, etc. If anything she'd usually waited on me on our previous visits, perhaps trying to show my parents what a good wife she was. Now she acted more like the mistress of the house and as if I were her manservant. She also called me "Johnny" and her "boy." She said, "Be a good boy and ...," and, "That's a good boy," repeatedly.

My father noticed the difference when we were left alone in the TV room while Tonya went to the bathroom.

"I can tell the honeymoon's over now!" he said. "She's turning into a typical wife—'Do this, do that, get me this, get me that!' " he joked.

To my surprise Tonya brought me a beer when she returned. I noticed it was only a little more than half full and I was about to remark on it, but Tonya leaned over quickly and whispered in my ear.

"My special home brew, only for you. Don't share it with anyone!"

I didn't put two and two together until I took the bottle in my hand and found that it was warm. I tipped the bottle back and tasted the familiar flavor of Tonya's pee!

Tonya smiled at me. I looked guiltily at my unsuspecting Dad. I was drinking my wife's piss in front of him, in the TV room!

"Johnny, why don't you help your Mom with getting dinner together?"

"But don't you usually help her?" I protested.

"Well, I'm feeling a little tired, honey. As you know, I didn't get much sleep last night. I don't think there's any harm in a husband doing a little 'woman's work' once in a while. I've seen you do some at home just this weekend. So be a good boy and take your drink in there and get to work! You've got your orders!"

My mother was certainly surprised to see me in the kitchen. Almost as soon as I started helping, Tonya appeared, holding one of my mother's frilly aprons.

"Johnny! If you're going to help, don't get stains on your nice clothes! Looks like the menfolk don't do much helping in the kitchen around here—all I could find you was one of your Mom's aprons, but better that than ruining your clothes."

She practically lassoed me with the apron straps.

"There! Don't you look cute! I may get you one of those for home! Somehow it's you!"

I tried to laugh it off as a joke while I blushed. Tonya went back to the TV room, leaving me and my Mom to get supper.

"Tonya's such a doll!" my Mom remarked. "She's just bubbling over today. She seems so happy. Do you two have some good news? Is she pregnant?"

"No, Mom! Nothing like that!"

"Well, did you guys win the lottery then? Did you get a promotion at work? What is it?"

"Can't a person just be happy?"

"Not usually," my Mom countered. "There's usually got to be a reason."

"She's married to your son. Isn't that a reason to be happy?"

"Not usually!" my Mom teased. "Must be something else! Well, whatever you're doing, keep doing it, because I've never seen her look so happy and satisfied. That's why I wondered if she were pregnant: you know how women get that 'glow.' She's glowing!"

I blushed at the thought of saying, 'She's glowing because she's been well-fucked by another man's big cock, Mom! She's finally getting enough cock, instead of the little worm your son's been trying to fuck her with! And she's happy with me because I gave her boyfriend a blow-job this morning!'

"And here you are in the kitchen and you've been waiting on her hand and foot. Sometimes when a man's wife is expecting, he'll pamper her like that!"

"No, we're not expecting! Can't a man pamper his wife a little? And in this day and age, shouldn't a man help out in the kitchen?"

"Well, aren't we all liberated? Maybe that's why she's so happy: she's got you whipped into shape finally! Even got you wearing a frilly apron!" My Mom chuckled, as if she were in on a female conspiracy with Tonya and they were getting a kick out of seeing me humiliated! "Here, you whip the potatoes, then set the table."

Soon we sat down to dinner. Tonya dominated the conversation, often cutting me off or even answering for me when one of my folks asked me a question: "Oh, Johnny's been doing this," or, "Johnny doesn't care for that kind of thing," or, "We are looking forward to...." It wasn't as domineering as it was dominant: she was so full of energy and confidence and I was hesitant, almost meek. Throughout the meal Tonya found reasons to continue to have me wait on her: to refill her drink, to get something from the fridge, to pass her a roll.

Sometime during the meal she excused herself. She came back holding my beer bottle, which had mysteriously refilled itself.

"Honey, you left your beer in the kitchen. I brought it for you. I hope it isn't too warm."

"Thanks, hon. I don't mind if it's a little warm," I said and took a big swig, confirming my expectation that it was another dose of her urine. I felt a little shiver go down my spine as the warm liquid went down my gullet, to mix with my Mom's pot roast. Tonya beamed approval at me that I was sitting at my parents' table drinking her piss. I felt a warm melty feeling wash over me as I realized that I was hers, and that I was pleased to be her plaything. I looked at her with adoration, ignoring my parents for the moment. Tonya covered up my spacing out by launching a new topic of conversation.

When we got back in the car, I told Tonya what my Mom had said. She leaned over and kissed me.

"She's right! I am so happy, babe! I'm sexually fulfilled for the first time in two years! That's a long time to go. But this time, I'm not just getting good cock. I also have a husband who loves me and would do anything for me! I have the best of both worlds: a gentle partner who's there for me, who'll stand behind me, who's devoted to me; and a lover who will fulfill my need to be fucked and possessed by a strong man. Not only that, but I am free to fuck any cock I take a fancy to! What woman wouldn't be happy?

"But I owe it all to you, babe. There's lots of fat cocks out there—well, at least there are for a woman as attractive as I am. But how many guys are there out there like you? How many husbands would tolerate their wife fucking other men, much less encourage her, participate in it, and get off on it?

"I'd feel so bad if I had to be sneaking off to fuck a lover behind your back, but I'd feel just as guilty if I did it with your knowledge but you were home dying of jealousy. If I knew it were tearing you up inside, how long could our marriage last like that?

"But you are amazing! You are actually getting off on my cheating on you, getting turned on by it, having orgasms watching me do it! So I don't have to hide it, don't have to feel guilty about it: I can really enjoy it, even share my joy with you and you can share your shameful joy in it with me!

"You are one in a million, Johnny! I couldn't do what you're doing! I couldn't stand it if you were fucking other women: I'd be torn up with jealousy. Can you see me licking some other girl's cunt to get it ready for you, the way you sucked Brian hard for me? Can you see me holding your dick up to her pussy or ass so you could ram it in her, like you did with Brian? I'd scratch her eyes out and cut your balls off first!

"Most people are naturally jealous: no matter what the situation or arguments pro or con, their instincts take over and they can't help themselves. It's a rare man like you whose love is so strong or whose masculine instincts are so weak that you could stand by and watch another man usurp your role. But you are even rarer: you actually like it! So why shouldn't I be happy? When I fuck another man, I'm making myself happy and making my husband happy! It's a win-win!"

Tonya rattled this all off with such excitement and glee that I couldn't get a word in edgewise. 'Free to fuck any cock I take a fancy to?' I thought. We hadn't really discussed that! We hadn't really mentioned whether there was any chance of a two-way street, for me to have sex with other women, but I guess that was out of the question. 'Masculine instincts are so weak'?

"Now, although I'd be jealous of another woman, your unexpected love for cocks has raised the question whether I'll be jealous of you having sex with other men. I'm happy to tell you that I didn't feel jealous at all when you were blowing Brian! In fact, it was exciting! So I'd be OK with that, as long as you weren't sneaking around behind my back. So as long as you only have sex with the men I bring home, or I have approval of the men you bring home, I think I can handle that."

"Tonya!" I sputtered out. "I'm not going to be bringing men home to have sex with! I'm not gay! I love you! I want to have sex with you! You asked me to suck Brian off! I did that for you!"

"Sure you did, but didn't you do it for you too? I saw how hard you got; I saw how much you enjoyed it! You didn't just blow him: you made love to his cock with your mouth! But baby, it's OK! I enjoyed it! I love you and I want you to be able to do the things that excite you, as long as they don't get in the way of you and me."

"Tonya! You've already got me as a gay slut! I'm not going to be out chasing cock!"

"But remember, babe, it's only been how long that I haven't let you fuck me? As the months go on, you're bound to get horny for something other than jacking yourself off. I'll help as much as I can by fucking you with the dildo, but you're going to start to lust for flesh and blood contact. I'm going to be giving you a regular diet of cum-soaked cunt and ass, but if you need some real cock in your mouth or your ass, I'm willing to share. Just don't do it behind my back and give me some say over who it is."

There was something about this conversation that was causing me real anxiety, but I couldn't put my finger on it.

"You seem determined to make me into some kind of gay gigolo! I never touched another man's cock until last night! Why are you pushing me into gay sex?"

"I'm not, babe. Well, maybe a little! It is fun to see what I can get you to do, to see how much power I have over you! What a trip it would be to make a man gay who didn't have the least inclinations that way! I'd be like Professor Higgins in My Fair Lady!

"But mostly I don't want any silly fears or embarrassments to hold you back from what you want to do or what makes you happy." Tonya reached over and started to unzip my pants and fished my cock out. She cradled it in her hands.

"Last night was the first time you jacked a man off or sucked his cock, but it isn't the first time you've thought about it, is it? You've told me that the idea excites you and it's made your little willie hard. You've masturbated thinking about it. You've come fantasizing about it. You've admitted as much to me."

I trembled as she stroked my cock, which had been excited off and on all afternoon and evening.

"Look how hard your cock is just from us talking about it! And you've admitted to wanting to do even more than touch one of those big cocks, or suck on it, or even have it come in your mouth. You've fantasized about being fucked by one of those big cocks! You've imagined what it would feel like to have a real throbbing manly cock up your ass, forcing itself up your bum, slamming into your prostate! You've wished your ass were a cunt, so you could take cock after cock into you and milk their cum out of them! You've wanted to feel the warmth of their cum squirting into your bowels like a semen enema!"

I was quivering with lust now, bucking my hips up into Tonya's hand. Her hand was too gentle, too slow. I was so excited, I needed to come. I wanted to come right now, in the car, in the middle of traffic.

"Tell me the truth, Johnny! Tell me you want Brian to fuck you. The next time you see him, you want to suck him hard and beg him to fuck you up the ass. You'll stretch yourself with the butt plug, thinking of him, thinking of his cock. You'll have greased up your ass beforehand, so his pole will slide into your ass and he'll be able to fuck you as hard and fast as he wants."

This picture Tonya was painting charged me with so much lust that I wasn't sure I could drive. I was practically convulsing, trying to get her to put me over the top.

"Tell me, Johnny! Tell me: is that what you want? Is that what has you so excited right now, thinking of that? Be honest! You can tell me anything: I love you! Do you really want my stud to fuck your ass? DO you want to be a girl for him? Not just once, but over and over?"

Oh, God! What was the truth? When I pictured Brian's cock, when I remembered what it felt like to suck him off, a wave of arousal swept over me! Or was it worse than that? Did it feel like ... longing? An ache? A need? What would it be like to be <u>fucked</u> by that cock? I had knelt down to suck his cock and it had felt ... satisfying. But to submit to being fucked by him.... To be dominated like that. To be helpless, opened up, invaded.... My stomach dropped like the elevator in the Empire State Building. An empty, feverish, hungry feeling.

"Maybe," I whispered. "Maybe ... yes!" My voice was a strangled, anguished croak.

"Yes what? Say it!"

"Yes, I want to suck his cock again! I want to taste his cum! And ... I want him to fuck me! I want to feel him shoot in my ass!"

"Yes! I know! Don't lie to me, babe! Let it all out! It's OK: I still love you!" With that she grasped my cock and began pumping it furiously. "Think of his big cock, stretching your ass, filling it. Imagine the pulses as his cock explodes in your ass, just as your cock is going to explode right now!"

"Oh shit! Argghhh!" I screamed as my cum shot out of my dick in thin, watery strings, over the steering wheel, the seat, my pants, and Tonya's hand. She reached out her other hand and grabbed the steering wheel to steady it, watching the traffic.

"Slow down, baby! You mashed the accelerator! Back off. We're OK. You're OK. We're almost home."

Tonya let my penis go and held her cum-covered hand to my mouth.

"Lick it off, baby, and imagine that it's Brian's cum. I know it doesn't taste as manly as his, but use your imagination."

I shakily pulled into our drive and parked. Tonya continued to scrape my cum off the steering wheel, the seat, and my pants.

"So let's not have any more nonsense about how you don't love cocks, baby. Go ahead and love them! I sure do! At least the big ones! I bet those will be your favorites too! Dream about them! Jack off thinking about them! We'll just have to share, so we'll have to be on the lookout for them. Thank God Brian has his friends Calvin and David, eh? Otherwise you and I together might wear out even a stud like Brian!"

"So do Calvin and David know … that I know? Do they know about last night … about me being there … about me watching?"

"I don't know how much they know, baby. They know that you caught me and Calvin and that I gave you an ultimatum to accept it or get a divorce, and that you decided to let me continue to fuck other men. I don't know if Brian will have told him about the watching part. I didn't tell him not to tell them about that, but I don't know if he will."

"Are you going to … fuck them with me there too?"

"Would you like that, Johnny? Would you like to taste some black cock? Would you like to see another DP close up—two at once? Or you and I could do them two at a time, eh? You could be warming one up while I fuck the other! Or one could be fucking my ass and the other could be fucking yours! Would you like to be looking each other in the eyes, holding each other's hand while we each get a cock in our ass?"

I closed my eyes and imagined that. My mind felt fried. I was speechless. My God, that did sound exciting—and terrifying!

"I know, baby, it's a lot to take in," Tonya interjected. "Your genius cock knows what you want, but your middle-class mind still rebels, is still hung up on what's 'normal.' Well, being deliriously happy and sexually satisfied beyond your wildest dreams isn't normal either! Having 15 orgasms a week isn't 'average.' Of course, we can't get ahead of ourselves. We don't even know that Calvin or David would go for that scene. Maybe Brian's way more open-minded than your average horse-cocked stud. Wait and see."

We didn't have to wait long. We went into the house and the message light on our answering machine was blinking. As I tried to clean up my pants and got ready to go out and wipe down the car, Tonya played the message. Of course, it was from Brian. He said that Calvin and David couldn't wait to get together again and "make our threesome a fivesome." And he wasn't talking about golf.

"That's guys for you, Johnny. Always thinking with their dicks. They don't care if you're gay, a transvestite, or have 3 dicks with fangs. All they care about is that they're going to get their rocks off and they can't wait! But I'm exhausted and U have some practicing to do before we can take that bunch on. I'll give them a rain check for later in the week. We might even wait until the weekend. We've got to work on your cock-sucking and ass fucking! They want you, Johnny, and they don't even know what you're capable of! We'll blow their minds!"

Tomorrow was a work day and we spent what little remained of the evening winding down and relaxing. As we got ready for bed, Tonya asked me to let her piss in my mouth again. A look of affection came over her as I lay on the floor and opened my mouth so compliantly. I could tell this act touched her somewhere deep and somehow I knew she would never tire of it. She sighed with pleasure as a licked the last drops of urine from her, and then she asked me to give her pussy and ass some relaxing oral worship.

As my tongue dipped into her anal flower I could not help but picture Brian's cock poised at this entrance, still held in my greasy hand. I recalled how her anus had looked stretched tightly around his shaft and how it had sheathed and unsheathed his sword. Forever now my own wife's ass would be owned by other men's cocks. It was a place she entertained her men friends. I could taste it, but it would never belong to me now. As bittersweet as this realization was, it did not keep those memories from firing my lust and quickening my dicklet.

Tonya also asked me to wear one of her nighties to bed and to sleep with her.

"I'd really rather sleep alone, but you need your rest and I know if you're by yourself, you'll end up masturbating half the night. I love seeing you in something frilly and feminine! It made me wet to see you in that apron this morning and at your Mom's house. When you do that, you're giving me a gift, Johnny. You're giving up your manhood, your manly pride. You're giving me the gift of humiliating yourself. You're wrapping your balls up in a pretty pink box with a bow and saying, 'Here, these are for you. I'm sacrificing them to show how much I love you.' When you put on a nightie or you wear women's panties, it's just a little way of doing the same thing as when you held Brian's cock up to my pussy."

So I put on her nightie. My erect cock pushed out the front and my pre-cum left a small wet spot on the shiny fabric. She snuggled up behind me and lifted the hem to cup my bottom. She snaked her fingers between my cheeks and stroked across my rosebud.

"Soon, baby. Soon!" she whispered and then cradled my cock as we drifted off to sleep.

As I lay waiting for sleep to come what preyed on my mind was my reaction to Brian's cock. When I had masturbated holding his cock to mine, that had been the most startlingly exciting thing I had ever felt. The sight of our two penises pressed against each other was so unnatural and yet so incredibly arousing! I couldn't help picturing it and remembering what it had felt like for our slippery cocks to slide against each other. It was a jolt to my system, like sticking my finger in an electric socket!

What did it mean that I had found that so perversely arousing? Was I starting to crave sex with men? If sucking Brian off felt that good, what would it feel like if he fucked me? The very idea sent a feverish excitement through me! My cock throbbed as I imagined what it would be like, to feel a real cock instead of a dildo penetrate me, to feel a strong male body envelop mine, to submit to him! I couldn't get the picture of his cock out of my mind, of how it had felt to suck on it, to feel it spurt in my mouth! I hungered to do it again! What was happening to me? I was so aroused I had trouble falling asleep.

Perhaps then it is no surprise that I had several disturbing dreams that night. I was a baby and Tonya was my nurse. She had a baby bottle for me and fed it to me. At first it was milk coming out of the bottle and then the taste turned to semen. Then Tonya wasn't holding a bottle anymore. She was holding a penis and feeding it to me. As soon as I finished one penis another took its place. Some of the penises gave forth milk and some of them spurted semen, but I sucked all of them hungrily. Tonya cooed at me.

"Eat it all and Baby will grow up big and strong! Well, not really. You'll grow up to be a sissy faggot!"

Later I had another dream. I went into a bar. Instead of beer taps there were women standing on the bar. The bartender went up to a woman with a beer mug and held it up to the woman's crotch and she squatted and peed in it. The men in the bar drank the girls' piss as if it were beer. In fact, men argued with each other over which girl's urine was the best. Some men swore by their favorite girl and wouldn't drink any other girl's piss.

When one girl ran out, another girl would be brought in to replace her and men who favored the new girl's urine would clamor for a refill. Fights sometimes broke out between men who wanted the same girl's pee. Before they drank, they'd clank their mugs together and toast, "To piss!" and drink heartily.

I waited to fill my mug until I saw that it was Tonya's turn. But when she got on the bar, a line of men formed in front of me. The men were excited, saying that Tonya's pee was the sweetest of all. Somehow she was able to fill mug after mug and the men went away happily to drink her piss down, crowing at their good fortune.

A man next to me inhaled the bouquet of his glass and took a swig and gave a great sigh of satisfaction.

"Ah! Now that's some good piss!" he exclaimed. He cradled his mug and savored the warmth of it through the glass and sipped at it.

But when it finally came my turn, Tonya was dry! She drank some water. to try to make some more piss, but somehow other men would always push into line ahead of me and I'd never get my turn....

-Day 24 Monday-

Tonya cuddled with me just before our alarm went off. The feel of our satin nighties rubbing against each other was strange but alluring. Tonya reached around me with one hand, cradling my penis, which soon rose to the occasion. With her other hand she stroked a finger across my anus, tickling it. She reached for the lube jar and soon snaked a finger deep into my rectum, probing for my prostate. She continued to play with my penis all the while, driving me to distraction and forging a connection between anal invasion and erotic stimulation. She had me more than halfway to orgasm when she suddenly stopped.

"Make yourself a mini-enema, babe, with my douche kit. Just make sure you're clean down there."

My dream had left me with an unfulfilled thirst for more of Tonya's pee. That, coupled with the frustration of the interrupted hand job made me throw caution to the winds.

"Tonya.... Could ... could I be your toilet again first? I just have to taste you again." I hoped I hadn't overstepped my bounds. Her delighted smile told me I was OK.

"It would be my pleasure! So you really like it, do you? Every time will taste different. Strongest in the morning, like now. Other times almost like water. Sometimes sweet if I've had a diet drink, or taste of what I've been drinking or eating. Tell me how it tastes, when you like it the best!"

Before she settled on my face she put a hand to my cheek.

"Oh, Johnny, you're such a dear! Who'd have thought that marrying a pin-dick would be my lucky day?"

Then she lowered herself to just above my face and her morning urine rushed into my mouth, hot, hard, and strong. She stopped when my mouth was full to let me swallow. Her piss was salty and bitter. But I was happy to prove myself the devoted husband. I opened my mouth for more. I felt its warmth fill my belly and I felt glad to have gotten the gift I'd been denied in my dream.

I got out Tonya's douche kit and used the enema solution from the jug. I mused that this routine certainly might help me feel more comfortable about my rectum becoming a "dual-purpose" organ.

Tonya kissed me as we exited the house for work.

"No jerking off at work today! They'll be time enough for sex when you get home, but you've got to give yourself a break or you'll burn out. Just concentrate on work today."

To my surprise her admonition worked. I was more focused at work than I'd been in weeks. And that was a good thing, because my sex-addled brain had let a lot of things pile up in three weeks.

I didn't even let myself get distracted when I got a text message from Tonya.

"Brian here. Loved his WE! Wait til Fri!"

When I got home, Tonya greeted me by dropping her drawers, flipping her skirt up and leaning over the table. She didn't say what I was to do. In the old days I'd have taken it as an invitation to do her doggie style, but I knew that I wouldn't be allowed that. Which left only one other possibility.

I spread her cheeks with my hands and admired the beautiful starburst of her asshole. It was subtly different than it had been. The reddish area was larger and it was not so tight at the center. There was a raised lip around the very center, where some of her stretched-out tissues now slightly protruded. The radiating puckers stretched out further. Her lovers' cocks had possessed it, used it, and changed it, making it theirs. It would never be quite the same again.

But it was my Tonya, her most intimate, secret place, even more than her cunt. And that made it beloved of me. I leaned forward and inhaled the musky smell of her crack. I had a hot, moist, earthy, sexy smell. I savored it.

Then I kissed her hole. My lips felt every fold, every crevice, every protrusion. I kissed it gently, caressing it with my lips. I laid little feathery dry kisses on it.

My tongue then slipped out, not wet and slobbery but almost dry, to touch and tickle and caress her anus. I traced little circles around it and tentatively dipped into the middle, not penetrating, only testing. I felt her muscle's rubbery tone and felt it twitch at my touch. I went back to kissing, now harder and longer.

Tonya hummed in satisfaction at my worship of her anus, then stood up, signaling that my job was done. She pulled up her panties and smoothed her skirt. I felt as if I'd passed a test and pleased her. I'd treated her as a goddess: her dirtiest parts were worthy of my devotion. I'd taken no liberties.

"Ohhh!" she shivered. "That was so nice!" she said, half to herself.

At dinner she told me that she and Brian had gone out for coffee and briefly discussed the past weekend. Far from being freaked out by my involvement, Brian had confirmed Tonya's diagnosis. He had been thrilled by his "conquest" and humiliation of his mistress's husband. As she'd predicted he framed my sexual submission to him as confirming his alpha male status and not as casting any doubts on his heterosexuality.

It was apparent that he'd wasted no time before crowing to his cronies in explicit detail, and it appeared Calvin and David were amazed and skeptical that I would stoop to such acts. But far from horrified, they were eager to witness my humiliation with their own eyes. And they were apparently willing to do anything which would allow them access to Tonya's magnificent cunt and newly fuckable ass.

Although Calvin and David had beseeched Brian for an immediate repeat performance, Tonya decided to put them off until Friday night. But she told them to clear their calendars for Saturday and Saturday night too! So she was delaying them by promising a two-day orgy if they'd wait!

"We'll need the time to get you ready! If we're going to keep three big cocks happy for over 24 hours, I'm going to need your help!"

Tonya had me wait while she strapped on the dildo. I started to get aroused just from watching her put it on!

"Imagine it's Brian's cock, babe! You want that cock so bad! You want to suck it. You want to please him because he's the big strong sexy man you wish you were. You can't offer him a cunt, so you have to offer him your mouth and your ass!"

Tonya's pep talk worked on my need to be good for <u>something</u>. I'd do it to please her, and impress Brian. So I glugged the dildo down, pulling it deep in my mouth and then I started to fuck it in and out. Now that I had experienced a real cock, the Cyberskin was a poor substitute. It had the rubbery consistency, but it lacked the warmth, the pulse, the smell of the real thing. But I would show Tonya that I was game. I tried to make love to this phallus the way I remembered caressing Brian's with my lips and tongue.

Tonya looked down at the glistening rod protruding from her crotch.

"Shame to waste this. It's all ready to go. Get yourself a douche and hurry back," she ordered. I rushed to the bathroom with my dick bouncing, in anticipation of more anal stimulation. I sighed as I lubed up my ass for the enema. My dick wept a drop of pre-cum.

"That's the spirit!" Tonya jibed when I hurried back, my hard cock preceding me. "I like to see a boy who can't wait to get butt-fucked!" Tonya inserted a glob of lube in my ass with one finger and I was already in a zone. She nudged my ass ring with the tip of the dildo.

"Now relax. Remember, this is what you want. Let this cock in, like you're going to let Brian's cock in your ass on Friday!" She pushed into me and I could feel my muscles tighten up involuntarily. Tonya started to force her way in, making me tense up even more.

"No, honey!" I begged. "Take it all the way out, then it'll go in easier next time. When it gets harder to push, pull out all the way for a second and then back in."

"That's a good faggot! Tell me how to make your ass into a cunt!"

Tonya inserted the dildo in again and it did go in more easily, but she pushed too fast again.

"Whoa! Take it out just for a second!" I asked. She slipped the cock out and then eased it in, almost reaching the base on only the third try. I could feel my ass protest, and I thought she was going to pull out again, but she only pulled halfway out and then buried the rod. I could feel it prodding the entrance to my colon uncomfortably, but Tonya only rocked into my ass, telling me that she was not going to pull out.

"Feel it, baby! This cock's going nowhere! Get used to it! Cocks belong in that sissy ass!" She continued to grind her hips against mine.

"Take one for the team, Johnny! Yeah, Brian's the quarterback, and Calvin's the running back, and David's the star wide receiver. You, you're on the punt team! You've got to try harder just to make the team! Show them how bad you want to make the team! Open up that ass!"

She reached around and grabbed my dick with her greasy hand and began to stroke me, which very effectively distracted me from the large phallus up my butt. Her hand felt like liquid fire on my cock. I moaned and rolled my hips, working my ass around the shaft of the dildo.

"Oh, yeah! His cock is going to love that! Hitting the top of your ass is going to feel so good to the tip of his cock! Feel how your ass grips his cock! You're going to milk every drop out of his balls with that ass of yours!"

Tonya started to slowly fuck me.

"I'm not going to give you a hot fuck, Johnny. This is training. I'm training your ass to open up when a cock tries to get in. I'm training your muscles to relax and let go. So we're going to go nice and slow, take our time. In fact, I'm going to stop with this cock way up in you. I'll just play with your penis enough to keep you hard and keep you hot to have a big cock in your ass on Friday!" She was just stroking my penis very slowly, almost teasingly.

"Oh, shit!" I hissed in frustration and I tried to fuck myself on the dildo, but Tonya grabbed my hips and held me still.

"Oh, baby! I'm glad to see that you want so bad to be fucked up the ass, but I want you to be still and relax. Just get used to feeling relaxed and sexy with a big cock filling your ass. Let's not fuck: let's just talk. Talk to me!"

"Tonya, why do you seem so bent on making me hot for these guys' cocks? You seem to want me to be gay!"

"That's a very good question. I've been wondering why that idea turns me on so much! And I think I've figured it out. It's because that is how you make me a gift of your masculinity! The most precious gift a man can give his wife is to sacrifice his manhood. It's the most personal, most precious thing he has, and when he gives it away to his wife, he is making the deepest, most meaningful sacrifice he can make.

"There are so many ways he can strip himself of his manhood for her: to give up intercourse, to eat his own cum, to wear feminine clothing, to kneel before his wife and let her order him around, to let her fuck him up the ass. Then to step aside while other men fuck his wife and then to be there and even encourage it, that is a deeper sacrifice.

"But to fondle another man's penis, to suck it, to let another man ejaculate in his mouth, and finally to let another man fuck him up the ass: these are some of the most profound ways a man can forfeit his manhood! There are a lot of cuckolds out there who can stand by knowing their wife is cheating on them and swallow their pride. But they don't have the devotion to suck off their wife's lover like you have, and they would never think of letting him have their anal cherry. To do these unwillingly would be a great enough sacrifice, but to make oneself want to do them, or, even better, to lust to do them, is yet another step farther and an even more perfect proof of his love!"

As Tonya gave this speech she continued to stroke my penis maddeningly and she punctuated her points by grinding the dildo into my ass or giving little mini-thrusts. Her technique was working, because my ass felt more and more relaxed, almost loose. As if to illustrate that fact she drew her cock all the way out and then slipped it back in. She continued.

"I know you're not gay, Johnny. If you were, then it would be no sacrifice. So it's a paradox: because you aren't gay, the greatest gift you can give me is to be gay! Not just to act gay, but to actually want to suck their cocks, to fantasize about it, to look forward to it, maybe even to dream about it! To find your cock hardening at the thought of cock up your ass, to feel your ass twitching at the thought. To feel your mouth start to water at the thought of eating their cum, to hunger for the taste, to thrill at the smell of semen!"

"And I guess another part is the bitchy part, I'm afraid. I like to see what I can get you to do! It's a power trip to see how much I can wrap you around my little finger and get you to do things you'd never have done on your own in million years! I know that isn't nice, but it's such a thrill to have that much power over someone!"

She began to pump the dildo into me more forcefully and her hand began to stroke my dick more insistently.

"So do you want what I want, baby? Do you want to prove your love to me by becoming my little gay husband? Are you willing to go gay just to please me? Do you feel the lust building in you? Which do you want more: to lick my cunny or suck on Brian's cock? Which excites you more: my dildo fucking you, or the idea of Brian spurting up your backside? Do you want my plain vanilla cunt, or do you prefer it oozing with Brian's cum? Maybe I'll make you choose: one or the other. Which would you pick?"

Her taunting was driving me insane. My ass was on fire with sexual electricity that went straight through my groin and came out my cock. I writhed to get more stimulation on my prostate as Tonya's grip on my cock was just loose enough so I couldn't get enough friction.

"That's it, baby, fuck yourself! Grind away on my cock!" But then she buried it all the way in and held me tight so I couldn't get more than a nudge and held my cock still. I shrieked with frustration.

"What's the matter, baby? Doesn't it feel good?"

"I need you to <u>fuck</u> me! I can't come like that!"

"Poor baby! You need a <u>hard fucking</u> so you can come? Here, I have a better idea. You fuck yourself on my cock!"

She pulled all the way out and I groaned in frustration. My ass felt empty, hungry, lonely.

"Don't worry, baby, we'll let you come. But you need to do the work." She lay down on the bed and ordered me to mount her. "You ride my cock. That way you can fuck yourself just how you like!"

I climbed on top of her and awkwardly aimed the dildo and sat down on it with a moan of satisfaction. There was no resistance: it filled an empty place I needed filled just then. I leaned forward onto my hands and began to rock back and forth, spearing myself with the phallus. It felt good. I angled my pelvis, seeking contact with my prostate. When the tip of the dildo touched it, I groaned.

"Oh, yeah! Oh!"

"Does that cock feel good up you, baby?"

"Oh! Unh! Hnh! Hnh!"

"I'll take that as a 'yes'!" She took my greasy cock in her hands, smearing my pre-cum over the head and down the shaft, making a slippery, gooey mess. "Think about Brian's big hard hot cock fucking your ass, baby! Isn't that going to feel so good? You want that, don't you?"

She let go of my dick and I gritted my teeth at the loss of the stimulation. I fucked myself more frantically on the dildo, trying to push myself over the top.

"Think of fucking my pussy with your little wiener, baby. Too little, barely touching the sides. Not stretching me, filling me. Failing me, polluting me with your little boy squirts."

She took my cock in her hand and began to stroke it.

"Now think of a big hard cock fucking your ass. Your ass is nice and tight, milking his cock, feeling so good to him and to you!"

Her hand was wringing wonderful sensations from my cock and I began to bounce spastically on the dildo.

"Now think of a big hard slick cock sliding in and out of your mouth. Your lips and tongue are massaging his cock marvelously. He's delirious with the sensations you're giving him! You're a winner!"

Tonya slowed her hand on my cock.

"So which do you want? The pussy? Or the cock? Loser at satisfying pussy or winner at pleasing cocks? Which one?"

I was fucking myself desperately, trying vainly to wring an orgasm out the dildo by jamming my prostate. The arousal coming from my ass was wonderful but without more stimulation from my cock, I just couldn't get over the brink, and Tonya knew it.

"Which do you want, Johnny, pussy or cock?"

I was suspended on the knife's edge for what seemed like an eternity. I rocked back and forth on the dildo, fucking myself deliciously, but Tonya moved her hand with my rocking, so that my cock was only being held and not stroked.

"Cock!" I growled. "I want cock! I want to be fucked! I want to suck cock!" I said, desperate to come now.

"That's right! Now pretend you are fucking yourself on Brian's nice warm, smooth, slippery cock!" She began to pump my dick the way I desperately needed. "Think of how good it's going to feel! Think of all the cock you can suck! Think of all the delicious creamy cum you can eat!"

And I did: I thought of everything she had said and my cock swelled, and the cum arrived at the base of my penis and I froze on the dildo. Tonya beat my meat furiously, knowing my come was imminent.

"Arggghhh!" I cried in animal lust and my cum splashed out over Tonya's hand and her stomach. "Oh, FUCK!" I groaned with each spurt.

"Oh, baby! Look at you! What a nice come! Oh, you get so excited when you think about cocks! I almost wish I had one, they get you so hot! You're going to make me jealous with those studs on Friday – and Saturday — and Sunday...."

I felt like a wet dishrag, but I knew that the show wasn't over just because I'd come.

"Oh, let's get this nice creamy cum and rub it all over my nice cock and let you lick your cum dessert off." I lifted off the dildo and Tonya scooped up the jism and rubbed onto the greasy cock. The cum kept sliding off the cock, until she started mixing it in with the lube and spreading it thinly over the dildo. She held it for me to lick and then had me suck on it. Then Tonya decided the spit- and cum-covered cock should go back in my ass for practice.

"That's what it'll be like after he comes. His hot jism will make it even slipperier. And then whoever does you second will find your hole all nice and juicy and wide open for him! Actually the second and the third fucks are in some ways better. No pain, just fucking!"

My ass was starting to feel a little sore from how hard I'd gone at it earlier, but the dildo did slip in with hardly any resistance and no real pain.

"Oh, yeah," Tonya enthused as she fucked my passive ass. "That goes in so easy." She planted the dildo deep within me and lay on top of me. "I love you, Johnny!" she told me. "No matter how much cock you suck or fuck, no matter how many men you give my cunt to, you are my soul-mate and I love you."

She withdrew the dildo again and made me clean it off with my tongue and mouth. Then she had me wash it off "extra clean," because she told me she was going to be using it solo later.

"This fucking and sucking has made me horny, babe. I want you to sleep in the guest room tonight, because I'm going to have some private time with Richard." However, some of the rest of the evening was spent with her editing the videos and pictures she had taken over the weekend. She gave me a flash drive with picture files and written instructions for another rush job for the photo shop.

I went to bed in another nightgown. I thought about her threat that this weekend her friends would be fucking my ass. I pictured all the porn videos I'd watched of men fucking men and my head spun and my cock throbbed. I felt out of control, as if my brain and body had been taken over by a demon. I couldn't get those pictures out of my mind and I couldn't cool the fever of arousal those pictures brought!

That night I had another dream. I was locked naked into an apparatus. My waist was belted to a seat and my hands were strapped to the arms of the seat. There was a suction thing around my penis that gently massaged and sucked on it. A video screen was in front of me. Various videos would come up, all sexual in content. Some were my wife being fucked or sucking off various men, some were of strangers. Some were of men sucking each other or fucking each other. Some were of me sucking off or being fucked by well-endowed men.

I was vaguely aware that there seemed to be a row of these cubicles and there were other men strapped into similar ones. A woman came along with a clipboard and she was explaining the apparatus, as if she were giving a tour.

"These collector tubes collect the secreted pre-cum. It turns out to be a remarkable substance if it is produced in the right conditions. It has many uses in cosmetics & medicines. It may seem ironic but the pre-cum of a frustrated male applied to the skin of a woman's face keeps the skin marvelously firm and supple. Perhaps God has a sense of humor!

"The problem, of course, is that under normal conditions, the male produces only small quantities of pre-cum at a time. But in this apparatus, we can artificially produce large quantities and we can increase the frustration level to where the pre-cum produced has a much higher content of the active ingredients. We keep the subject highly stimulated and we prevent him from coming, so that he starts producing large quantities of pre-cum. Anal stimulation is used periodically to increase the output."

The woman pushed a button and I felt something push into my ass from the seat bottom. It felt like a small butt plug and it began to vibrate softly. I felt it settle near my prostate and I felt pre-cum ooze up my cock and spill out the end.

"What do you use as the videos?" the visitor asked.

"We try to find a mix which is maximally stimulating to the subject without inducing boredom from showing the same thing too much. We keep track of the pre-cum output to see what videos are the most effective. Sometimes they bring their own, or their wives or partners bring in homemade videos. Those are often the most productive. You'd be surprised at what works. Anal sex videos consistently out-produce vanilla videos. We have ostensibly heterosexual males who produce the most when shown gay male porn, for instance.

"This fellow (referring to me) is a good example. You can see by his chart that vanilla porn does almost nothing, watching other men fuck his wife is about equal to watching gay porn, but watching himself in gay activity doubles his output over that."

"Where do you get the subjects?"

"Some are criminals working off their sentences, some are paid, but a surprising number are volunteers!"

"Volunteers! How can that be?"

"Well, most of those are volunteered by their wives. They're in some kind of sub-dom relationship and this is part of the wife's discipline."

"Do they need any special diet?"

"Oh, yes! They need to eat cum and drink female urine. Those are fed into their cubicles through those tubes you see on each side. If their pre-cum output drops, they get a signal which to drink. They need only turn their head and suck it out of one tube or the other."

"How long do they stay?"

"It depends on their contract. The best pre-cum comes from prolonged periods of production and frustration. The fellow I was talking about is a champ. His wife has signed him up for a solid week!"

"How long has he been strapped in so far?"

"An hour...."

-Day 25 Tuesday-

The next morning Tonya wakened me by nudging the dildo against my lips. It smelled of her juices, which were liberally smeared on it, and of lube, telling me she'd employed it on both holes. Even though I was still half-asleep she bade me to suck on it.

"Just lie there and suck on it, babe, and dream of big juicy cocks! When you're done, wash it off and preserve it, but you keep it in here for practice. I give you permission to practice whenever you want, as many times a day as you want! Friday isn't long from now!"

I lay there as she had told me to and sucked on it, like a baby with a pacifier. Her permission to "practice" predictably excited me. How many wives say, "Now you run along and play with your dildo! And if you masturbate, remember to lick it up!"? I have to think there'd be fewer divorces if more wives did, though.

One thing I'd have to say in my defense is that if I wasn't able to satisfy Tonya with my little dick, it wasn't due to lack of libido. Despite having come less than 12 hours before and having barely awakened, her permission to practice had my perverted brain in a fever again. I supposed that the more times I stuck that cock in my mouth or up my butt, the sooner I'd get used to it.

I pulled my knees up and brought the dildo to my nether opening. It still felt huge despite the incursions of just last night. But in my excitement I pressed the bulb against my sphincter and forced it in. My muscles spasmed in complaint, so I pulled it out momentarily, only to stab it back in. One more tactical retreat relieved the pain and I drove the dildo in up to its base.

I groaned at the uncomfortable pleasure of feeling my rectum filled with cock. Even more uncomfortable was the image of Brian's pubic hair tickling my ass cheeks that came unbidden into my mind. As unexpectedly thrilling as his man-flesh filling my mouth had been, how much more exciting would it be to be fucked with a real cock instead of this vinyl replica?

I stroked my penis now, quivering with delight. I alternated between these two sources of pleasure, fucking myself with the dildo and wringing voluptuous sensations from my greasy erection with my slippery hand. The cock slipped easily in and out now. With almost no warning my spunk was spurting over my chest and I writhed in tormented ecstasy. Was I really a cock-whore now?

"Wow, I tell you to practice and you don't lose any time, do you?" came Tonya's voice from the door of the guest room (or was it 'my' room now?). I froze like a kid caught with his hand in the cookie jar. I quickly pulled the dildo out and began to sit up, embarrassed to look at her.

"Stop, Johnny! Lie back down! It's OK! You haven't been 'caught.' I just came to see if you were ready for breakfast. I guess you sort of are!" she said, as she scooped up a fingerful of my cum and held it to my lips. "Eat your breakfast, little birdie!" Tonya said in motherly tones, as if she were speaking to a toddler. I sucked it off her fingers. She took the dildo out of my hand and rolled it in the strings of cum on my stomach. She held it to my lips and I licked it off. She dragged it repeatedly through my jism until there was none left, just of film of cum and lube.

"I had no idea you'd be so eager! We could have started your cocksucking on our honeymoon! Poor baby: all those cocks you could have sucked and fucked, and all the cum you could have eaten! And all the big cocks you could have watched fuck me! Well, we'll just have to make up for lost time." She kissed me and I tasted the lube on my own lips. "Hurry up or you'll be late to work! No more masturbating until tonight!"

At my place at the breakfast table sat a glass with the yellow of Tonya's morning urine. I drank it. Tonya gave me the flash drive she'd saved things on and instructions for the photo shop and told me to take them there on my lunch hour and to pick them up later.

Work was harder that day. My real job was sucking and fucking and attending my adulterous wife: what was I doing here? But I told myself it would do no good to get fired, so I buckled down and slogged through without too much daydreaming. But I felt as if I were in exile.

At the photo shop I detected a smirk from the cashier and knowing looks exchanged among the help as they handed me more wrapped poster-sized packages and a wrapped framed picture. I paid an outlandish bill for the rush service and special handling and felt a blush warm my cheeks. 'That's the guy in the pictures!' I imagined them guffawing after I left.

Tonya'd beaten me home and she was eager to unveil her handiwork. One poster was the direct comparison shots from various angles of Brian and me holding our penises side-by-side, with his dwarfing mine in every dimension. Another poster was another montage that showed me holding Brian's cock to Tonya's cunt, to her ass, me kissing and then sucking Brian's cock, and finally me holding our two cocks shaft-to-shaft. They were larger than life-size and shocking in their lewdness. They were practically a "highlight reel" in stills and blow-ups.

Tonya rubbed the front of my pants, pleased to find me hard.

"Pretty hot pictures, huh?" She had me hang them immediately in the "guest room," augmenting the earlier posters. I had a feeling these would be permanently on display now, at least until we had company other than Tonya's lovers.

After dinner Tonya "assigned" me some solo "practice." She set me up in front of the laptop.

"You're going to practice 'edging,' " Tonya told me. "It's a very good discipline for a cuckold to learn. It keeps you keen to fulfill your duties. And it gives you the horny state of mind I need to mold you into the husband I want!"

She started a video she'D constructed out of the weekend's activities, cut in with older stuff and videos she'd downloaded off the Internet.

"I had to subscribe you to a couple of gay sites, to get some good man-on-man cocksucking and butt-fucking clips for you," Tonya informed me.

"Now go ahead and pull your peepee while you watch these. But if you feel you're about to come, you have to stop. Then let yourself cool off until you're out of danger. Then you can start in again. But be careful not to go too far: go slower, or take breaks, or do it left-handed. I want you to keep yourself on the 'edge' of coming, but you mustn't come.

"If you think you might have slipped, bite your lip or clamp down on your muscles and try to hold off! But don't dare come, whatever you do! See how long you can keep your willie hard and weepy. If the video is too exciting you might have to leave off stroking yourself entirely for a while. Let's see if you can go an hour!"

At first I didn't think that would be too hard, but after ten minutes my cock was red and my groin felt congested with blood, as if things were backing up. In the next ten minutes I two close calls. I found I couldn't judge just by the hardness. If I left off jerking for more than a minute, I'd start to wilt. But almost as soon as I started stroking again—bang—I was on the verge of coming again after about 30 seconds, even if I weren't even completely hard yet.

I guessed that edging is so unnatural that my dick was going to try to come and give the plumbing some relief. Maybe a constant hard-on was cutting off circulation to some places, or maybe my storage vessels were full to overflowing. Like they say in Viagra commercials, "Seek medical attention for an erection lasting more than four hours." But I hadn't even made it to 30 minutes!

After a half-hour Tonya came to "help."

"You probably can't keep stroking with your whole hand, Johnny," she advised—as if she were an expert on cock-pulling! "Try just tickling it with your fingertip." I shuddered as she demonstrated.

"Or just tickle the rim here," she said and ran a finger around the edge of my cockhead. "I read that some boys just grab it here, down by the base of the shaft." She slipped just two fingers down against my pubic hair and pumped it gently. "Not so many nerve endings down there.

"Tell me if you get too close now," she said as she continued to milk me. "Concentrate on the video. My, look at that nice big cock!" she said, referring to the gay video playing. "Wouldn't it be tasty to wrap your lips around that piece of meat!"

She continued to pump me slowly and gently at the base.

"Now say aloud to yourself, 'I want cock! I want cock!!! I love cock!' You need to say it, hear it, think it, feel it!"

"I want cock," I whispered uncertainly.

"Good!" She gave my cock a full-length stroke and then resumed the base-only massage. "Again!"

"I want cock," I parroted, a little louder. "I want cock."

"Look at that gorgeous cock! It's so perfect! So long, so thick, so pink. Look at it and feel yourself wanting it. 'I want that cock!' "

"I ... want ... that ... cock!" I breathed.

Tonya gave my dick another two good strokes and I shuddered.

"Yes! Look how beautiful it is! Anyone would love that cock, man or woman! You don't need to gay to admit that that cock cries out to be sucked. It's gorgeous! How good would it feel in your mouth? Why shouldn't two men enjoy sex with each other? Who are they hurting? Let yourself enjoy it, Johnny. Say it: 'I want that cock.' Feel it!"

"I want that cock!" I said, falling under Tonya's spell. "I want that cock!" Hearing myself say that made a thrill of illicit excitement go through me. I felt on the verge of shooting.

Tonya sensed it and snatched her hand away and bit my shoulder.

"Don't come! Just look at that cock! Feel how hard you cock is! You want it! It excites you! You crave it! Your cock burns for it! But don't come!"

I held my breath as I felt my cum pooling at the base of my cock, ready to spurt. I clamped down on my muscles desperately, as if I were holding my bladder, trying to squelch my orgasm. My cock swelled and I teetered on the brink. But then the urge passed, leaving my groin uncomfortably congested with blood.

"Good job, baby! That cock makes you so hot, but you controlled your lust for it." Her eyes turned back to the screen. She paused the video on the frame of the actor's large, rampant penis.

"I'd love to fuck that cock, Johnny! But that cock doesn't want my cunt. It wants your mouth and ass! I can't compete with you for that one. I can't please that cock, but you can! That's your department!"

Tonya un-paused the video and resumed very gently pulling my painfully sensitive dick.

"Nice deal for you: with your little dick and less-than-he-man physique, you wouldn't get much action from these studs on your own. But using me as bait you can attract a regular stable of horse-cocks to suck and fuck to your heart's content!"

"But I'm not using you as bait! That's is all your idea!"

"You mean you want to attract them all on your own? You might have to femme it up a little bit. You could maybe attract them as a twink or a she-male: you're never going to do it as a hunk."

"No! I mean, the whole gay thing is your idea!"

"Maybe so, but judging by your hard-on, it's an idea you've warmed up to! But why put labels on it like, 'gay'? Can't men just enjoy the pleasure that another man's cock can give them? You know, throughout history men have always had sex with other men. It wasn't even considered 'homosexual' until recent history. Whenever women weren't available, men always turned to each other. They knew that cocks don't care about the gender of the mouth or the ass they're in. Maybe the bisexuals have the right idea: sex is sex. Why rule out half the human race? The more the merrier!"

My near-orgasm had released a copious amount of pre-cum and there were strings of it dripping off my cockhead lewdly. Tonya had to wipe her hand off to keep from getting too slippery. I still had 15 minutes to go and it seemed as if it were going to be an eternity.

I don't know if I could have kept myself from coming on my own, but Tonya took over, expertly gauging when to stop stimulating my poor prick and when it was safe to resume.

Whenever the video switched to gay anal sex, she coached me to say, "I want that cock. I want that cock up my butt!" I felt my asshole twitching in sympathy with the actor in the video.

"Don't you feel so empty, babe? Doesn't your ass long to be stretched and filled by a nice fat cock?" I closed my eyes and I could almost feel what I imagined the receiver in the video was feeling, even though I'd only ever felt a dildo. How much more satisfying would a real cock be? My ass wouldn't be feeling a lifeless dildo: it would feel every twitch of his excitement, the swell of his organ preparing to shoot, the hot wetness of his cum discharging deep into me.

It wouldn't even all be sensations: it would be a relationship. Knowing my ass had enticed that out of him—how hot would that be? And maybe even hotter—knowing a man had taken me. Feeling that completely dominated. Feeling a strong man take possession of me, inside and out. Surrendering myself to a man. Being that helpless....

Tonya watched me sink into that fantasy and knowingly released my dick, as it swelled dangerously close to orgasm from the arousal coming from that fantasy more than from her hand.

"You want it, babe!" she murmured in my ear, not wanting to intrude too much into my reverie, but only to deepen it. "When he comes in your ass, that will be your triumph! At that second you'll be the King of the Hill, not him! He'll be in your power, humping your ass frantically, like a wild animal! He'll be helpless to do anything but let your ass milk his manhood out of him! He'll think he's won, but at the moment he comes, he'll be a brainless lunatic for those few seconds, reduced to jelly by your luscious asshole!"

Whoa! I shuddered thinking of that and my cock twitched perilously close to orgasm. My power to seduce a man, to make a big stud putty in my hands: that was the power the female of the species usually wielded and thrilled in. The man might be the hunter, but the prey could be a trap, a lure, like the spider at her web. Then was the stud the conqueror or the conquered?

"Well, that's an hour, baby! You made it!"

"Arrgghh! Can I come now?"

"Oh, no, baby! Don't waste all that sexual energy with just a dirty little orgasm! Use it for your training! I want you to practice your cocksucking and butt-fucking,. You'll be ultra-motivated now. But your cock is off-limits! I don't want to catch you touching it until I say! I have a plan for how you can practice on your own while I relax."

Tonya took the laptop and set it to play gay cocksucking videos, then gave me the dildo.

"Work on that for a while. Try to mimic whatever the slut in the video is doing. When you've had enough I'll come back and we'll work on your other end. But no touching Little Johnny!"

Tonya was right about one thing: an hour of edging had my brain swimming in a fog of sexual arousal. I was ready to do anything.

I watched the videos and tried to copy the techniques I saw. It was a weird experience to be mimicking what I was seeing. It was almost as if I were in the movie myself. My cock was so hard I wondered if I could come just from watching. Tonya was right about another thing: watching these men seeming to enjoy what they were doing made it seem less and less taboo. These men certainly were into it.

That didn't escape Tonya's notice when she returned. She took my hard-on in hand.

"I guess you like the videos I picked!" she said as she stroked me. "Don't stop! Let me watch you."

I continued to ape the actor in the video.

"Oh, shit, that's hot! Johnny, I can see that you're putting your heart into it!" She started to talk to me in her hypnotic patter.

"You love to suck cocks. You want to take their meat in your mouth. You long to feel them squirt their jizz right into your tummy. It will be so hot and sexy." She was like a snake charmer mesmerizing a cobra. It didn't hurt that she continued to jiggle my tormented penis.

Then she took the dildo and began to fuck my mouth with it while she deliciously toyed with my dick. She fingered my pee slit while she sawed the phallus in and out.

"Very good. Keeping your cock nice and hard helps you get into it. Now let's get your other end ready. Go use your douche!"

I scampered off to the bathroom. When I returned I found that Tonya had strapped the dildo to our headboard, with several pillows behind it to hold it out. It hung there in midair obscenely, almost menacing. She'd brought the laptop back to the bed.

"Let me grease you up and we'll see if I got the height right." I crawled on my hands and knees and she inserted a finger and then two in my backside. How quickly my anus accommodated itself to her invasion! I found my cock soon throbbing again and myself welcoming her thrusts and twists.

"Now back yourself onto this. The height looks right, but you be the judge. I want you to be able to fuck yourself by rocking back and forth."

I backed into the tip of the dildo, startled again by how thick it felt. Even after her preparation my muscles protested the intrusion and complained. I rocked forward, slipping the rubber cock out of my behind, and then immediately rocked back, spearing my anus again. The muscles still strained against the invader, so I backed off again. On the third thrust I worked two-thirds of the shaft into my rectum. The next rock forward only unsheathed the dildo partway and then I drove it in to the base on the next thrust. I rested against the dildo, letting my sphincters adjust to being stretched wide.

"That's right, baby. Now enjoy the videos I downloaded for you. Give yourself a good fucking. But no touching your peepee! I don't think you'll be able to come just from fucking yourself, but we'll see. Add more lube whenever you need it." Tonya cued up the show she'd prepared for me, of gay hunks fucking more effeminate men—"twinks."

My cock thrilled at the twin stimulation of the video and the dildo in my ass. Of course I couldn't help but see myself as the fuckee in the video and anticipate that Brian would be servicing me like that in three days' time.

I began to fuck myself more forcefully as my dick begged for release. I tried to angle my pelvis to bring the dildo against my prostate. I jiggled. I jabbed. I fucked myself faster, slower, harder, deeper. My ass started to feel hot, loose, sexy. The dildo slipped in and out easily now and I was truly enjoying the feeling of it filling and penetrating me. Every stroke was luxurious now. My cock was dripping pre-cum liberally now, leaving a wet spot on the towel beneath me.

But I couldn't come! My cock felt like a hot dog on the grill, ready to split, and my groin was so congested with blood that I must be on the verge of popping a blood vessel.

Just then the video changed to a different scene. This was obviously from a cuckold website, because now there was a wife in the scene. She was taunting her husband, telling him that since he was such a wimp, she thought it only fitting that her lover butt-fuck him—if he wasn't a man, he must be a woman, right? The husband in the video was begging his wife to spare him this humiliation, but she wouldn't hear of it. In fact, she masturbated her husband while taunting him and used his stiff erection as proof that he secretly looked forward to being sodomized.

I found this video even more arousing than the last one. The idea of the wife leading her husband to be sacrificed was perversely compelling to me. I watched with rapt fascination as the wife first fellated her lover to hardness and then greased his pole for her husband's deflowering. Of course the husband cried for mercy as he was being penetrated, but eventually he was clearly enjoying his fucking. He leaned back to meet his tormenter's thrusts.

His wife was stroking him as she continued to taunt him, pointing out how much he appeared to be enjoying her boyfriend's prick up his behind. I shuddered with envy as the camera zoomed in on her greasy hand sliding over the husband's engorged, but thoroughly modest, dick. I was sure that I would explode if Tonya were even to grip my shaft for five seconds now.

The wife commanded her husband to beg her boyfriend to fuck him and to please come in his ass. She orchestrated for her husband to come just after her lover had clearly unloaded into her spouse's bowels.

I had stopped my self-fucking to concentrate on the video, but now that it had reached its climax, I resumed pistoning the dildo in and out of my rectum. I closed my eyes and concentrated on the sensations the cock was creating in my behind, while I pictured myself as the husband in the video. My cock quivered with arousal as the mental and physical stimulation combined.

"I knew you'd like that one!" Tonya whispered in my ear. I had been so intent that I hadn't even heard her come back into the room. "Fuck yourself, baby! Fuck yourself on Brian's gorgeous meat!" She lightly cradled my dick in her hand, not even grasping it, just letting it lay on her hand, teasing me. I groaned with the need for just a little more stimulation to make me come.

"Feel how desperately you want it, baby! You want that stud to fuck you! You want to be his! You love that he's stronger than you, that he's so manly. You want him to take you, to possess you, to use you, to love your ass. And you want to drive him to orgasm with your pretty ass! Tell me! Tell me how badly you want it!"

I was driving the dildo into me in long luxurious strokes. I wanted to feel every inch of it, feel it penetrating me, stretching me, inflaming me. What would it feel like to have a real flesh and blood penis there, connected to an aroused, lusting man, striving to fill me with his hot cum?

"Oh, God, I want it! I want him to fuck me! I want it!" I gasped out in my lust.

"I know you do, baby!" Tonya replied, and she gripped my cock and began to massage it with frustratingly short strokes. She wanted to bring me to the edge as I frantically fucked myself on the dildo.

"And what does that make you?"

"A ... faggot!"

"That's right! That makes you a faggot! Say, 'I love cock! I'm a faggot!'
"

"Unh! Tonya, please!"

"Say it!"

"Unh! I—unh!—love cock! I'm a faggot!"

"That's right!" She increased her strokes and commanded, "Come now, thinking of Brian's cock!"

I exploded with a strangled scream as all the pent-up cum from nearly two hours of stimulation spurted out onto Tonya cupped hand. Stream after stream burst out of me in copious quantities.

"Oh my! Look at all that cum! I think we've found what really turns you on! I don't think my poor little ol' cunt ever got that much cum out of you! It looks like we both need a big cock to get off!"

Before I'd even pulled my ass off the dildo, Tonya held the handful of cum to my mouth. As I licked it off, she stroked my head, as if she were rewarding a dog who'd done a trick.

"That's a good boy! Keep fucking yourself while you eat up this girly-cum. This weekend we'll get you lots of manly cum, babe. We've got three horny studs and I'm sure they'll be happy to let you and me share."

When I finished cleaning her hand, I pulled off the dildo. Of course, she insisted I clean the dildo off with my mouth, even though it had just been in my own ass.

"Certainly the boys will be expecting you to clean them up after, so you might as well get used to it," Tonya reasoned. I found I was indeed getting pretty inured to the taste of the lube, to my surprise.

"My, this has gotten me a little hot and bothered," Tonya told me. "I think I'd like to use your talented tongue for myself now. I know I've only got a cunt and ass, not a cock, but you used to like them pretty well, if I recall."

As drained as I was, I couldn't let Tonya think I has lost interest in her charms, so I fell to licking her pussy as enthusiastically as I could in my post-orgasmic state. She wanted me to lie on my back so she could sit on my face and I did indeed enjoy being drowned in her labia. But my cock couldn't rise to the occasion again so soon, and Tonya noticed that.

"Well, my cunt isn't full of another man's cum or stretched wide by a monster cock, so I suppose it's less exciting for you." I tried to protest, but Tonya cut off my words by smothering me with her pussy. After a few minutes of that she reversed positions to put her ass to my lips and I munched on that orifice, drawing some gratifying groans from her

"This is nice, but I need some cock!" Tonya finally declared after a few minutes. "Clean off that dildo and bring it back to me!" she ordered.

When I brought the dildo back I asked if she wanted me to go into the other room.

"No, you might as well stay. I may want your help. Get me the butt plug." She inserted the butt plug in the rosebud I had so nicely moistened and relaxed and then began to fuck her pussy with the dildo. Soon she was moaning and groaning with arousal. I felt like a fifth wheel, just standing there while she ignored me, but soon I found that very awkwardness was exciting me. Somehow whatever she did that said, "You're not man enough for me," paradoxically aroused me! I began to fondle my penis.

"Oh, shit! Fuck!" Tonya exclaimed as she drove herself into an orgasm. She continued to fuck herself to another climax, ignoring me. My eyes were drinking in the erotic scene of my voluptuous wife consumed with passion, masturbating herself right in front of me.

"Get me the smaller dildo!" she barked at me, startling me, as it appeared until then that she'd forgotten I was still in the room. I pulled the smaller dildo from her drawer and handed it to her.

"Lube it up! I need it in my ass!" she growled, as if her lust had turned her into a different person. I clumsily uncapped the lube and smeared it on the dildo, quivering at the thought that soon it would be entering her ass. She pulled out the butt plug and threw it on the towel, still stained with my pre-cum from earlier. She extracted the dildo from her pussy and then, with a satisfied sigh, she sank the small dildo into her bottom with one slow thrust. She began immediately to gently fuck herself in the ass with the small dildo, giving out moans of desire.

"Oh, yeah! Oh! So good! Fuck me, Brian! Fuck my sweet ass!" she crooned to herself. "That feels so good!"

Then she began to work the larger dildo into her pussy. The slowness and hesitation with which she did this testified to the tightness of the fit and the stretching involved in accommodating both cocks at once. It was clear that there was some discomfort from her pained expression and grunts. But gradually pleasure appeared to gain the upper hand and she was soon working both dildos in and out of herself in a perverse syncopation.

"Oh, God! Oh, yes! Oh, YES! God damn!" she cried in ecstasy at the dual stimulation. "Fuck me! Fuck me!" I was mesmerized by the sight, my cock starting to thicken again and drooling pre-cum.

"Johnny," she called, snapping me out of my masturbatory trance. "I need you to fuck my ass with the small dildo! I need a hand for my clit!"

With a trembling hand I took the base of the small dildo and began to thrust it in and out of her gripping greasy hole. Tonya took her hand and began to rub her clit furiously, shuddering with the overwhelming stimulation. Almost immediately, she began convulsing in orgasm. I could feel her contractions through the dildo in my hand.

"Don't stop!" she cried and I resumed fucking her ass while she fucked her pussy with the other dildo. "Oh, God! God, I need more! Johnny, fuck me with both dildos!" she commanded.

I took both dildos and awkwardly began to piston them in and out of her in alternating rhythm. Tonya grabbed both her breasts in her hands and began tweaking her nipples, moaning in voluptuous pleasure. She writhed in her ecstasy as I fucked both her openings with the dildos. I was in awe of her capacity for sexual arousal.

After a moment she dropped one hand to her clit and within seconds another wave of orgasm was rolling over her.

"Oh shit! Oh shit! Oh God! Fuck! Fuck! Fuck!" she cried as I felt her muscles spasm around both cocks. "Oh God! Oh, stop, Johnny! Just stay still!" she ordered.

I held both dildos crammed into her distended orifices. Tonya grabbed both breasts again and seemed to be wringing the last pleasurable sensations out of the tail of her orgasms.

"Ok, take them out," she said and I slipped both shafts out, each glittering with a different lubricant. "Lick them off, baby. Lick my lovers off. Whew! They've satisfied your wife quite well," she said dreamily.

I sniffed the larger dildo, redolent with the powerful scent of Tonya's pussy juice. My cock continued to stiffen as I savored the smell and taste of her juices while I licked off the dildo. Then I took the other dildo and smelled the scents of her ass and the lube. 'This has been in my beloved wife's ass. It has pleasured the ass I love,' I told myself and I licked it off with equal devotion. Then I took them to the bathroom and cleaned them and returned them to her drawer.

Tonya still lay on the bed in a swoon of satisfaction.

"Come here, baby. Let's cuddle," she said. She took my head in her hands and clutched it to her chest.

"Do you hate it, baby, knowing that I need a big cock? Do you hate seeing how much pleasure a big cock gives me, even if it is fake one? That I can get much more pleasure even from a fake cock than your little real one?

"Or do you love it? Do you love knowing that I'll always need a real man to take care of me? Do you love seeing a big cock fucking me, seeing my cunt stretched open, seeing another man's cum dripping out of me? Does that thrill and satisfy you in a way no plain vanilla fuck ever could? Do you look forward to the next humiliation, hoping it will be even more glorious than the last? Are you glad now to be a cuckold? Are you happier being a cuckold than you ever could have being an ordinary husband? Would you go back to what we had then if you could or would you choose to be a cuckold?"

I didn't know what to say. "I don't know.... I really don't know."

"Well, that's good enough, babe. That answers the question, doesn't it?"

I knew what she meant. If I didn't know, it meant that I really did accept all of this. If I wouldn't jump at the chance to take it all back, I must be wanting what was happening.

Or was I just addicted to it? It was like a drug. It was intoxicating. It gave me highs that I could never have from "normal" sex or a normal life. And the more I had, the more I wanted it. It had literally taken over our lives. But even so, now I couldn't imagine walking away from it. I needed it. There was no question of whether we would continue or not. It was only a question of when, how much, how much more perverted would it get? Were we out of control? Were we on a path to crash and burn? I knew I wasn't in control. I was at Tonya's mercy. I had to pray that she was in control and she would keep us safe.

Yet another question nagged at me.

"Baby, why—uh—why did you want me to call myself a faggot?"

"Ha! Oh, yeah, that gets you in the goodie, doesn't it? That's why, baby! That's the scary, humiliating, exciting question, isn't it? 'Am I really gay?' That would be more shameful than being a cuckold, or drinking piss. I want you to torture yourself with that, because you get off on the humiliation. The lower you are in your own and others' eyes, the more turned on you get!"

"But do you really think I am?"

"Who knows, baby? If you don't know, how am I to know?"

That was not the answer I wanted to hear.

When we got ready for bed that night, Tonya strapped on the dildo and had me wear a nightie again. She snuggled up to me in bed, slipping the dildo against my crack. It underlined her questions about whether I accepted our new life.

"Baby, I've been thinking about what you asked," I whispered, "about whether I wished we could go back to how things were."

"Yeah? And what have you thought?"

"I was thinking about whether there are things I miss about, er, our old life, and I realized it's been so long now I've almost forgot what it feels like—er, felt like—to... um... put my dick in your pussy. But I know it felt good. I do sort of miss that."

"Are you sure, babe? Are you sure it was as good as you remember? I mean, you're pretty small, so it wasn't exactly a tight fit. Not like your hand, that you can make as small as you need to get good friction. And aren't you forgetting those inklings you had that you weren't satisfying me, those doubts, those sinking feelings that you weren't man enough for me? Did those feel good? I know it always bothered you that I didn't come from you fucking me. When you think about the old days, think about that.

"Think about how you were failing me, trying to be a real man when you aren't. What about those times you couldn't get me excited at all and my pussy was dry? You don't have to worry about that now when you're jerking off: you just grab up some more Vaseline and you're back in business.

"Isn't it much better now to see my pussy getting plowed by nice big cocks and know your wife is satisfied? And isn't it better to get all hard and excited about being a cuckold? And think about all the pleasure you've gotten already from being butt-fucked, and you haven't even had the real thing yet!

"No, don't start thinking your weenie's getting back in my cunt, baby. That's ancient history now. Start thinking about how nice a cock's going to feel in your ass or a cock down your throat."

"OK," I said. But it bothered me still, because I really could hardly remember what it had felt like....

We drifted off with Tonya spooned against my back. But my traitorous mind went back to the videos I had watched. What would it be like if it were a man who was cuddling me? What if it were a real penis that stiffened against my ass? Would it be good to feel myself held in his muscular arms? Would I itch to open myself for his cock, long to feel his meat saw in and out? My dickie stiffened and I felt a wave of submissive arousal course through me. It took a while for sleep to overtake my fevered brain.

-Day 26 Wednesday-

Maybe my doubts had worried Tonya too, because she seemed more affectionate the next morning. She kissed me in bed and joked with me, poking me all over with the dildo, calling me a "cock-hungry minx" who was going to seduce all the good men and cheat her of all the cock she needed.

When we got in the bathroom she asked me to drink her pee, but she made a point to tell me how special it was to her that I would do that for her and what a warm feeling it gave her, as if to reassure me. And I was eager to do it too, to reassure myself that I was special to her and to be close to her pussy in one of the few ways I still could. Then she made breakfast for us both and the rest of the morning we were like any other couple.

When I got home from work Tonya was already home. She met me at the door and had me greet her by pulling down her panties and kissing her anus. I did it almost without thinking, accepting that as normal for us. I realized that by being denied intercourse I had become hungry to be in her pants any other way I could. Kissing her ass was no longer a submission or humiliation for me: it was a way for me to be intimate with her. But dinner and dishes and TV were shared and, again, Tonya seemed to want to reassure me that there was still some normalcy in our lives. Until a little later....

"Honey, I hope you won't be upset, but I've made some plans to go out tonight while you do some more of your practice."

"Go out?"

"Well, baby, it has been Sunday morning since I had any real cock. I thought I could wait until Friday, but I don't think I can. And as much as I've enjoyed what you and I have done, once you've had a real cock you'll understand that it just isn't the same with a dildo. And, well, Brian and his friends, they haven't even had that. So I've agreed to meet them at the club."

"I thought everything was going to be here from now on."

"Well, I thought so too, but I've changed my mind. I think if I brought them back here, it would take away from Friday and, besides, I need to have some freedom."

"Some freedom? You mean other than the freedom to fuck other guys under my nose?"

"I was afraid you'd be upset. But yes, I need the freedom to come and go as I choose. We don't have to be bound together hand and foot. We do plenty of things together. It won't hurt for me to do something on my own now and then."

"You mean do some<u>one</u> on your own, don't you?"

"Oh, dear, you were doing so well and now you're so jealous all of a sudden! Well I guess you cuckolds have to go through stages of learning to accept your lot. Now I ask you: if I let you dictate who I could fuck and where and when, would you really be a cuckold? Or would I be your whore? The wife's freedom is the very basis of the cuckold relationship. By definition it is a one-way street."

I had no comeback to that. She had me. I was behaving in a very "un-cuckold-like" fashion.

"Now I think it's a good thing that I decided to go out tonight without you. You need to be reminded of your place. Maybe I've been too easy on you or too generous. Use that jealous energy during your practice tonight. Channel the humiliation of your wife going out to get fucked and leaving you home to masturbate into an erotic high. Think about me getting miles of pipe laid while you beat off and use that to get off!"

I didn't feel very sexy right then. But as I watched Tonya get dressed to the nines and put on her "fuck-me" make-up, my traitorous dick started to get her idea. And as she assigned me more cock sucking and butt-fuck practice and told me I could watch videos and masturbate to my heart's content, my erection betrayed that I could not oppose her.

There was something irresistible about having one's wife give him permission to masturbate. It seemed so wrong that it was unfailingly exciting. I wasted no time getting out the dildo and cueing up the laptop. I added a twist of my own by putting in the butt plug while I did my cocksucking practice. That way I'd already be loose when I started the butt fucking. Tonya had exhorted me to take my practice seriously.

"There's only two days to D-Day," she'd reminded me. "You don't want to disappoint Brian, or me—or yourself."

A while into my practice I wondered if Tonya had left the club yet. In other words, was she fucking anybody yet? Certainly they weren't going to waste much time drinking or dancing when they could be doing the horizontal polka. But who knew how long she was going to be out? Maybe she wouldn't even come home tonight! Maybe there was no hurry.

Although the butt plug made it easier to get the dildo in my ass, I never ceased to be amazed how big that dildo felt every time I tried to take it. There was always a period of adjustment to the size before it became comfortable. And then a period of warming up before it became pleasurable. And then a period of amazement that a cock up my butt could feel so damn good! I plunged the dildo in and out, marveling in the feelings shooting from my rectum to my cock. How was it that gay guys had kept this a secret from the rest of us?

I grabbed my cock and began to jerk off. It was distracting having to fuck myself and beat my meat at the same time. I wished for a second that I had someone else to fuck me with the dildo so I could concentrate on my cock. But I didn't have long to think because soon I was squirting cum over my chest. In my post-orgasmic haze I thought, "I was sincerely wishing for someone to fuck my ass...."

I cleaned myself up the "cuck-fashioned" way, by eating my own cum and licking the dildo off. I actually thought to myself, "At least eating someone else's cum will be more exciting than eating your own, and licking off a real cock will be more exciting than licking off a dildo." What comparisons!

I worried a little bit that watching my "highlight reel" in the wake of an orgasm would actually dull my excitement for the highlight reel, so I decided instead to prospect through some of the new videos that Tonya had downloaded from the cuckold and gay sites. I found that she had downloaded some with definite domination and S-M aspects. I watched in fascination at one where the husband had to address his wife as "Mistress" and had to bow to her and her lover. The cuckold husband submitted to being spanked and whipped and trampled by the wife and her lover. Did Tonya plan that for me, or did she just wonder if that would turn me on? As little as I wished for that to happen, my cock responded to the perversity by tingling. My hand found my prick and massaged it even in its limp state..

The next video was a gay scene, also with bondage and domination. The sub was chained and blindfolded. He had clamps placed on his nipples and ball sac. The sex was accompanied by verbal degradation and presented as a punishment rather than lovemaking, as if the sub were being raped, orally and anally. I was appalled to find that this scene was very arousing for me, just as I had been aroused by the cuckold husband being forced to submit to anal intercourse in the video I'd watched last night. Somehow the sub being unwilling made it more exciting for me. I was pretty sure that I didn't want to be raped or beaten, but the ideas certainly turned me on. I jerked my cock furiously and came for the second time that night, draining my vital fluids into my palm.

The last part of the gay scene ended with the dom forcing the sub to let him urinate in his mouth! Although I was excited by Tonya peeing in my mouth, I had no such desire to allow Brian or any man to do it! We'd never discussed limits, but I hoped this video didn't give Tonya any ideas!

The last video I watched was of a bisexual husband, who participated in a three-way with his wife and her lover. This video included man-to-man kissing and fondling, as the husband made it clear he was as attracted to the man as to his wife. I wondered if this really were a cuckolding video, as the man certainly wasn't giving up his wife: he was gaining a lover! But, tellingly, this video also didn't excite me much. So being a cuckold or submissive was the key to my arousal, not the homosexual activity.

I looked at the clock and by now there could be no doubt but that Tonya was at this minute having sex with another man (or men!). Here I was at home jerking off (with her permission!) and my wife was enjoying being plowed by the large cock of a better endowed man—with my permission. I decided to be there in spirit, and I cued up the video of the night Calvin and David came over—only a week ago, although it seemed like an age ago. I had never felt I had any biases, but the sight of Calvin forcing his black cock into Tonya's anus brought my weary penis somewhat back to life. Stroking my prick to the rhythm of his cock stretching her rectum filled my groin with delightful feelings.

But the double penetration was the climax. Watching Tonya's body convulse with unbearable pleasure confirmed for the umpteenth time that I had no chance to compete with these men. I was a plow horse (or a pony?) up against thoroughbreds. I could not bring her to those exalted heights of ecstasy. And I could not deny her that to save my pride or satisfy my jealousy.

With those thoughts in my brain, I wanted to spill my worthless seed for the third time that night, but I just couldn't get there. After two orgasms not long ago, I couldn't keep hard, even though the video was arousing mentally.

But I'd had plenty enough "practice" for the night and I prepared for bed. It was eleven, but I had no illusions that Tonya would be home soon. She had three men to satisfy and two holes to fill.

I could only doze fitfully. I had a dream. Tonya came home carrying a bucket. I looked in it and it was two-thirds filled with semen.

"I didn't want you to miss eating any of it, so we caught it all in this bucket and I brought it home for you." In the dream she crammed a funnel in my mouth and drained the bucket into it. "Don't want to spill any," Tonya said.

About 1:30 am I heard the front door open and hall light went on. Our bedroom door opened and Tonya called my name softly.

"Johnny? I'm home! Are you awake?"

I turned over and turned on my bedside lamp. Tonya's make-up was smeared and her dress had been put on hurriedly. She stood with one hand pressed tightly to her crotch.

"I've got a present for you!" she sang brightly. "I've got loads and loads of fresh man-cum up me and I know it's your favorite! Get it while it's hot!"

She pulled off her panties, which were soaked in cum and she threw them toward my face.

"Here's an appetizer. Don't waste a drop!"

I picked up the panties and held them to my nose. They reeked of sex: raw, powerful, animal sex. Tonya's juices had flowed, and mixed with it was the strong smell of men's spunk. The smells excited me irresistibly. Obediently I began to lick the men's scum off the fabric, then sucked the cloth into my mouth to vacuum all the fluids from it.

"Yes! Get it all, babe! I tried to hold it all in, but their cocks stretched me so much, I couldn't. But there's still plenty for you. They came like fire hoses, baby! And I came like gangbusters!"

She shinnied over to me on her knees and loomed over my face. She waited for me to open my mouth wide and then she took her hand off her crotch. In the light of the lamp I could see my bride's cunt lips were red and stretched. Her vagina opened wide, like a mouth—no longer a slit. And immediately a stream of cum began to drool out. I stretched open my mouth and reached up my tongue to accept my wife's offering of her lovers' spend. Glob after glob dripped out of her pussy. I swallowed and opened wide to accept the next flood.

"God, I love this moment, baby! This is my homecoming! I have to get my satisfaction from other men, but when you suck my cum-fill puss, I know you still love me! I know that this is my home even if I get my sex elsewhere. I need you to do this every time, to suck my cheating snatch clean every time I fuck another man, to tell me that it is OK, that you accept my need. And to prove that you want me to do it. You want me to have the joy you can't give me. You want to be my hero in any way you can."

Her words inflamed me and I went at her cunt with ravenous hunger. I licked her labia clean and plunged my tongue deep into her distended pussy, sucking the continuing gouts of cock cream from deep within her, deeper than my poor dick would ever reach. The unmistakable taste of semen excited me and  made me lust for more. Tonya began to hunch against my face and I moved up to suck on her clit and lash it with my tongue. She gasped and I felt her pussy contract and shudder with an orgasm. Her womb pushed forth another wave of cum then, forced out by the spasms within her. I gagged at the unexpected flood.

"Oh, that feels so nice, baby! Your mouth is so gentle, like a woman's mouth. You're so loving, so soothing. Get out all that nasty jism! Clean up all the evidence of your wife's unfaithfulness!"

She threw a knee over my head and repositioned herself with her buttocks in my face.

"Don't worry, baby, I didn't let my other end go to waste. I'm pretty sure the boys are going to give my backside equal time, that is, unless they decide they like the back door better! They say it's so tight that it feels like I'm going to choke their kielbasas right off! But they seem to like it! I can't decide which I like better either. As big as they feel in my cunt, they feel twice as big up my ass! And bigger IS better, you know!"

There was no mistaking that her backside had suffered an assault. It was reddened for an inch all around and the pucker seemed three times as wide as before. Of course it was shiny with lube as well as smeared cum. As I watched it I saw Tonya strain and squeeze out a blob of cum. I sealed my lips around her anus and sucked as she squirted out dribble after dribble of lube and semen.

I dipped my tongue into her hole and felt the looseness of the muscles, as my tongue penetrated easily, scooping more sperm into my mouth. I thrilled to feel my tongue easily burying itself entirely within her rectum and I felt a sensation of intimate connection between us. Tonya moaned with pleasure to feel my tongue straining up her anal canal and sensing my eagerness and excitement. I plunged my tongue repeatedly into her and she began to squirm with enjoyment of the sensations.

Tonya dismounted me and pulled me to her side.

"Oh, baby, you love my ass, don't you? Even though it's just been reamed and defiled by other men's cocks and sperm, after it's convulsed with orgasm around their pricks, even when it is stretched and leaking their cum, you still love it with all your heart and soul! You'd rather kiss my ass than kiss my mouth! God, I love you! What did I do to deserve you?"

She kissed me and hugged me and I felt on top of the world. With who know how many loads of cum in my stomach.

"I'm gonna kiss you goodnight on your mouth, but I want you to kiss me good night on my asshole, because I know that's what you really want to do. From now on that will be Our Kiss, because the way you love my ass makes me feel like the special-est girl in the whole world!"

How well she knew me. They could fuck her ass, but only I could really love her ass! I burrowed down to her posterior and I planted soul kiss after soul kiss on her springy rosebud. Tonya sighed with delight.

Again the thoughts that filled my mind as I drifted off were not on Tonya, but on her men. I thought of my eagerness to swallow their semen. The taste of their cum on my tongue thrilled me! My cocklet stiffened at the warm thought of my tummy filled with sperm!

-Day 27 Thursday-

I woke Tonya with more kisses on her behind, which pleased her. Tonya announced that we would be going shopping after work to prepare for our special weekend. I assumed she meant to pick up drinks and snacks and food for meals, but when we got to the mall she pulled into the department store lot. First we went to the men's department and picked up three terrycloth robes in extra-large. Tonya said we needed to be accommodating hosts and robes would be the uniform for the weekend, "for easy access!"

Then we went to the women's department. Tonya looked through a number of filmy women's robes. I thought she was looking to pick up something extra sexy for herself. But finally she held up a pink filmy lacy robe in a size too large for her and held it up to me!

'That'll appeal to them," she whispered to me. "It makes your being another man—technically anyway—less threatening to them. It will also work into them accepting the homo stuff as domination rather than gay. I've got some other ideas to go along with that. Try this on."

"Right here in front of everyone?"

"Oh, get over yourself! Who cares if a few people raise their eyebrows and think I'm shopping for my transvestite husband? You're gonna have to work on getting over your worries about a little gender bending this weekend!"

I sputtered but pulled on the robe, feeling fantastically foolish.

"Oh, the color is perfect for you! That's it!" Tonya enthused. I took it off as quick as I could. "Now for something to wear under it."

"I thought 'easy access' would call for nothing under it."

"It would if you had tits and a cunt, but you need more help!" Tonya horrified me by looking through bustiers and corsets, but she was disappointed to find nothing in my size. "We might have to shop on line for that," she decided ominously. So she settled for looking through camisoles and chose a pink lacy one to match the robe. I was thankful she decided I didn't need to try it on. While we were in that department she decided to buy three different baby doll nighties in different pastel shades for me to sleep in.

We did some grocery shopping and then went home. Tonya immediately wanted a fashion show. As soon as I put the camisole and robe on she frowned with disappointment.

"The hair's got to go. It spoils the whole effect. You can't have hair sticking through a filmy camisole. Don't know why I didn't think of it earlier. Your little winkie will look even smaller and more infantile without any hair! It'll look like a ten-year-old's next to theirs!" She clapped her hands and squealed with delight. "Let's do it right now! We may have to redo it tomorrow to be perfectly smooth, but I want to see how you'll look!"

She took a pair of hair clippers and had me stand still while she sheared off the larger part of my pubic hair and body hair. I was shocked at the difference in how my cock looked. It seemed so naked and immature. We went into the shower and she lathered me up and went at my body hair with a razor. I trembled as she worked on the hair on my scrotum, I was so afraid she'd cut me. When she was done I looked at myself and I did look like a boy with a five o'clock shadow.

"Big improvement!" Tonya declared as she looked at her handiwork. "Brian will be blown away, since he saw the 'before'!" She had me turn around, and then, to my discomfort, she asked me to bend over.

"This is the view Brian will have before your deflowering. Tsk, tsk. There's some hair around your brown-eye there. I think that might be too sensitive to shave, might really detract from your enjoyment of your fucking. I think we've have to wax! You're gonna get a Brazilian!"

So I submitted to the indignity of Tonya applying wax all around my asshole while I bent over and spread my ass cheeks out.

"Oh, I like that pose. That's how we'll have you present yourself to Brian," she said as she brushed on the wax. " 'Please, sir, will you fuck me up the ass? I do so want to feel your fine cock up my butt!' " she mimicked.

Tonya's taunting had the predictable effect: my cock quickly jumped to hardness as I imagined the scene she painted: myself trembling with anticipation, offering my ass to Brian to defile.

The pain of pulling off the wax felt like a hundred needles, but Tonya was overjoyed with the results.

"Oh, your ass is as smooth as a baby's bottom! It looks so vulnerable, naked like that! I want to fuck it myself! But not yet!"

The skin around my ass hurt like fire, but the sensation of smoothness was startling. It made me feel "more naked than naked" somehow. It really was as if my ass were now even more defenseless and inviting. Tonya applied some soothing lotion, especially for post-waxing.

She took me into our bedroom and had me sit at her make-up table.

"Now, I'm not going to make you up like a girl, at least not for tomorrow. I just want to give you the least little bit of a feminine air, so subtle they won't even notice consciously, but their cocks will!" To my dismay she applied brown eyeliner and just a brush of mascara. "Just a bit, to give your eyes a little bit of a sexy look, but not enough so they'll notice you're wearing make-up!" She'd found a lip pencil just the shade of my lips, and used it to make my lips look a little plumper. "All the better to suck cocks with!"

I looked at myself in the mirror and I had to admire Tonya's handiwork. If I didn't know what to look for, I wouldn't have noticed any of the changes, but there was no doubt that I looked "prettier" and there was something feminine about my face that you couldn't quite put your finger on.

"I won't have to suggest it: they'll be thinking of fucking you on their own!" Tonya enthused. I was startled to find that the idea of being alluring excited me deeply. A little shiver went up my spine.

"Do you like it, Johnny?" she asked as she ran her fingers up the underside of my erection.

"Yes," I choked out, my mouth dry with arousal. "Thank you."

"You're welcome! My pussy is all wet looking at you! We have to practice! It'll be your dress rehearsal!"

Tonya strapped on the dildo and donned one of the robes we had bought, playing the man.

"Get over here, faggot, and suck my dick!" she said in a deep voice. I knelt at her feet and took the dildo into my mouth. My head bobbed on her cock like a kid with a popsicle. I soon had the cock all covered with my slobber.

" 'Tonya, he's so eager! He's a natural born cocksucker. Probably been a closet fag this whole time. No wonder you can't get a decent fuck out of him!' " Tonya continued, mimicking a man's voice.

I applied some lube to the phallus with my hand.

" 'Oh my, he knows how to jerk a cock off by hand too!' " Tonya said in a deep voice, then answered herself in her own voice. "He's had plenty of practice at that!"

I grabbed Tonya by the hips and pressed forward onto the cock, taking it as deep as I could. I smelled Tonya's excitement. I lingered only a second and then pulled back.

"Oh, shit, that is so hot!" Tonya exclaimed, forgetting her role. She thrust her hips forward, seeking to bury the cock in my mouth again. I held her hips at bay so I would be able to control the penetration and then swallowed the cock again.

"Oh fuck!" she cried before I pushed the cock back out. Tonya was overcome with desire. She thrust her hand under the base of the dildo and began to frig her clitoris. I pushed my mouth onto the dildo, pressing it back against her hand, trying to excite her further. I began to mouth-fuck myself, slamming the dildo against the back of my throat.

Tonya grabbed one breast with her free hand, while she continued to masturbate with the other. I grabbed Tonya's hips and pulling them toward me, trying to keep the cock pressed against the back of my mouth. I could feel her body was jerking with arousal, trying desperately to fuck my throat. The cock was twisting and moving and I fought not to gag. I felt my throat spasm and tears filled my eyes. I had to pull back off the dildo and take a breath, and then I took the head back between my lips.

"Unh! Unh! Unnnhhhh!" I heard Tonya exclaim as her orgasm washed over her. I kept the dildo held firmly between my tongue and the roof of my mouth to protect my throat from her jerking hips. I reached quickly between her ass cheeks and stroked her asshole, provoking a moan and another jerk of her hips from her.

Tonya was driven now, her orgasm only whetting her libido.

"Bend over the arm of the couch!" she ordered me firmly. Quickly she slathered lube into my asshole and had two fingers in me, stretching the muscular bands. " 'I'm gonna fuck you, faggot! I'm gonna come in your ass!' " she said in her man's voice.

Hardly had she said that before I felt the dildo pressing into my ass. My ass burned from the waxing, but she expertly opened me up with short jabs and withdrawals, gradually pushing in further and further. My cock was leaking like a faucet and I was eager for her to penetrate me. Soon the whole dildo was in me, more easily than it had ever gone before.

" 'How do you like that, faggot?' " she asked. " 'How do you like having a real man's cock up your ass? Probably feels like homecoming to a fairy like you, eh?' "

"It feels wonderful," I admitted. I relaxed into enjoying the cock tickling my prostate and prodding the top of my rectum, deep within me, but almost as soon as I began to enjoy it, Tonya slipped the dildo out of me.

"That's enough for now!" Tonya said in her own voice. "Don't want to steal the thunder from the real thing." I almost whimpered with disappointment. "And no jerking off tonight! I want you so horny you can't stand it! You may watch your videos if you want, or surf your cuckold or gay websites, but if you touch yourself, you have to stop as soon as you feel the edge. Don't even dare come close to shooting. I want you full of cum and desperate to shoot tomorrow night!"

She sat down on the couch, the dildo leering up from her crotch, shiny with lube. "I'm going to keep this on and you keep your robe and camisole on. Clean me off with your mouth!" I knelt down and licked and sucked the dildo clean. "Oh my, you do look like the cutest little fag boy! Look at your naked little wiener, so hard and so cute! Here, hand me the camera! I need to get some pictures of you sucking me off and your faggy little face and your Mexican hairless! Yes, it's a tiny little hairless cock, just like a Chihuahua!"

She snapped away with the camera, making me pose in different positions. Throughout the night she had me kneel at her feet and suck on her dildo some more, or she would have me bend over and she would finger-fuck me for a couple minutes, then made me lick her fingers clean. I was very horny. I did cruise some of the cuckold and gay websites as she had offered, and my cock stayed hard most of the evening. Seeing all the cocksucking and butt-fucking there almost desensitized me to it. No one on those sites found anything strange about a man lusting for cock!

She had me put on one of my new baby doll nighties to go to bed. She kept the dildo on and snuggled up behind me again, slipping the cock against the crack of my ass.

"Baby, I'm so happy with your makeover! You make the cutest little sissy! Those men won't be able to decide who they want to fuck more, you or me! They'll have so much fun comparing and making up their minds!

"Your dress rehearsal went fantastically! You are making me so proud and happy! I'm going to cream watching Brian's cock slip into your ass! Then once your cherry is broken, who knows what we'll do? Maybe we can have a tandem: one guy can fuck me while the other is fucking you! Wouldn't that be a mind-blowing kind of togetherness?"

Tonya was so brimming with happiness that I couldn't help but be infected. The satiny material of the new nightie felt sexy against my skin and I felt safe and loved in her arms. My cock ached with unrelieved arousal, but overall I was happy and excited. I drifted off into a warm and pleasant sleep.

That night I dreamed Tonya was get remarried. She was dressed in a wedding gown that was like a bustier, exposing her breasts, and it stopped at her waist, leaving her bottom half bare. Her train was divided, each half coming from each hip, so her naked ass was framed by lace. Her mother and father both led her up the aisle, where Brian was waiting for her. He was wearing a tux, but it was open in the front, exposing his cock.

As Tonya's parents reached the altar, her mother looked at Brian's package and said, "Well, this is more what we had in mind for a son-in-law! A real man, not like Whatshisname, you know, Pin Dick. This one's hung more like your father," and she fished out her husband's large cock to demonstrate, as if people did that all the time, like making a muscle to show off your workout regimen. She apparently became distracted, because she fell to fellating Tonya's father while the ceremony continued.

"Who comes to give this woman away?" the minister asked and suddenly everyone was looking at me. Apparently I'd failed to learn my part of the service, because I didn't know what I was supposed to do.

Tonya whispered to me *sotto voce*, "C'mon, Johnny, this is your part!"

Embarrassed to have everyone staring at me I stammered out, "I do," and Tonya smiled.

"And do you give her away of your own free will and without reservation? And do you agree henceforth to forever hold your peace?" the minister asked me.

"You bet he'll be holding his piece, because I sure won't hold it!" Tonya cracked.

"Y-y-yes," I choked out.

"So as this man has freely given up his claims to the virtue of this woman..." (I wasn't sure if the minister's voice sounded a little sarcastic on the word 'virtue.') "...it is altogether fitting that she should be released from her wedding vows and be free to give herself to another man. Or a man," the minister said looking down at me. "Did you bring a ring?" he questioned.

"I did!" Tonya volunteered and she bent over an spread her ass cheeks wide, exposing the ring of her anus.

"And who will lube this ring so that this man may enter into anal matrimony with this woman?" queried the minister.

"I will," said Calvin, also in a tux, acting as best man. He dipped his fingers into a silver pot on a silver tray and plunged his black fingers into Tonya's rectum.

"And who will wet this penis to prepare it to enter this woman's promised land?" the minister intoned.

Again they were all looking at me, waiting for me to add my blessing. Their eyes felt like an irresistible pressure on me and I was too weak to resist. I stumbled to the altar and got down on my knees. I took one long look at Brian's rampant cock and then took it into my mouth, slobbering all over it.

At this point I heard my mother's voice and I realized that my own parents were there.

"I've never been prouder of him than this moment," my Mom said tearfully to my father. "Look how hard his little sissy clit is, with that big cock in his mouth!" she continued, her hand on my father's sleeve.

"The family has asked that all who bless this union join hands in starting this couple on their new life." And Brian's cock was being taken out of my mouth and Tonya's mom and dad, Calvin, David, Audrey, and I all had our hands on part of Brian's shaft and were holding it to Tonya's greased hole.

"Ass fucking's the best!" Tonya's mom gushed, and with that Brian speared Tonya's ass with his thick meat.

"I now pronounce you man and wife!" the minister announced. "You may fuck the bride!" Everyone cheered. Brian began pistoning in and out of Tonya while the ceremony devolved into an orgy, with Audrey fucking Tonya's dad, Calvin fucking her mom, and the minister blowing David. I was the only one without a partner, so I began jerking myself off. But at that point I woke up from the dream, to find myself in bed with a painfully engorged dick.

-Day 28 Friday-

Tonya told the men to come over about 8. We both showered and Tonya had me shave all over again, and then she had us both take a thorough enema.

"We don't want any surprises!" she said.

Then she made up my eyes the way she had before and put on her own make-up, a dramatic style just this side of "hooker."

She was excited and happy, like a giddy schoolgirl. "The men are coming, baby! Enough cock for both of us! Aren't you excited? I can't wait!"

Just after 8 the doorbell rang. Tonya told me to watch through a cracked door. She greeted the trio at the door in a robe that covered up a skimpy negligee. She kissed Brian deeply and then hugged Calvin and David. Calvin took the opportunity to grab a generous handful of her ass possessively, while he pressed her to his front. David boldly hefted one breast through her robe and tweaked the nipple suggestively. Tonya moaned and rubbed David's hard-on through his pants.

"Did you bring anything to the party?" she asked huskily.

"You bet, babe!" David answered eagerly, cupping his crotch and giving it a couple of tugs.

"Oh, goodie!" Tonya cried. "You boys make yourselves comfortable and we'll get this party started. Why don't you get those constricting clothes off first and put on these robes?"

"What an accommodating hostess! But I thought your husband was going to be here. Where is he?" Calvin asked.

"He's a little shy, Calvin. I mean, when you see him *au naturel* you'll see that he's got a lot to be modest about, or maybe it's what he doesn't have! But we won't let him hide. I mean, he agreed that since it's his shortcomings that force me to go outside of our marriage to be satisfied, he has to show that he accepts and even supports what I'm doing.

"Now what would you fellows like to drink?"

"Beer for me," Brian decided.

"Me too," David chimed in.

"7&7 for me," Calvin answered.

"I'll be right back with your drinks and Johnny," Tonya told them and left for the kitchen.

"Two beers, and 7&7, and a white wine for me, Johnny," she commanded me. I put the drinks on a tray and followed her back into the living room like a waiter.

"Haw haw!" Calvin guffawed when he saw my outfit, the pink lacy camisole and robe set.

"Shee-it!" David exclaimed.

I burned with humiliation. I could feel my cheeks hot with blood. My heart was pounding and my brain was fuzzy. It took all the willpower I had to fight an impulse to run and hide. "Embarrassment is the death throes of your male ego,' Tonya had said. It wasn't being dressed as a sissy I should be embarrassed of, she had said, but I should be ashamed of all the years I had pretended to be a man. Being paraded as a sissy is something I should get used to. "Be proud to be a sissy, Johnny! It shows you have the courage to face up to what you are!" she'd said. I forced myself to endure it, as a punishment and as my admission ticket to what was to follow.

"Whoa!" Brian said in surprise. "That's new!" He turned to his mates and explained. "He wasn't dolled up like that before, although, given his position, I can see that it's appropriate!"

"What kind of freak is this guy?" Calvin asked.

"Oh, it's all my idea, Calvin," Tonya said. "I thought it would help remind him who the real men are in this house," she said, rubbing Calvin's muscular chest. She turned to me and I stood there like a deer in the headlights. "But I think he does like what I picked out." She parted my lacy robe to reveal my turgid penis.

"Oh my," Calvin commented, always the one who was quick to say whatever he was thinking. "I can see why you need some strange! That's small even for a white boy!"

"Hey!" Brian and David said in unison.

"Present company excepted, of course," Calvin laughed.

"I should say so!" David said in mock affront.

Tonya sat between Brian and David and took hold of their cocks, one in each hand.

"I've got no complaints about either of these white boys!" Brian and David smiled as she worked their shafts, sliding the loose skin over their hardening cores.

I felt awkward just doing nothing, so I gave each of the men their drinks and then stood there, not knowing what to do with Tonya's wine, since she "had her hands full."

"Johnny, come look at these beautiful cocks. Aren't they gorgeous?"

"Uh ... very nice," I stuttered.

"Oh, you don't know how nice until you feel them in your hand, or your mouth, or your cunt! Of course, you already know that—you're acquainted with Brian's pole. Here, give me that wine and you feel David's cock. Wrap your hand around it and tell me that doesn't feel like the nicest hunk of man-meat?"

Tonya let go of David's prick and took the wine. David looked at me expectantly, obviously proud of his manhood. It stood out stiffly. It was paler than Brian's, because of David's blond coloring, but the head was pink and there was a pink line down the underside.

With trepidation I reached out and took the shaft in my hand. 'I'm holding a man's cock again!' I thought and I shivered. After years of holding my own dick it was a momentary shock to feel how his organ filled my hand. It felt unnatural to me, as if this couldn't be a real cock: it had to be some magnified model for a biology class.

But it was real. So real, so alive. I could feel the heat, the pulse of his blood, the firm give of real flesh. My own cock jumped in sympathy.

"Isn't it nice?" Tonya said. "Can't you see why a woman would so much rather have that cock in her than your little worm? If you were me, which would you rather have, that cock or yours?"

I didn't reply, so Tonya went on.

"Stroke it. Feel the shaft. Feel the weight, the length, the girth."

I did as she asked. This was only the second man whose cock I'd touched, so it was still strange to me. I was watching my hand on it, as if I were watching someone else. With reverence, almost lovingly, as if it were a rare piece of Greek sculpture, I ran my hand down to the blond pubic hair and then up to the rim of the pink head. David closed his eyes. I ran my hand up and down it, turning my hand to feel every part of his shaft, to feel the veins and ridges.

Oh, my God, this was exciting! Half of me was so nervous that I couldn't feel anything, but part of me was getting really turned on! There was something undeniably exciting about doing this forbidden thing! I shouldn't be excited to touch another man! But I was!

David sighed.

"Shit, this is hot!" he murmured.

"Whose cock would give me more pleasure? Which cock would satisfy me, his or yours? Who should I fuck: him or you?"

"Him," I admitted quietly, not taking my eyes off the bizarre sight of my handing milking a man's penis.

"Then get him ready for me! Suck him hard and get him wet, because it'll be a tight fit!" Tonya commanded. "Calvin, would you take a video of this with my phone?" she asked.

I looked at the erect member I held and imagined taking it into my mouth as I had Brian's. With a start I saw a bead of pre-cum form at the slit, undeniable proof that David was aroused by my attentions.

Tonya leaned toward Brian and began French kissing him, while Brian's fingers stroked her cunny and began spreading her nether lips.

"Hurry, Johnny," Tonya moaned. "I'm going to be ready for him any minute." Her hand went to Brian's shaft.

I was borne along by the Roman orgy atmosphere. I was amazed to realize that I wasn't feeling jealous to see Brian kissing and fingering her: I was aroused. I couldn't wait to see somebody fuck her and I hardly cared who it was.

"C'mon pansy-boy," David goaded. "You heard the lady. Get busy."

I turned back to the hot flesh in my hand. I licked my lips and took a deep breath. I realized that I wasn't really reluctant, just embarrassed. I wanted to suck that cock. I was going to become a cocksucker once again. Say goodbye to my masculinity and my "husbandly rights."

I opened up my mouth and lowered my head to his crotch. I felt the heat of his manhood as I closed my lips around the head. 'Oh!' I thought in surprise. 'So thick! So warm! So silky against my tongue.' I felt a mini-convulsion of arousal shoot through me! God, this was good!

David moaned in pleasure as I sucked his knob to the back of my throat and pressed his shaft against the roof of my mouth. I gathered my saliva in my mouth to wet it thoroughly. I licked up the sensitive underside and began to suck up and down. I gathered some of the slickness on one hand and began to stroke the shaft in unison with my mouth.

What was I doing? I asked myself. Am I a slave doing his mistress's bidding? Or am I wanting this? I had another man's cock in my mouth! It was the absolute horror of every teenage boy's nightmares! How could I be doing this?

This was the fourth time I had had sucked a man's cock. I bobbed my head on David's shaft and thrilled as I felt it slide in and out, filling my mouth. It took my breath away! It felt so sexy! It was hot! The very wrongness of it was erotic electricity. The thought that I was stiffening this cock so that it could soon be stretching my bride's cunt made it even hotter. The only thing I could think of better would be to keep the cum for myself!

I felt the quivering life in the flesh in my mouth, felt every vein, every ridge, every bump. I wanted more. I let it out of my mouth and began to lick up the shaft, trying to get at all of it. I ran my lips up and down the length of his penis from his pubic hair to his glans. I wanted it hot, wet, and slick. I licked more pre-cum from his slit and curled my tongue-tip around the ridge of his knob.

I could smell a definite murkiness wafting from his pubic hair and balls. I breathed it in deeply. It was a manly scent, much different from Tonya's, but it was a very sexual odor.

I felt David's cock getting harder, the skin stretched tighter and smoother. I felt his blood pulse in it. My own penis throbbed in sympathy.

"God, he's good!" David said.

"Look at him go! He loves it!" Calvin marveled. "Maybe your cunt isn't really his taste, Tonya!"

Tonya broke her kiss with Brian to disagree.

"Oh no, he loves to eat my pussy too. Although he does seem especially eager when it's full of Brian's cum, come to think of it! But when you're a pin-dick, you learn to make the most of your mouth. Get that pansy mouth over here, Johnny! Get me all nice and ready for that cock you're sucking!"

I felt proud to hear David groan in protest when I let go of his erection. Tonya scooted herself to the edge of the couch, presenting her cunt to me. I could already smell her heat and her labia had started to swell. I eagerly smashed my mouth to her crotch, anxious to both lap up her juices and to prove that I was at least as enthusiastic about pussy eating as cock sucking.

I relished the powerful scent of her excitement and the erotic taste of her secretions. Her pussy already felt hot and swollen under my lips. Performing in front of this audience made me all the more eager to plunge my tongue into her slit and suckle her clit.

"Oh, God, baby, that's so good! But I need a cock, a man's cock. I need to be full and to be fucked right into my womb! But you can't furnish that. What should we do? What do you want me to do about it?"

I assumed the question was rhetorical, so I kept licking, but Tonya wanted to hear it out loud.

"Tell me, Johnny! Tell me what to do."

I lifted my pussy-smeared face from her pubes.

"You should fuck David."

"Is that what you really want? You're my husband. You don't want to fuck me yourself? You'd rather I let David fuck me?"

"I ... I can't.. satisfy you. I ... I want you to fuck David."

"Well, but he hasn't asked me. You ask him. Ask him to please fuck your wife for you. I mean, he's doing your job. It's a favor."

It was so humiliating—but I was so aroused! My brain was soaked in lust. I would have done or said anything she told me to.

"Um, David ... uh ... please ... please fuck my wife for me."

"Happy to, bud! Anything for a pal!" David laughed.

"Get him wet and hard, baby, because it's going to be a tight fit. Then aim him. Put his cock right up to my pussy."

David knelt in front of the couch and I dipped my head to take his manhood into my mouth again. I slobbered all over it, preparing it to slide into my wife's oozing portal. I took the thick shaft in my hand and pointed it at Tonya's vagina. My hand trembled slightly, I was so excited. David leaned forward and I directed his tip into the center of my wife's hungry cunt. His cock dwarfed her opening and I marveled at how she'd ever accommodate it.

"Hold it, baby," Tonya ordered me, "so you can feel it going in!" David pressed forward and I watched Tonya's lips cave in with the pressure. David eased back and then pushed again and, through my hand on his hard shaft, I could feel Tonya's cunny start to stretch.

He was so long that I could easily keep my hold on his cock while he tried to get the first inches into my wife's pussy. He pulled back and then thrust forward and with a gasp Tonya felt him push halfway in. With my hand still on him like a conductor, he pulled out again and then slammed home, squeezing my hand out of the way.

"Oh, David! Oh! God! It's so good! Your fucking cock feels so good! Fuck me!"

I watched with bated breath as he began to slowly plunge in and out of her. Tonya hunched her hips forward to take him more deeply into her center.

"Johnny!" Tonya cried, "Kiss me! Kiss me while another man fucks me!" I sat next to Tonya and she kissed me savagely, devouring my mouth frantically.

"Oh Shit! Oh shit! His cock feels so good in me!" she said breathlessly. "So deep! So thick! Oh, God, I love it, Johnny! I want you to kiss me while I'm dying with another man's cock inside me!" She continued to mash her mouth against mine, delirious with pleasure and with the perversity of what we were doing and her total victory over me, shattering the bonds of our wedding vows!

But I reveled in it too! I reveled in her heat and in my own surrender. I wallowed in my own debasement, participated in my own submission to Tonya and to these men. I returned her kisses and I reached for her breast, to tweak her nipple and help David's fucking drive her to ecstasy. Tonya broke our kiss.

"Look at me, Johnny!" she gasped. "Look how much I crave his cock! His cock is driving me wild! Love me for how much I love a big cock! Love that I will always fuck other men! Your wife's cunt will always drip with the cum of other men!"

She closed her eyes and arched her back to press her breast further into my hand. I kissed her harder and squeezed her breast firmly. I thrilled when she responded by moaning and hunching her pelvis at David, frantically seeking to orgasm around his organ. Soon she was no longer kissing me but merely moaning into my mouth, her consciousness collapsed into her lust to milk his man-seed from him.

Then she was shrieking with her release. Through my hand and lips I could feel the intensity of her convulsions as orgasm rippled through her uterus. David could feel it too and his thrusts became savage, rocking her whole body. Then he froze and gave a guttural roar as he emptied his balls into her womb. No long swim for his sperm, starting several inches closer than mine ever had and shot forcefully even farther into her tubes.

The primal power of what was happening was overpowering. The urge to impregnate a nubile female and the female's quest for the best possible seed orchestrated this scene. Only the hormonal tricks of modern chemistry kept me from being the witness to David siring a baby on my wife this night. The thought of his potent sperm inches from her eggs strangely fired my lust to almost unbearable intensity. I reached for my rampant dick and almost swooned with arousal as I grasped it.

"That's it, baby," Tonya murmured. "Enjoy it. Whack your little peepee whlle the big man's cock fills up your wife! You love it, don't you? You love being my little cuckold husband!"

I closed my eyes in humiliation as Brian and Calvin chuckled at my pathetic wanking. But I kept pumping my penis because Tonya was right. I did love it. I was in erotic bliss, like a drug high.

"Get ready, Johnny! When David pulls out, the buckets of cum he just pumped into me are gonna come gushing out. As my husband, it's your job to see that we don't make a mess."

She reached out and laid her hand on my cheek and looked into my eyes.

"And it's your job to show my cunt that you still love it. Even when it's full of another man's cum. Even when it's stretched wide by a bigger, manly prick. Even when it's convulsed in ecstasy around another man's cock!

"Show me how much you love me, husband!" she cried as David rolled off her. I fell on my knees in front of her. Immediately a gush of semen appeared between her red and swollen inner lips. Without hesitation I dove at her crotch and sealed my lips to over the opening and tasted the foreign taste of David's spend.

I'd rather had my face buried in her pussy than to endure the looks from the other men. But I was also mad to taste another man's semen! I lapped up David's cum like cream. I sucked it into my mouth, tasting it on every part of my tongue: strange, bitter, unnatural.

"Oh, that's not right!" David opined. "I could never do that!"

But I loved it. The oh-so-distinctive taste of cum had become an aphrodisiac for me. Maybe it was the undeniable fact that I was humiliating myself in front of superior men, or ... what? I daren't think. But there was no getting around the fact that I was exulting in the flavor of a another man's semen on my tongue.

"Get used to it, hubby, because that's how my pussy is going to taste most of the time. That's going to be the taste and feel of your wife's cunt from now on. Whatever pleasure you'll be allowed to give me will be while you're vacuuming up the spill of another man who's cuckolding you."

As I heard her words I tried to show her that I would be a willing servant to her cunt. I sucked and licked at her cavity enthusiastically.

"Jesus, what a tool!" Calvin mocked. "I like pussy, but not covered in another man's spooge!"

"There's no accounting for taste!" Brian pointed out sagely.

"Whatever gets your rocks off," David generously agreed. "Besides, don't look a gift horse in the mouth. His loss is our gain."

"True that!" Calvin confirmed.

"Oh, that's nice, baby," Tonya crooned. "There's nothing like the caress of a good cuntlapper's tongue after a hard fuck! Sometimes a pussy wants to get fucked and I've got men for that, and sometimes a pussy wants to be loved, and I've got my sissy boy for that!"

Tonya pushed my head away.

"Lie down on the floor, baby. Let's make sure you don't miss a drop. That would be a shame."

My heart leapt as once again Tonya's pussy loomed large above me, filling my view, becoming my whole world. I felt her thighs press against my cheeks and her distended pussy lips settle on my mouth. I grasped her luscious ass cheeks in my hands and suckled at her twat like a babe at the breast. Her lover's jism was mother's milk. I jumped as Tonya reached behind her and clutched my erection and pulled on it, as if to urge me to my task.

Indeed with the help of gravity more sperm did drip out of her gash in small dribs and drabs.

"Oh, baby, you're getting me hot again already! You're going to force me to fuck one of these other gentlemen. Is that what you're trying to do, to drive your wife like a whore into the arms of yet another man?" She intoned these words in mock horror at the impropriety of the suggestion. "What else am I to do when you inflame me so and yet offer me no solace, since your own loins are clearly not up to the job?"

She got up and went over to Calvin, who had up to then been a patient spectator. She took his thick ebony rod in one hand while he took her breast in his. The contrast of his black hand on her white flesh sent a surge of arousal through my groin. Tonya planted her mouth on his and they began to suck on each other.

Tonya broke the kiss long enough to instruct me.

"Clean up David too, honey. Taste the pussy juice on his tool!"

David smiled as I crawled over to between his knees. His half-hard cock was still bigger than my stiff one. It glistened with a mixture of Tonya's cream and his own ejaculate. I reached out and took his shaft in one hand and felt the slick juices, and, under that, the lingering spongy firmness of his excitement. I stopped for a second to admire the handsome organ and plumb my own feelings. Was this simply obedience? Or admiration? Or lust?

I felt all of them mixed together. I did want to please Tonya. But I also could not help but feel in awe of the sexual prowess of these men, so much better equipped to satisfy my wife. At least if I could participate in some way, I wasn't simply being disregarded.

I took his cockhead in my mouth and thrilled again at its warmth and how it filled my mouth. I was aroused by the satiny slickness of the delicate skin and the way their sex juices made it slip so easily across my tongue. I sucked the now-familiar taste of cum and pussy off the head and the powerful smell of raw sex filled my nose. I moaned as I felt my own pleasure.

"Suck that lollipop, Johnny," Tonya urged me. "Get it nice and hard so he can put it in my ass later!"

I ran my hand tightly up his shaft and was rewarded with a dollop of cum extruded from his pee slit. I dipped my tongue down to lick the drop off and David sighed with satisfaction. I proceeded to lick up his shaft with the flat of my tongue, collecting all of Tonya's honey and David's sperm. I plunged his cockhead to the back of my throat and sucked hard, trying to gobble as much of his penis into my mouth as I could. David hummed in pleasure.

"Oh, Tonya, you're right: his soft mouth is delightful! What a nice soothing aftermath to a fuck! So relaxing and ... invigorating!"

"He has more talents than you'd even guess, fellows. Johnny, come over here and taste some African fuck-stick. Do you think you'll taste a hint of licorice?"

Calvin looked down with a domineering air. He was clearly getting off on the idea of a white man debasing himself by taking a black cock in his mouth. He grinned down at me, as if to say, 'Who's the slave now?' He handed Tonya's phone off to Brian.

Tonya had already excited the black man to hardness. She pumped it a few more times and a pearl of pre-cum oozed out of the pink slit.

"Lick up his pre-cum, baby. Tickle his helmet with your sissy tongue!"

Tonya's taunting raised the temperature in the room. Everyone was staring at me and the tip of Calvin's penis. My pink tongue snaked out and I lapped up the drop of clear liquid. I then licked around the rim of his cockhead, almost teasing. Calvin hunched his hips up, seeking more contact and I obliged by taking the head of his black dick in my mouth and sucking hard on it. I pressed the hard flesh against the roof of my mouth with my tongue and then pushed it against the back of my throat.

"Oh, yeah!" Calvin sighed, now in honest pleasure rather than mockery.

His cock felt hot and thick in my mouth. I thrilled again at the unique consistency of cock meat: spongy on the outside with a center of steel, hard and soft at the same time. It was smooth but with a topography of ridges and veins. As a man I knew the delicious sensation that my mouth had to be sending through that oh-so-sensitive flesh. That sympathy urged me on, to stroke his shaft with one hand while I feasted on his knob. He was uncircumcised, so the extra looseness of his foreskin and the pinkness of his cockhead were new to me.

"That's it, baby!" Tonya congratulated me. "Eat that meat! Isn't it tasty?"

"Mmmm," I wordlessly agreed.

"Do you want to see that chocolate pole fuck your wife's ass. baby? Would that excite you? Do you want to see your bride straining to put that cock where it was never meant to go? Would it turn you on to see her so full of lust for him that she'd let this black man sodomize her?" She turned and held her ass cheeks apart and showed me her hole, no longer as small or tight as it once was, but more wrinkled and red from recent invasions.

"Do you want to help, to get him nice and hard, to lube him up, to lick my ass to get me hot for him? Tell me! Tell him!" She reached back and took my dick in her hand and stroked it, making me shudder.

I took Calvin's cock out of my mouth and I looked at it, and then I looked at Tonya's ass leering at me, and I looked back at the rampant cock in my hand. Did I want to see this black battering ram sawing in and out of my wife's ass? You bet I did: I could hardly wait!

"Yes!" I hissed, surprised at how easy it was to say. "Please let me see him fuck your ass. Please, Calvin," I said to his phallus, not able to look up at his face, "please use my wife's ass for your pleasure, but please let me watch!"

"Sure thing, brother!" Calvin answered. "I'll be happy to fuck your wife's sweet ass!"

Tonya planted her luscious globes between me and Calvin's pride. She began to stroke Calvin's staff. while she pushed her rear at me.

"Johnny, lick my ass and get it ready for this black butt-buster!"

I pulled her cheeks apart and inhaled the heady aroma of her cleft mixed with the pussy juice and cum which had dripped into her crack. It was like a pheromone factory and I took a large whiff before I planted my lips on her anus. I kissed her pucker with ardor and then I slipped my tongue into her starburst. Her ring tightened and then relaxed and I probed her rectum. I stretched my tongue, trying to drive it as deeply as I could, a tiny part of the way Calvin's penis would soon reach.

"Lube me, baby! Prepare you wife to be butt-fucked by a back stud."

I got up and grabbed the lube jar and crammed first one, then two, then three fingers into her accommodating hole.

"Now Calvin, Johnny. Grease up his pole. Kiss it first!"

She moved out of the way. I leaned down to kiss the tip of his cock and somehow that seemed dirtier than anything else we'd done: an act of affection rather than lust.

"Kiss it again!" Tonya ordered, always quick to pick up on whatever was my vulnerability. "You love it because it's going to make you a cuckold again, to humiliate you, and that excites you more than fucking your own wife!"

I tried to feel what Tonya was telling me to feel, to feel gratitude, respect, admiration, and even love for this man's long thick cock. I bent down and kissed it again, then another time, and then another, for good measure. With a little shiver I realized that Brian was getting this all on Tonya's phone too! The feeling of humiliation and perversity made my cheeks burn again. But I also felt lust: I lusted after a man's sex! I felt flushed and lightheaded. Then I began to slather lube on Calvin's cock, making it shine lewdly. The slippery sliding of my hand over his penis sent a scary thrill through my scalp and down my spine. I gasped with the power of it.

Tonya got on all fours and spread her legs to offer Calvin her backside.

"Put him in me, Johnny! Place his cock at my asshole!"

Calvin shinnied up to her ass on his knees and I took hold of his cock. Tonya's ass was gleaming with lube and standing partway stretched open by my fingers, but Calvin's cockhead dwarfed it. I aimed his knob at the center of her rosebud and pulled it gently forward, my pulse pounding in my ears.

"Johnny's never had me there, Calvin," Tonya told him. "He's seeing you fuck me in a place he never has and never will, though he's my husband and I'm his wife. I give my ass to you, Calvin, and he does too!"

I felt Calvin's cock meet her ass and start to push into her. Through my hand I could feel her flesh resist the invasion. Calvin started to bump forward and back, pushing his way slowly forward with my hand still cradling his rod. I let go and stepped a half-step back, unable to take my eyes off the junction where their flesh met.

"Oh, fuck, you're so big!" Tonya gasped, but she pushed back, trying to take his organ in past her protesting muscles. "Fuck me, Calvin! Fuck my cheating white ass! Make me your white ass whore! Rape my ass with your black fuck-stick!"

Calvin needed little encouragement, but Tonya's ass had trouble keeping the promises her mouth made. Calvin drove forward and Tonya shrieked in pain.

"Oh, shit! Ow! Ow! Just hold it! Hold it!" She panted and I could tell all her focus was on relaxing her sphincters to take that salami. Her face was screwed up in concentration and I saw her anus clutching Calvin's shaft.

"Take it out ... just for a second. Please, just help me take it," Tonya pleaded.

"Your ass is so tight, you tight-ass white bitch!" Calvin gibed. But he pulled back.

I stared in amazement at the gaping hole in my wife's bottom. Her anus shrank immediately, but it remained open the width of a dime, already stretched too much for it to snap all the way back.

"Put more lube on him, Johnny," Tonya panted. I thickly slathered more lube on Calvin's already glistening cockhead. I grabbed another fingerful and stuck two fingers up Tonya's backside.

"Oh, yeah, Johnny. You really want to see me take that black cock, don't you? Be my ass whisperer, Johnny. Tell me how much you want to give my ass away, to prove what a cuckold slave you are!"

I was unsure what Tonya wanted but I took her cue. I lay down next to her and I stroked her back and began to talk to her in a soothing voice."

"You can do it, babe. You can take that big cock up your bunghole." Calvin began to push back into her. "You need it. You need a real man to fuck you, to own you, by taking your most forbidden place. Show me how much you need it. Show me that this black man owns you, even owns your ass.

"Put me in my place. Show me that I will always only be your cuckold—that I may be your husband but your body will belong to other men."

With that Calvin drove almost all the way into Tonya's ass without any protest. He stopped there and let her feel him deep in her bowel. He hunched against the resistance so she could feel his thickness and his depth.

"Oh, shit! Johnny! I'm so full of cock! It's so different from my cunt. I can feel every bit of it! It's so there! Why did I deprive myself this to put up with your pathetic squirming?

"Unh!" she grunted as Calvin began to pump his penis in and out of her rectum.

"Oh, baby, your white ass feels so good!" Calvin exulted. "After your faggot husband's excellent blow-job, I don't know how long I can take this!"

Tonya was still concentrating, clearly straining to get used to the girth of his rod in her inner sanctum.

"He's fucking my ass, Johnny! A big black man has his big black cock up your wife's ass! Aren't you proud of me? Go ahead and beat your little white dick! I want you to enjoy giving your wife away to other men! I want you to come when he spurts his strong black seed into my ass!"

I got up and stood where I could see his cock disappear into that tight ring of flesh and then reappear, her ass clutching at it. He was fucking her now with long, deep strokes, getting into a rhythm, building up to his climax. Tonya started pushing back against him more and more energetically and I knew her ass was opening up. She was enjoying her anal rape now.

My hand was still slick with goo and I cradled my stiff prick and began to pump it. I sighed with the exquisiteness of the feelings that my hand could coax from my much-maligned organ. It felt as if Calvin's and Tonya's fucking were sending electricity through the air and heating up both my brain and my penis. I saw out of the corner of my eye that Brian was fondling himself and David's recently discharged cock was reawakening itself at the scene.

In my mind I strived to obey Tonya's order to focus on my cuckolding. I said to myself, 'That's my wlfe. Another man is fucking her. Fucking her ass. His big black cock is 8 inches up her ass. He's giving her pleasure that I will never give her in places I will never go. And here I am beating my meat at the sight.'

Pre-cum wept out of my slit and added itself to the greasy slickness of the lube. My dick swelled, straining to feel the friction of my stroking hand. I closed my eyes to revel in the sensation. With my eyes closed I was assaulted by the sounds of Tonya grunting with every plunge of Calvin's meat into her bowels and the sound of his thighs slapping against hers. Calvin was grunting too, but grunting with the pleasure that Tonya's ass was squeezing out of his love rod.

I opened my eyes and was overcome again by the sight of a black stud plumbing my wife's bottom. Tonya was digging away at her clitoris with one hand while she rocked back into every thrust of the black man's cock into her. My penis swelled near to bursting.

"Oh, shit!" Calvin roared. "Oh, fucking shit! Fuck! Fuck!" he yelled as he drove himself into Tonya's ass and released his load. Another obscenity burst out with every spasm.

"Oh, God! Fill my ass! I can feel your cum, so hot, so deep! Mark me as your bitch! Take my ass!" Her submission devolved into a series of moans as her own orgasm broke over her.

Oh, God, I longed for her ass to be spasming around my cock! The poignancy of the distance between us wrenched at my heart. It was his cock in her, it was him her ass was milking, it was his cum defiling her. I was a cuckold. My insides twisted into a knot, but at the same time, my cock exploded in climax, spurting my unwanted sperm into my free hand. I watched the pathetic strings of my semen land on my palm and looked up at the contrasting scene of a man and a woman locked in carnal embrace.

Tonya and Calvin collapsed to one side, his cock still buried in her rectum. Calvin reached a meaty black hand around her and took her milky white breast in his fingers and massaged it possessively. He thrust his pelvis forward, reminding her that he still penetrated her body, while he kneaded her nipple.

"Oh, Calvin!" Tonya sighed. "What a fuck! What a man!" she said, almost breathless. "Your cock feels so good in my ass now! It doesn't hurt at all! I just feel nice and full, it's so nice and big!"

"Your ass is one sweet fuck, babe!" responded the muscular black man. "I could get used to that!"

"Did you enjoy it too, Johnny?" Tonya asked, craning her neck to look at me. "What have you got in your hand there? Another squirt from your little winkie? Well, you have to clean up your own messes, little man! Lick that mess up so you can get down to soothing my poor black-fucked ass!"

"God, that's gross!" David muttered as I licked the thin puddle of ejaculate off my palm.

"Johnny, kneel down here. I want you to suck Calvin clean right after he pulls out of my ass, 'Hot from the oven,' as they say. Don't worry, I won't let any of his tasty sperm leak out while you're cleaning him off."

With a mixture of post-orgasm resignation and cock-hungry anticipation I got down on my hands and knees. Calvin rolled away from Tonya onto his back, his snake slithering out of Tonya's greasy ass. Tonya's butt hole yawned open like an angry red mouth, a half-dollar sized chasm where her dainty pucker had once been. Immediately white cum and lube began to gush out but Tonya slapped her hand over her anus to stem the tide.

Calvin's cock had lost some of its mass, but it was still an impressive slab of meat. It was coated with a sheen of unappetizing jelly, no doubt liberally mixed with some of his semen. I saw no point in delaying the inevitable and I took his cockhead in my mouth. I was assailed by the now-familiar taste of lube, but also the musky man-smell from his sweaty crotch, mixed with a faint scent of Tonya's pussy juice that had leaked from her cunt as they fucked.

Despite having just come, I felt a twinge of arousal as my mouth was again filed with another man's penis. Calvin trembled slightly and I realized that his cock would be supersensitive so soon after his shoot, so I gentled my ministrations. I sucked at his slit and was rewarded with a taste of the last drips of his jism leaking from his manhood. I took a moment to savor the fact that his cock was in my mouth now, but seconds ago had been buried in my wife's ass. I felt a strange connection to Tonya through this phallus that we were sharing.

Or that she was sharing with me. She had found it and attracted it and aroused it and now was giving it to me to appreciate. I held it in my mouth and paid my homage to it, and then I dutifully licked the long thick shaft clean of all the lube. I kept my eyes down, concentrating on the penis itself, but I couldn't help but think of the large black man it was attached to. I pictured his linebacker body and myself, huddled on my knees, dwarfed and humbled. But strangely I didn't shrink from the image. A warm sensation enveloped me. I felt almost ... protected, as if by submitting to him I were safe now. I was surrendering. After you surrender, you're safe, right?

"You do that real nice, boy," Calvin intoned. "You're real handy to have around when a man wants to fuck some white strange!"

"Now eat some black cum from my white ass!" Tonya ordered. She rolled on her back and pulled her knees up to her chest, still holding one hand over her anus. I crawled between her thighs and she pulled her hand away, exposing the distended hole that had once been her virgin brown-eye. I sealed my mouth over her hole and immediately she extruded a glob of sperm and lube into it. I swallowed the mass and quickly she was pushing out another blob. I sucked at her hole and licked up the greasy coating surrounding it before I stuck my tongue deep into her rectum. The taste of cum and lube were strong there, mixed with the musky smell of her crack. Her bottom was so stretched, I could barely feel the sides of her ass around my tongue.

Tonya purred her pleasure at the sensations my oral probing was giving her.

"Oh, yes, love up my adulterous ass, baby! Kiss the ass that just cuckolded you; kiss the ass that loves another man's cock in it; that is filled with another man's cum! Know that you are only the set-up boy and the clean-up boy for the real deal!"

I followed her instructions, sucking hungrily at her asshole. I could feel her pushing out, trying to feed me her lover's spunk. I loved how her anus was alive against my mouth, clenching and opening! I repeatedly plumbed her hole, reaching with my tongue as deep as I could, still nowhere near where her black lover's cock had deposited his load. I found myself savoring the taste of another man's semen, now so strongly associated with perverted lust and insane arousal!

Brian knelt down and kissed Tonya.

"I'm the only one who hasn't come yet, and it's my turn!" he complained.

"Oh, babe, you are the pièce de resistance. I'm saving a special surprise for you!" Tonya countered. "It's almost your turn, but I have to get something first." She pushed my head from her ass and got up. "I'll be right back!"

I wondered what "treat" she was talking about. She hadn't shared this plan with me. I heard her going into her bedroom and in a couple minutes she reappeared.

"What do you think of my cock?" Tonya asked. She was wearing the dildo and harness! She strutted around the room, showing off her toy. She walked up to Brian and grabbed his erection, holding it against the dildo, to show that it was very nearly the same size.

"You're such a pervert!" Brian teased in mock horror. "What are you planning to do with that thing?"

"Well, you've all fucked my ass—well, not Johnny, but the rest of you. I've got such a nice cock; don't you think I should get to fuck somebody's ass with it? Turnabout is fair play, after all!"

"Get away from me with that thing!" Brian protested.

"Well, who then? Who would be the most fitting person for me to try this out with?"

"Not me," said Calvin. "No way."

"Don't look at me," David chimed in.

"Well, Johnny, it looks like you're elected! After all, since I've got the bigger cock, if we're going to fuck like a proper married couple should, doesn't it only makes sense that I should fuck you?"

"I don't know…," I equivocated, playing my part in Tonya's drama.

"You got off on watching me get ass-fucked. Don't you want to know how it feels? After all, you have a prostate and I don't. I understand it can be quite stimulating for some men."

"I thought this was about you getting some big cock," I countered.

"But, baby, I don't want you to feel left out! And besides, this will go a ways toward turning you into the wimp cuckold that I want you to be. I want to make sure your male pride never rears its head again, so that you'll never try to get in the way of my fucking any man I want. I want you to prove to the world that you're no kind of real man. That way the thought of competing with men like these studs here will never enter your head."

Tonya walked over and started stroking my ass cheeks suggestively with one hand.

"I want to fuck you, baby! I want to fuck you tonight, right here, right now, in front of them! I want you to give yourself up to me." She slipped her hand into my crevice and began to finger my anus. "Will you, babe? Will you give yourself to me? Do you love me enough to give up your false pride and surrender yourself to me?"

She was like an Indian snake charmer. She made it sound noble, attractive, inevitable.

"Suck my cock, baby! Get down on your knees and suck your wife's cock!"

Without answering her questions aloud, I answered them with my actions. I knelt down and took the dildo in my mouth and began to make love to it. Tonya twined her fingers into my hair and held my head as it bobbed on her phallus.

"Oh shit, this is hot!" Calvin whispered. Out of the corner of my eye I could see that Brian was watching intently. His penis jutted out in front of him and he was stroking himself. David Had taken over the filming, but he took his recovering cock in hand. Calvin took a sip of his beer, but he never took his eyes from the tableau.

"Lube my cock up, baby. Lube it so I can fuck you with it," Tonya said, making it sound like the most exciting thing anyone could hope for.

Without questioning I stumbled to my feet and located the jar of lube. I pulled out a large glob of lube and smeared it all over the dildo by taking it in my hand, as if I were masturbating it.

"Doesn't it feel good, baby? Don't I have a nice big, long, thick cock? Don't you wish you had a cock like that? If you did, you could fuck me with it. I'd love it if you had a cock as nice as mine, instead of your little pee-pee. Well, in a minute you will have a cock like this! Won't it feel nice in your ass? It'll fill you up and it will rub against your little prostate and feel so good! You'll know what it feels like to be a woman and have a nice cock fill you up."

"Feel your own cock, baby. Feel how little it is compared to mine. Rub that lube all over your little wee-wee. Yours is so soft and thin and little."

Tonya had taken the lube jar from my hand and dug out a medium glob on two fingers and dove into my crack, finding my anus with her finger tips. She took my greasy cock in her other hand and milked me while she began to smear the lube on my pucker and stabbed a fingertip into me.

"Surrender to me, Johnny! Put yourself in my power! I know you want to. Inside you are a weakling, Johnny. Trying to be a man is such an effort, always trying to be strong. Give it up, Johnny. Let go of it. Give in to me, Johnny. Put yourself in my hands. You can relax."

By now she had two fingers deep in my ass, while her other hand was pumping my cock, which was pitifully limp, owing to my recent orgasm.

"Little-dicked guys always know that they aren't meant to lead, that they can't really compete with the real men. But the world keeps telling them that they have to be strong, that they have to compete, have to fight for dominance. But it is such a strain, so hard. It's such a relief if they give up, give up the charade, and accept their place! It is such a blessing for those guys if they find a strong woman who accepts them for what they are and lets them be the weak, submissive one."

Tonya took her hand off my cock and pushed me over the arm of the couch, leaving my ass sticking up in the air. She reached between my legs and took my soft organ in her hand again, while she continued to fuck my ass with two fingers. Now her three lovers could clearly see that she had two fingers knuckle-deep in my ass. She pulled another dollop of lube out of the jar and crammed it in my butthole.

"When a weak man submits to a woman, his submission needs constant reinforcement to withstand the propaganda from society that he should be strong and be the 'man of the house.' Symbolic actions help him learn his new role and accept it. Like allowing his wife to take lovers. Eating his own cum and the cum of his wife's lovers. Licking and kissing her ass.

"But one of the most powerful is allowing his wife to be the one in their relationship who does the fucking and letting her fuck his ass! It is so powerful because to allow her cock to enter him he has to let go and be helpless and vulnerable: he is physically surrendering at the same time he is mentally and emotionally surrendering."

During this speech Tonya was demonstrating my surrender by plunging her fingers more and more deeply and energetically into my ass, stretching it in all directions.

"Will you surrender to me, Johnny? Will you let me fuck you? Do you want me to fuck you?"

"Yes…," I whispered.

"You have to say it, baby. You have to say it and you have to ask me to do it."

"Yes … I will let you fuck me. I … surrender to you. I want you to fuck me. Please do it. Fuck my ass!"

With that Tonya raised the dildo to my leering greased hole and put the tip into my rectum. No amount of finger-fucking could prepare for the thickness of the dildo and I gasped once again at the feeling of it stretching my hole unnaturally. Tonya pushed in a couple inches and then expertly backed off to let my muscles relax. She pushed in and out, massaging my sphincters into surrender. Every stroke stretched me wider and every stretch was uncomfortable and my ass strained to keep the invader out. But she was not to be denied.

Tonya drove in and out in a slow, inexorable rhythm. My ass clung tightly to the dildo, straining to relax enough to let her plunge in unimpeded. She finally buried the dildo fully in me, her thighs meeting mine, her pubis grinding into my pelvis. She stopped there, knowing that my anus was stretched to the max and she hunched into me. Then she began long strokes, almost pulling all the way out on each backstroke. I could feel myself start to relax and let go. The dildo started to slide in with ease and each thrust felt better and better.

"Do you like it, baby? Do you like my cock? Do you like me fucking you?" Tonya demanded.

"Yes!" I hissed. "Oh, God it feels good! Yes! Fuck me!"

Tonya gave me my wish and started fucking me more energetically. Now her cock was shuttling in and out like my ass was a cunt. Then she slowed.

"You know the only thing that could make this better?" she asked. "Wouldn't it feel better if this were a real cock? Wouldn't you like to know what a real flesh and blood cock feels like? Would you like to feel a real man's cock in your ass? Like Brian's? When Brian fucks my ass it feels wonderful, Johnny. He has a magnificent cock. Well, you know that. You've sucked it: you've tasted his cum."

Tonya withdrew the dildo to where only the tip rested in me, keeping my anus stretched. I groaned at the feeling of emptiness.

"I'd like to see Brian fuck you, Johnny. To be fucked by a real cock, by a real man: that's the best kind of fuck. I want you to feel that, to feel the same cock in your ass that I've had in mine. I want to share that feeling with you, babe!

"And I want to drain that last shred of male pride out of you. To suck another man's penis, to suck down his cum, to put his cock in your wife's cunt and ass, those are all humiliating. But to let him fuck you, to make you his bitch, to let him make a woman out of you: that is the ultimate surrender to another man!

"I want you to do that now! I've got you all ready, nice and stretched out, nice and horny. And we've got poor Brian all hot and bothered, made him wait while everyone else got off. He'll fuck you like a wild stallion!"

She tickled my asshole with the tip of the dildo and turned her head to look at Brian.

"Brian, you would be doing me a great favor to fuck my husband! I know you aren't gay, but you would be doing me an honor by being the man that takes my husband's virginity. It would prove forever than you are the alpha male and his superior. Put him in his place so that he can never deny you access to my cunt or ass!"

"Jesus, Tonya, you've got me so horny now that I'd fuck a knothole pretty soon! Whatever you say, doll. If you want me to fuck him, I'll fuck him!"

Turning to the other two men, Tonya said, "I want Brian to be the first, but I want each of you to fuck him before the weekend is out. I want him to know in a way that he can't deny that he is inferior to each of you, and he must submit to each of you as well as to me. And I don't want any of you to play the gay card and say that the guy who fucked him is a closet homo. I want you all in on it. Otherwise you can say goodbye to fucking my luscious pussy and ass."

Calvin and David looked at each other and shrugged.

"If you put it that way, I guess we're in," David said. "Don't want to lose out on that pussy and ass." Calvin nodded his consent.

Tonya tuned back to me and diddled my ass with the dildo.

"How about it, Johnny? Do you want to feel what's it's like to have a real cock in you? Do you want to submit to the man who first cuckolded you?"

I hesitated. Why? I knew what I would say; I knew what was going to happen. It was inevitable. It was a runaway train. But I guess those shreds of male dignity were rising up in their death throes. Was I going to let another man fuck me? Did I really want to feel another man's cock in my ass, to feel a man squirt his seed in me like I was a woman?

All those gay pornos I'd watched played in my brain, all the hung guys fucking twinks and the twinks moaning and fucking them back as if it were the greatest feeling in the whole world. I'd been fucked by Tonya and I'd come like gangbusters with her dildo in me. What would it feel like to have a real cock in my ass, to feel a real man rutting away, to feel his cock spasm and his cum spewing into me? Oh, God, here was my chance! I wanted to find out!

Tonya kept up a maddening tickling of my ass, with the dildo just a couple inches in, moving back and forth just a half and inch, stimulating me but withholding the satisfying penetration, as if to tease me.

"Yes!" I groaned. "I submit! I want to feel his cock in me! Please Brian, fuck my ass!"

"Good girl!" Tonya whispered incongruously as she pulled out.

I waited impatiently, my ass open and empty, stuck up in the air, as Tonya lubed up Brian's cock and then placed the tip at my anus. It felt his cockhead touch my oh-so sensitive hole. Oh, God! That was a man's cock that was going to go into me! This was it. A man was going to fuck me! I was going to be fucked for real!

"I want to hold you and feel you go into him!" Tonya confessed to Brian with glee in her voice.

I felt the warm spongy head of his cock start to cave in my sphincter. It felt so different from the dildo. For all the technology that was supposed to mimic real flesh, there was no mistaking Brian's cock for Cyberskin. It was hot and throbbing with his pulse and quivering with his excitement. To me it felt like electricity, knowing this was no dildo, but another man's real cock!

I knew that every sensation I was feeling was mirrored in Brian: he was feeling my ass flesh squeeze him; my ass was pleasuring this cock. I was going to be fucked by a man! That knowledge made this overwhelming, and unlike all the times Tonya had fucked me. This was a real fuck. I was really being fucked! I was a man but I was being fucked by another man!

Brian did not have to warm me up: Tonya had done that for him. He worked his cock into my ass quickly, each thrust plunging another two inches deeper until he hit the top of my rectum, sending a twinge to my stomach. Oh, my God, I have man's penis in me! He began long slow strokes.

"Oh, shit, babe! You got me so horny, I'm not gonna last long!" Brian cried. "God that feels good! I needed to fuck so bad! Oh, shit, that's so tight! So hot!" he babbled.

His horny words stoked my arousal. A shudder went up my spine and I knew I was truly into being fucked now. I felt my ass heat up and let go. Brian started to fuck me in earnest, striving for his orgasm. His thrusts were faster and faster, harder and harder, and I wanted it now. My ass felt like it was melting and the friction of his strokes just felt better and better. I was being fucked! I was startled how good it felt! Oh God! It was so good! Oh! Oh! How could it feel this good! I had never felt anything like it! It felt so ... wonderful!

I started to push back to meet his thrusts, and I could hear the slap of his thighs hitting mine and feel the thud of his groin hitting my ass cheeks. I wanted his cock as deep in me as it could go. I wasn't pleasing Tonya now: I was enjoying being fucked! I was grunting with every slam of his cock into me and I heard him grunting with his effort. My still-limp penis hung down and swung uselessly below me with each thrust.

I loved the feel of Brian's warm body against my ass, his solid thighs pressed into mine. I could feel his body over me, emphasizing how much bigger and stronger he was. I began to sink into the warm feeling of giving myself to him, giving myself to another man in the most intimate way a man could.

I felt myself surrender to the feeling of helplessness—and it was wonderful! I just let go and my whole world was his cock going in and out of me. I could do nothing but accept him, accept his manhood—and I loved that! I loved feeling like he owned me, owned my ass! I didn't have to be strong, couldn't be strong. I wanted to be weak, wanted to let this strong man possess me! A warm feeling spread through my whole body, like I was filling up with melted butter!

"Oh, God, baby, this is so hot! I am getting so turned on!" Tonya shouted and I glanced over to see her frantically scrubbing her clit with lust. "Fuck him, Brian! Fuck the shit out of the sissy boy!"

Tonya words seemed to inflame Brian and his thrusting became wilder and then he was shouting incoherently, "Fuck! Fuck! Fuck!" I felt him bury his cock in me and then I gasped as I felt his organ pulse with his ejaculation. I felt a sympathetic shudder go through me as I was overcome with the knowledge that he had filled me with his hot seed! I could feel the warmth of his cum spreading from the end of his cock deep within me. I got goose bumps and my brain seemed to turn to jelly. Suddenly I felt limp all over, as if I had no bones. Brian collapsed on top of me, his cock jammed to the hilt.

Oh God! I'd been fucked! Fucked by a man! I'd been fucked like a woman. And it felt ... wonderful! I felt so ... used, so ... limp ... wrung out ... satisfied!

Out of my fog I hazily heard the sounds of Tonya orgasming, presumably by her own hand. I felt Brian's weight on top of me, but I didn't want to move. His cock felt good in me and I didn't want him to take it out. The heaviness of his body pressed against me and the warmth felt good, strangely comforting. He felt so strong, solid, masculine. I felt small, weak, helpless ... and I liked it! Tonya had talked about the relief of surrendering and I was feeling that now. I had totally surrendered to Brian and given him my body. And it felt good! I was his in this moment and I felt protected. I was loving the feeling of being his possession!

"Oh, shit!" he exclaimed and he started to push up off me. I groaned as I started to feel his cock sliding out.

"Wait!" Tonya cried. "Don't' pull out yet! Just a second." I heard her get up and then she told Brian he could pull out. He staggered away with a groan.

"Jesus H. Fucking Christ! Damn, what a fuck!" he declared.

Then I felt something rigid against the top of my thighs.

"We don't want to waste any of this yummy cum, do we? Your first butt-fuck, Johnny! We need to toast that!" I put two and two together and realized that what I was feeling was a cup or a glass that Tonya was holding to catch the cum that was dribbling out of my destroyed asshole. Brian had thrown himself down on the coach in front of me and I gazed on the shiny ramrod which had so recently been buried in my bowels. It was softening, but still a proud emblem of superior manhood.

"Babe, you're closing up. Not all the way, mind you, but if we want to get all of Brian's delicious juice, you'll need to push it out. Here, squat down over this cup and squeeze it out, you know, like you were, uh, going to the bathroom?"

I obediently got up and lowered myself over the custard cup she'd fetched from the kitchen. I watched in amazement as glob after glob of lube and the unmistakable pearly white of semen blobbed out of my backside. I hardly felt like I had any control of my sphincters. As I tried to squeeze out Brian's spunk, it felt like my whole insides would come out with it.

Tonya held the cup up to my lips and tipped it toward me and I watched as the goop oozed down the sides of the cup and fell into my mouth. I dimly heard Calvin and David swearing their disgust. I tasted the same flavor as I had so recently savored coming out of Tonya's bottom, but I shivered with the knowledge that it had been squirted into me rather than her. Tonya obligingly scraped the cup with her finger and fed me the rest of the mixture.

"Now thank the nice man who fucked you, baby, and lick off his wonderful cock!" Tonya urged me. "Did you like your fuck, babe? Was a real cock better than Tonya's dildo?"

"Yes, yes, Brian's cock was much better!" I admitted sheepishly. "It ... rubbed me ... places." I shyly looked at Brian and murmured, "Thank you." My cheeks burned with embarrassment at what I was saying. But I felt ... what? Warm. Loved?

"My pleasure!" Brian laughed and Calvin and David roared. "Man, Tonya, you really warmed him up! That was ... wow! He's got a great ass!" He laughed and gave Tonya a high five.

"May I clean you up?" I asked him. I wasn't sure why I asked him. I hadn't asked David, I'd just done as Tonya ordered me. But this felt different now. Well, we'd ... been intimate....

"Sure, that'd be nice," Brian replied.

I looked at his cock differently now—with … affection? Gratitude? Love? I eagerly took it into my mouth, somehow not repelled by the fact that it had just been withdrawn from eight inches up my own ass. I tasted the flavor of Brian's cum dribbling down it. I held it in my mouth and really let myself enjoy the warmth and feel of it filling my mouth. I caressed it with my tongue and lips, taking pleasure in its slick satiny skin. This was the cock, no, the <u>man</u> who had fucked me, taken my anal virginity had … made love to me?

Brian squirmed a little, but I sensed he was enjoying it rather than being uncomfortable. I cradled his cock in my hands and licked it thoroughly, removing as much of the lube and cum as I could. I even sucked some of the goo off his dark pubic hair and some that had oozed down to his hairy sac. I had to hold his balls in my hands to do that and I thought of the sperm still held in them and wondered how much more of his spunk I would be eating and from where.

"Wow, I don't know about you boys, but I need a breather," Tonya suggested. "Let's get something to eat and drink and see where the rest of the night leads us!"

I could barely summon the strength to stand up. It felt as if I didn't have any bones. I felt as if all the strength had been drained out of me. As I walked to the kitchen I could feel my ass feeling wet and greasy and loose. But it didn't bother me. I reveled in it! 'I've been well-fucked!' I thought to myself and the thought made me feel warm and muzzy and relaxed.

Although I'd come earlier, I realized that I hadn't come from Brian fucking me, but I still felt wonderfully satisfied, rather than frustrated and horny. Is that what women meant when they said they enjoyed intercourse whether they had an orgasm or not? I almost felt tipsy, like that giddy, happy feeling when the alcohol just hits you and relaxes you. Euphoric. Glowing?

It felt as if submitting to Brian in that way had ripped all my armor off. I was weak and vulnerable, like a turtle without its shell. But I wasn't scared. I almost felt liberated. It was like Tonya had said: I could give up trying to protect myself: I'd been defeated already. I had a warm, goofy, happy feeling. I looked at Brian when no one was looking and I felt … what? Connected to him. Connected in the most primal way. As if I belonged to him now. But that didn't bother me. It … what? … sent a warm shudder up my spine. I sort of <u>liked</u> belonging to him! Like a schoolgirl crush! I didn't know what was happening to me, but it didn't scare me, at least not yet. I felt happy!

Everyone pulled their robes back on. Normally I would have felt a little foolish to be putting back on the feminine camisole and robe Tonya had issued me, but no one else seemed to care. I looked at the pink and lacy outfit and I felt ... well ... I hoped Brian thought it was pretty!

We ate and the four of them talked just like a group of friends at a pool party, rather than a cuckold fuck-fest. The main difference was that they all liberally helped themselves to fondling Tonya's ass or tits or pussy, or giving her French kisses, without any restraint or apology. Her body belonged to all three of them, to use as they felt, and Tonya seemed fine with that.

Their joint complicity in agreeing to have Brian fuck me seemed to have forged a bond and an ease in the group. If that was OK in this group, what wouldn't be OK? I knew some Rubicon had been crossed when David called me over and said, "I think I'm ready for the next round. Johnny, why don't you get me ready to fuck Tonya's cute little behind? I think she might still be nice and relaxed from Calvin's fuckpole. I don't mind a little sloppy seconds."

He threw open his robe and slouched back in his chair, clearly presenting his meat for me to minister to. Apparently the idea of the wife's husband as harem eunuch and fluffer didn't bother him at all. Tonya's eyebrows went up and she smiled like the cat that ate the canary. She was delighted at David's comfort in using me. That's exactly what she wanted: all the cock she could get and her husband as a sexual gofer. Her experiment was a smashing success.

I felt an odd hesitation. I had to resist the urge to look to Brian, as if I had to ask his permission. I mean, I was his now, right? It was almost as if I'd be being unfaithful...?

Tonya must have sensed my momentary reluctance, for she came over an started kissing me and sweet-talking me.

"Won't you, baby? Do it for me? David's got such a nice prick. It would feel so nice in my bottom, squishing around in there with Calvin's cum! You can suck his jizz back out when he's done." She started handling my traitorous penis, which had started to fill as she painted that picture.

"Please, baby? Show me how much you love me by sucking David's gorgeous cock nice and hard for me?"

That's right. I didn't really like sucking cocks, did I? I was just doing it for Tonya, right?

David didn't really need that much help to get ready for Tonya. He was already at three-quarters staff when I knelt between his legs and took his large cockhead in my mouth for the second time that night. Again I was surprised at the unexpectedly pleasant sensation of the warmth and aliveness of his cock as I sealed my lips around it. The was a real live penis, not a dildo. I could never get over how much bigger it felt in my mouth than I expected. And I was startled again at how much it aroused me to be sucking it!

As I sucked his cock to full hardness I was struck by the similarity of my posture to a supplicant at prayer. It was as if I were a worshipper at the altar, making my devotions to this superior penis. The thought sent a shiver through me and I could feel my arousal spike. Yes, these superior penises were my gods and I was an unworthy follower kneeling down to show respect for them. I could not help but acknowledge their superiority. This penis deserved to be honored, served, even loved.

These cocks deserved my respect and devotion ... and affection. I should be honored to be asked to service them, honored that they would fuck my wife, honored to swallow the cum that flowed from them. I slid David's penis in and out of mouth. Oh, that felt so nice! I took my mouth off David's cock and admired it, licking every ridge and vein with the tip of my tongue. I was rewarded with a quick intake of breath from him.

"Look at that whore!" Calvin burst out, half-disgusted. "He can't get enough of Dave's meat! He must be a faggot!"

I didn't let Calvin deter me. It was all part of the cuckold's lot. My job was to suck this cock as well as I could, to suck any cock Tonya told me to, to serve any cock worthier than mine. If they called me a faggot while I sucked their prick or ate their cum or watched them fuck my wife, so be it. Cuckolds have to get used to being humiliated. I could hear Tonya's voice in my head, 'Do you have to be a faggot to love sucking cock?'

While I continued to blow David I was inspired to cradle his balls in my free hand and think of all the cum stored in them. David seemed turned on by that. I rolled them around gently.

"Damn, Tonya!" Dave exclaimed. "You sure he hasn't been practicing behind your back?"

"No, I keep him on a pretty short leash. But you know what they say: when you love what you do...."

They all laughed but I didn't let it faze me. All I heard was that I was doing a good job.

Tonya came over and started petting me. She caressed my nipples and ran a finger up the underside of my now-hard shaft.

"You do love it, don't you, Johnny? It's so wrong, so dirty. Boys aren't supposed to like sucking cock! Bad enough to be doing it at all, but doubly wrong to get hard from doing it, to be excited about having a man's cock in your mouth. But why not? Why shouldn't enjoy it? But are you getting it ready for Tonya's ass, or do you want him to come right in your mouth? Or do want it for your ass?"

She ran a finger between my ass cheeks and started tickling my anus with her talented fingertips. She rubbed back and forth across the opening while she toyed with "Little Johnny." My newly hairless anus seemed even more sensitive than it had been. I moaned while I continued to feast on David's erection. What did I want?

Brian's cock had felt so good fucking me, and submitting to him had touched something deep inside me. I felt a warmth rush across my whole body as a thought of that again. I felt melty all over, like my bones were going away. The idea of David's cock fucking me....

Tonya dipped a fingertip into my opening and mini-fucked me just to the first knuckle.

"You've never had David in your ass. I bet it would feel so good. But then, he's never shot in your mouth before either. You've tasted his cum out of me, but not straight from the spigot, all hot and strong. I guess the question is whether you're more gay or more cuckold? Maybe your biggest turn-on is to see him plug your wife's ass while you beat off. Which, baby? Which do you want more?"

I answered with David's cock still filling my mouth.

"I don't know!"

"Hah! That's the real pervert's torment, isn't it? So many ways to degrade yourself, so many taboos to break. But you can't do them all at once! If you suck off that cock, it can't fuck you. If it fucks your wife, you can't suck it off. Choices, choices! Good thing we have so many nice cocks here and lots of time and lots of cum."

She pulled David's cock out of my mouth and he groaned.

"I'll decide. My ass is lonely and watching you suck David so hungrily has got my cunt so horny. I want a cock in each hole! I want a DP!"

She started kissing David and grabbed hold of his glistening prick.

"You get Calvin up to speed while I lube up for Davey here," Tonya instructed me.

I was supposed to be a reluctant submissive husband, but being passed around like a two-bit gay whore made me vibrate with excitement! Going from Dave's pink phallus to Calvin's black cock was no sacrifice. I was a lucky guy to have so many big thick cocks to suck, I thought. I didn't hesitate this time. I was determined to show Tonya that I was game, and anxious to have my mouth filled with cock again. Calvin's penis was half-hard already, but I sucked it to life. I felt proud as it grew in my mouth.

"A good blow-job is a thing of beauty," Calvin sighed, apparently dismissing easily any homosexual implications to what we were doing. "Get my piece all ready for your lady, cuck boy!"

His put-down only increased my energy. I twisted and turned my mouth around the meaty head of his penis, licked up the underside, and drove the head deep against the back of my throat.

I looked over and David was already easing his member onto Tonya's back entrance, clearly more easily than Calvin had earlier. Tonya was already moaning with pleasure rather than straining to admit him. I wondered how Calvin would gain access, as David had Tonya on all fours.

Calvin answered my question by getting up and crawling under Tonya, shinnying so that he was under her now. He stopped to kiss and fondle her dangling breasts before he started to try to find her vagina with his cock.

"Unh! Johnny ... unh ... get over here and put Calvin in me. He can't see what he's doing," Tonya commanded.

I had to reach in from the side to take Calvin's ebony rod in hand and held it to Tonya's puffy pussy lips. I paused momentarily to heft its thickness in my hand. Then I aimed it as Calvin creeped back and then began to penetrate her.

"Oh, shit!" Tonya exclaimed as Calvin's dick tried to find room to enter her. Oh, God! Oh, shit, so ... much ... cock ... in...!" She was sandwiched between the two men, helpless as their cocks both drove into her.

"Shit! Shit! Shit! Shit!" she gasped.

"Jesus! That's so ... fucking ... weird!" Calvin reported. "Fuck! I can feel him fucking her ass!"

"Too much!" David crowed.

"Get your mouth on my cock!" Brian barked at me. "This is too hot for me to just watch!"

His penis was already hard and I licked a drop of pre-cum from his slit. I knew that I wasn't just following orders. I was eager to have Brian's cock in my mouth again. I wanted to suck him. I felt that warm thrill pass over me that I had felt from his fucking me, that feeling that I was connected to him. I wanted to serve him. I wanted to belong to him.

'His cock is my god,' I told myself. 'I serve my master. I want his cock. I want to please him.' Oh, God! "My master"! That was so hot!

Brian was frantic with arousal from watching Tonya take two cocks at once. He didn't want to wait for me to suck him off. He wanted to fuck my mouth. He grabbed my head and pushed his cock to the back of my throat. I started to gag but Brian hardly noticed. He continued to fuck back and forth, heedless of my distress. I realized he was going to use me for his pleasure whether I could handle it or not. I tried to relax and let it happen.

I dimly heard Tonya grunting and groaning as Calvin and David ravaged her twin holes. I daren't turn my head and all I could see was Brian groin pumping at my face. But I heard Tonya go over the edge.

"Oh, shit! Arrggghhh!" she cried in ecstasy. Her orgasm thrilled Brian and his thrusts became jerkier. My jaw was getting sore, but I knew I would not have to endure much longer.

Brian froze and I felt every twitch as his cock swelled even more and then I felt it spasm, as his cum shot straight down the back of my throat. I pressed his shaft with my tongue and he shuddered at the overwhelming stimulation.

"Oh, fuck!" he yelled and pulled back, depositing the next spurt of cum on my tongue this time. I sucked on him as if I were sucking a thick milkshake through a straw. Then I reached up and grabbed his shaft so that I could lick all around the head. I was proud that I'd brought him off! I felt my chest swell with an unfamiliar emotion and found myself kissing his penis several times before I let it go.

Brian stumbled away, and then collapsed on the floor, spent. He lay on his back, spread-eagled, panting.

'I did that to him!' I thought to myself and smiled. I savored the taste of his spend in my mouth.

"I hope you're not full, because I have something for you!" Tonya announced. She straddled my head and lowered her dripping cunt to my mouth. Her gash hung open, red and soupy, and I tasted the cum Calvin had deposited there. The acrid taste was no longer strange or repugnant to me. It was a special taste, just for me. I licked it up eagerly, savoring it.

Then she swung herself around to give me access to her also-gaping asshole, and she squeezed dollop after dollop of David's cream into my mouth. I accepted her anal load without a thought. I just sucked and licked her ass clean, as naturally as I'd kiss her good night.

"You're probably thirsty too, aren't you, Johnny? Why don't we show the boys your other talent? Open wide!" She lifted herself up a couple of inches so that the men could see what she was doing.

"Do you want it, Johnny? Are you thirsty? Do you want Tonya? Tell me you want it."

"Please, Tonya, may I ... drink your piss?"

"No!" Calvin exclaimed.

"Too much," David muttered, shaking his head in disgust. "You two are something else!"

Brian had seen it before, but he just shook his head, like he still couldn't believe it, or maybe couldn't believe I'd do that in front of Calvin and David.

Tonya closed her eyes and immediately a cascade of her hot piss filled my mouth. As I swallowed and felt her hot urine flowing down to my stomach I realize why she'd been so eager to do this. It was our special bond and it brought us back together after our separate sexual experiences of the last few minutes. But this time her pee mixed with the cum of three different men that I'd swallowed tonight.

"God, I don't believe it. He's drinking her damn piss!" David burst out. "Oh, man!"

"That's fucked up!" Calvin agreed.

"They think you're a perv, Johnny," Tonya pointed out. "That's something coming from two guys who just DP'd another guy's wife! You've sunk pretty low in their eyes."

I guess I couldn't argue with that. I was a pervert. I answered the charge by licking her pussy clean once her last few dribbles had ceased. I maybe a pervert, but at least I was Tonya's pervert. I looked at the three studs and I now saw something that didn't look like triumph or amazement: maybe pity or disgust?

"Don't forget your other clean-up job, Johnny," Tonya reminded me.

I crawled over on my hands and knees. I couldn't look them in the eye, so I just concentrated on their spent penises. I smelled Tonya's pussy juice strong on Calvin and the musky smell of Tonya's ass on David. I missed the feel of stiffness of their earlier erections, but even limp their cocks were works of art and I gave them each my full devotion.

Tonya curled up next to Brian on the love seat, then tangled their legs together and kissed him deeply.

"I don't know about you young bucks, but I'm all in," Tonya announced. "Even three gorgeous cocks aren't enough to keep me from falling into a coma after that.

"But first I think Johnny deserves a reward for all his good service tonight,. Lube up and sit back, Johnny, and beat your little meat for us. You'll be the solo finale for tonight!"

I felt another wave of humiliation as I saw the smirks on their faces. Although I'd obviously masturbated in front of them earlier, I'd been focused on Tonya and oblivious to all else. Now they'd all be watching me. I'd be the pathetic jerk-off, literally. To my horror my traitorous cock rose to the occasion, always willing to help me embarrass myself yet again.

I dutifully scooped up some lube and applied it to my stiff little willie. I sighed as the familiar thrill of my slick fist shuddered through me. I closed my eyes and sank into the sensations, letting the sights, sounds, and smells of the evening roll through my mind in a lewd kaleidoscope.

"Open your eyes, baby," Tonya commanded. "Keep beating your little thingy, but be aware of where you are and what you are doing. You're jerking yourself off in front of your beautiful wife! Instead of fucking her cunt or ass, you're fucking your fist! You're beating off in front of three men who've just fucked your wife or will soon. Your ass is sore from where another man's fucked you. Your stomach is full from six loads of cum—well, plus a few dribbles of your own—plus your wife's hot piss."

Each sentence was like a blow, grinding the shreds of my ego into dust. But each blow pumped my dick harder and sent shock waves through my spine up to my sex-addled brain.

"You're a cuckold, my dear! You stand by and watch while other men fuck your wife—and you get off on it, don't you? Against all that is natural, instead of rage, you feel lust! Instead of throwing them off and sticking your hard cock into your wife's pussy, you stand by and take your cock into your hand! Instead of grabbing a knife to cut off their balls for defiling your bride, you want to suck their cocks hard so you can watch them do it again! Instead of throwing your unfaithful wife's ass out into to the street, you throw yourself down on your knees to kiss her adulterous cunt and taste the manly cum that leaks out! Instead of protesting your manhood, you wear a girlie nightie to let everyone know what a wimp you really are!"

I cringed at every description, but I pumped my prick faster with every word.

"Say it, Johnny! Tell us how much you enjoyed every bit of your humiliation!"

"Yes!" I choked out with effort. "I enjoyed it!"

"It excited you, didn't it? More than anything else you've ever done, didn't it? And you want it to go on and on, don't you?"

"Yes!" I gasped.

"Then I think you need to thank us: thank me, thank them, for fucking me, for letting you suck them, for fucking you, for their tasty cum—all of it!"

My cock was so hard it hurt. I had to slow down stroking to be able to speak.

"Th-thank you, Tonya, for letting me ... watch ... them...."

"..'real men'...," Tonya corrected.

"...watch real men fuck you ... and to ... let me see how utterly superior they are!"

"You're welcome," Tonya gloated.

'Thank you for ... fucking my wife and giving her the real sexual pleasure a real man can give a woman."

"Our pleasure!" David and Calvin replied.

"Thank you for letting me ... suck ... your superior cocks and taste your superior cum," I choked. "And thank you, Brian, for taking my anal virginity ... and letting me feel what it feels like to be fucked ... by a ... real man!"

At that moment I felt my own cum arrive at the base of my penis like molten lava. I gasped and then I felt the spasms shake my groin and semen spurt weakly from the end of my dick and fall over my greasy fist. I groaned and belatedly tried to catch the second and third squirt with my left hand and to dam up the dripping cum so it wouldn't fall to the floor.

"Marvelous, Johnny! A fitting end to tonight's show," Tonya praised me. "Now lick up your goo: don't make a mess!"

Mortified at the spectacle I had made of myself, in a daze I obediently licked the bitter, watery ejaculate from my hands.

"You fellows throw evens and odds. The two who match may sleep with me tonight. The odd man gets the guest room. Johnny, I'm afraid you get the couch."

I didn't even rate the "guest" bedroom anymore, much less the master bedroom (Mistress bedroom?). I noticed a wet spot on the couch, so I fetched a towel and a blanket.

I lay there waiting for sleep to come and my mind raced with all that had happened. I'd let a man fuck me! As I thought about that my ass tingled. I could recall every sensation of having Brian's penis inside me, feeling it open me and stretch me. I'd loved it! I trembled to feel again what it had been like when my anus had relaxed and really accepted him. I sighed to remember how good that had felt! It was ... satisfying ... satisfying in a way unlike anything I'd ever felt before! Just imagining the feeling again took my breath away. It was so ... sexy. So ... arousing. I couldn't get the idea out of my head. I had loved it! Oh, I was in trouble!

Two questions swirled about in my head: why did it excite me so? And how could I make it happen again?

Despite the rude accommodations, I finally fell asleep and slept the sleep of the dead.

-Day 29, Saturday-

"Wake up, sleepyhead! Tonya's got your breakfast!"

I woke with a start to find Tonya clambering over my head and lowering her seeping gash to my face. Her labia hung down and her cunt yawned open, glistening with her dew and the milky evidence of her morning exertions. The smell of sex was like a slap, it was so strong, now a fermented mixture of yesterday's leavings and new deposits. Despite my demeaning position, my dick began to swell as the rank aroma filled my nostrils.

I pressed my mouth to her pussy and the strong taste assailed my tongue. The leftovers of yesterday added an acrid flavor that cut through the taste of fresh globs of man-cum now dribbling out of her cunt. I sucked her offering and from the volume of ooze guessed that both of her bedmates had shared her already this morning!

"Tell me, Johnny, now that you've tasted it several times, which do you prefer: licking my clean pussy before I've fucked a big stud, or do you actually prefer my used pussy, with another man's cum oozing out of it? Which gets you hotter? If you could only have me one way or the other, would you rather eat my pussy only after a real man has used it? Or would you rather have it 'unsullied' by the spunk of a big cock?"

It was a startling question. Of course I did eat her pussy even when a man had just used her. But did I prefer it that way? Would I rather another man used her first? Would I choose a life where I only got to eat my wife's pussy after another man had marked her as his bitch?

It was a hard admission but I knew what the truth was.

"Like it is now," I mumbled, my face smeared with her juices and the seed of Brian and David. Her cunt reeked of powerful pheromones. It was like sexual heroin.

"I thought so!" Tonya said to herself. "So given a choice, you'd rather wait until a real man had fucked me, so you could lap at a well-fucked pussy and savor the taste of semen! You're hooked on it! You really need and want me to fuck other men!

"Here's some juice to go with your cream," Tonya warned me and soon the salty stream of her morning urine hit my tongue. I swallowed desperately to keep from drowning as she peed and peed. She jumped off me as soon as I'd licked her clean of the last drops of urine and imperiously commanded me.

"Now that you've had your breakfast, go and rustle us up some eggs and bacon and toast. These boys are going to need their strength!"

Tonya was right about one thing: my "breakfast" had killed my appetite temporarily. My poor stomach rebelled at the unhealthy mixture that filled it now. I put the frilly apron I'd worn last week over my robe and nightie. Calvin and David roared when they saw me in the apron and smirked at me as if I were mental. I was surprised to find that it didn't bother me to be made a laughingstock or to act as the foursome's maid. Why shouldn't I be? I was getting used to my subservient position.

I wasn't hungry until the rest of them had almost finished eating. It wasn't until I was serving them their second and third cups of coffee that my stomach felt as if I could handle some eggs and toast. I was sure I'd be getting my fill of "sausage" the rest of the day.

After I'd finished eating my real breakfast Tonya and Calvin came up to me.

"Johnny, I'm proud of you that you let Brian fuck your ass last night. I know you enjoyed it, but that wasn't really the point. The idea was to submit to Brian and to let him use you for his pleasure. But now I want you to take your pleasure from being fucked up the ass.

"David and Brian have already had some fun this morning, as you know. But Calvin was in the guest room and he's ready to go again. But I want this fuck to be all about you discovering all the joy you can get from a cock, for you to enjoy that feeling of a man filling you and rubbing you way up in there. I want you to be in control, to milk all the pleasure you can get. You call the shots. You tell Calvin how you want him to fuck you: slow and easy, fast and hard, shallow or deep, short or long. You be in charge.

"Calvin tells me he has great control. He can hold back and go as long as you want, as fast as you want, as deep as you want. I want you to get in touch with what you want when a man is fucking you, to find what feels best to your ass. Don't worry about him. Don't just let him fuck you: use his cock to get your ass fucked exactly the way you want."

Brian came up holding the enema bag and hose, so they'd planned this. Tonya took it and made it clear she was going to give it to me right there in the living room! That was more humiliating than being fucked, or drinking piss, or sucking cock! No privacy or respect was to be left to me. Tonya had me draw up my knees and present my helpless, hairless anus to them all. They watched as she inserted the nozzle and filled my colon with the warm solution.

"We'll get you all clean and relaxed so you can really enjoy your fucking!" she cooed. I squirmed with uncomfortable fullness as she made me lie there and wait. But soon she let me waddle to the bathroom to empty myself with relief.

I came back to the spectacle of Tonya mouthing Calvin's big black cock. The sight no longer startled me, but the contrast of my wife's lovely face and this massive black penis sent erotic shivers up my spine.

"Don't worry, baby," Tonya assured me, licking the pink slit at the end of Calvin's organ, "I'm only warming him up for you. The poor boy's been neglected all night!"

"Oh, suck it a little more, baby," Calvin begged, but Tonya only kissed the underside tenderly.

"Johnny's ass will take good care of you, don't fret!" she chided. "Do you want him doggy style or missionary position, Johnny? You call the shots. How do you want him to fuck you?"

I gulped. I hadn't thought about that. It'd never been up to me so far. I was uncomfortable being in charge.

"Er, whichever way Calvin would rather," I answered.

"No, babe, you have to choose. Calvin will do you whichever way, but it's your call."

"I guess on my back would be more relaxed than on my hands and knees."

"Good! It'll be more like he's the man and you're the woman," Tonya interpreted. "You won't be able to move much, so he'll be fucking you that way. OK, lie on the chaise and I'll lube you up, baby." I lay on the chaise, my ass at the edge of the cushion, and I pulled my legs up as I had for the enema. Nervous as I was, my damn dick was already hard. It stiffened more as Tonya speared my ass with her lubed fingers.

"This is going to be so good, baby. Calvin will be your man. He'll fuck you as long as you want, just how you want." She reached up and greased my cock with her other hand and began to stroke me in rhythm with the fingers in my ass. In less than a minute I was moaning with delight as her fingers sent sparks back and forth from my ass to my cock.

"God, you love to be fucked, don't you? You love to be fucked as much as any woman does! And what does any woman long to be fucked with? A little boy dicklette?"

"No...," I admitted.

"Does she want to be fucked by a dildo?"

"No."

"What does she want to be fucked with?"

"A big cock ... a real man's cock...."

"And what do you want to be fucked with? Two fingers? A dildo? What do you want to fill you up, to fuck you to rub your prostate?"

"...a ... cock. A ... big ... hard ... cock...," I gasped, delirious with what she was doing to me.

"Do you. want Calvin's cock up your ass right now?"

"Yes!" I hissed. "God! Yes!"

"Beg him then," Tonya ordered, stilling her fingers to drive me crazy.

"Please! Fuck me with you big black cock!" I cried.

I felt his cockhead replace Tonya's fingers at my opening, but he just pushed against my anus and did not enter.

"Open your eyes, Johnny!" Tonya commanded. "Look at the big black man who is going to fuck you, as his cock enters you. Look at him and know that you want his cock just as much as I want his cock. You hunger for this. It will feel so good inside you!"

I opened my eyes and looked at this muscular black man looming over me. I did want him; I wanted his cock. I needed to feel that hot thick meat in me, fucking me, taking me. I was ready for it.

As soon as Calvin knew I was watching him, he began to press into my ass. God, he was so big and I gasped as my sphincter stretched and pain made me wince.

"Oh! Wait! Hold it!"

Calvin immediately stopped and began to pull back. The pain immediately eased.

"Stay there! Oh, go in again!" I wanted to feel that cock in me! The pain began again but not as bad. "OK, keep going." Discomfort, but I gritted my teeth. "Hold it there!" I squeezed my muscles and let go, to get them to relax. The strain eased.

"Pull it out and then go in again," I husked. "Unh!" I grunted as his cock slithered back out and then pressed past my sphincters again. "Keep going!" I begged him and gulped as his magnificent penis began to fill my rectum completely. Calvin began to make mini-fucking motions to relax my ass, pressing inexorably deeper and deeper. I sighed as I felt him reach the top of my rectum. "Oh, God!" I exulted, "That's all I can take! Oh! Just ... let me feel that! Oh ... it's so big ... so full.... God!"

Tonya reached between us and milked my cock. I'd almost forgot about that organ, so focused on my ass.

"You love it, don't you?" she whispered. "You love feeling that big cock in you!"

"Oh, shit!" I exclaimed in inarticulate admission.

Calvin began to gently fuck me in long slow strokes. Oh, it was so big! So big! But, oh, it felt so good! I squirmed and groaned in pleasure and Calvin knew to keep doing what he was doing. I could feel his cock rub my prostate, sending awesome sensations to my little cock, making it painfully hard. Although it almost felt like too much pleasure, but I couldn't bear the thought of stopping either. I writhed in delicious torment.

Calvin sadistically kept up a maddeningly slow steady rhythm, stroking my ass from the inside, from my anus to the top of my rectum, in l-o-o-o-n-g delightful strokes. I shuddered with a warm melty feeling all over, the same feeling I'd had last night after Brian fucked me. I felt my hairs stand up. My ass went loose. I had a sensation of complete surrender and helplessness. But it wasn't a feeling of being in danger. It was a feeling of being open but safe. I loved feeling ... weak ... passive ... feminine! I loved feeling helpless ... taken...! Ohhhhh!

But soon the slow gentle fucking wasn't enough. I wanted more.

"Oh, God! Fuck me! I want you to really fuck me! Hard and fast now!"

"You want a <u>man</u>? You want a <u>man</u> to really <u>fuck</u> you, Johnny?" Tonya teased.

"Yes, oh, it feels so ... unh!"

Calvin was happy to oblige. He began to pound into me in a fast jabbing rut. His cock stabbed into the top of my rectum, sending twinges to my stomach. But I exulted when I felt his pelvis smash against mine. He was so big, so strong, so manly. I was so weak by comparison. He could do what he wanted with me, if I were willing or not.

"Oh, God, yes! Fuck me!" I cried. Calvin was like a machine now, pounding into me, and I wanted every thrust. I wanted to feel <u>used</u>! My cock felt like bursting and I grabbed it and began to beat it.

"That's it, baby!" Tonya cried. "Go for it! Let Calvin fuck you over the top!"

My hand flew over my cock. The heat Calvin was stoking in my ass seemed to flow like lava to the base of my penis and then hesitate for an agonizing second. And then it was flowing up my cock and I came, in ropes of cum shooting over my belly. I was in delirious rapture!

"Oh! Ow! Oh! Oh! Oh, shit! Oh, God! Fuck!" I babbled in a cry of too much pleasure, sexual overload burning out brain cells and nerve endings. I groaned as Calvin continued to pound into me.

"Oh, please, stop now!" I pleaded. "Too much!"

"Oh, baby, we can't leave Calvin hanging!" Tonya scolded. "You've had your fun, but now the man has his! That's the woman's <u>place</u>, to be used for the man's pleasure! Let yourself be his woman!" She started scooping up my squirted cum with her fingers and bringing the warm acrid goo to my lips. I reluctantly licked my own semen off her hand while Calvin continued to plumb my ass.

"Maybe he'd come sooner if you helped him," Tonya helpfully suggested. "Maybe he'd like you to feel his pecs and nipples."

I doubted Calvin would appreciate my caresses, but I wanted him to finish. Tentatively I reached out and cupped the rippling muscles of his chest. It was like a dream to see my white hands on his black skin and to know I was fondling another man like a woman might.

I was glad Calvin's eyes were closed so that we did not have to acknowledge what we were doing. But it seemed to be working: the pace of his fucking became more forceful. Encouraged, I took each of his ebony nipples between my thumb and forefinger. The comparison with all the times I'd tweaked Tonya's nipples was blowing my mind. I was making love to a man!

I didn't know how the gayness of this sat with Calvin, but physically he responded. His fucking became frantic. I continued until, with a roar, he buried his penis in my ass and I felt his cock throb and fill my bowels with his man-seed.

"Oh, fuck!" he gasped and I felt a schizophrenic flash of pride that my ass had pleased him. He hunched hard into me, as if he couldn't get far enough in. I felt an after-shock spasm go through his cock.

"Shit! Fuck!" he gasped and I knew I'd milked him good. That thought sent a warm shiver and a happy afterglow through me! But I think it surprised and disturbed him a little how much he'd enjoyed it! I suspected he'd wanted to do it mostly to further humiliate me, but he hadn't expected to get off on it so much!

Calvin pulled out and I winced at the sudden empty feeling. My ass felt bereft. I reached down to catch the spate of cum that was sure to start leaking out of me, only to find David nudging my hand away with his greasy penis.

"Sloppy seconds time, Johnny!" Tonya crowed. "It'd be a shame to waste a nice stretched and lubed asshole! Of course, David's already come once this morning, so he might take a bit longer. Give him a good squeeze so he gets some friction."

David's cock slid into me effortlessly. Thankfully Tonya'd lubed him up liberally and he was soon sliding in and out easily. Even despite my post-orgasmic blahs, I was shocked at the thrill that went through my rectum to be filled again! If I'd wanted to be used, I was certainly getting used! David's strokes were ... comforting? What was I feeling? Without the frenzy of my own urge to come, I had time to explore my emotions. This man's body was thrusting into mine and I felt ... useful? I was serving Tonya and her men. This man wanted me ... or my ass at least ... and ... it felt good to be ... wanted.

The slickness of my open and cum-drenched asshole seemed to excite David.

"Oh, man, Calvin, you really opened him up for me! His ass is so loose and slick! Can you handle more cock, Johnny? Oh, yeah!"

"Fuck him good, Davey!" Tonya urged. "Fill him up!"

Tonya snaked her hand out to my limp sissy cock and slathered lube on it. She began to tug on it, despite its flaccid state. She couldn't coax a hard-on out of my poor penis, but her touching me still felt good.

"Show David a good time, baby. He's got a nice cock. Make it good for him. Play with his nipples like you did with Calvin."

I reached up and cupped his pecs. I think more than the stimulation, he got off on seeing me following Tonya's orders. Before I did anything more he already began to pound into me harder and faster. The way he looked at me it felt like an act of conquest, that he was fucking me to show that he could, that I was his toy.

What made my mouth go dry was how I was getting into the sensation of being his toy! I caressed his nipples as Tonya had ordered. I felt his chest muscles rippling as he thrust and I was acutely aware of his masculinity. I pressed up more firmly and felt the solidity of body, so different from a woman's. The wrongness, the taboo of that shocked my conscience, but it thrilled my libido. I was having sex with a man!

I had an urge to excite David, to make love back to him. I experimented with squeezing his cock with my stretched ass muscles. I was rewarded with a moan. I started rhythmically squeezing and releasing his cock. Tonya leaned down to whisper in my ear as she played with my dick.

"You like David's cock in you, don't you, babe? You still want more cock, even after you've shot your wad! Think of it! Last night was your first real cock and now you're having your second one of this morning! Do you want more cock? Are you addicted to it? I want you to be, baby. I want you to love my boyfriends' cocks just as much as I do. I want you to look forward to them coming over, to their staying the night. That way you'll never say no to me. I'll be in charge, because I'll control the supply of cocks, the cocks you need."

Tonya's perverted monologue sparked a response in me. My abused prick tried to swell in her hand.

"Think of it, baby. You know these cocks are superior to yours. It's a small step from acknowledgement to admiration. You have to admit: they are impressive cocks. Feel how full David fills you! Feel how deep it goes, how it feels! Imagine how good it will feel when it throbs with orgasm. How satisfying that will be to feel that hot cum way up inside you!

"It's only another small step from admiration to adoration. Their cocks are beautiful: they draw you. You want to see them, be close to them, touch them, stroke them. You want to feel their hardness, their heat, the blood throbbing in them.

"And it's only another small step from adoration to addiction. You want it so much, you never want to be away from it. You want it to be a part of you. You can't get enough of it. You want them in your hand, your mouth, your ass: everywhere!"

Tonya's words inflamed me. I could imagine, could feel everything she said. My cock half-hardened and the cock in my ass was no longer an invader but a lover. I could feel my rectum grasping it, trying to milk the joyous spurt out of it! I was welcoming this violation of my gender and my identity.

I reached up and caressed David's nipples again, this time with affection. I thrilled again at the strength, the mastery I felt in his body. I spoke the words that thrilled Tonya: "Fuck me."

Two words, not shouted, but said quietly, firmly. But they spoke volumes. I wasn't being fucked any more. I wanted David to fuck me.

David groaned as I kneaded his nipples. I wasn't after my orgasm: I wanted his. I wanted to feel his manhood throb in me, to feel it spurt its life deep, deep in me.

"Fuck me," I repeated quietly. "Give me your cum. I want you to fill my ass with your cum."

The seriousness of my tone did something to David. He began to pound me harder.

"Yes! Feels so good!" I groaned. "Fuck my ass, David! I love your cock in my ass!"

With that David became frantic. He couldn't fuck me hard enough! If he hadn't already come not long ago, he'd have given it up already. Only seconds later I felt him freeze, buried to the hilt and then came my sweet reward! His cock throbbed and I felt a hot wetness as he spilled his semen into my rectum.

I gasped with delight at every spasm of David's manhood and the spreading heat deep within me. I marveled at Tonya's genius. This fuck, so soon after the last one, hard on the heels of my orgasm, had been totally different. I wasn't frantic. But that allowed me to experience this fuck in a deeper way. I wasn't relieved, exhausted. This fuck had taken me to another level. I was high. I was floating on a sexual cloud and David's cum felt like a gift to me! I wanted to be their sex object!

David was panting roughly, but no oaths poured forth. He groaned as he pulled out and I grimaced as the empty, lost, incomplete feeling returned. My hand shot to my gaping ass to dam up the flood of cum ready to erupt.

I had my wits about me now enough to guess what would come next. Tonya released my stiff four-and-a-half incher to grasp Brian's 8-incher and slather lube on it. Without letting Brian's cock go, she pulled him over and guided his thick cockhead to my stretched opening. This time I greeted his cock as an old friend and it slipped easily deep within me, filling that empty feeling!

"Oh, yeah," I murmured, no longer embarrassed or self-conscious. Tonya had won. I wanted this cock. I wanted my third ass-fuck of the morning! I reached up and put my hands on Brian's chest and felt his muscular torso as he started to hump his cock into my ass. It no longer felt sore or tight. I only felt satisfaction. Brian's cock satisfied a hunger that Tonya had awakened. I let myself enjoy every stroke, enjoying the full-empty-full syncopation. I enjoyed Brian's slowly mounting arousal, thrilled as his thrusts became more rapid and jerky, and groaned as he emptied his man-juice into my boy-cunt!

I'd been so into Brian's fucking me that I'd practically forgotten Tonya, until I felt her breath in my ear.

"Three loads of fuck-juice in your ass, baby! Imagine all those spermies swimming around! The essence of three real men in you! You only started ass-fucking yesterday and you've already pulled a train on your second day! Just the caboose left!"

I felt a quiver of anxiety. Caboose? Was there another man here? What else was Tonya going to spring on me?

I turned my head to find that Tonya had strapped on her harness and was sporting a new, odd-looking dildo. It had a definite upward curve with almost a hooked bulb on the end. As Tonya stepped back I caught sight of a wire and what looked like a battery pack coming out of the base of the dildo.

"What is that?" I asked.

"It's a G-spot dildo."

"But men don't have a G-spot."

"Oh, I think you're going to find out different!" She pushed my hand from my anus and pressed the dildo easily into my gaping ass. The reason for the odd shape of the dildo became clear to me once it was about 4 inches in. The upward curve pressed the bulbed end of the dildo hard against my prostate. The jolt of the sensation it produced made my jaw drop and my cock throb. Tonya gave it a few strokes, prodding my prostate, sending overwhelming sexual shocks up my penis.

"Oh, God, Tonya, that's too much!"

"You ain't seen nothin' yet!" she warned and her hand went to the battery pack. A second later the whole dildo began to vibrate. The sensation against my prostate was like touching a live wire.

"Arrggghhh!" I cried and writhed, trying to move the dildo away from my gland. My cries were greeted by cackles from the men and a laugh from Tonya. My cock swelled alarmingly despite my discomfort. Tonya did not relent but instead began fucking me with the quivering dildo, raking it repeatedly across my prostate while the vibrations turned my sphincters to mush.

I moaned and squirmed as my sexual arousal shot up like a rocket. Much longer of this and I'd either have an orgasm or a stroke! Before I realized it, my orgasm ripped through me. It felt as if one of my balls might shoot out my dick. I only squirted a thin watery stream. But I was sure some part of my brain must have come out too.

"Owwww! Ow, ow, ow!" I yelled at the violence of my ejaculation, which was greeted by another burst of mirth from my audience. I thanked God that Tonya snapped off the vibration.

I was panting for air and limp as a dishrag. Tonya lay her body down on top of me and kissed me tenderly,

"Now everybody's fucked you, Johnny! You belong to all of us," she murmured. "Your ass is going to crave cock from now on. But first you've got three man-loads of cum and a pansy squirt to clean up." She lifted up and started wiping up my watery spray off our stomachs and feeding it to me. I moaned as she slipped the dildo out of my ravaged anus and groaned at the feeling of it gaping open.

"Get me that cup," Tonya asked Brian and he handed her a small custard cup. I could feel cum already starting to leak out of my ass and wet my cheeks, but Tonya pressed the cup to my bottom and caught it.

"Up you go," Tonya urged and she pulled me up, keeping the cup positioned to catch all the oozing semen. "Now squat down and squirt all that nice cum into the dish, baby. Three big man-loads. Push it out or you'll be leaking all day!"

Meekly I squatted in front of my three fuckers. I gasped as the first squeeze started a gush of stringy white glop.

"Good girl! Oh, you really milked those studs! They'll have to rest up before they have any more for Tonya!" I could feel my insides churning and soon I pushed out another load of man-cream and watched it plop lewdly into the cup. With every push more dropped out, a little less each time, but soon the bottom of the cup was covered. Tonya wiped my ass with her finger and put it to my lips to lick clean. She briefly disappeared into the kitchen and reappeared holding a spoon.

"Hm! Lots of good manly cum for Johnny! Open wide!" The men laughed as Tonya dipped up a spoonful of the pearly white liquid and raised it to my lips. They laughed again when I close my mouth on the spoon, sucking their ejaculate off of it. The strange taste screamed at my instincts, "No!" but my sex-addicted brain only felt the satisfaction of accepting this gift from my Mistress and the cocks of the men who cuckolded and dominated me.

Spoonful after spoonful filled my mouth. The quantity forced me to really taste the men's semen over and over. When Tonya could scrape no more out with the spoon, she ordered me to lick the cup clean. I did so without hesitation, a little wistful that there was no more.

To my surprise Tonya did not tell me to suck the three men clean. She reserved that honor for herself, going from man to man and licking and sucking them in turn.

"Thank you for fucking my husband," she said to each of them. "Thank you for helping me train him to be the perfect cuckold husband." Each man murmured their response with their cock in my wife's mouth.

The fuckfest seemed to have tuckered everyone out, so we lounged around lazily, drinking coffee, reading the paper, and watching Sports Center on ESPN.

I found myself in a strange, happy mood, given what I'd been through. My ass throbbed pleasantly and it sent a warm glow all over my body. I felt totally relaxed, as if it might be dangerous for me to walk around, for fear I'd just melt to the ground. I had an uncanny feeling of goodwill toward the three men who had fucked me, as Tonya had said, a feeling bordering on "admiration." I felt connected to them now, as if we had a special bond. Not the bond of a friend or a lover, but the bond of a vassal to his liege. They were above me, superior to me, and I was honored that they'd used me. I basked in reflected glory of their magnificence.

"It's a nice day out," Tonya announced. "I'd like to go to the pool and show off my three stud boyfriends!"

I shuddered in surprise. I thought this was going to be our secret! Was she going to advertise her infidelity to the world? Was I to be the laughingstock of the neighborhood?

"Are you going to announce to everyone that you're fucking other men?" I protested.

"Johnny! Jealous pride doesn't suit a man who just let three studs fuck him up the ass—and enjoyed it! You agreed that you weren't going to stand in the way of my getting what I need from other men. Well that doesn't stop just at fucking. A girl likes to show off her man. She likes to dance with a manly man. She likes a virile arm around her.

"Since you're not man enough to give me all that, I'm going to get it elsewhere. There's other things you provide me that they can't: love, security, affection, tenderness. But manly stuff is their department. If you can't handle that, then maybe this cuckold thing won't work. Maybe we'll have to get a divorce."

"I don't want that! But do we have to parade it in public? I'm just asking to keep it behind closed doors."

Tonya stared sternly at me.

"Excuse us, gentlemen. Johnny and I need a minute." She led me into the bedroom ... er, her bedroom.

"Johnny, do you believe I love you?"

"Apparently not as much as you love other men's cocks!" I shot back.

"Oh, God, you're right, I do love a real man with a big cock! I didn't realize how much! But I've also found that I love cuckolding you! I love being in charge. I love pushing your limits and seeing what it does to you.

"Forbidden fruit is sweeter, Johnny! Every time I fuck these studs is better, hotter, because I'm married to you! They're fucking your wife's cunt, your wife's ass. It makes me the worst kind of slut and I love it!"

She looked me in the eye and a serious look came over her face.

"But it's not just about me, baby. It's about you too. Even if I would go back to being your faithful wife, could you be happy? Could you go back to fucking me, knowing that you could never gratify me? Could you stick your little wiener in me and shoot your wad, know that while you were rutting away that I was hungering for a real fuck from a real cock? What would that do to you, knowing you were just using my body to masturbate with for your selfish pleasure with no chance of pleasing me?

"I know you, baby. You're too good a person to do that. It would eat you up. Sure, you'd do it: your lust would take over eventually, but afterwards there would be an awful feeling of failure and guilt. We'd make love—well, no, it wouldn't be making love, would it? Let's say, you'd fuck me, but it would be less and less often. You'd feel worse and worse every time you gave in to your lust and used me. You'd be tortured by fears that I'd go out on you behind your back or that I'd leave you. Hell, eventually you'd probably be impotent. We'd drift apart. We'd end up divorced or miserable together."

She reached out and stroked my face.

"At least this way you can feel <u>proud</u> of the sacrifices you are making for me! We're being honest with each other. We're doing this together."

"But can't we just keep it in private?" I begged.

"Baby, one of the best things about this has been the tremendous feeling of freedom. It's as if I've been holding my breath for two years and now I can breathe! I can gulp big lungfuls of air; I can run; I can jump! I don't want to go back to holding my breath again!

"Baby, I don't want to sneak around. I don't want to hide. I'm not going to tell everybody I meet, 'Hey, we had an orgy at our house this weekend! Hey, I fuck my husband up the ass with a dildo!'. But neither am I going to skulk around, have Brian park two streets away and sneak away in the middle of the night. He's gonna park in our drive and come in the front door. If the neighbors notice his car was there all night or all weekend, let them think what they will. We're not breaking any laws. If I want to kiss Brian on the front porch when he comes and leaves, I will. If I want to grind against him when we dance, I will.

"And if I want to go to the pool with him in my skimpiest bikini and let him put suntan lotion on my back, I will. You're just going to have to get used to it. In fact, I think your being there along with us will be good for you, to work at whittling down that pitiful male ego of yours. Who would have thought a guy with such a little dick and who enjoys being fucked up the ass would put up such a fight about going to a pool?"

I felt something crumbling inside me and I knew I couldn't win, no matter what I said or did. I decided instead to take advantage of the moment of frankness on her part to ask a question that still kept weighing on my mind.

"Why do you want to make me want cocks so badly? Do you want me to be gay?"

She laughed.

"Oh, Johnny! Oh, there's lots of reasons. How do I explain them all in a way that makes sense? For one, it's another limit and challenging those limits is so scary and exciting! To get you to suck a cock or let a man fuck you is one limit, but to get you to <u>want</u> to suck a cock, to get turned on by another man's cock, that's a whole other limit. To get you to want to be <u>fucked</u> by another man, that's even better! To get you to hunger for cock, to dream about cock, to scheme about how you can get cock, to feel incomplete when you can't get cock, that will take you to a place you never imagined!"

"So it's just to be perverse?" I asked.

"Well, of course! But not just that. It's also out of guilt a little bit. I've deprived you of something very dear, to be able to fuck your wife—or any other woman, for that matter! That's a lot for any man to give up, even a small-dicked man like you. I guess I feel I owe you something to replace it, something erotic and exciting. Manly cocks give me so much pleasure that I want you to get that pleasure too.

"Of course, there's also a pragmatic aspect. I you enjoy big-cocked studs, you're not going to try to stand in my way. You'll be just as eager for these get-togethers as I am.

"Another reason, and probably the darkest, is that it gives me the upper hand in our relationship. If you're addicted to cocks, if you can't wait for me to invite some studs over, how are you going to tell me that I can't do this or I can't do that? If I have videos of you declaring how much you love a hard cock up your ass, how could you threaten to divorce me or to expose me to my family or my boss?

"But the biggest power it gives me is psychological. Any heterosexual man who develops an addiction to cock is deep down horrified at it. It weakens him, because he feels like a pervert. He feels out of control, at war with himself. He knows it is wrong but his traitorous penis stiffens at the thought of cock! His ass twitches at the thought of being filled with cock! He can't keep his eyes off other men's cocks in the urinal or locker room!

"He's horrified that he can't get hard for pussy anymore. He stops going to heterosexual porn sites, but he can't stop himself from going to gay sites. Even when he's looking at heterosexual porn, his eyes are on the man's cock and he's imagining that he's the girl! He feels schizophrenic when his body thrills at a cock throbbing in his mouth or his ass and his heart sings with joy when that cock fills him with man-cream!

"That weakness, that self-disgust makes him putty in a woman's hands! Because his worst fear is that his lust for cock makes him a monster to her, that no woman will want him. So any woman who accepts him despite his cock-lust is like a goddess to him. He worships the ground she walks on and will do anything for her!"

I was dumbfounded. It was like your opponent in a game explaining his whole plan of attack ahead of time, but you are helpless to stop him. Tonya was explaining how she was going to pervert and dominate me, but she had no worry that telling me would "give the game away." She was sure it would work even if I knew all about it—or that it had already worked and it was too late for me to stop it!

"I guess the last reason is that I think we've discovered that you have a need to be humiliated. A lot of cuckolds seem to have that. Nothing gets them as horned up as when they are embarrassing themselves, lowering themselves, appearlng weak, appearing perverted! So in a way, the more homosexuality goes against the grain, the more wrong it feels, the more thrilling it will be for you!"

We rejoined the men, who must have known about Tonya's plan beforehand, because they all had bathing suits and had changed into them. They all wore surfer-type suits, which surprised me. I expected Speedos. But then I realized that as well-endowed as they were, a speedo would be pretty uncomfortable, as well as obscene. I put on my boxer-length suit.

When Tonya came out of the bathroom my jaw dropped and I popped a boner. She was wearing one of the sexiest suits I'd ever seen, a suit I'd never laid eyes on before. It was two tiny triangles on top, that made her boobs look as if they were fighting to pop out, and the bottom was a thong with a back that was about the width of a piece of masking tape, not concealing her ass cheeks at all. I wasn't sure if that suit was legal in our city. That suit said one thing: "I fuck!"

A protest rose in my chest and died there. Tonya's recent lecture stifled it. This suit said, "Don't pay any attention that I'm married! Look at my tits! Look at my ass! Wouldn't you like to fuck me? For a good time, call Tonya: 555-1212." Tonya was backing up what she'd said: she was going to do as she liked, regardless of my humiliation—or even because of it.

The men whooped and whistled and swore and Tonya ate it up. She twirled and posed and rolled her hips to their catcalls, like a stripper at a burlesque show. Men are funny: even though they'd just seen her buck naked, somehow the skimpy bikini was even sexier.

She ordered me to pack fixings for a picnic lunch while she had the men fill an ice chest with beer, wine coolers, and sodas. We jumped in David's SUV. I was in the third row seat with the cooler. Tonya sat in the back seat, lying against Brian's chest, his arms around her. Tonya was his girl and David and Calvin were his henchmen. I was the toady.

It was a nice day and a Saturday, so the pool was crowded, making it inevitable that some of our friends and neighbors would be there. Tonya walked in brashly holding hands with Brian, while Calvin and David carried the cooler between them and I carried the picnic basket.

We all sat together and through the afternoon we all hovered around Tonya like drones and the queen bee. But Brian got the chair next to Tonya, she asked him to put on her suntan lotion, and she let him towel her off after they got out of the pool. No one from this planet could think anything but that this was her boyfriend.

Tonya's suit caused a lot of sensation among the onlookers. Every male's eyes were glued on her. Women's reaction ranged from shock to envy to scandalized to disgust. But nobody had the nerve to call the cops or the pool manager.

In the water Tonya and her men frolicked like high school kids, splashing and dunking each other. As if by mutual consent, I did not try to join in and no one invited me to. Brian and David had a little diving competition, each trying to outdo the other and impress Tonya with their athleticism. Brian was the more muscular of the two, but David was the more graceful diver. Tonya pronounced it a tie, gave them each a smoldering kiss, and said that she'd present them with their prize later!

A few neighbors and acquaintances stopped by our group and I was forced to introduce our "friends." I couldn't tell if it was my imagination, but I thought I saw some raised eyebrows and sideways glances exchanged, as Tonya held hands with Brian or made a point to put a hand on his arm or thigh as we exchanged pleasantries with our visitors. I hoped the sunny day might obscure the blush of embarrassment as I stood there like a fifth wheel.

Tonya made no attempt at any kind of cover story to explain the men's presence, introducing Brian as someone she met recently through work and the other two as his friends, "but we've gotten very close in a short time!" I could see our acquaintances wondering how close that was.

Tonya returned from the pool locker room and handed me a half-full beer bottle.

"I haven't forgotten about you, baby. I thought all this sun might be making you thirsty!"

I felt the warmth of the contents through the glass and knew the amber liquid was not warm beer.

"Drink up, baby," Tonya urged me. I took a swig and the contrast between the expected cold beer and warm piss shocked my tongue. Rather than thirst quenching, it was salty with a little sweetness from Tonya's diet sodas. It wasn't too bad to drink.

"Does it remind you of St. Pauli Girl? Because it's all girl! All natural!"

I quickly swigged the rest down. It amazed me to feel my penis start to swell from being made to drink urine in public, in front of our neighbors and friends, even though they were unaware. But I knew and the idea apparently excited Little Johnny.

Tonya surreptitiously ran her hand down the front of my swim trunks and confirmed her hopes.

"Oh, I see somebody likes that brand! You're a connoisseur, Johnny!" She kissed me and I wondered if she could smell her urine on my breath. Strangely I felt better even for that little scrap of attention.

As the session wore on, my embarrassment and humiliation started to sting less. I guess you can get used to anything. With my attention no longer on wondering what would happen next or what the other pool-goers would think of me, I was horrified to find that my eyes were not fastened on Tonya and her scandalous bikini. I found myself watching her lovers, watching their muscular and athletic bodies as they jumped off the diving board or frolicked in the water. They were specimens for sure. Everything a man should be, physically. And my eyes wandered to the front of their swimsuits. I knew they were everything a man could want to be down there too.

And ... and ... as images of their erect penises flashed before my mind's eye, I could feel my own begin to harden! I couldn't help but remember what their cockheads had felt like passing under my lips! I could almost feel their shafts fill my mouth and press against the back of my throat. The sensation of their slick lengths sliding back and forth was so real it was like a tactile hallucination. My mouth began to water, as if I hungered for that man-flesh again! And ... my sphincter flexed as I relived the feeling of being stretched, filled ... possessed!

As Tonya headed back toward our lounge chairs I startled, as if waking from a dream. I felt a sick feeling in my stomach as I came back to reality and realized I had been ... what? .. daydreaming? Fantasizing? Wanting?

We headed back to the house. David let Calvin drive and Brian and he sandwiched Tonya in the back seat. They took turns French kissing her and pulled her scrap of a top up so they could maul her breasts. David slipped his hand down her suit and started fingering her cunt. By the time we pulled in our drive, Tonya was moaning and hunching her hips. She pulled her top back over her nipples hurriedly and scrambled into the house. She and the two diving champs immediately continued their making out on the couch, sans suits.

"Johnny, make me an enema. Since these two tied, I've decided they should both get me at the same time. So bring the lube too."

By the time I got back with the enema bag, Tonya was in position, on all fours and fellating Brian while David fingered her pussy. She moaned as I inserted the enema nozzle and filled her ass with warm water. With regret she scampered to the john to release the liquid but hurried back. She lay Brian down on the couch.

"Johnny, hold his cock straight up so I can sit on it." I took Brian's rigid member in my hand an sighed as I felt it silky / steely thickness in my hand. I was glad my swimsuit concealed how my dick sprang to attention at the brief contact with Brian's cock. Tonya's cunt was already wet and engorged, making it easy to aim Brian's cockhead at her vagina. Despite her excitement, she had to work his girth into her until she was sitting on his pubes.

Tonya lay her boobs down on Brian's muscular chest, exposing her beautiful star of an anus.

"Please get me all ready for David's cock, baby. Brian's already filling me, so you'll need to stretch me and lube me good for me to fit David's meat in my ass!"

I applied a dollop of lube to Tonya's pucker, uncomfortably aware of being a half-inch away from Brian's cock, already buried in her pussy. When I pushed my finger up Tonya's ass I'd be stimulating Brian through the thin tissue separating her two tunnels! Skittishly I scooped up a fingerful of lube and worked it into her rear. Both Tonya and Brian moaned.

"Oh, that feels so nice, Johnny! Johnny, tell me, do you want David to fuck my ass right now?

"Uh ... yeah," I stumbled.

"How come?"

"Because you're really hot to fuck him and I want you to be happy."

"But wouldn't you like to fuck my ass? You're right, I'm hot, I'm turned on, ready to fuck. You've got your finger in me: wouldn't you like to stick your little willie in my tight ass? You could be practically rubbing it against Brian's cock! Wouldn't a cock-loving pansy like you love that?"

"But I know I could never satisfy you with my small penis. You need a big cock to fill you up. You ... you've been out showing off your body to all the guys at the pool and all that male attention has got you all hot. You've been flirting with your ... boyfriends ... all afternoon and you love it, especially since you did it all right under the nose of your cuckold husband. You're dying for a good fuck now and I'd just be a disappointment."

"Oh, God, baby, you are making my ass feel so nice. But you're my husband. Don't you deserve my ass more than David?"

"No, baby, you deserve more than I can give. David won your ass fair and square in the diving contest. I wasn't even in the running. He's the one you want, so he's the one I want you to have."

"Have what?"

"Have his cock ... fuck your ass."

"Oh, baby, my ass is ready for that big cock. Grease his cock up and tell me how good it feels in your hand. Then tell me how good it's gonna be in my ass! You know!"

I pulled up a glob of lube and began to smear it on David's pole. I took it in my hand and began to stroke it, covering it in grease.

"Do you like how his cock feels in your hand, Johnny?"

I closed my eyes and let myself feel it.

"It feels so different than mine. So much bigger. Longer. Heavy," I described. "It's spongy, but underneath that it is hard, strong. It's so warm. It's ... sexy. Exciting."

"You like it, don't you? You like to touch it. It's so manly, so powerful."

"Yes, it is," I agreed, and I let myself feel that, let myself enjoy the sensation of it sliding through my hand. "I love how it feels!"

"Oh, God, put it in me! I want it in me!" Tonya commanded. I pulled the head toward Tonya's gooey anus and watched David press it against the ring of muscle. The whole area caved in as her ass struggled to stretch around it. David goosed her teasingly and then pushed forward. Tonya whimpered and David rocked back and forth, relieving the pressure momentarily and then thrusting forward.

"Ow! Ow! Ow!" Tonya protested, but David knew there was nothing for it but to get past it. He began short fucking motions, gradually edging further and further up her ass.

"Oh, Jesus! Oh, God!" Tonya exclaimed, as she was split by two large cocks at once. Brian sought to distract her and he cupped her full breasts and began to squeeze and tweak them. Her attention divided, Tonya let David press himself into her ass completely.

"Oh, shit, I've got two cocks in me! Oh, God! This is how I want to die, full of big long hard cocks! Oh, fuck me! Fuck my ass! Fuck my cunt!"

David and Brian began to each thrust in their own rhythm, overwhelming Tonya's nervous system.

"I always want big cocks! All the time! No more little boy cocks! Oh God!" she yelled. "Tell me, Johnny, tell me you only want me to fuck other men's big cocks, that it excites you to see me fuck other men's big cocks!"

My dick stood out in my suit like a tent pole as I watched my wife squirm with these two sausages crammed in her. My mouth was dry. I took a deep breath.

"Oh, God, Tonya, it is so sexy to see you fuck them! My little dick is so hard! I want to see you fuck their big cocks. Please, please only fuck other men's big cocks from now on!" I cried.

"Come here, cocksucker!" Calvin roughly addressed me. He had his trunks off and he was casually stroking his black meat. "Bring that pin dick over here. Put it next to Mandingo here. This is what your wife's talking about. A real cock." His black cock looked like a different species it was much bigger than my white worm.

"Yours doesn't really measure up, does it? Why would a fine woman like that marry a little wimp like you anyway? She needs a man. Hell, looks like even then she's so hot she needs two or three! Ha ha! Well, your wife's well taken care of, but I'm feeling left out. Show Calvin how much you like big black cock!"

Without hesitation I dropped to my knees between his legs and I stared at the erect cock in front of me. Tonya told me she not only wanted me to suck cock: she wanted me to love sucking cock. She basically told me she wanted to mind-fuck me that way. Was her plan working? Did I crave sucking this cock?

It was almost, "If you have to ask, you've got your answer." Was that cock beautiful? Was it sexy? Did I want to lick it, mouth it, kiss it, suck it? Would it feel good, taste good, thrill me? I thought of all the feelings and fantasies I'd had at the poolside. The feeling of his cockhead, the sliding of his shaft through my lips! God, yes, I wanted it!

I closed my eyes and took the head in my mouth. Mmm! The spongy-hard slick warmth of it in my mouth was exciting. I could feel his arousal as I caressed the knob with my lips. I pressed the underside with my tongue and stroked the sensitive ridge with the tip of my tongue. If I was going to be a cocksucker I was going to be a good one.

And, hell, I might as well enjoy it too.

I threw myself into making love to this cock with my mouth. I ran my open lips up and down the shaft, covering it with my saliva, making it slippery. I flicked the slit with my thumb while I continued to mouth the shaft from all sides. I was rewarded by feeling Calvin squirm with arousal and I felt my own penis throb in sympathy.

I leaned back and continued to stroke the spit-slick shaft with my hand. Tonya was right. A gorgeous cock was a thing of beauty, a powerful sexual instrument. My being a man didn't change that. Sex was sex. Why shouldn't I enjoy sucking a nice cock, if I could? Wondering if her spell was working made me think about how this black penis felt in my hands. The silky feeling of my hands stroking it, the feel of the ridges and veins against my skin, the pumping of his blood, the growing warmth, the quiver of his excitement, the pride I felt in seeing a pearl of pre-cum form at his slit: these were all stirring. I bent down to taste his pre-cum, licking his pee slit with the tip of my tongue.

The knowledge that I was arousing this black man stoked my own excitement. I wanted to please him, to push his buttons. My own cock was hard, straining. I dove onto his prick and drive it to the back of my throat. He started squirming and I could feel his cock getting harder. I took the head in my mouth and I start suckling it like a tit. 'C'mon,' I thought, 'Give it to me! Give me your cock-milk! Feed me!'

"Oh, yeah," Calvin gasped. "Oh, fuck your faggot mouth! Suck my black cock, you fairy! Shit! Here it comes!"

I felt his cock swell another size and I felt the spasm with my hand. Suddenly hot cum filled my mouth, white gold. I felt four spurts and I was swallowing down his black seed. There was no denying the thrill of feeling that eruption, the very stuff of life striving to make a new life. It fascinated me, like the primal fascination with fire, or lightning, or a hurricane. And I had unleashed that. I controlled it. That was cool!

I knew how sensitive my cock became as soon as I came, but I didn't want to let go of Calvin's penis just yet. I cradled it in my mouth, gently sucking on it, milking the last few drops of precious sperm from its tip. Tentatively I pushed the head to the back of my throat, trying to get as much of his cock in my mouth as I could.

"Goddam! You suck cock as good as any girl! Some bitches can't get it out of their mouth fast enough when you come. And some dumb ass bitches keep sucking on it like you never came. You did it just right. I guess you know what a man likes! A bitch just has to guess!"

"Yoo-hoo, Johnny! Cleanup on Aisle 7!" called out Tonya. David had pulled out of her and was slumped on the sofa. Tonya was still mounted on Brian, holding a hand over her stretched asshole. I relinquished Calvin's penis and walked over to the couch. Halfway there I decided to surprise Tonya. I dropped in front of David and took his greasy and softening prick in my mouth. I tasted his cum smeared all over his cock and vacuumed the last drops out of his penis.

"Damn!" said Tonya. "I guess I'll have to learn to wait my turn! Looks like he'll go for the cock over a girl every time!"

I played along, taking my time to lick and suck David completely clean. To tell the truth, I wasn't minding communing with his delightful cock, just what Tonya was accusing me of. Tonya pulled herself off Brian's rod and quickly clamped her other hand over her gaping pussy.

"I suppose you'll do him next!" she said in mock impatience. "I'll just wait over here until you're ready for me!"

I inhaled the aroma of Brian's cock, drenched in Tonya's fragrant juices and his own semen. With relish I took his now-spongy flesh in my mouth and tasted the mixture. Brian groaned as I sucked gently on the head and extracted a few more droplets of cum from his slit. But I wasn't just about clean-up duty this time. I wanted to savor his manhood. I tongued his rim and licked all around the head, then. I laved his shaft up and down with my tongue.

I took my time, knowing Tonya wanted me to commune with her lover's' cocks. I almost felt as if I'd turned a corner. Why shouldn't I enjoy it? I wasn't getting any pussy, that was for sure. Take away the taboos and the fears, why not? My cock certainly didn't mind. It was leaking pre-cum copiously.

When I finished, Brian got up and I lay on the couch. I knew that Tonya would prefer to sit on my face so that she could both dominate me and deposit as much of her boyfriends' jism as possible in my mouth. Her cunt was an intoxicating mixture of the aromas of two days of fucking, with sperm of three different vintages. But I wasn't resisting. I was looking forward to drowning myself in the sperm of these he-men. I wanted to serve Tonya, but I was eager to serve them too! I lapped hungrily at her pussy while Brian's spend trickled out.

Then she reversed her position and placed her red and wrinkled anus to my lips. My tongue easily entered her and encountered the taste of

David's semen and the slipperiness of globs of lube. I thrilled at the thought that her anus was being stretched to accommodate these men's cocks more and more easily, almost like the Story of O! In a way she was modifying her body for their pleasure. I drove my tongue into her as far as I could in the excitement of that idea. Here I was, cheerfully offering up the virgin ass of my bride to the cocks of these dominant males! A shiver went down my spine. I might as well take delight in being a cum whore if had to be one anyway.

The sexual tension was lulled for the time being and we turned on the TV and channel-surfed. Tonya again made it clear that Brian was the alpha male, as she sat in his arms and let him hug her and toy with her tits and ass. After a while everyone but me had pulled on a robe. Tonya directed me to put on the frilly apron and start making dinner and see that everyone had drinks or snacks. I tossed a salad and baked some potatoes and grilled some burgers on our patio.

I was glad that our backyard had some privacy, as Tonya had me out there with just an apron on, with my backside hanging out. Tonya and the men took turns laughingly smacking my exposed ass for laughs. I blushed some, but actually the touch of the men's hands on my ass sent a warm shiver up my spine! It was as if their smacks signaled that I was a sex object, their sex object. Their hands on my bottom made my asshole twitch with the memory of their much more intimate invasions.

The group was lighthearted and jovial as they discussed how to spend the evening. They all decided that we should go to the dance club. Tonya expected that Audrey might be there and maybe some of her friends.

Tonya let me help her pick out an outfit to wear to the club: low cut, skin-tight, short, with a half-cup bra and thong panties. To my horror she insisted on putting some eyeliner and mascara on me, "to give you a little bit of a metrosexual look. Maybe you'll get some action of your own, babe!" For her part she went all out on the false eyelashes, eyeshadow, blusher, and lipstick, to the point of a Betty Boop look.

As we walked into the club I was struck the same way as I was at the pool: Tonya was the star and we circled her like planets. Her sexual allure was the gravity that pulled four men along with her as surely as if we were on leashes.

On Saturday night the club was loud, crowded, and hot. We were lucky to find that Audrey and two of her friends had staked out a booth, although her friends had already attracted a couple of dance partners. We crammed in as best we could, stealing a couple of chairs from nearby. Tonya made no effort to disguise her interests, sitting Brian on one side of her and Calvin on the other. David squeezed next to Audrey, as they were already "acquainted."

It was suggested, if course, that I stand the first round of drinks for everyone. Luckily the fellows were satisfied with a couple of pitchers of beer. Once everyone had drinks, the girls wanted to dance. Tonya grabbed Brian as her partner for the first dance, but she ended up dancing with all the guys, as did Audrey. As if they'd all agreed ahead of time, no one asked me to dance or even commented on my not dancing, as if I weren't there. Her friends seemed satisfied with the guys they'd picked up earlier, so it began to feel as if Audrey had de facto become a member of our little troupe.

I found somehow that the dance club made me feel worse than our private orgy. Here I was almost forgotten. The men were paying all their attention to the women. I was feeling ... jealous?

Of course as Tonya got a couple of drinks in her, the dancing started to look more like foreplay standing up. She danced plastered against whomever was her partner, whether facing him or backing up to him, grinding her groin or ass against his crotch. In her defense it was only slightly more lewd than what a lot of the other couples were doing. It was a rather uninhibited crowd.

When I came back from the bathroom I found Tonya and Brian unabashedly French kissing in our booth. I sat down and stared at the dance floor, trying not to watch them. Once again my peter turned traitor, stiffening in my pants as if humiliation were an aphrodisiac. Blood surged to my cheeks and my dick in equal measure as I sat feet away from my wife making out with another man in public.

Just then Calvin deposited Audrey in the seat next to me and headed to the john.

Audrey took in the scene in our booth and shook her head. She leaned over toward me and said to me, too low for Tonya to hear.

"Why do you let her do that to you, Johnny?"

My cheeks turned redder and I looked down at the floor. What should I say? How could I explain what I couldn't understand myself? I looked at her with a look of bewilderment and desperation.

"I love her. I love her and I'll do anything not to lose her," I said. That sounded about right. It sounded half noble and half pathetic. That was me in a nutshell.

"You'll even put up with that?"

"That's not half of it...."

"Oh shit! You mean...?"

I swallowed hard and looked down, saying nothing, but my silence told her all she needed to know. My cheeks burned with embarrassment.

"Jesus!' Audrey exclaimed.

"What can I do? I can't stop her. I don't want to lose her! I have to ... make compromises."

"Compromise? What do you get out of it?"

"It's hard to explain...."

"Damn! I don't know what to think! You're either a wimp or a saint! I don't know which."

"Neither do I, Audrey!" I cried. "Maybe both."

I looked up and saw Tonya and Brian looking at us, having come up for air. They could tell we were having some kind of intense discussion. Tonya broke the tension by scooting sideways and announcing that she needed the loo and inviting Audrey to accompany her. They were gone for what seemed like a long time. When they came back Audrey looked flushed and flustered and Tonya look like the cat that ate the canary. Tonya sat next to me for the first time that night and kissed me full on the lips.

"What's going on?" I whispered to her.

"I told Audrey a little bit about our 'party.' She's very interested to find out more about our new 'lifestyle.' I invited her to come back to our house. She's thinking about it. Order her another drink to help her make up her mind!"

"You told her everything?"

"Not everything, no. I don't think she'd believe everything if I told her! You need to see that kind of thing with your own eyes! But I told her enough to whet her appetite! Hey, don't blame me: you started it! She told me you told her Brian was banging me and I had your permission!"

"Well, I didn't exactly say that. She sort of guessed and I didn't deny it."

"Well, I think it'll be fun if she comes along, so just get used to the idea."

I obediently ordered Audrey another margarita. Audrey was flashing me looks and then brashly raised her glass and proposed a toast: "To Tonya and Johnny!" Brian, Calvin, and David raised their glasses enthusiastically and downed their beers. Audrey practically chugalugged her margarita, which suggested to me that she'd made up her mind to come.

"Let's get out of here!" she declared and we headed out to David's SUV. Audrey piled in the third seat with David, and Tonya was between Brian and Calvin in the back seat. I'd had the least to drink, so I was elected to be the chauffeur, of course. Tonya started trading off kissing and fondling Brian and Calvin right away. Not far out of the parking lot I heard a zipper and at a stoplight I turned around to see Tonya giving Calvin some head.

"God, Tonya!" Audrey exclaimed. "You weren't kidding! Watch out, you'll get us arrested."

"Wait 'til you get a taste of this licorice stick, Audrey, and you won't be able to control yourself either!"

"Vanilla ain't bad, either!" she responded and began kissing David.

I was amazed that Tonya managed to divide her attentions equally between Calvin and Brian, going from fellating the black man to letting Brian suck her tits, pulling down her top to give him access. I heard Audrey moaning from the third seat, suggesting that David had slipped a finger in her panties. The pheromones in the car had me light-headed and my cock standing at attention. I ran a couple of yellow lights getting us home as fast as I could.

When we pulled in the drive, everyone scrambled out, rearranging their clothing as best they could. We gathered in the living room. Tonya immediately told me to get everyone a beer.

"So Johnny, you don't mind if Tonya fucks these guys?" Audrey asked me point blank.

Before I could answer, Tonya jumped in.

"Show her why I have to go outside my marriage, Johnny. Show her Little Johnny."

I looked at Tonya pleadingly, hoping she'd stop me, but she stared back unflinchingly. I began to undo my belt and skim off my pants. I forgot that I was wearing women's satin panties. Until Audrey burst out laughing.

"He's gay? That's it?" I blushed as I realized that Audrey was more shocked by my pink panties than she had been by Tonya blowing Calvin in the car.

"No, he's not gay—or at least we're not sure. The panties were my idea. It's what's in the panties. Show her, Johnny."

I quickly pulled off the panties, uncovering my cock, which had softened with my nervousness.

"Get it hard, Johnny. Show Audrey what I had to settle for for two years. Audrey, why don't you rile David up, so we'll have a real cock to compare Johnny to?"

Mortified I took my dick in hand and began to stroke it, while Audrey unzipped David and fished his snake out. David had also lost some of his starch at the oddness of the situation, but he soon rallied as Audrey used her hand to encourage him.

"Sit next to Audrey, honey, and let her compare you two close up."

The thought of Audrey touching me brought my dick to full mast.

"Go ahead, Audrey. Feel Johnny's prick, then David's and tell me if you ... er ... 'grasp' the problem!"

Audrey took my penis in her hand and I stifled a moan. She was the only woman other than Tonya who'd touched my cock in years. I could already see a droplet of pre-cum peek out of my slit. Audrey helped me and gave my shaft a couple of strokes. Then she reached back to David's boner and hefted it.

"Oh my! That's a big difference! David must have at least twice as much meat as Johnny. I see your point."

"And that's just in your hand. Imagine the difference in your cunt!" Tonya pointed out. "Here, you two. Stand up. Bring your cocks side by side. Or, I mean, bring David's cock next to Johnny's peepee!"

David and I awkwardly stood face to face, our penises sticking our straight in front of us, and brought them side by side. David's clearly extended at least two or three inches farther than mine.

"That's the difference between his cock filling you up to the top, banging into your cervix with every thrust, girlfriend, instead of feeling a little worm squirming away inside you," Tonya told us.

"Oh, I've had the pleasure of David's," Audrey said. "I see what you mean about Johnny."

"So tell Audrey what we decided to do about it, babe."

I looked down while I spoke.

"We decided that Tonya deserved to fuck men who could satisfy her..., men with bigger cocks."

"And what do you do while I'm fucking them?"

"I watch."

"And?"

"I ... masturbate."

"You come too, while you watch them fuck me, don't you? It excites you to watch a real man fuck me. And what do you do after?"

"I ... eat your ... pussy...."

"No! You're kidding!" Audrey gasped. "With their ... stuff ... in there?"

"And what else do you eat?"

"Their cum. I suck out their cum."

"Oh, Jesus, this is making me wet!" Audrey cried. "I've got to see that!"

"And that's not all," Tonya promised. "But that's enough talk! Time to put Johnny's mouth where my pussy is!"

Tonya pulled down her panties and lay back on the couch, her pussy obscenely exposed as she hiked up the hem of her dress.

"Come here, Johnny, and get me ready to fuck one of these studs."

My nakedness allowed everyone to see that my dick was standing tall with arousal through all these revelations and despite the fact that I was being ordered to help my wife commit adultery. My cock bobbed as I walked over between Tonya's splayed legs and began to lick and suck her cunt. All of the dancing, foreplay, and sex talk already had her pussy hot and wet, so there was little need to get her "ready." She merely wanted to flaunt her control over me and demonstrate my participation in my own cuckolding!

Tonya began moaning with arousal. She was already halfway to an orgasm.

"OK, Johnny, you pick my man for me. Get them nice and hard and wet for me first, will you? Pick your favorite cock for me to fuck."

I was nonplussed at her command. She was showing off for Audrey. Did I have a favorite cock? I guess it would be my first, the alpha. I went to Brian and began to unbuckle his belt, while he took off his shirt. I pulled down his pants and underwear and his thickening cock sprung up at my face. As Audrey gasped, I took Brian's penis in my hands and dropped to my knees and guided it into my mouth.

But despite having Audrey there and being on display in public, my main emotion was not nervousness this time. My chief feeling was excitement to have a hard cock in my mouth again!

"Oh, Jesus! He is a fag!" Audrey declared.

As I worked my mouth wetly all around the head of Brian's rod, I heard Tonya explain.

"No, there's a difference between liking cocks and being gay. I introduced Johnny to cocksucking—and I think he really likes it—but I don't think he's into men. It's more like a fetish. You can get off on baby bottles and diapers without liking actual babies, you know?"

"You were right, what you said at the club—if you'd just told me I'd never have believed it!" Audrey exclaimed.

"Believe it! Oh, baby, that looks so good! Put him in me!" Tonya commanded.

Inwardly I protested having to leave off making love to Brian's cock. But Audrey watched with her jaw dropped while I led Brian over by his penis and used its bulbous head to nudge Tonya's dewy labia apart. I held his cock, slick with my saliva, pointed at her yearning vagina.

"Tell us what you want, Johnny. Ask Brian to do what you want."

"I want you ... to fuck my wife. Please fuck her!"

With that Brian pressed his sword into Tonya's scabbard. As eager as she was to accept it, as always the girth of his manhood had to push through the resistance of her swollen tissues and stretch her open. Tonya grunted with the effort and with the satisfaction of his penetrating her.

"Oh, fuck me, Brian! Fuck me with your magnificent cock! Johnny, you beat off! Show Audrey how much you get off watching your wife fuck another man!"

I could feel relays in my brain short-circuiting. Just as Tonya had said, humiliation was an aphrodisiac to me, and performing in front of Audrey was overwhelming! The power of Tonya's control over me and the intoxication of my mounting sexual arousal swept away all my civilized instincts and inhibitions. I opened the lube and applied it to my rigid peter as if in a dream. I saw Audrey watching me and I knew I was humiliating myself in front of her, but it was impossible to stop myself.

I trembled with the delight of my greasy hand on my cock. Seeing Tonya positively writhe under Brian was deliriously exciting! I watched his thick cock pull out of her cunt, shiny with the juices of her arousal. I vibrated with joy at the sounds of her animal lust for him. They were a sexual god and goddess whose mating lit up the stars.

I felt my own orgasm building and I was glad to lay my poor tribute at their altar. I cried out as my cum rushed up my shaft and splattered out onto my palm. I whimpered: the humiliation of coming in front of Audrey drove my excitement to new heights! I thrilled to debase myself further by licking up my semen, adding the acrid taste of my own cum to the tortured joy of the experience.

"Ewww!" exclaimed Audrey.

As I came back down to earth I could tell that Tonya was coming down off her orgasm while Brian neared his. In my mind I urged him on and I smiled as his thrusts and cries signaled that he was unleashing his army of sperm into her womb. Only the absence of an egg in her uterus kept this from being the ultimate union, the planting of a new life as the product of their passion.

I waited patiently while Brian enjoyed the afterglow of feeling her cunt hugging his spent cock, trying to milk the last of his semen from him. Finally he rolled off her and I hungrily took his hot wet cock in my mouth and eagerly sucked Tonya's juices and his ejaculate off it. Again I was inspired to think of his cock as the attribute of a god and myself as the lucky acolyte allowed to attend it.

His cock clean, I descended on Tonya's sloppy cunny and joyfully buried my face in her slick flesh. I feasted at the ooze coming out, thrilling at the strong taste of Brian's cum. After a couple minutes Tonya indulged me by turning over to plant her pussy on my face and squeezed out more globs of Brian's deposit.

All of this was accompanied by a cacophony of Audrey's cries of amazement and disgust.

"God, it's as if he likes it! He must be gay!"

In my altered state I considered her calumny a badge of honor. Her disapproval proved that what I was doing was above and beyond the call of duty, was a sacrifice of noble dimensions.

I looked over at Audrey to find, to my amazement, that she had her own dress hiked up and her hand in her panties, scrubbing away at her clit. A large wet spot darkened the crotch of her panties. Despite her cries of disbelief, the scene had obviously stoked her own lusts! Next to her David was less frantically stroking his stiff erection.

"Why don't you let Johnny help you with that, Audrey?" Tonya leered. "He's very good at it. I guess he hopes to make up in enthusiasm what he lacks in endowment!"

I stared at Tonya in wide-eyed wonder. She was going to let me eat out another woman? Audrey seemed equally incredulous.

"You want your husband to lick my pussy?" she exclaimed.

"Sure! The least he can do is warm you up for one of the real men."

Audrey looked at me quizzically, but then her oozing pussy made up her mind for her. In a flash she shoved her panties down and scooted forward to the edge of the love-seat. She lay back and spread her legs, proffering her pudendum for my attention.

I moved toward her with cautious reverence. It had been years since I'd seen a live pussy other than my wife's! I could hardly believe my luck. As I neared it the powerful scent spoke of Audrey's arousal at the sex show she'd just seen! Her aroma was different from Tonya's but still extremely sexy. Her pubic hair was sparser than Tonya's, but I was excited to see that she wasn't clean shaven. Bald cunts were a fad of which I heartily disapproved.

I wanted to admire her pussy longer, but she was so aroused that I was afraid to make her wait. I bent down and planted a kiss on her clitoris and was rewarded with a gasp, as if she hadn't really believed I would suck her. I pressed my lips hard against her labia and gently sucked them into my mouth, tasting her juices for the first time. I thrilled at the idea that I was in a very small way turning the tables on Tonya, that I was cheating on her with another woman!

I made bold to wrap my arms around her thighs and I drew her crotch hard against my mouth. I sucked up her dew greedily and dipped my tongue into her center, seeking more. I heard her softly moan and I knew I was pleasing her. I drove my tongue as deep as I could into her vagina, lapping up her juices, and I licked up to her clitoris again. I pulled her bud into my mouth and flicked at it with my tongue. I could feel her shudder with pleasure and grind her pelvis against my face.

I looked up and found Tonya pulling Audrey's dress over her head and unhooking her bra. Then I was astonished to see Tonya take one of Audrey's breasts in her hand and caress it. Audrey gasped with pleasure. Tonya leaned over and kissed Audrey's moaning mouth full on the lips. I was mesmerized by the erotic sight, but Tonya had more tasks for me.

"I think Audrey's more than ready for a cock now. Why don't you pick one for her? And get it hard and wet like you did for me"

I knew she'd had David before and I didn't know how she'd feel if I foisted Calvin on her, so I decided to play it safe. I chose David. I saw Audrey smile as I knelt between David's legs and began to suck on his knob. A little thrill went through me as I enjoyed the sensation of sucking a hot erection again. My little penis started to rally at the arousal I was getting from this oh-so-forbidden act! I licked a glob of pre-cum off its tip, so I knew David was ready too. I gave his cock a few good sucks and then I motioned for him to mount Audrey.

Audrey watched with rapt attention as I guided David's tool up to her pussy. Tonya had been stroking Audrey's clit as she suckled at one tit. As I drew David's cock to Audrey's slit, Tonya took two fingers and kept Audrey's labia apart, making Audrey's vagina leer open. I shivered at the perversity of the scene before me. Tonya and I were a team orchestrating Audrey's fucking!

David's big cock more than filled Audrey's opening. Audrey moaned as she felt his head stretch her entrance and demand admission. I still held his shaft as her prodded at her vault, collecting her juices to lubricate his way. With several jabs he managed to bury himself in her and he groaned in satisfaction.

"So full! So good!" Audrey exulted. "So big! Be gentle!" David was horny enough to ignore this plea and he began to slowly pump his prick in and out of her. She winced and groaned but soon she was crying out in pleasure and growling at him to fuck her. After that, all could be heard was both of them moaning. Tonya continued to stroke Audrey's nipples with her fingers, which drove Audrey wild and was so sexy to me that I could only stare in amazement!

"Come, baby, come hard on that great big nasty cock!" Tonya urged.

Audrey was so turned on that she sounded as if she were in pain. Then her orgasm ripped through her like a seizure. She was bucking up into David, as if she wanted his cock to come out her back, she needed it in her so much!

David could not hold back after that. Soon he was screaming out his own climax, pumping his cum deep into her.

"Good girl," Tonya whispered to Audrey. "Milk every drop from that big cock!" David was panting with exertion.

"Shit! I came so hard ... I think I strained something! Oh shit, that was hot!"

He rolled off Audrey and Tonya clamped her hand over Audrey's cavern, holding the cum in. She began to kiss Audrey, first in little pecks all over her face and then kissed her deep on the mouth. It was as if she were rewarding Audrey or congratulating her on her initiation into our circle. But I suspected her initiation had only just started.

I bent over and took David's ebbing erection in my mouth and delighted at the new taste of Audrey's spend mixed with his. I licked every inch of his cock and even sucked the goo out of his pubic hair.

"Audrey," murmured Tonya, "time for Johnny to do his thing."

"Oh, God, no, I'll be gross down there!" she protested.

"Oh, no, baby, he loves it! That sloppy mess is like candy to him! He'd rather lick a well-fucked pussy than an empty one. Tell her, Johnny."

"Um ... uh ... well, it's so sexy then. All your juices ... and it's all engorged and your lips are all full ... and your ... vagina is so wide open...."

"But it's got his cum in it! You'll be eating a man's cum!"

Well it's ... it's not so bad. It's ... it's sex, pure sex. It's got some power ... something primal about it. And ... well, it's dirty. A dirty, forbidden, taboo thing to do."

"He gets off on that, babe! He's kinky. He's got a tiny little thingie, so he's got to get his kicks other ways. Trust me, you'll love it! Once you get over the strangeness, you'll want him to do it every time. The feeling of power Is awesome! Your cunt is gaping, dripping with cum and this guy is begging to eat it up! The more disgusting you think it is, the more of a rush to think that he's willing to debase himself just to eat your pussy!"

Tonya locked eyes with me. She silently mouthed the words, 'Beg her.'

"Um ... Audrey, may I please eat your pussy? I'd love to eat David's cum from your pussy. Please?" I felt a twinge of anxiety. I was afraid she'd say no! Tonya wasn't the only one who wanted me to do this. I was looking forward to tasting the strong flavor of David's hot cum.

Audrey didn't answer, but Tonya pulled her hand away from her opening and started kissing Audrey on the mouth again. I took my cue and quickly latched my mouth onto her pussy, catching the gush of cum that came out. I thrilled at the strong taste of semen. I looked up and Tonya was Frenching Audrey and cupping one breast while tweaking the nipple. I sucked for all I was worth on Audrey's cunt. The stink of her arousal was overpowering and I reached my tongue as deep as I could, reveling in the stretched openness of her tunnel. There could be no doubt that a big cock had been here. This was a cunt my poor prick could never produce.

Audrey began to moan and hunch into my face and I realized that Tonya and I were bringing her to another peak. I drifted up to her clit and began to suck and flick it with my tongue. Tonya moved down to suckle at one tit while fingering the other one and Audrey began to groan. Seconds later she was crying out in orgasm as her cunt convulsed against my mouth.

"Good girl," Tonya repeated, as if encouraging a new student who had mastered a technique.

"Oh, God!" Audrey panted.

"If you think that's good, Audrey, you've got to mount his face. Johnny, lie down," she told me. "Plant your cunt right on his mouth, babe," she told Audrey. "Ride his face! He likes that. He likes to drown in your pussy! He wants to get every drop of David's cum he can."

Audrey looked a little dubious, but she squatted down as Tonya told her to. I again entered the blissful state where a pussy was my whole world. Audrey's thighs gripped my cheeks and I was submerged in swollen female flesh. I may have missed out on getting a big cock, but men who don't go down on women are missing one of the best things on God's green Earth. Gravity added to the engorgement caused by her arousal and the thick heavy feel of her labia on my mouth and on my lips was Heaven.

Towering over me and feeling my eagerness quickly overcame Audrey's initial hesitation.

"That's it, pin dick! Eat the pussy your dick will never touch! Taste the cum a real man put in there! Feel how he's stretched my cunt!"

She said all the right things to fire my lust. My prick started to swell yet again.

"Look, Audrey, he's getting excited! Make him masturbate while he eats David spew out of your cunny!"

"Yeah, pansy boy. Beat your little willie while your mouth is full of another man's spunk!"

I was happy to oblige. With Audrey's pudendum covering my face and my hand on my Johnson, I was in an erotic haze. There was no urgency, since had come not long ago. It was laid back.

But Tonya had more tricks to show Audrey. She pulled Audrey up off of me and the kissed her, breast to breast and pussy to pussy. Then she bade me to get up.

"Calvin's been waiting patiently, but we mustn't be ungracious hosts, darling. What do you want to offer him? My cunt? My ass? Your mouth? Your...."

I cut her off.

"Your ass!" I interjected.

"You want this black stud to fuck your wife's ass?"

"But Tonya," Audrey interrupted, "he's so big! You're not gonna let him do your ass! He'll tear something!"

"Oh, you'd be surprised what a horny gal can get in there. Don't worry, I've already taken all these guys in my ass! It wasn't easy, but once you get used to it, butt fucking might become one of your favorite things. It's so dirty, isn't it, Johnny?"

"Johnny's fucked your ass?"

"You answer her, Johnny," Tonya insisted.

"Er, no, I never have."

"What I meant was that Johnny likes how dirty it is when I let other men fuck me up the ass! I think it's his favorite thing. Which turns you on more, Johnny, to watch another man fuck my pussy or my ass?"

I looked down at the floor. I saw my cock stiffen as Tonya humiliated me.

"Um, your ass," I answered.

"How come?"

"Um, because, like you said, it's dirtier. More slutty. More forbidden. And because you never let me do it. So you're giving them something you never even gave me."

"And that excites you? I would think it'd piss you off," Audrey commented.

"I can't explain it either. But it does."

Tonya came over and started rubbing my nipples with both hands, expertly tweaking and stroking them, to arouse me to where I'd do anything she told me to do.

"So beg me, Johnny. Beg me to let you watch Calvin fuck my ass. Tell me how much you want it."

I shuddered at the sensations her fingers were causing and the excitement her words were inciting.

"Unh! Uh, please ... Tonya, let Calvin fuck your ass. I want you to."

"Anything to please. my husband!" Tonya teased. "But it's up to you to get me ready. You get the enema and clean me out. Then you relax me with your mouth and fingers and lube me up for Calvin."

"Oh shit! This is wild!" Audrey exclaimed. "What'd I get myself into here?" she asked.

"A pot of jam, babe!" Tonya smirked.

When I came back with the prepared enema, I found Tonya already Frenching Calvin and stroking his ebony erection. Audrey sat on his other side and Tonya handed the black cock off to her. Calvin was equally happy to turn to Audrey and stick his tongue down her throat.

"Hang that up, baby," Tonya said, referring to the enema. "I want you to eat my ass a little first. I love to feel your tongue up there."

"He's gonna put his tongue up your ass?"

"Oh, Audrey, he loves my ass. The dirtier something is, the more Johnny loves it. He'll eat yours too if you want."

"Oh my!" Audrey replied with stunned amazement.

I knew what Tonya wanted me to do, so I lay on the floor so could sit on my mouth, planting my face firmly between her cheeks. I quickly set to plumbing her sphincter, plunging my tongue as deeply as I could.

"Mmm, that's nice," Tonya cooed, squirming on my tongue in delight. "Nothing like a big cock, but nice." She rocked and undulated, seeking more stimulation. "There's something about having someone licking your asshole that is so wrong, so dirty, that I just love it!" Tonya gushed. "Mmmm," she purred, rocking against my face. I felt her sphincter grab my tongue and then relax, welcoming my licking and probing. My dick pulsed with renewed excitement.

"Oh, I'm all ready for my enema now, baby!" Tonya announced and she lay down and pulled her knees up, exposing her already loosening rosebud. I slipped the enema nozzle in and released the valve.

"Unh!" Tonya grunted. "Mmmm," she hummed as she felt the warm water fill her. "You're so good, baby, getting my ass all ready for my black lover to fuck. C'm'ere and let me give you a kiss." Tonya put her. Hand behind my head and kissed me. Deeply. "I love you so much for giving my ass away to a big manly cock! That makes you such a dear, my cuckold husband."

Tonya rested a few moments and then jumped up to release the enema in the bathroom. She then lay down again on her back.

"Lube me up for my ass-fuck, hubby," she directed. I pushed one, then two greasy fingers into her, while she hummed and purred. I could see Audrey wide-eyed at the sight of my fingers stretching Tonya's bottom easily, sawing in and out freely.

"Now get Calvin all ready, Johnny. Give him a little oral and then grease him up. Audrey, why don't you keep one hand on Calvin while Johnny works?"

Audrey obediently held Calvin's shaft straight up while she watched his knob go into my mouth. Calvin moaned as I pressed the sensitive spot just below his slit with the broad of my tongue. Audrey kept one hand at the base of Calvin's cock, but I saw the other sneak down to stroke her clitoris, which fired my lust further. I sighed and slipped into a brief sub-space as I forgot about everything for a minute except how good it felt to have Calvin's black cock in my mouth.

Then I shook myself back to the situation. I grabbed the Vaseline and I applied lube thickly, spreading it evenly up and down, stroking Calvin's beautiful organ. For a few more moments this big African cock was all mine! I took the opportunity to savor the feel of its soft-hardness against my palm and fingers. I felt Calvin's hips start to squirm.

"Put him in me, Johnny!" Tonya urged. She pulled up her knees, exposing her glistening and eager anus. Audrey was rapt, watching as I held Calvin's greasy penis and placed its head squarely at Tonya's starburst. Calvin pressed forward and Tonya grunted. Her whole anal area dipped in like the caldera of a volcano.

"It'll never fit!" Audrey warned, until Calvin's cockhead pushed through the ring of flesh. He stopped and fucked back and forth, teasing Tonya's muscles. He pushed in another couple of inches and Tonya gasped and panted, willing herself to relax. Audrey winced and shook her head almost imperceptibly, no doubt in disbelief at the thought that her own rectum could ever stretch to admit such a monster.

"Tonya, he's going to hurt you!" Audrey exclaimed, unable to stop herself.

"Unh! Umph!" Tonya grunted as her asshole strained to accommodate such a large cock. "Oh, it isn't easy, but it's worth it. Once you get ... unh! ... used to it, it feels ... so ... good! Oh, God!" she cried as Calvin reached the top of her rectum. "So deep!" Tonya gasped. "So full! So big! Oh God!"

Calvin grunted and began slowly fucking my wife's ass in short strokes, almost massaging her bowel with his scepter.

"Oh, it's so there. I can feel every millimeter! Oh God! It's ... it's invading your insides. It's taking you, possessing you! Oh, God, I love it! I'm your whore, Calvin! I'm your ass-fucking whore! Fuck my adulterous white ass! Show my wimp husband who owns this ass!" Tonya was almost growling now.

I watched in fascination as my bride's reddened anus once again stretched tight around that black shaft like a rubber band at its limit. Her ass sunk in at every in-thrust and stretched outward as Calvin pulled back. Tonya was pulling her knees back tight to offer her ass and open herself as much as she could to this invasion.

I grasped my own rampant erection with my greasy hand and shuddered with the perverse pleasure that watching my own cuckolding gave me. Why? Why did this feel so satisfying, so compelling? To give my wife away, to masturbate in front of others while acknowledging my own inferiority and helplessness? To willingly participate in opening her ass and placing my rival's cock into her? My throbbing cock and the transcendent joy it gave me was my only answer.

I sneaked a glance at Audrey and thrilled to see her wantonly rubbing her own pussy. She grasped one tit with her other hand and pulled at her taut nipple. I saw her plunge one finger and then two into her cunt, bringing glistening drippings out.

Now Calvin was fucking away without restraint and I could see his cock slipping out with less and less resistance.

"Oh, yes!' Tonya exulted. "Oh, it feels so good! Oh, I only want big long cocks in my ass! Rape my ass, Calvin! I want to feel your cum in my ass!"

Tonya looked at me.

"I want your cum too, Johnny. Show me how much it pleases you to see another man fuck my ass, to see him pleasing me like you never could! Bless this union with your spunk! Come in your hand while Calvin comes in your wife's ass!"

Her words sent chills down my spine and a fire up my penis. I shuddered and I felt my dick swell and then spit my meager ejaculation onto my cupped palm. I jerked with convulsive release for the second time in a short while.

Tonya smiled and lay back and closed her eyes, swallowed up by the frenzy of Calvin's assault on her bowel. As I stared at the translucent puddle in my hand, I heard Calvin bellow. I looked up to see him straining to push his cock deep into Tonya's colon as his cock spewed his seed into her.

"Oh, God! Oh, oh, oh!" Tonya exulted as she felt his hot cum shoot deep in her. Her head whipped back and forth deliriously as she spasmed around his rod.

"Jesus!" swore Calvin as his sensitive penis felt Tonya's orgasm ripple through her rectum.

"Fuck! Fuck! Shit!" exclaimed Audrey as her hand wrung an orgasm from her clitoris. She plunged two fingers into her slit, probing her G-spot, squeezing another shudder from her body.

Tonya lay spent, her eyes closed, head lolling to one side. Languorously she opened her eyes and looked at me as out of a daze.

"Baby, I love you so much that you gave me that," she whispered just loud enough for me to hear. Her regard zeroed in on my cupped hand.

"Show me what you've got there, baby."

I stretched out my hand tentatively. Tonya smiled.

"Oh, that's good, baby. You love me enough to get excited when you see me getting a good fucking. You bless our union with your little offering there. Give me a kiss while Calvin still has his big cock up my ass. Mind, don't spill!"

I leaned down and our mouths met and Tonya kissed me deeply, tenderly. She reached up and stroked my cheek with one hand.

"Johnny, tell me you're done with jealousy and male pride. Tell me you release me to fuck anyone, anywhere, anytime I like. Tell me you give up all husbandly claims to my cunt or my ass or my mouth."

"I do. You're free," I choked out huskily, looking into her dewy eyes.

"Except for the cum in them. Tell me you will eat every drop of cum that other men shoot in me or on me. You'll suck or lick up every drop as a token of your love for me and your acceptance of being a cuckold."

"I will," I said, squeezing my eyes shut, overcome with the bizarre closeness with her that I felt at that moment. I really did love her. Could this perverse lifestyle really make our hearts one?

"Oh, baby, you make me so happy!" Tonya told me with joy in her voice. She took my cum-filled hand in hers. "Let me feed you your cum, dear heart!" She held my hand flat and lifted it to my lips, where I was forced to lap it up like a cat licking up milk.

"Cum is our sacrament, baby," she instructed me. "Cum is the glue that joins my heart to yours! Taste it! Cum is the flavor of our love for each other! With every tongueful, say, 'She loves me. Tonya loves me with all her heart. Her cunt and ass belong to other men, but her heart belongs to me. She fucks them, but she brings the cum to me!' "

I wished our love tasted better, but I'd eaten so much that I was getting used to it. I'd tasted a lot of things worse and I was starting to associate this taste with being part of a fantastically erotic situation. I could sense that I was starting to crave it. I mean, nobody ever liked their first taste of coffee, Scotch, or bleu cheese. Maybe cum is an acquired taste, only fully appreciated by the connoisseur. I liked it better when it was warm: the puddle in my hand had already cooled. I liked it lots better when I was tasting it while sucking on Tonya's beloved cunt or ass ... or from the cocks of the studs surrounding me.

It didn't take many licks until I had my palm clean as a whistle. Tonya capped my obeisance by kissing the center of my palm soulfully, approving of the job I'd done.

"Now lick my lover clean, Johnny. Show your appreciation for the pleasure he's given your wife. Show that you really respect and admire his magnificent manhood."

Calvin pulled out of Tonya's ass and I was awestruck at the yawning chasm he left behind. Tonya's ass didn't look like an anus anymore. It looked like a wound or a mouth. I could see an inch into her rectum, seeing the bright red of it, so different than the pink of her pucker. It was shiny and glistening with the lube and then I saw a glob of white jism starting to collect and threatening to flood out. I instinctively reached to catch it, but Tonya beat me to it, clamping her hand over the gaping orifice. She whimpered at losing her hold on Calvin's cock.

Calvin's penis was impressive even at half-mast. I should feel resentful or disgusted or angry, but I only felt excited. This cock had given my beloved much pleasure. I love Tonya. I had to be happy for the delight this rod had produced in her. I worked at sincerely wrapping my head around that idea as I wrapped my lips around the head of his cock.

I sucked at it, tasting the film of his cum, the lube, and the musk of Tonya's bowel, mixed with the overflow of juices from her aroused cunt. I took it deeper into the back of my throat and felt his meat fill my mouth. I suckled at it, enjoying its manly strength, wanting to feel one with it. I squeezed it with my tongue, milking it for the last drops of his man-juice. Calvin moaned in post-orgasm sensitivity.

"God, what a faggot!" Audrey protested. "Look at him suck that nigger cock!"

"You're right, Audrey. Cuckolds do tiptoe the line. Do they suck cock to submit to their wife and acknowledge the superiority of her lover, or do they just like to suck cock? Every cuckold is tormented by that question, especially when his little peepee gets as stiff as a board every time he even thinks about sucking cock! But I prefer to think he's showing his love for me and his respect for Calvin.

"But there's also his appetite for humiliating himself. Remember, a cuckold has a need to prostrate himself, to show he's no threat, no competition. He's eager to surrender before the fight's even started, because he knows he'll lose. What better way to show that he's no man than to take the woman's role, to suck his rival's penis? So in a way he's sucking out of fear. But then why is his little dicklet so hard? Out of relief maybe?"

Kneeling between Calvin's legs, his penis in my mouth, I felt these words like lashes of a whip, beating the last shreds of my self-respect to dust. I was a wimp, a loser! What better place for me than this? It was all I deserved. And Tonya was right. Part of me was eager to surrender. I was afraid to fight for her. I was glad to give in and be safe. If you didn't fight, could you ever really lose? The Japanese have a saying, "The nail that stands up gets hammered down." I never stood up: I would always be the one who lay down—or knelt down.

But another part of me was enjoying this more than submitting to it. Yes, I was surrendering my manhood by sucking cock, but it was a sweet surrender! I felt that same feeling I had had when I was being fucked by Tonya's lovers: a feeling of complete and utter surrender. It felt so good, it almost hurt my heart to feel the poignancy of that release. To give up, give in, let go, and let a man's strength and power surround and suffuse me. Submitting to that masculine force stirred something deep within.

I shivered and felt a warm, melty feeling course through my whole body. Calvin's penis in my mouth became like a tit, and I was a babe sucking strength and sustenance from his manly strength. It was my connection to his energy. I finished licking his shaft clean with loving devotion.

"Come here, baby. Don't listen to mean old Audrey. I know you love my pussy more than those big meaty cocks." She pulled my head down and kissed me affectionately. "Here, show Audrey how much you love my ass, especially after a big hard cock has jizzed in it."

Tonya pulled her knees up again and I rolled her ass upwards to bring it to where I could eat it comfortably. Tonya pulled her hand away and held her cum-smeared fingers to my lips for me to lick clean.

I looked down at her poor asshole, which had hardly closed while I had laved Calvin's cock. It still gaped open the width of a golf ball. But now a pool of slimy cum collected in the opening and began to slide out between her cheeks. I quickly swooped to dam the flood with my tongue and sucked the sweet semen into my mouth. This cum was hot and runny. I felt Tonya's anus ripple and I realized she was trying to feed me Calvin's sperm, to propel his spew into my mouth.

Surrender. Surrender.

I welcomed this abasement. I was loving my wife's body and surrendering to her lovers at the same time. I kissed and sucked at her anus. I was making love to my wife in the only way I could. I could demonstrate my devotion with my mouth even if I could not with my puny dick. I would show her by sucking and licking her ass eagerly and being glad. I would demonstrate tenderness and affection that she craved, even as she craved Calvin's strength and domination.

The thought glimmered in the back of my mind that I was demonstrating my devotion to her lovers by treating their sperm as a gift. That idea sent a shiver down my spine.

I was pleased to hear Tonya murmuring in satisfaction at the job I was doing.

"Oh, Johnny, that feels so good. My poor asshole needs your TLC after Calvin's battering.

"Audrey, that's why I'm so glad I married Johnny instead of some he-man. A girl needs tenderness too, a partner for her heart, not just for her cunt. If a girl is lucky and plays her cards right, she can have both. Oh! That's nice! I'm the luckiest girl in the world!"

My heart swelled to hear Tonya's praise, even as her lover's sperm leaked into my mouth.

"Here, Johnny, let's make sure you get all of your treat," She got up and settled her ass on my face so gravity would help her dump all of Calvin's black cum out of her ass. I could feel her straining to expel as much of his load as she could. Slowly her asshole was closing, amazing organ that it was.

"Audrey, I haven't showed you another one of Johnny's talents yet! Come watch!

"Open wide, hubby!" Tonya lifted off my face and hovered a few inches above my mouth. I opened my mouth as wide as I could.

A few drops of piss fell into my mouth and then it was a jet of urine hitting my tongue and spraying against the back of my throat.

"Jesus! Tonya! Stop! That's gross! Oh shit, that's gonna make him sick!" Audrey cried.

"Oh, he's drunk lots of my piss and it's never hurt him," Tonya responded. "In India the yogis drink their own piss as some kind of health thing. They think it helps recapture vital minerals and trace elements. Mahatma Gandhi drank his own piss. I don't guess drinking my piss is any different."

My cheeks burned to know that was doing this in front of an audience, especially another woman. It seemed dirty in a way that would make Audrey regard me with disgust.

"It's very weird at first, Audrey, but once you've done it, it's such a rush! That he's drinking my piss—it makes me feel like a queen. I mean, if my piss is his nectar, I'm like a goddess.

"You should try it. I'm sure he'd drink yours if I told him to, wouldn't you, Johnny?"

"I guess," I mumbled. Yet another thing I'd never even dreamed of. But my damned dick tingled at the idea!

"You want me to piss in your husband's mouth? That's what you're telling me?" Audrey objected.

"It's a power trip you'll never forget. Strike a blow for womankind, if you please," Tonya urged.

"No! That's crazy!"

"You've surely had plenty of guys piss on you, figuratively! Now you can piss on one, literally! You'll never look at a man the same again!"

"I don't know...."

But Tonya knew Audrey pretty well. She'd have her share of man troubles. Her argument seemed to have hit the right button, because Audrey's whole demeanor changed. I could see the wheels turning: not being a pervert, but getting even with all the men who'd hurt her. She could get into that.

I lay there like the bathroom fixture I was, while Audrey tentatively put one foot on either side of my head and carefully lowered her pudendum toward my face. I dutifully opened my mouth wide, which excited her amazement. She looked me in the eye.

"So you want to drink my piss, eh! Do you like the taste? Or do you just get off on the submission? Are you one of those masochists?"

My mouth was going dry and my thoughts were mixed up. My cock was trying to stiffen and was intoxicating my brain with sexual arousal. I did want it. I wanted her piss. I wanted to see it shoot out of her vulva. I wanted to feel its hot stream. I wanted to taste its salty bitterness and its femaleness—her hormones or pheromones or whatever. There was an essence there, an essence of woman.

"It's ... not the taste," I sputtered out. "It's ... it's the idea. It's ... sexy somehow. The taste is ... not too bad."

"So you want it? You want my piss? It turns you on?"

"Yes!"

"OK, you got it!" And with that I saw her strain. I waited and nothing came. She was concentrating. I guessed that she was having a hard time letting go. She closed her eyes and held her breath.

I felt a few dribbles hit my tongue, then a spurt, then nothing. My cock throbbed and I wanted more. Then there was another spurt, then a stream. I felt her hot piss filling my mouth and I strained to swallow it without closing my mouth. The stream stopped for a moment and then another jet hissed out.

"Oh, fuck!" Audrey exclaimed as she looked down at her urine filling my mouth. "He's really swallowing it! Damn!"

"And look at this!" Tonya suggested. Audrey twisted her head around to see Tonya holding my half-hard cockette.

"Well, if you like it that much...," she said. Audrey turned back and concentrated on emptying her bladder.

When the last drops finished, Audrey tried to stand up, but I grabbed her waist and pulled her pussy down to my mouth. I licked a few drops of salty piss from her urethra and labia and planted a kiss on her piss hole.

"Wow!" Audrey exclaimed and she seemed taken aback by the experience.

"What do you think?" Tonya asked.

"You were right! It is a rush!" Audrey enthused. "It gave me goosebumps!"

Tonya took my hands and pulled me up into a full frontal hug and a deep kiss.

"See, these cuckold pansies have their uses! Johnny will surprise you again and again, Audrey. Nothing's too low for him! He's got unplumbed depths."

"No, I think you've plumbed them all!" Brian cracked, and they all guffawed, except Audrey, who had no clue what he was talking about.

It was getting late by now, so Tonya suggested that Audrey stay the night, as she promised she still had a few more surprises she'd like to show Audrey the next day. They threw odds and evens and Calvin ended up sleeping with Audrey and Brian and David were in with Tonya. Audrey didn't balk, so I guess dark meat wasn't a problem for her.

I ended up on the couch again. 'We might need to move into a three-bedroom house,' I thought to myself. How did this get from Tonya needing a bigger cock to fuck to needing three at a time?

Before she went to bed, Audrey startled me by coming over and giving me an affectionate hug and a kiss.

"Thank you for a once-in-a-lifetime experience!" she whispered. She laughed as my "little peepee" sprung to attention and she gave it a playful pat. As she walked away I wondered if my accepting her pee made her feel a special connection between us. It certainly was a powerful experience for me.

I realized that I was beginning to think of her as having the same status above me as Tonya did, as if she were a Mistress. Tonya and I hadn't really talked about our relationship being a dominant-submissive one. I mean, she didn't make me kneel at her feet or call her "Mistress Tonya," and she didn't call me "slave." But there was no doubt that she was calling all the shots and I was doing everything she asked.

I thought about Audrey's strange affectionate gesture and it made me think back to the unexpected feeling I was feeling toward Brian after he fucked me. Audrey had talked about having "goosebumps," and I realized that that described the strange warm shiver than had come over me since that ultimate surrender of my will and my body.

That night I had another dream. I dreamed that Tonya came to me very serious and told me she had something very important to ask me. She asked me if I truly loved her and if I'd do anything for her. In the dream she glowed, almost as if she were a goddess, and that is the way I felt about her, that I could deny her nothing.

In the dream I told her that I worshipped her and I would do anything she asked. She looked me in the eyes and asked me if I would undergo "the Operation." In the dream it was possible to transplant a man's penis onto a woman and this was something some men and women did.

Everyone didn't do it, but it wasn't rare either: something like 10% of couples did it.

It was considered a great honor for a woman and a great sign of love and devotion that a man would give a woman his penis. Most men didn't want to do it, so a woman usually had to cultivate a man for a long time to make him so in love with her and so devoted that he would make that sacrifice. A woman would "groom" a man for years, hoping that eventually he'd worship her to the point of giving up his manhood.

In the dream I was scared, but I was honored to have Tonya willing to accept my penis. I wanted to show her my devotion and so I said yes.

I woke up after the operation and I felt the bandages and knew I had no penis or balls anymore. My only sexual organ now was my ass. Tonya was in the bed beside mine and I went to her side. The operation only transplanted the penis. Tonya had followed tradition and had my balls encased in acrylic and hanging as a pendant around her neck. Her new penis was covered in bandages, right above the top of her vulva.

In the dream I was filled with love for Tonya and proud of the sacrifice I'd made. She put one hand over the pendant, holding it to her heart and she kissed me and cried.

"Oh, baby, thank you! Thank you!" she sobbed.

As soon as the doctors let us, we tried out her new penis. I gave her a blow job and she shot off in my mouth. Her semen was only seminal fluid made by the transplanted glands, without any sperm. Tonya cried with joy at her first penile orgasm. She couldn't wait to fuck my ass, and I loved finally being able to have her fuck me with a real penis.

Of course, Tonya wanted to try out her new equipment with men who had penises, engaging in 69 and masturbating her cock while an intact man fucked her. But the real upside of the Operation was allowing her to be fully bisexual and to enjoy fucking women too. Tonya let me watch her first fuck with a woman. I watched her make love to Audrey in the dream. Unable to masturbate the normal way myself, I had to get off by fucking myself with a dildo while Tonya fucked Audrey with my old penis!

-Day 30 Sunday-

After that dream I woke up Sunday with a hard-on and feeling exhausted, as if I'd run all night. The images that stuck with me were the pleasure of being fucked by Tonya with a real penis and the excitement of watching her fuck Audrey. And the idea of being so under Tonya's spell that I would even let her have my penis!

When I awoke the only voices I could hear sounded like Tonya's and Audrey's. I heard talking a laughing coming from the bathroom. A little while later they both came out wrapped in bath towels. I got the strong impression that they'd taken a shower together! My dick saluted the idea with an erection.

The girls walked hand in hand to the kitchen, where they poured themselves orange juices and made toast and a pot of coffee.

"Where are the guys?" I asked.

"I think we wore them out!" Audrey replied. "They're still sleeping. Want anything?"

"I think I know what Johnny'd want," Tonya interrupted. She took one of the juice glasses and held it to her pudendum. Then she squatted and squirted a third of a glass of her piss into it. She held it up to admire the pale yellow color in the morning light. She turned to Audrey.

"That's not much, but that's all I got. Why don't you top it off, Audrey? It'll be like a V-8!"

"Tonya, you're so relaxed! I don't know if I can go, here in the middle of the kitchen! What if I miss the glass?"

"Then Johnny'll lick it up off the floor! C'mon, you can do it!"

Audrey took the glass and tentatively slipped it under the hem of her towel as she squatted down. She concentrated with her eyes closed, trying to relax.

"I think it's coming...," she said and then I heard a hiss of pee into the glass, then another hiss, and then some dribbles. A few moments later she pulled the glass out. It was three-quarters full of golden liquid. She handed it to me.

"Thank you," I said. I was somehow touched by Audrey's willingness to indulge Tonya and me, even against her instincts.

Audrey gave me a look as I took the glass from her, looking for sarcasm or sincerity. I think it surprised and pleased her that she saw nothing in my face other than gratitude.

I took the glass and felt the heat of their bodies through the glass. It excited to me to think that their essences joined together in that glass. I drank down their piss, savoring their mixed flavors. I smelled their urine in between sips, as it wafted up the back of my nose.

Watching me drink both their urine together seem to excite and unite the two women. They turned to each other and hugged as their lips joined in a passionate kiss. Watching my wife kiss another half-naked woman with whom she'd just gotten out of the shower was all my lesbian fantasies come true! My cock went steely with arousal.

"Tonya, you're a she-devil! You're bringing me over to the Dark Side!" Audrey said, but she sounded almost grateful. "You're making me hot!"

"Oh, Audrey, I hope so!" Tonya replied. "There's more I want to show you. Do you want to see more?"

"There's more?!?"

"Oh, yeah!"

Audrey hugged Tonya to her and lay her head on Tonya's shoulder.

"Yes, I think I do! I trust you."

Tonya hugged Audrey to her in a crushing hug, almost sisterly. Then she tipped Audrey's chin up to look her in the eyes. They kissed again. Clearly their tongues were exploring each other's mouths in a very unsisterly way. I watched transfixed. They broke their kiss and looked each other in the eyes for a long moment and then broke their embrace.

"Come here, Audrey," Tonya said, leading her over to me. "Look at his cute little wiener. It's all stiff! Feel it."

Audrey was shedding ever more of her inhibitions. She grasped my erection lightly.

"Give it a tug and I'll show you what a little dickie like that is good for."

Audrey began to gently pump my cock. It felt wonderful. Tonya reached out and lightly stroked my nipples, sending shivers through me.

"Would you like to make us some breakfast, Johnny? I have a feeling Audrey and I are going to need our strength today. Would you make us some eggs and sausage? We like sausage—especially big, thick kielbasas! But right now a little breakfast sausage like yours would be fine. Make enough for our boyfriends too. They'll need their strength and they'll probably wake up when they smell the food." All the while she was toying with my nipples and Audrey was milking my prick. A bead a pre-cum formed in my slit.

"Y-y-y ... uh ... sure...," I stuttered, unwilling for the stimulation to end.

"Oh, look, Audrey!" Tonya gushed, "You got him leaking! Squeeze some pre-cum out of his peepee and feed it to him."

Audrey giggled, obviously getting off on her tutorial in humiliating a man. She carefully squeezed my cock between her fingers from the base to the tip, wringing a glob of clear fluid out of me. She collected it between her thumb and forefinger and lifted it to my lips. I took her fingertips into my mouth, which somehow felt as erotic as licking her cunt had been last night.

She said, "He'll eat that too!" But at least she didn't exclaim that it was queer or disgusting this time.

"OK, off to make breakfast," Tonya ordered, swatting my behind. Of course I donned the frilly pink apron, which caused Audrey to giggle again. As I busied myself, Tonya explained to Audrey, "See, that little willie is good for controlling him. If you keep that little thing stiff, he'll do anything we want. And I mean anything!"

"After what I've seen, I believe you!" Audrey responded.

"And you still haven't seen all of it yet!"

"God, Tonya, what else do you do? Dogs? Horses? Midgets?"

"Don't give me any ideas! But there's still more possibilities just with the players at hand!"

True to Tonya's prediction, the smell of eggs and sausage links eventually roused the men from their slumbers. Tonya and Audrey and I wore silky feminine robes, while the men wore terry cloth ones. We enjoyed a relaxed breakfast, although it fell to me to wait on everyone, of course.

After breakfast it seemed that Tonya's teasers had piqued Audrey's curiosity.

"So, Tonya dear, what are these other surprises you have in store? You said that cuckolding, sucking, cum-eating, asshole eating, and piss drinking are not all?"

"Oh goody! You're game for more?" Tonya answered.

"Why stop now? I'm already going to Hell for what I've done so far! Might as well get full value for my ticket!" she replied insouciantly.

Tonya hugged her with joy.

"I can't wait!" Tonya said, giggling. "Wait right here!"

Only a minute later Tonya returned. She had her robe open to reveal that she had strapped on a dildo that I hadn't seen before and harness.

"Oh, shit!" Audrey exclaimed. "What are you going to do with that?!"

"You mean who am I going to do with that, don't you? I've never made love to a woman, my dear, but I was hoping to make love to you!"

Audrey was taken aback again. She looked at Tonya in shock and fascination. Tonya stood where she was and waited for Audrey to make the first move. The men held their breaths, wanting very much to see a girl-on-girl sex show, but instinctively knowing that guffaws and catcalls might blow their chance. The very sight of Tonya wearing the dildo and harness had my dickie at attention and I saw a couple of the other guys shift meaningfully in their seats.

It was Audrey's move. She moved toward Tonya, her eyes flitting from the jutting phallus to Tonya's eyes and back to the dildo. She tentatively reached out and touched the fake penis. She flinched as she grabbed it.

"Oh! It feels ... so real!" She jiggled it gingerly, feeling the Cyberskin move so realistically over the underlying firmness. "It's like you really have a cock!" She looked over at me and continued, "And yours is bigger than Johnny's too!" she giggled.

"Well, I want to keep my girlfriend happy, after all," Tonya admitted.

Audrey pulled at the dildo to see how firmly it was held in place. Tonya sighed.

"The other end goes inside me! So when you pull it, it feels good!" She closed her eyes and purred. I realized why the dildo looked unfamiliar to me. Tonya had bought a double-ended one.

Audrey took the hint and started pulling and pushing on the fake cock. Then she put her other arm around Tonya and began to kiss her while she continued to fondle the dildo. She looked for all the world like a frisky girlfriend stoking the passions of her boyfriend.

"Oh, baby!" Tonya gasped. "That feels so good!"

"You are making me wet, Tonya!" Audrey breathed. "I've never had a woman want me like that! Feel me!" Tonya reached down between them, her fingers probing between Audrey's nether lips. My cock jumped at the sight!

"My God, girl! You're gushing!"

"It's you, babe. You and your cock. You look so dirty and so hot! I want it! I want you to fuck me!"

"Oh, God, I want to fuck you too!"

Tonya drew her fingers out of Audrey's cunt and they shone with Audrey's wetness. She brought them to her lips and sucked Audrey's juices as if they were ambrosia. She then reached her hand into Audrey's half-open robe and took one delicious tit in her hand and caressed it, pulling a moan from Audrey.

"I've always wanted to know what it was like to feel another girl's tits!" Tonya admitted. "They feel lovely! No wonder guys are so gaga over them!"

Tonya attacked Audrey's mouth with her tongue as she tweaked her nipple and pressed her breast. Audrey moved her free hand from behind Tonya's back and reached for Tonya's breast. I took my own cock in hand and began to stroke myself as I saw the other men's hands disappear into their robes.

Tonya broke their kiss and lowered her head to Audrey's tit and lifted her hard nipple to her mouth. Audrey moaned as Tonya suckled at her breast. Tonya's other hand dipped into Audrey's honeypot and smeared her leaking juices onto her clit and began to toy with it. Audrey began to grunt and press her groin against Tonya's hand. She pulled Tonya's cock harder and Tonya groaned in her turn.

"God, I need you to fuck me, Tonya! I've never made love with a girl, but I want you to make love to me now!"

I gasped and began to stroke myself harder. I couldn't believe how hot this was! Tonya could direct XXX videos! All four men watched in silence, hushed by the intensity of the scene in front of us.

Audrey lowered herself to the floor and reached for the dildo jutting from Tonya's pubis. Tonya covered her like a blanket, but then pushed herself up so that her breasts hung over Audrey's. She let her nipples just barely touch Audrey's, then moved them side to side, so they brushed together. I shuddered with excitement to see them breast to breast, a double dose of smoldering female sexuality, like two high-voltage wires touching! Audrey arched her back with delight.

"Why have I never tried this before?" whispered Audrey.

"You're so beautiful," Tonya murmured. "I want to fuck you and see you come on my cock!" The dildo rested on Audrey's belly and Tonya reached down to stroke Audrey's pussy. "Do you want my cock? Do you want a girl to fuck you?"

"Oh, yes!" Audrey cried. "Please! Put it in me! I want to feel it in me!"

"Open up for me then. Spread your legs! Show me what a whore you are for my cock!"

Audrey whimpered and pulled her knees to her chest and then reached down to part her cunt lips for Tonya. She held her pussy wide open in a gesture of need and surrender. Tonya gasped at the lewd display and then grasped the dildo and raked it through Audrey's oozing gash. She wet the end of the prod with Audrey's juices and then pressed it into her slit.

Audrey cried out in relief and delight as she felt the cock pierce her. She bucked up, impatient to impale herself on the shaft. She grunted as her cunt was stretched by the thickness of the dildo. Tonya worked it into her in short in-and-out jabs.

"That's right, baby, take my cock!" Tonya urged in a low voice. "Doesn't it feel good? Your cunt loves my cock! I'm gonna fuck you nice and slow, because I want you to love every second of it."

Tonya continued to gently fuck her until Audrey gasped as the phallus reached her cervix. Tonya kept up slow short undulations, while she started to rain kisses on Audrey's face.

"God, you're beautiful, baby!" Tonya told her. "I want to kiss your beautiful face and suck your beautiful tits and fuck your beautiful cunt!"

That was too much for me. My cock swelled in my hand and I spurted.

"Shit!" I cursed as cum spilled into my palm. "Shit! Oh! Oh!" It felt good, but I wanted it to last and last!

Audrey pulled back her knees, trying to open herself up as much as she could, welcoming Tonya's cock into her body.

"Fuck me! Fuck me, Tonya!" she cried. She reached up and palmed Tonya's boobs, as if to remind herself that it was a woman fucking her, not a man. "Your cock feels so good in me! Unh! Unh!" she grunted as Tonya picked up her pace.

"Oh yes! Oh! Hnh! Hnh!" Audrey babbled. Tonya also began to pant, as her exertions moved the dildo's other end in her vagina and its base kneaded her own clit.

"Come for me, baby! Come on my girl-cock! Give me your cum, baby!" Tonya demanded, as she started giving Audrey long hard stabs with the fake penis. "Look at me, baby, as you come! A girl is fucking you! You're coming for a girl!"

Tonya knew what buttons to push. Audrey opened her eyes and looked at her and almost immediately began the convulsions of her climax. Those words did it for David too, as he groaned and ropes of semen splashed onto his stomach and chest.

Tonya was grunting at the double stimulation of seeing Audrey writhing in orgasm under her and the continued rubbing of the dildo on her clit. She reached down and worked her fingers under the base of the dildo and found her nub. Audrey felt the change in rhythm and realized what Tonya was doing. She began to tweak Tonya's nipples and craned her neck to pull one nipple into her mouth. Tonya groaned and stopped thrusting, concentrating on bringing herself to climax.

"Suck me!" Tonya urged Audrey, who redoubled her efforts to suckle at Tonya's breast. Moments later Tonya began to buck and tremble and her incoherent grunts signaled her completion. Then she collapsed on top of Audrey, who began to cover Tonya's face with kisses.

"Shit!" David exclaimed as he looked at the gooey mess his ejaculation had made. He looked over to see me finishing licking my own cum off my hand. "Johnny! I almost forgot: that's your department, isn't it? Don't you love to eat this shit? I've got a treat for you then!"

In my post-orgasmic letdown I wasn't exactly champing at the bit, but I wasn't going to let that chance go by either. I went over to David. His half-hard cock was the most tempting place to start. As I lifted the head toward my mouth I felt a twinge of arousal. To my surprise I found myself getting turned on again! It looked so ... delicious ... to me.

I felt his cockhead fill my mouth and I found its spongy firmness and smoothness thrilling! I milked a few drops of cum from its head and then spent a few moments enjoying suckling at it like a baby at the bottle!

"Mmmm, that's nice," David murmured. He reached out and tousled my hair and I felt a warmth go down my back at the affectionate gesture. David was rewarded by my licking his shaft up and down. I was getting turned on again! Licking up his cum sounded ... yummy!

I began to lap up his pearly rivulets. The taste was strong, unmixed with Tonya's or Audrey's juices. It took many licks to vacuum it all up, giving lots of time to savor the taste. It didn't taste great, but the flavor was starting to appeal to me! Mostly it was just perverted that I was tasting it at all, which made me want to do it more, and made my cock half-hard again, despite having just come mere minutes ago.

"That's it, cuck boy, enjoy your dessert," David gibed. But the joke was on him: I _was_ enjoying it! 'Whatever you do, don't throw me into that briar patch!'

Tonya had pulled out of Audrey and they lay side by side, the indefatigable dildo leering obscenely from Tony's crotch.

"Look, the boys enjoyed the show!" Tonya pointed out to Audrey.

"Yeah, they did. I'm raring to get in on this!" Brian announced.

"Hold your horses!" Tonya told him. "I have something very special in mind for you. How'd you like Audrey's anal cherry?"

"No way!" Audrey protested, jumping to her feet, as Brian, in contrast, nodded his eager assent. "I've never had any guy's prick in there, much less a horse cock like one of these guys! They'd rip something! It'd hurt like hell!"

"Not if I prepared you first," Tonya countered, her hand suggestively palming the shaft of the dildo.

Audrey's eyes dilated a telltale moment before she remembered herself.

"No way! That thing is no pin-dick! That's a good-sized cock! It'll never fit up my ass!"

Tonya got to her feet and took Audrey in her arms.

"Baby, I'll be gentle. I was your first girl. Now I'd like to be your first ass-fuck! I know how it feels. We'll go slow. I guarantee that once you relax, you'll love it! You saw Calvin do me: it's a feeling that just isn't like any other. I want you to have that feeling, babe!"

Tonya pulled Audrey close and ran her hands up and down her back and then took her ass in both hands.

"I want this ass, baby! I've had your cunt and I loved it! Now I want to see my cock fucking your ass!"

Audrey shivered at Tonya's lustful declaration. I had to remind myself that women could have one orgasm after another. If Audrey were a guy, she'd be satisfied with one fuck. But could one orgasm just whet her appetite for another?

"Oh, Tonya! What are doing to me? Are you hypnotizing me or did you slip me some Spanish fly? You're making me wet again! I can't resist you! What's next? Whip and chains?"

"Shhh! It's a secret!" Tonya said, laughing. "Whatever it is, I guarantee you'll love it!" She kissed Audrey fervently and her hand went to Audrey's snatch to confirm the wetness there. Audrey moaned into Tonya's mouth as Tonya's fingers found her clit and then dipped into her opening.

"Oh, fuck!" Audrey growled at the instant fire Tonya sparked in her loins. "You're gonna turn me bi!"

"Back at you, babe!" Tonya replied, and her hips rolled with arousal as she felt the heat in Audrey's cunt for her.

"Johnny, please prepare an enema. I believe Audrey wants her ass fucked!" I hurried to the bathroom and ran the water nice and warm and added some buffering salts to make it gentle. I emerged from the bathroom carrying the bag, hose, and nozzle. Tonya had Audrey lying on her back on the sofa. She kissed Audrey and stroked her tummy.

"We're gonna get you all clean and relaxed. Pull your knees up and let me see that cute little pucker I'm gonna fuck!" Audrey shyly pulled her knees to her chest, exposing her rosebud. Tonya took her ass cheeks with each hand and bent over and planted a big smooch right on Audrey's anus!

"Tonya!" Audrey protested. "Now you're going to kiss me with that mouth?"

"I think your ass is lovely!" Tonya proclaimed. "And I know you showered this morning, because you showered with me!" confirming my suspicions. She reached for the lube and dabbed some on Audrey's asshole and gently began to circle the opening, massaging the lube in. "Doesn't that feel nice? It's so sensitive, so many nerve endings." She dipped just the end of her finger in the middle. "Open up, little girl, and let Tonya in!"

Audrey was still evaluating how it felt. Tonya turned her finger, coating all sides with the slippery lube and Audrey gave a small whimper.

"Oh, that feels so wrong! If your finger feels like that, how's a cock going to fit in there?"

"You'll see."

Then Tonya slipped the enema nozzle in and released the stopcock. She stroked Audrey's stomach as the water flowed in. Tonya snaked a finger into Audrey's pubic hair and toyed with her clit to distract her from the unusual sensations in her gut.

"Oh, that's so embarrassing!" Audrey said about her public enema.

"OK, babe, go to the bathroom now." Audrey got up gingerly and awkwardly waddled off to the bathroom. A few minutes later she tiptoed back to the living room and obediently lay down on the couch again.

Tonya kissed Audrey and spoke softly to her.

"Babe, give yourself to me! Open up to me. Trust me. We'll take it slow."

Tonya took a fingerful of lube and daubed it on Audrey's anus, circling it and massaging the muscle. She took another fingerful and pressed it in the opening just up to the knuckle and then turned it to spread lube all around. She could feel Audrey's sphincter tense up and squeeze her finger.

"We're taught all our lives that our asshole is dirty, gross, sickening. We're taught to hide it, cover it, not to let anyone see it or touch it. It's more private than even a vagina or penis. A husband or wife can touch our vagina or penis, but no one is supposed to touch our dirty, disgusting asshole!" While she distracted Audrey with her dissertation, Tonya had started to very gently fuck Audrey's ass with tiny in-out motions.

"We're not even supposed to touch our <u>own</u> asshole, except with toilet paper or a washcloth. Maybe so we don't discover how delicious it can be? It is our most private, most personal, most secret part of our whole body. So even touching it is a violation. Entering it is an ... invasion!"

With that Tonya inserted her whole finger.

"Our minds and bodies are programmed to fight any penetration! It's gross; it's dangerous; it's wrong; it's embarrassing; it's too personal! More personal than fucking someone!"

Tonya kept her finger buried in Audrey's ass, but put her other arm behind Audrey's head and drew her up into a kiss.

"But that's what makes it so wonderful! When you let someone in to that personal, hidden, scary, embarrassing place, you've opened up to them in a way you never have before! You've bared your soul, let your defenses down, put yourself in their power—at their mercy! You've said, 'Take me' in the most powerful way you ever could! 'Take me: I trust you with all of me, good and bad; even the dirty, shameful, secret parts of me I will show you, admit you, give to you!' "

Tonya took my breath away! She put into words all the strange thoughts, emotions, and urges I had had around anal sex!

Tonya kissed Audrey deeply while she finger-fucked her ass insistently. Audrey's hips started grinding up and down, as if she were fucking herself on Tonya's finger. My cock hardened to steel at the sight.

They broke their kiss and Audrey looked Tonya intensely in the eyes and spoke in a husky, lust-drunk voice.

"I want you to take me that way!"

I've told you: Tonya knows what buttons to push. After that speech it was a wonder we didn't all start shouting, "No, fuck me!" "No, me!" But to our credit we were all frozen in silence, sensing the fragility of the moment.

Tonya deeply kissed Audrey again and then started stretching her asshole sideways, pulling it this way and that, and then running her finger all around the inside in larger and larger circles. Quickly she scooped up lube on two fingers and plunged them into Audrey at once. Of course, Audrey's anus resisted the doubled girth.

"Ow! Oh, that feels so weird!" Audrey groaned.

But Tonya pulled out and went back in, out and in, soothing the muscles. She turned her fingers to spread the lube and massage the sphincters. Soon two fingers were taken as easily as one.

"Oh, baby, you're doing so good! I can feel you relaxing, letting Tonya in! Tonya loves you and she's gonna make your ass feel so good!"

Audrey was quiet now, concentrating, trying to get used to the sensation and not knowing how to fight the instinct to clamp down and push out, how to let in. I knew from my own experience that this is where the wanting runs up against the inconvenient fact that asses aren't really designed for fucking. Cunts are designed for two-way traffic. "In" is like falling off a log for cunts (I'm guessing), but not for asses.

Tonya took a chance and lubed up a third finger and pressed it to Audrey's bum. Audrey grunted. Three fingers is beyond anything a sphincter is designed to stretch around. Tonya needed to talk her good game now.

"Ass-fucking is about going where you didn't think you could. Rebelling against what you've been taught, your instincts. Going past your limits. When you can do that you're free! You can do whatever you want to do, go wherever you want to go, be whoever you want to be!" By the time Tonya finished, her three fingers were in Audrey up to the hand. Tonya started jamming them into Audrey in a fucking motion.

"I've got three fingers in your dirty ass, baby! I think you're ready for my cock!" Tonya crowed. "Do you want my cock up your ass? Do you want me way up there? Do you want me to fuck your ass?"

"Unh! Hnh! Unh! Oh! Yes! Please! Fuck my slut ass!"

Tonya descended on Audrey's mouth and kissed her hard, almost violently.

"God, I love you! I am gonna fuck your ass so good and you're gonna come and come! You're gonna feel my cock tickle your tonsils!"

Tonya turned Audrey around so that her ass was at the edge of the couch and she knelt in front of the couch, bringing the looming dildo to just the right height. She slathered lube all over the dildo, so it glistened evilly.

"Here I come, baby!" Tonya declared and she nudged Audrey's anus open and began to press inside.

"Ouch! Oh! Stop!" Audrey cried. "It's too big!"

Tonya backed out and then pressed the tip of the cock halfway in.

"Relax, baby! You gotta stretch to take my cock. It'll get easier and then you'll love it!" She pressed forward again.

"Unh! Unh! God! Oh! Oh!" Audrey grunted, clearly straining. She relaxed as Tonya withdrew the dildo again and then immediately thrust it in again.

"You have to take my cock! I want your ass, Audrey! Give it to me!" Tonya growled. She pulled out and stabbed in and then repeated the cycle. Audrey protested less each time. Then Tonya pushed in and only backed halfway out and pushed forward again, burying half the cock in Audrey's ass. She stopped there and gently mini-fucked Audrey in short, massage-like undulations.

"Feel it, baby! My cock is in your ass! I'm in you! I'm fucking your ass! You're letting me in your ass!"

Audrey had a look of stress and discomfort on her face. She strained to take the girl-cock where no cock was ever meant to go. Part of me sympathized with her—I knew just how it felt. But most of me identified with Tonya and I felt myself overcome with fuck-lust. 'Fuck her!' I shouted in my head. 'Fuck that ass!' I wanted to see her conquered, taken, debauched.

I'm sure Tonya felt the same way, but fortunately she was able to rein herself in and she continued to milk Audrey's ass with the dildo, letting her get used to it. She never stood still, but neither did she plunge in heedlessly. She even pulled out all the way a couple times, as if to give Audrey's ass a moment's rest, only to plunge in again. With infinite patience she worked closer and closer to getting the whole dildo in Audrey's bottom.

"So tight!" Audrey moaned. "So big...." Tonya gave a couple more gentle prods and then she pressed forward until she saw Audrey wince.

"Oh! What's that?!" Audrey squeaked. Tonya poked at her and Audrey whimpered. "Oh, shit, you're in as far as it can go!"

"No, babe, but almost!" She jabbed forward and Tonya's pelvis met Audrey's.

"Oh, fuck! Of, fucks that feels ... shit! ... weird!" Audrey exclaimed.

"I'm all the way in, babe. You did it! You took my big cock in your ass! My cock's touching the top of your rectum. I'm all the way in!"

Tonya kept gently fucking, now staying mostly buried, just moving in and out a couple of inches. Gradually she began to fuck faster and harder. Audrey's head lolled back and her face was intent, no longer in pain, but not yet in ecstasy. Tonya noticed the change and began longer strokes. Audrey shuddered and began to breathe faster. Her mouth opened and a low moan came forth.

"Oh! Oh! Oh! Oo-oo-oh!" Audrey moaned. "Oh, fuck! Oh! Oh! Oh, shit!"

It was happening. The pain was turning to pleasure. Her ass was no longer fighting the invader. She was accepting the inevitable. She was surrendering. I knew the delicious feeling. Soon she would be begging for more.

"Oh God! Oh God!" she whimpered. "Oh shit! Oh God, Tonya! Oh, fuck me! Oh shit! Fuck my fucking ass!"

"Yes!" Tonya crowed an began to fuck Audrey in earnest. "Take it, baby, take it!"

"Jesus!" Audrey yelled and she reached down and stuck two fingers in her cunt and drew out juices to smear on her clit. "Shit! I'm gonna come! Here it comes!"

Audrey began bucking into Tonya, driving the cock harder into her ass and then she was screaming out her orgasm.

"Come on, baby! Come as I fuck your ass! You want my cock up your ass!"

Audrey was grunting and shrieking in ecstasy as Tonya pounded in and then gradually slowed and stopped. She lay her body down on top of Audrey and begged for her lips. Audrey bent her head forward to accept kisses from her lover. She was smiling and giggling.

"I don't believe that! That was ... that was ... I don't know what that was...!

"You're a hot fuck, Audrey! And now you're an ass slut!"

"Brian, get over here!" Tonya barked.

"My poor ass! He's even bigger, Tonya! Give me a break!" Audrey protested.

"No, babe, your ass will never be more ready than it is now. I got you all warmed up. After you've taken his fuckpole up your ass, you'll never give my poor girl-cock a second glance."

Audrey groaned as Tonya slipped out of her ass.

"See, you miss a cock up there already! Strike while the iron is hot, Brian!"

Brian already had his cock obscenely lubed and glistening. Audrey's asshole was gaping open, a raw red mouth, but the difference in girth meant Audrey's ass had to stretch yet more. Audrey grunted with the strain as Brian's cockhead squeezed into her.

"Oh, God, stop! Oh, I just can't take that!" Audrey claimed. To Brian's credit he backed out and tickled Audrey's anus with his tip.

"Oh, baby," Tonya crooned, "think how good a real man is going to feel in there! Your ass will be gripping his cock like a boa constrictor! Think of all the pleasure you'll be giving him. And think of what it'll feel like when he shoots his hot cum in there! Think of how much cum is bubbling in his balls after watching our hot lesbian action!"

"OK, OK. But take it easy until I say so." Brian pressed in and Audrey cursed.

"Oh God! Ow! Ow!" Brian wisely pulled out to gain Audrey's trust, hesitated a moment and then pushed in again. Audrey only grunted this time and he stopped, letting her feel his thickness. He pushed forward another inch and Audrey grunted but did not cry out. He backed up almost out and then pushed in three inches and stopped there, just jiggling back and forth.

My cock throbbed at seeing the rubber band tightness of Audrey's anus around his shaft. I could tell how tightly she was gripping him by the way her skin clung as he pulled back and forth.

"Oh, babe, you're almost got half of him in you! You're doing so good!" Tonya encouraged.

'Is there a Girl Scout merit badge for ass-fucking?' I wondered. Tonya leaned over and began to French Audrey, while one hand strayed down to stroke Audrey's pussy. Audrey moaned into Tonya's mouth.

Brian forged ahead with short slow fucking motions, gradually burying six inches into Audrey's bottom.

"Damn!" Brian cursed at the delectable feel of Audrey's ass gripping his cock.

"Oh God, it's so big!" Audrey gasped. "I can't take any more!"

But Brian continued to slowly fuck her, almost in slow motion, but his strokes grew longer and longer.

"Oh!" Brian moaned. "So ... nice ... tight ... hot...," he panted out as his thrusts started to be long enough and fast enough to wring delicious sensations from his buried penis. He began to lengthen his strokes to where he almost came out and then stabbed deeply into Audrey's ass.

"Unh! Oh! Unh! Ahhh!" Audrey grunted as Brian's thrusts hit the top of her rectum. His longer and harder thrusts were starting to heat up her ass. I could tell her ass was on the verge of surrender.

Tonya began to probe into Audrey's drooling pussy with her fingers, wrenching a whimper from Audrey. 'No fair!' I thought to myself. 'You're going to give her brain damage!' It was like a mini-DP. Tonya went even farther by latching her mouth onto one of Audrey's tits and Audrey began to make strangling animal sounds.

Brian passed over from being a lover to being a fucker as the pleasure he was getting from Audrey's clutching ass took over his brain.

"Oh fucking shit!" he cried. "My God, your ass feels ... so ... GOOD! Oh, Jesus! Oh! Oh!" His thrusts became frantic and jerky.

"Oh God, oh God, oh God!" Audrey cried incoherently. "Oh shit! Oh fuck! Oh, fuck my ass! Fuck my damn whore ass!"

Tonya crammed her fingers into Audrey and began to finger-fuck her as fast as she could, while bumping Audrey's clit with her thumb. Audrey began growling and crying and writhing. It was like watching a tornado.

"Oh fucking God!" Audrey cried and arched her back and came.

"Oh shit!" Brian yelled as her ass spasmed around his slamming cock. He only lasted another few strokes and then he thrust forward and shuddered, blasting his sperm into Audrey's bowels. He too was reduced to grunting and growling as his precious seed spilled itself into the infertile tunnel, never to find an egg.

"Ahhh! Ohhh!" Audrey whimpered as she felt his spasms and the hot jets of semen coat her rectum. "Oh ... my ... God!!" she proclaimed.

Again Tonya devoured Audrey's mouth, as if to claim Audrey's ecstasy for her own, like the symphony conductor taking a bow, taking credit for the whole orchestra. They broke the kiss and Audrey gasped.

"That was awesome!" She remembered whose cock was in her ass and looked at Brian and credited him. "You were awesome!" Brian smiled an exhausted smile.

"Now your behind is going to feel a little roughed up, babe," Tonya explained. "That's when a well-trained cuckold comes in handy again. He can be so soothing." She crooked her finger at me.

Having been mostly left out of this scene, I felt eager to play my role. The idea of a gush of hot cum streaming out of Audrey's butthole did not dismay me. I was looking forward to it. I was inspired to kiss Tonya affectionately before I knelt down at Audrey's knee. Brian pulled out of Audrey's ass with an audible <<schlurp>>.

I was torn between sucking Brian's magnificent cock clean and licking out Audrey's ass. But the gush of jism that threatened to cascade from Audrey's gaping hole made my mind up. Brian could wait, but that cum wouldn't. Audrey groaned at the void left by Brian's withdrawal, but she stopped as soon as she felt my mouth fill the breach.

"Oh, God, he's really going to...," started Audrey, but left unfinished as I quickly licked up the hot semen dribbling down her crack and feasted on the swollen, tender ring of anal flesh it came from. Audrey purred as she felt me suck the oozing sperm and my tongue snake into her entrails seeking more: more of the precious fluid and more of Audrey's sexy rectum.

"You love to eat cum now, don't you, Johnny?" Tonya asked. "Which do you like better: cum that's been shot into a woman's cunt or ass, or cum straight from a big, thick cock?"

I didn't know how to answer that, do I just kept sucking Brian's cum from Audrey's bunghole.

"It's a tough choice, isn't it? One has the advantage of being the product of a hot fuck—especially since you're not even eligible to fuck anyone yourself. But the other is hot, straight from a superior male's cock that you worship. I guess you love both, don't you?

"Audrey," Tonya said, pulling her friend upright, "Johnny will miss some of his treat unless you get up." She maneuvered Audrey to sit on my face. "Push out the cum, babe."

"Oh, God, I feel like all my insides are going to fall out!" Audrey moaned.

"No! Just a lot of Brian cream he shot up your bum! Squirt it out! Feed Johnny what he craves!"

I could feel Audrey's anus twitch and push and indeed a few more dollops of jism were deposited from her backside onto my tongue. I licked her gratefully, feeing the still-open ring of her ass wide but gradually shrinking. I kissed her puckered starburst repeatedly.

Audrey rose up off my face. She saw my chin and lips covered with the slimy combination of lube and cum. She raked a little of it toward my mouth with her finger and then stuck her finger in my mouth to clean it off. I was shocked that she bent down then and licked my chin and lips clean and kissed me! Then she reached back and gave my stiff dick a squeeze.

"Poor Johnny! He's the only one who doesn't get a fuck!" Audrey cooed.

"Oh, you're right," Tonya agreed. "Whatever should we do about that?"

"Should you or I give him a pity fuck?" Audrey asked.

"With that little thing? That would be a piti_ful_ fuck, not a pity fuck! No, Johnny deserves a different kind of fuck."

Tonya disappeared into her bedroom and reappeared holding "Richard." She slipped it into the unhooked harness and walked up to Audrey and began to hook it around her waist.

"What are you doing?" Audrey protested.

"You said Johnny deserved a fuck. Well, he doesn't have the equipment, but now you do!"

"You want me to fuck his ass?!"

"Oh, I think he wants you to! Don't you, Johnny?"

The sight of Audrey wearing the big dildo was stupefying! After all, I'd seen Tonya wearing it before, but the picture of her buckling this penis on another woman had me awestruck.

"Yes, please!" I whispered.

"Unless he'd like the real thing better!" piped up David, standing up next to Audrey, his cock standing straight out in front of him just like Audrey's dildo.

"No! He wants my cock!" Audrey played along, grasping the base of the dildo and thrusting her hips out.

"Not when he could have a real flesh and blood cock, complete with real cream!"

"But I'm the only one except Johnny that hasn't got to fuck anyone yet!" pleaded Audrey, much to Tonya's delight. "I wanna try this out!" she said, shaking the cock jutting from her pubis.

"Hold on! No need to fight! You both can fuck him!" Tonya suggested.

"Well then I get to go first!" Audrey asserted. "I call dibs on Johnny's sissy ass!" she laughed.

"Sure: warm him up for me" David jibed. "After I'm done with him, he'll need a break!"

"I'll get his enema," Tonya offered. Audrey had me get up on the couch and she began rubbing my ass and toying with my rosebud as if she did this every day.

"Do you enjoy having your ass fucked, Johnny?" she asked. Despite everything I'd already done in front of her, somehow being asked to admit it was still embarrassing.

"Um ... uh ... yeah, I guess. It ... you know ... it rubs my ... uh ... prostate. That ... uh ... feels pretty good."

"So I guess the bigger, thicker, harder cock the better, eh?"

"Um ... I suppose."

"Isn't that pretty gay? I mean, butt fucking...."

"But I love Tonya! The other ... it's ... it's just sex. Just physical." I said it, but the warm, goofy feelings I had had made me wonder.

"Oh, I see. You're not gay—you're just a slut!"

A slut. I was sucking any cock, pussy, or asshole set in front of me; I ate cum; I drank piss; and I took cock up my ass. 'Slut' sounded about right.

"Yeah, I guess so."

"Well, it's good work if you can get it!" she ended brightly as Tonya returned with the enema. Tonya did the honors and I took a trip to the bathroom. When I came back I found Tonya waiting for me with the lube.

"I thought you'd lube Audrey's cock up and show her how much you want her cock by sucking her off!"

I started by sucking the dildo first. Audrey got a laugh pretending she could feel my sucking, but after a couple of minutes it was clear that she was getting turned on by watching me fellate her.

"Suck my cock, boy!" she urged me.

"Yes, he's quite a talent. I'm gonna have men lined up at my door, but I won't know whether they've come for me or him!" Tonya boasted.

"What a slut! Let me fuck his whore ass!"

"Make him beg for it," Tonya told her.

"Yeah! Do you want my cock, Johnny? Do you want me to fuck you? I've got a bigger cock than you. Do you want it?"

"Yes!" I gasped out. My erection told her that I wasn't just role-playing.

"Well beg me then! What do you want?" Audrey was getting into it.

"Please ... fuck me! I want you to ... fuck my ass with your cock!"

"What are you?"

"I'm a slut!"

"Would you let anyone here fuck you?"

"Yes!"

"Would you suck anyone here?"

"Yes!"

"Do you drink piss and eat cum?"

"Yes, yes, yes!"

"You are a slut! Tonya should whore you out and make some pin money."

"You mean 'pin-dick money'!" Tonya laughed.

Audrey slapped some lube on the dildo and pressed some into my ass with two fingers. She was a little rough about it, but I was too horny now to mind.

"Put in three fingers!" Tonya instructed. "That cock's thick. Make his pussy nice and wet for you!"

Audrey worked me open. It felt so good! I love having my ass played with!

"Please! I want your cock!" I begged.

Tonya and Audrey exchanged a raised eyebrow look that said, 'He really is a slut!'

I felt the head of the dildo at my entrance and I wanted to back onto it, but I couldn't move with my legs pulled up. All I could do was pull back harder on my knees to open myself up as much as I could.

Audrey pushed forward and I felt the thick dildo wrench my ass apart. It hurt, but I gritted my teeth and stifled my cries. I wanted it in me. I didn't want to wait and I didn't want her to be gentle. I wanted her to take my ass.

I couldn't help but grunt and strain as my sphincters tightened around the thick cockhead, trying instinctively to force it out. But Audrey, encouraged by my lack of protests, pushed ahead. For all her solicitousness, she was an aggressive fucker! I remembered how much she'd got off on peeing in my mouth. She apparently had some scores to settle with men.

"You're gonna take it, boy!" she growled. "You're gonna take my cock! I'm gonna fuck your faggot ass!" She began to pump in and out, working the dildo deeper into me. I jumped as it hit my prostate and my dick tingled with sexual charge. I squirmed to rub her cock against the gland. It was still a mixture of strain and pleasure, but, oh, what pleasure!

"You like it, boy? You like my cock?" Audrey demanded.

"Yes! It feels so good...."

"So good up your ass?"

"Your cock ... feels so good ... up my ass!" I gasped.

"Up your faggot ass!"

"Up my faggot ass," I repeated.

"You're not a real man, are you, Johnny?" Tonya chimed in. "You're a pansy who loves being butt-fucked, aren't you? You don't fuck women because you want to be the one being fucked."

"Yes! Yes!" I gasped. "I'm a faggot pansy!"

Audrey started fucking me harder and my ass started to feel hotter and looser and sexier.

"Oh fuck! Oh, oh, oh!" I moaned. "So full! So good!" Audrey started banging me with long hard strokes that felt better and better to me.

"Oh God! Oh God!" I cried.

"Jack yourself off!" Audrey demanded. "Come with my cock in your ass!"

Tonya offered me the lube and I smeared it thickly on my cock. I arched my back with ecstasy as the slippery friction sent shock waves through my nervous system.

"Jerk your cock and say, 'I'm a faggot. I'm a sissy. I'm a sissy faggot!'" Audrey insisted. I would have done anything she asked at that point. I trembled as the words formed on my lips.

"I'm a faggot," I said softly. "I'm a sissy."

"Louder!"

My brain was on fire with the ideas she was planting there, mixed with the incredible feelings coming from my ass!

"I'm a faggot. I'm a sissy faggot. I want ... cock up my ass! I want cock in my mouth! I love to eat cum!"

With that my orgasm erupted. I screamed in release as my cock convulsed and spurted onto my stomach. I growled out animal groans of orgasm as my ass spasmed around the thick shaft of the penis. Audrey stopped fucking me and looked down on the wreck she'd created.

"Feed him his mess," Tonya instructed.

Audrey hesitantly wiped up some of my runny goo with her fingers and shoved it at my mouth, dripping some on my chest. In my sexual daze I eagerly accepted her gift. Seeing that, she quickly gathered more of it and held it to my mouth like honey to be licked off.

"Was that nice, baby? Did you like Audrey fucking you?"

"Yes," I sighed out of my post-orgasmic haze.

"But now you've had your come, but David hasn't had his! Will you still let him fuck you, even though you've already come?"

"Uh-huh," I agreed.

"You still want his cock in your bottom? Even though you won't be able to come again so soon?"

"Yes. I ... just want to feel it ... feel him come. In me. I ... want him to ... use me. Use my ass."

"Yes! You want to make love to a man! Because that's what every girl wants: to know that it is her charms that are exciting a man, to feel him lose it because of her power over him! Audrey can fuck you; she can violate you; she can open you; but only a man can give you that!"

Tonya got me up and turned me around on all fours with my arms on the arms of the couch.

"Now beg David to fuck you!" she ordered. "You've made it clear this is as much or more to please you as him, so you should invite him."

"Please, David, I want you to fuck me," I said, even though I couldn't see him behind me. "I want to feel your cock in my ass. I want to feel you come in me!"

"Yes, slut! Here you go!" he replied.

"Put it in for him!" Tonya suggested and I reached back and found the greasy shaft of his cock. I pulled it to the bullseye. I felt his thick cockhead prod at my anus and press in. He easily penetrated after Audrey's work, although I could feel his cock stretch me to overcome the slight retraction that had already taken place.

I really did want it. It felt so good going in, filling me up after the emptiness of Audrey's withdrawal. The sensation of his thighs hitting my ass and his cock hitting the top of my rectum was divine. I let out a gasp of delight! 'Fuck me! Fuck me!' I implored him silently in my mind.

David had no hesitation. He began long, strong strokes and I loved it! This felt heavenly! Even though my cock couldn't even manage to get half-hard, I was loving the feeling of being fucked by a real cock again. 'Do me! Do me!' I shouted inside my head. 'Don't stop!'

Tonya leaned down next to my ear and whispered to me, while she stroked my hair.

"You love it, don't you? You love a man's cock fucking you! How could a man who loves that ever hope to satisfy a woman?"

Her words, meant to humiliate, only excited me more! Being on my knees gave me the freedom to meet David's thrusts with my own. I began to rock back into him, driving myself onto his sturdy prick, slamming my ass into his groin. I thrilled as I heard him moan in response to my ardor! I wanted it harder, faster, deeper. I did want a man! I wanted to be fucked by a man!

Tonya stood up.

"Look how he wants it! No wonder he couldn't satisfy me! The faggot was dreaming of a big cock up his ass while I was wishing I had one up my cunt instead of his thingie!"

David was past hearing her now. He was reaming me and I was hungry to feel his blast.

"Fuck me! Fuck me! Fuck me!" I cried out loud what I had been screaming in my head. I wanted to be fucked and I didn't care who knew.

My lust put David over the top. He rammed into me and held my ass hard to his pelvis. I felt his cock convulse in my colon. 1, 2, 3 hard squirts were accompanied by a strangled groan of completion.

"Oh, fuck!" he gasped in exhaustion. "That.... It felt ... so good right from the start ... loose ... hot ... ready...." He groaned again as I squeezed my ass down on his cock, wanting to hug that beautiful penis with my rectum, milking the last drops of cum from him.

"I do think Dave likes sloppy seconds!" Tonya laughed.

I was exhilarated to feel the hot sensation of his sperm coating my bowel. I hung my head in fatigue and surrender to the glorious feeling surging through my body.

Was I really gay? How could I love this so much and be straight? But I didn't love David. I didn't want to kiss him, didn't want to cuddle with him. I just wanted his cock to fuck me! But it did excite me to know that it was a man on the other end of that cock, not a girl with a strap-on. I liked to feel a big strong masculine man taking me! I decided to stop worrying about it and decided just to enjoy it. If it didn't bother Tonya, then why should I stop?

"Don't pull out yet, David!" Tonya told him. "Audrey, get a glass! Hold it to his bottom when David pulls out!" I heard a tinkle of glasses and then I felt David's cock slipping from my ass. I groaned at the loss, the emptiness, the feeling of my ass gaping open wide.

"He misses your cock, David!" Tonya smirked. I felt the cold glass against my taint.

"Squeeze it out, baby," Tonya cooed, "and Audrey will feel you a nice treat!" I could feel the goo trickle out of me and I pushed. "That's it, baby. That's a good boy!" she chuckled. "Or is it 'good girl'? 'Good sissy'?"

Audrey brought the collected slime and held the glass to my lips and tipped it into my mouth. It tasted strongly of lube as well as semen. Despite the taste, my thought was that this was my trophy. I was proud that I had satisfied a man, excited his lust!

"Lick the glass, babe," Tonya told me.

"Fuck! I gotta get mine too!" Calvin growled and he was in front of me, his ebon cock erect.

"Do you want more, babe?" Tonya asked. "Do you still need more cock?" I looked at the stiff black penis in front of me. It was proudly erect, skin stretched tight. I admired its size and shape. It was a beautiful specimen of what a man's cock should be. It deserved admiration. It could pleasure a cunt, an ass, a hand, or a mouth. I thought of how it would feel between my lips, in my mouth, against my tongue, and my mouth started to water. Shit, yes, I wanted more! I had discovered that cocks thrilled me and I couldn't get enough of them!

I licked and sucked at Calvin's cockhead and I thrilled at its heat and firmness. Calvin impatiently crammed himself to the back of my throat. I gagged, but inwardly thrilled at his eagerness to use my mouth. I startled him by taking his muscular ass cheeks in each hand and energetically bobbing my head on his cock. I alternated tantalizing his sensitive spots with my lips and tongue with taking him in as deeply as I could. I could tell this excited him and I suspected he would not take long.

I was surprised at the thrill I felt in having his solid ass in my hands. It was so different from the soft feel of a woman's padded behind. His butt was a rippling mass of muscle. And I had this strong man in my power! I let him know that I was blowing him, that he was not fucking my face. I was making love to his magnificent cock.

I felt his cock quiver and I knew his climax was coming. I wanted to taste his cream, so I waited until I felt his cock swell and I pulled back. Then he was flooding my mouth with his potent sperm! I sucked his cockhead like a baby nursing, swallowing his gift greedily.

"Oh, man!" Calvin gasped as he pulled out of my mouth. I grabbed his prick and squeezed a few more drops of his jism out onto my tongue. "That's some good cocksucking! You sure he's straight, Tonya?"

"No, I'm not sure at all! He sure seems to have developed a taste for cock in a big hurry! But I still love him, whatever he is!" She kissed me, tasting traces of Calvin's cum in my mouth.

That seems to bring a natural end to the weekend. Everybody had come so many times that we were all exhausted. They all made plans to go out dancing again Wednesday night.

After they all had left, Tonya sat down with me. She pulled me into her arms and laid my head against her chest. She stroked my hair and face, as one would comfort a child.

"Baby, I want you to know how happy I am! I guess you're finding out for yourself how wonderful it is to be fucked by a real man's cock! It is so satisfying, a satisfaction I haven't felt in over 2 years! I want you to know the sacrifice you are making to give up your rights to my pussy is totally appreciated. I know you are swallowing your pride to acknowledge, in front of these men, in front of Audrey—well, practically in front of everyone if you consider the club and the pool—that you aren't man enough for me. It takes a kind of strength to admit how weak you really are. And to do whatever it takes to make your wife happy."

She reached down and took my exhausted penis in her hand.

"I'm so glad you have let yourself enjoy their cocks too, to suckle them, to let them fuck you up the ass. That lets you understand how wonderful those cocks are and how satisfying a big thick cock is in a way nothing else in the world can be!"

Despite everything my dick started to stiffen in her hand! She looked at it and looked at me and kissed me.

"Oh, you do understand! Look, you're getting aroused again even thinking about those gorgeous cocks reaming your poop chute! You can maybe feel a little bit of that deep satisfaction I feel when my cunt or ass are being stretched and filled by those beautiful cocks! It's like you've been trying and trying keys and none of them fit—and then one fits and the lock turns and it opens something wonderful beyond that door!"

My cock was erect now, threatening to exude a drop of pre-cum even. Why was I aroused to hear my wife recite how much better her lovers made her feel than me? Oh why?

"I've been thinking about why that should be. Why is it SO good? Why should a couple of inches longer and thicker make all the difference, enough that I'd be willing to risk my marriage to get my cunt plowed by a bigger dick? It's not random, it's not perverse. It's Nature's plan.

"Nature has implanted an imperative in every woman to find the sperm which will ensure that her children will be the best they can be, to ensure the survival of her genes, to promote Life itself. It is her most basic need, the point of her whole existence. Everything else—beauty, health, food, a home, money, social standing—are in the service of that goal.

"And Nature has decided over the millennia that guys with bigger dicks are the superior sperm donors. They are the bigger, healthier, stronger, more aggressive, more competitive men—the winners. And their children will be the winners too. So Nature has planted a desperate need in every woman to find those bigger cocks and get fucked by those cocks and harvest that seed so she can have those men's babies.

"And Mother Nature, being a woman, rewarded the woman for finding those cocks by giving her such mind-bending orgasms that she can't wait to get fucked by those big cocks again! She'll cheat on her husband; she'll betray her best friend; she'll wear high heels and push-up bras and lacy lingerie: whatever it takes to get that big cock up her cunt again!"

'Being sexually satisfied certainly made Tonya wax philosophical!' I thought.

"What about me?" I asked. "Where do I fit into Nature's plan? If getting a big cock is what life's all about, why didn't you marry one?"

"Oh, baby! Don't get your feelings hurt! In fact, I'm really saying that it isn't about you at all, not you as a person. It's about instincts. I'm saying that it's very primitive. It has nothing to do with how I feel about you! I love you! It's as little about you as if I needed a blood transfusion and I needed Type O blood and you were Type B. It's something Nature has programmed me to need, like I need air or I need vitamins!

"But there are good reasons I married you and not one of those cocks. There's more to raising children than getting the right sperm. Children need care: they need a roof over their heads; they need food; they need clothes; they need love: they need parents. Those big cock guys aren't good at that: they're too busy trying to find more cunts to fill up; the more, the better. I want you to be my partner, to parent my children!"

"So am I some kind of a freak? Nature must have screwed up with me: I'm sitting around masturbating while my wife is being fucked by other men. My sperm aren't going to father any babies. How does that fit into Nature's plan?"

"Well, that is a little harder to explain. I've read some theories on those cuckold websites. I guess the answer is that you little-dicked fellas have got to be a little sneaky, since you start out with a handicap. It's all about 'sperm competition' "

"Huh? How does that explain what I'm doing?"

"Well, when two men fuck the same woman close together, their sperm are in competition. The sperm that gets to the egg first gets her pregnant. Which one wins depends on a lot of things: how much of a head start the first one has, how much sperm were deposited and how far up the vagina, how acid or alkaline her vaginal juices are, how thick or thin her vaginal mucous is, how long it's been since her last orgasm, how long it's been since the last sperm were deposited in her vagina. Did you know that if the woman has an orgasm during intercourse, she's more likely to get pregnant?"

"Yeah, I think you said something about that before."

"Well, unfortunately, that's not in your favor either, because women report they have more and more powerful orgasms with their lovers than with their husbands. So it looks like the wives would rather get knocked up by their lovers than their husbands!

"It's sort of controversial, but some researchers think that the sperm actually fight with each other in the woman's cunt, that they kill each other or at least block each other from getting to the egg. But some of what determines which one wins depends on how lively the sperm are, how old they are—that is, how long they've been sitting in your balls waiting to get shot out!—how many sperm are shot out, etc. Some scientists think that masturbation is a way to make sure you have good fresh sperm ready to compete—it gets rid of your old sperm. But you don't want to masturbate too much, or you'll use up all your bullets!

"Well there's a lot of factors that determine how much cum you have ready to shoot out, and how much you shoot, and how strongly you shoot it, and a lot of those are psychological. If you've been thinking about sex all day, your body generates more seminal fluid and gets more sperm ready. If you expect to have sex that night, ditto. If you know your wife is ovulating and there's a better chance to get her pregnant, you'll make more sperm. Your body gets you ready for what your brain thinks is coming."

'Wow, she's really studied up on this!' I thought to myself.

"Well, getting back to you, the cuckold husband: if a man thinks his wife is cheating on him, he knows his sperm are going to have competition. So what does he do? Does he rush home and confront his wife and threaten to kill her and her lover? Well, he might if he's a big strong manly alpha male. But not if he's an average beta male! He doesn't have much chance of beating the alpha lover in a fist fight, does he? He'd probably get torn limb from limb. That won't help him get his wife pregnant, will it? So how does he fight? The only way he can: with his sperm!

"What does the beta male do? He masturbates! Masturbates? Why? So that his troops will be young, fresh, and lively! He's got to get rid of his old lazy sperm and get ready to go home and fill his wife with some blitzkrieg sperm. And how does his body get him to masturbate? By making the idea of his wife cheating on him exciting! So when he suspects his wife is unfaithful, what does he get? A hard-on!

"Even though he is scared and angry, he can't help but take his cock in hand and beat off while he's imagining his wife fucking another man! He feels crazy: 'I think my wife is an adulterer and it makes me horny?' But it's his body's way of making sure he's ready for the sperm competition! All day long every time he thinks of his wife is another man's arms, he gets a woody! Instead of wanting to kill his wife, he can't think of anything but rushing home to fuck her! Why? Because his sperm have to compete with the lover's sperm, so he needs to generate as much cum as he can, and he has to get home as soon as he can to get his sperm in the race!"

Tonya looked down at her hand lazily stroking my cock. My penis was hard and copiously oozing pre-cum! She smiled at the silent confirmation of her scenario.

"So the suspicion that his wife is unfaithful has his brain in a sexual tizzy! He's as turned-on as he's ever been! He feels crazy. 'Do I want my wife to cuckold me?!? It makes me so hot to think of her cheating on me!?!' But it really is that his body doesn't care if his brain understands what is happening. It doesn't matter if he knows why he's doing what he's doing: it just matters that he does it.

"What happens when he gets home? He can't wait to get his wife in bed, which is unusual. After all he's a beta male, not really known for his high sex drive. His wife is reluctant for two reasons: one that she knows she still has her lover's cum dripping out of her and she doesn't want to get caught, but more important is that she wants to get pregnant by her superior lover and doesn't want her husband's weak sperm in her cunt to queer the deal! So she'll try to put him off, but her husband will probably insist, since he's in a fever to get his sperm in the race.

"But if the wife can't easily get out of sex, she's likely to submit to her husband's wishes, because she doesn't want to excite suspicion. Plus she knows her lover's sperm have a crucial head start.

"Unbeknownst to her, her lover's sperm have several additional advantages. Her lover's longer cock has deposited sperm farther up in her vagina than her husband has ever reached. Knowing that his sperm will probably have competition from the husband, the lover's body has unconsciously known to shoot more cum into the cheating wife than he would with his own wife. As a result the lover found his ejaculation more powerful and satisfying than his usual marital orgasm, reminding him why he so likes these affairs with other men's wives!

"And the cuckold's wife had orgasmed with her lover—several times in fact—even though she almost never orgasms with her husband! Her orgasms changed her blood flow and vaginal mucosa to give the lover's sperm smooth sailing!"

By now Tonya's story and her hand had me writhing on the verge of orgasm myself. My dick was a mess of pre-cum drooling out of my slit. I moaned and rolled my hips in torment. Her scenario was so true to everything I had done and felt when I knew she was going to be fucking another man! Every detail about the lover's superiority, his sexual prowess, and the husband's helpless Inferlorlty made me more aroused! Tonya, sensing that I was getting ahead of the story, slowed and lightened her masturbating strokes, grinning at her power over me and how she knew every button of mine to push.

"To the wife's horror the first thing the cuckold husband wants to do is to taste her vagina! She struggles mightily against it, saying she's not showered, she's probably smelly, but the husband insists. Why? Does he like to eat sperm? No, he does it for two other reasons. One is evidence: he has to know if his suspicions are true. He needs to know if this is a sperm competition, so his body can know if he needs to deposit the maximum load of sperm.

"And the taste of her cunt will give him clues as to how long ago she fucked the other man: the longer ago, the more vital it is to put his largest army in the field. If the cum is fresh, he'll have the best odds of overcoming the slight time advantage. So the fresher the cum he tastes, the better he likes it!

"The second reason is defense: the more of the other's man's sperm he can suck out, the less he'll have to compete with. So the more strongly her pussy tastes of semen, the more ravenously he needs to eat it! How does the cuckold's body persuade him to this unappetizing task? Same answer as before: by making it sexually exciting!

"For reasons the cuckold cannot fathom, he is obsessed with the idea of eating his wife's unfaithful cunt! Even as he imagines it is dripping with the disgusting slime of his rival, the idea of smelling, eating, and licking his wife's cummy pussy makes him wild with lust! And when he finds that her cunt reeks with the smell of sex and jism, his cock stiffens near to bursting and he is transported with a burning desire to suck every drop of his enemy's manly juices into his mouth!

"He feels schizophrenic: his own drive to devour another man's sperm feels like eagerness! Again he asks himself, 'Do I like this? Do I want to eat cum? Am I glad to I find my wife has cuckolded me? Do I want her to cheat on me?' But he can't stop, because his body knows he needs to do it to win."

Tonya looked at me with a look of pity and tenderness.

"Oh, poor baby, it is torture for you, isn't it? Nature is so cruel! You are driven by all these powerful feelings and urges and you're left totally in the dark trying to figure out what they mean! You're helpless to resist but all the while you're left fearing that you're crazy or perverted or gay! I feel so sorry for you: that has to be so hard for you!" She squeezed by cock, ironically reminding us both of who was the puppet master pulling my strings. "But it is a sweet agony, isn't it? It is joyful torture! An eager pain! It is so exciting and it gives such delight even as it terrifies!"

"The cuckold's wife notices another difference. His cock is as hard as it's ever been and his thrusting is longer and more powerful than it's ever been! Why? Again the answer is defense! By long hard thrusts he is trying to rake out the other man's cum! His cockhead is designed like a scraper, to catch cum behind the rim and pull it out! The more thrusts and the longer thrusts he has, the more of his rival's sperm is raked out!

"Another reason is that he desperately wants his wife to orgasm, to give his own sperm the advantages that she had given her lover. But in the poor cuckold's head, all <u>he</u> knows is that this fuck is more lustful than he's ever felt! Again it seems to him that his wife's cheating on him has <u>excited</u> him, that she is <u>more</u> attractive now rather than less! Again he wonders what is wrong with him, that he finds his wife's infidelity so arousing, as if he <u>wants</u> her to cuckold him!

"And this theme is underscored by his orgasm, which is one of the best he's ever had! His body has produced more sperm to better compete with his rival's, and his body knows that he needs to shoot it as hard and as far as he can to overcome the head start that the lover's spunk has. Both of these combine to give him the most powerful orgasm he can remember! To his surprise and delight, his wife may have also climaxed, which she rarely does with him normally. Unbeknownst to him, this is only partly because of his lasting longer and being more energetic. She was also relieved that she seemed to have gotten away with her infidelity if her husband's loud groans of orgasm are any indication. The other part is that, having gotten away with her infidelity his time, she was fantasizing about her lover and anticipating their next rendezvous!

"As the days go by, this dance snowballs in ways that are delightful for the wife and bewildering for the husband. The wife, unconsciously eager to be impregnated by her superior lover's sperm and emboldened by the apparent success of her first dalliance, arranges to meet with her lover more and more often.

"Her husband, sensing his vulnerability, is more and more preoccupied with sexual thoughts and driven to have intercourse with his wife more and more frequently. He is almost exhausting himself with masturbation and intercourse at two to four times his usual frequency. He is tortured by the fact that the fantasies that excite him while he is masturbating and fucking are now always of his wife being fucked by another man!

"In fact, when he imagines his wife actually getting <u>pregnant</u> by her lover, he is even more excited, to his horror! Why? Because that threat is the ultimate threat that spurs his body to its sperm competition efforts! So when he imagines that his wife has become pregnant by another man, he is even more driven to masturbate and to fuck her!

"Imagine that the cuckold suspects his wife is seeing her lover one afternoon. In his eagerness to come home to 'play defense' as soon after the lover leaves as possible, he sneaks away from work. When he gets home, he finds a strange car in his driveway. Fearful of losing a physical confrontation, he sneaks into the house and, unbeknownst to the lovers, he actually observes them in the act!

"Of course all men find watching sex exciting, but something else is going on here. The cuckold's body knows that his wife is getting a dose of competitive sperm and that he'll need to make his deposit soon. His body also knows his excellent timing means he will have a great chance of competing successfully. So his body wants to quickly generate the largest load of sperm it can! It does this by shooting massive amounts of testosterone into his bloodstream and flooding his nervous system with sex signals to get an emergency semen supply generated.

"What the cuckold experiences subjectively is that seeing his wife actually in the act has him even more excited than ever before! It is like the heroin of sexual stimulation! It seems to him that he is actually enjoying watching his wife being fucked by another man—more excited than he ever was when she was faithful! It seems to him that he gets off on her fucking other men more than he gets off on fucking her himself!

"The cuckold is caught in one of the worst flaws of human logic: if two things go together, we can confuse cause and effect. He doesn't really want his wife to cheat on him or get pregnant by another man, and he doesn't really want to find her cunt filled with strange cum and to eat another man's semen. The actual cause and effect is that excitement is what he needs to try to win a sperm competition.

"But all he knows is that when he imagines or finds these things, he gets excited and actually has more sexual pleasure! So in his fallacious logic he starts to think that he actually wants her to cheat on him, that he wants her to be pregnant by another man, that he has developed a taste for sloppy seconds and cream pies! His big brain has gotten in the way of his little brain!"

"But doesn't that mean he loses?" I wondered aloud. "If he got confused that way, wouldn't his wife always end up knocked up by the other man and wouldn't his genes always finally lose out? Why would Nature allow that to happen? And if it always worked out that way, why wouldn't every man end up a cuckold?"

"Well that's a good question. I guess it depends a little on how many alpha males and beta males are out there, how attractive the wife is, and how potent the husband's sperm are, etc. The husband does have an advantage of having more access to his wife. So some of the time his sperm win the competition.

"And remember, this is just the scenario when we're talking about a very desirable wife—let's call her an 'alpha female'—married to a beta male. If the wife isn't that attractive, maybe she can't get an alpha male. And if the husband is an alpha male, his best strategy is just to threaten to kill any guy that touches his wife—and to fuck every woman he can get. I suppose the cuckold scenario is the most likely when the wife is very hot to begin with and the husband is a pretty weak specimen. That's sort of a volatile situation, isn't it?" Tonya said, looking me in the eye and arching her brow.

"You've got to remember that this all evolved in caveman days, long before the invention of birth control. Evolution hasn't caught up to condoms and birth control pills. People still have all these primitive instincts even if the woman can't really get pregnant, since she's on The Pill. But even then Nature has a way of making girls 'forget' to take their birth control pills and getting couples to get so hot that they 'get carried away' and fuck without a condom."

"But what about our situation? How does your 'survival of the fittest' argument lead to a man helping his wife cuckold him? And how could survival ever lead to him sucking off his wife's lover or letting her wife's lover fuck him up the ass?"

"Well, for that one I think there could be a simple explanation and a complicated one. The simplest explanation is simple defense. If he can get his rivals to squirt their seed up his ass or in his mouth, those sperm can't knock up his wife! For that matter, that would be a good reason for him to offer his wife's ass for their use as well: you can't get pregnant going up the old dirt road!

"So Nature would have a good reason to encourage the cuckold to take as much cum as he could for himself. Again, the simplest way for Nature to do that is to make cocksucking or getting fucked up the ass arousing for the cuckold! The poor schmo is secretly terrified that he's turning gay, but he's really just unconsciously trying to keep the competition off his wife's bod by offering his own! Because of that he has the strange combination of seemingly having an insatiable appetite for sperm, while being disgusted by the idea of being gay and still being attracted to his wife!"

"I guess that makes sense … except when he's sticking the stud's cock into his own wife's cunt! That certainly isn't the way to win a sperm competition!"

"Well, I suppose not. Simple survival might explain that. In the face of a superior man wanting his woman, the beta male might be best to surrender rather than fight. If he fights, he might not only lose, but he could get maimed or killed. I don't mean Brian would ever hurt you, but back in prehistoric times when all these instincts got imprinted that definitely could happen. But if the cuckold surrenders, he could offer up his wife to the better man to win his trust and still hope to sneak his sperm into the running behind the big guy's back. So the willing cuckold route could be a stealth plan, sort of a Plan B.

"The other thing that evolutionary scientists are looking at is that a person's instincts might be to save his tribe's genes, even if his behavior doesn't lead to any of his own sperm making a baby. Remember, in caveman times, most of the people in your village were pretty closely related to you, so they'd have a lot of the same genes. So if something you did helped your tribe's genes to survive, more of your genes would survive too.

"So it might be a genetic survival strategy to offer the best females to the best males, even if you didn't get to bed any of the best females yourself. So cuckolding might be a kind of selfish 'sacrifice for the good of the team.' Nature might reward you with a good orgasm for masturbating and spilling your inferior seed while you cheered on your wife to get knocked up with some really good sperm!"

"Of course another possibility is that it really is a perversion; that is, somehow the survival instincts have gotten far off on the wrong track. Maybe the drives are healthy, but they've got the person off onto a dead end road and he can't get off. I mean, obviously alcoholism kills people, many before they can reproduce, but they're addicted to the thrill the drink gives them and they can't stop. For instance, it could never be in your survival interest to eat your own sperm, but maybe you've gotten so addicted to the sexual arousal of eating other men's sperm that you can't help yourself."

Tonya began to masturbate me in earnest again. She took the pre-cum leaking from my prick and made it into a gooey lubricant for her hand. She used her thumb to rub my sensitive cockhead and tickle my slit maddeningly. I shuddered and squirmed in her hands.

"The poor cuckold is caught in a web, where all his natural instincts point in ways that go against everything he's been taught. Where he's been told that a man protects his woman, it gives him delirious pleasure to give her away to a better man! Instead of longing to plunge his own cock into his wife's cunt, he burns to watch another man fuck his wife! His greatest joy is when he knows that a real man is pumping his sperm into his bride during the time of her cycle when she's most fertile and he imagines that seed rushing to find his wife's egg and plant a baby in his wife's womb! The ultimate defeat in the game of life becomes his deepest wish!

"Think of it, baby! Think of Brian's, or Calvin's, or David's seed sprayed deep in my cunt, my receptive body welcoming his cum, my womb sheltering an egg waiting for its mate! Imagine his potent sperm finds my egg and his baby begins to grow in your wife's tummy! Picture my belly swelling with pregnancy, knowing that your poor spunk hasn't been near my cunt in months! Imagine that my pregnancy doesn't disgust you: it fills you with lust! Your cock springs to hardness at the sight of my bulge! The knowledge that that 'baby bump' is another man's child sexually excites you! You can't think of it without grabbing your dick and beating off in joy at the thought!"

"Oh! No! No-o-o-o!" I cried, but my cock quivered in Tonya's hand and my cum sprayed out in a weak fountain onto her other palm. My prick convulsed and pumped but only a small puddle formed in her hand.

"Yes! The idea <u>does</u> excite you! Even after three days of debauchery, thinking of me pregnant with another man's baby drives you to spill your seed! And you want to taste it, because the taste of cum is becoming something you crave. Taste it to your heart's delight, husband!" She held it to my mouth and I lapped it up, tasting the difference from the virile spend of her lovers. Tonya moved her hand to let me get every drop, as if she were giving me a treat, like letting me lick buttercream icing from a spoon. She cooed at me, "That's it, baby. That's it, lick it up! Lick your impotent essence!"

My sleep that night was tormented by dreams of a pregnant Tonya. I dreamed of her flouncing around the house naked or half-naked, showing off her bulging tummy proudly. Despite her condition she continued to have sex with her lovers, vaginally, anally, and orally. In the dream she encouraged me to masturbate and shoot my wad over her protruding stomach. Later we took a little black baby home from the hospital, to be greeted by little brothers and sisters who looked like miniature Brians and Davids!

Maybe Tonya was right. Maybe deep primitive instincts had intersected with our circumstances and we were on a runaway train with no way off. My heart and brain were roiling with conflicting thoughts, feelings, and urges. We had already gone so far into unknown territory that I was completely lost and disoriented. I no longer even knew which way was up, much less who I was or what I really wanted.

All I knew for sure at this point was that Tonya still loved me and I still loved her. In a crazy way we were closer and more devoted to each other than ever, no matter whose sperm was leaking out of our mouth, cunts, or asses! I did not know where this roller coaster ride would end. All we could do was to hold onto to each other for dear life and see what was over the next hill!

## End of Book 2

## The Husband to Feminized Cuckold Saga

In each book John plunges further into his cuckold journey. John tells in his own words how a seemingly normal man descends a slippery slope by imperceptible degrees, discovering thoughts, urges, and impulses he never would have guessed. John's narrative reveals insights into the cuckold's psychology, tortures, and delights.

Continue Johnny's and Tonya's adventures!

Book 3: *Breeding Time at Gender Bend*

Book 4: *The Cuck 'n' Bull Club*

Book 5: *Over the Gender Divide*

Printed in Great Britain
by Amazon

28137521R00126